TEMBO

H. P. Oliver

MYSTERIES IN HISTORY

Copyright © 2015 Steven O. Eitzen

HPO Productions
8698 Elk Grove Boulevard, Suite 1-271
Elk Grove, California 95624

Cover art and book design by Steve Eitzen

Printed in the United States of America

ISBN-10:0988833174
ISBN-13:978-0-9888331-7-3

DEDICATION

For Tiare and Wendy in appreciation
for their inspiration and enthusiasm.

AUTHOR WEBSITE

You are cordially invited to visit the author's website at
http://www.HPOliver.com for many free features related to
this and other H. P. Oliver books. These include a unique
Visualization section providing illustrated quotes from
TEMBO that will increase your reading enjoyment by allowing
you to "see" parts of the story.

(http://www.hpoliver.com/BOOKS/TEMBO/VISUALIZATIONS/index.html)

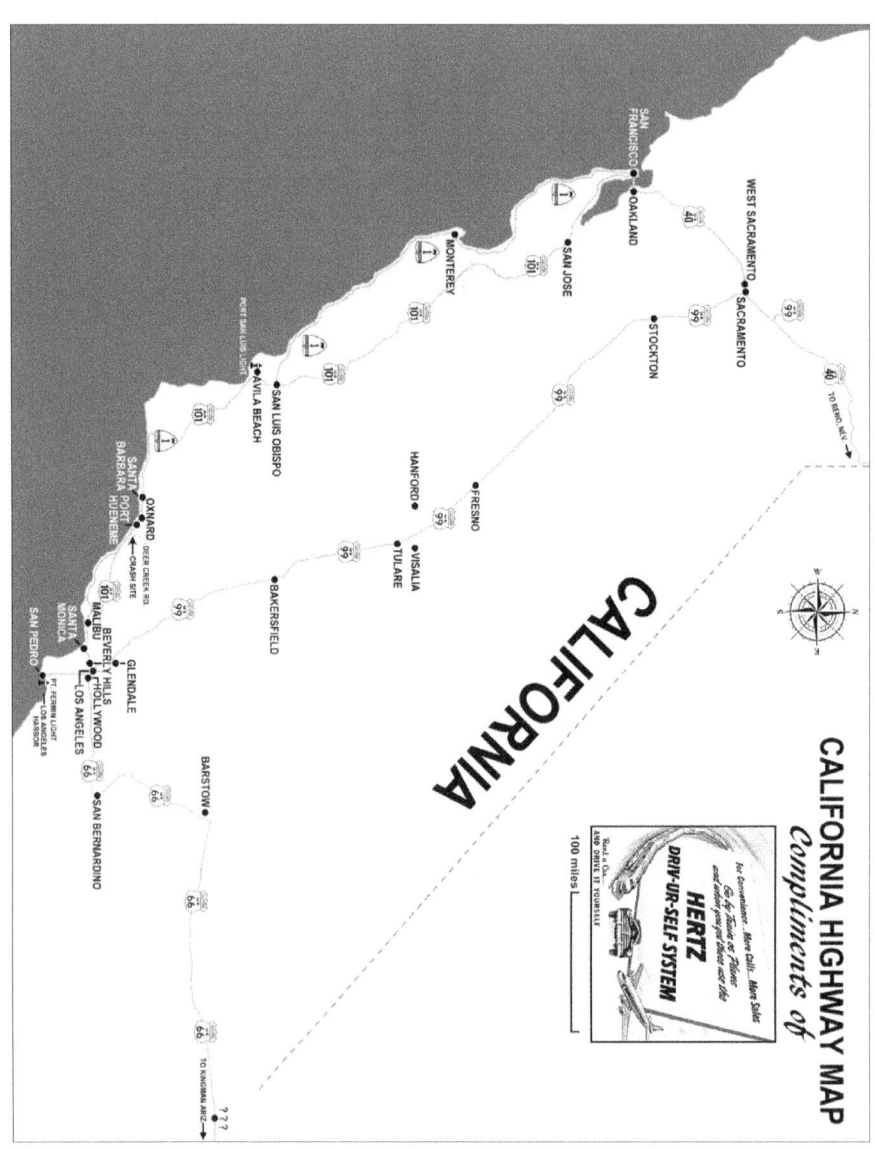

CALIFORNIA HIGHWAY MAP
Compliments of

HERTZ
DRIV-UR-SELF SYSTEM

For Convenience... More Calls... More Sales
Go by Train or Plane
and when you get there use the

Wait a Cue
AND DRIVE IT YOURSELF

100 miles

CALIFORNIA

SAN FRANCISCO
OAKLAND
SAN JOSE
MONTEREY
WEST SACRAMENTO
SACRAMENTO
STOCKTON
PORT SAN LUIS LIGHT
AVILA BEACH
SAN LUIS OBISPO
HANFORD
FRESNO
VISALIA
TULARE
BAKERSFIELD
SANTA BARBARA
PORT HUENEME
OXNARD
DEER CREEK RD.
CRASH SITE
SANTA MONICA
MALIBU
BEVERLY HILLS
HOLLYWOOD
GLENDALE
LOS ANGELES
SAN PEDRO
PT. FERMIN LIGHT
LOS ANGELES HARBOR
BARSTOW
SAN BERNARDINO
TO RENO, NEV.
TO KINGMAN, ARIZ.

???

ACKNOWLEDGMENTS

The author gratefully acknowledges Hollywood Heritage, Inc., the Water and Power Associates Museum, and the Burbank Historical Society as valuable resources in researching the background for this story. Also, the author is grateful to Miss Bette Davis for her autobiography, *This 'N That*, and to good friend, Gary Weisenberger for his invaluable help in the telling of this story.

PLEASE NOTE

This novel occasionally refers to individuals and groups with terms that are considered disrespectful and inappropriate in today's society. These terms, however, were in common usage during the historical period in which this story is set and are included here solely for the purpose of accurately depicting the attitudes and customs of the day.

One

Spicer Investigations – 1st National Bank Building, Hollywood

It was a hot, muggy Monday morning in the glamour capital of the world—the kind of day they have in the Deep South where you feel like you need another shower before you finish drying off from the one you just had. Both of my windows were open and I was putting up with the racket from the street two floors down in the hope a stray breeze might find its way into my office. So far none had.

The only part of me that was at all cool was my upper lip, the former residence of a mustache I grew when I got out of the Army about seven years ago. It was one of those thin little William Powell staches that are all the rage now. It got shaved off because while spending the weekend with Susan, the redheaded angel, she used her feminine wiles to convince me how much more handsome and debonair I'd look without it. I'm a sucker for feminine wiles.

Unfortunately, shaving off the mustache was about all I'd accomplished so far on this miserable Monday. Since I was, as we in the detective business put it, between clients at the moment, I was sitting at my desk waiting for one to show up. Hopefully it would be a well-to-do citizen with social or political aspirations who'd done something very stupid and ended up in a jam from which he or she— the gender mattered little—could only be extricated with the help of a clever and discreet private investigator.

Since waiting for clients doesn't require a whole lot of mental activity, I was doing some daydreaming about the aforementioned weekend I'd just spent with the aforementioned redheaded angel named Susan. Susan has emerald green eyes, an infectious smile, and enough charm to make a real angel jealous. In fact, the very first time I saw her I thought she actually was an angel.

I can be forgiven for that slight error in recognition because at the time I was just coming out from under an anesthetic the doctors had given me while they patched a hole in my head made by a very large bullet that bounced off my thick skull rather than imbedding itself in my brain as the lunatic who shot me intended. Susan was there when I woke up because she is a nurse at the private and exclusive Santa Barbara hospital where the aforementioned surgery took place.

Susan and I have seen a lot of each other since then because I still wasn't entirely certain she wasn't an angel, and because, for some reason beyond my understanding, she seemed to enjoy spending her time off with me. Thus, we had entered into a relationship that had yet to become complicated by expectations of what the future might bring.

Such were the sort of pleasant thoughts bouncing around my brain when I heard the tinkle of a small bell I installed on my outer office door to give warning that an evil doer, or even a client, had arrived. Hoping for the latter, I unstuck my sweat-damp shirt from the leather desk chair and arrived at the inner office door just as someone knocked on it.

I opened the door and invited Miss Frump into my office. I didn't really think her name was Miss Frump, but it was a moniker that fit her to a T.

The young woman had a plain face without the slightest hint of makeup and her hair was pulled into a tight bun in the manner of an old fashioned schoolmarm. She wore a simple black skirt with a hem that came to a point below her knees that hadn't been considered stylish for a few decades. The upper half of Miss Frump was covered with a white blouse that had a high collar fringed with the tiniest hint of lace. She also wore a short black jacket. The jacket was immodestly unbuttoned, perhaps as a small concession to the heat.

Miss Frump introduced herself as Lillian Bouvier, which she pronounced boo-vee-aay, emphasis on the final syllable. I invited Miss Bouvier to have a seat in one of my two upholstered armchairs, which were formerly property of the Hollywood Hotel across the street and had been acquired for my use when the hotel swapped them for newer models.

When we were both comfortably seated in our respective chairs, I said, "Now, Miss Bouvier, how can I be of service to you?"

Staring at me through a pair of the most practical wire-rimmed spectacles I have ever seen, Miss Bouvier said, "Mister Spicer, I doubt very much that there is any service you could provide that would be of the slightest use to me. I am here at the behest of my employer."

Behest—she had actually used the word "behest." I tried to remember the last time I heard that word used, and decided it was entirely possible that I had never heard the word used in an actual conversation.

I said, "I see. Okay, who is your employer and how can I be of service to him or her?"

"My employer is interested in hiring you to find something that was stolen from her."

Aha, a clue! Miss Bouvier's employer was a "her." Thinking it would be nice to have a little more to go on, I said, "Miss Bouvier, I'm afraid I can only give you half credit for that answer because you failed to include the name of your employer."

"That omission was intentional. My employer wishes to remain anonymous in this matter."

"Then we might just as well have a friendly chat about the lovely weather outside because I do not accept cases from clients who wish to remain anonymous."

Lillian Bouvier stuck her nose in the air and looked around my office as if seeking the source of an unpleasant odor. "Mister Spicer, judging by your office, it does not appear as if you are in any position to turn down clients because of a minor principle."

"Miss Bouvier, knowing for whom I am working is not a minor principle. As for my office, I choose to spend my money on more important necessities. Fine imported single malt Scotch, for example."

She stared at me, her eyes made large by the lenses of her glasses, and kept on staring at me. I was very near to picking her up and throwing her bodily from my office when she finally said, "Mister Spicer, may I please use your telephone to call my employer?"

"Sure, as long as your employer isn't somewhere that can only be reached with the assistance of a long distance operator."

Haughtily, she said, "I assure you it is a local telephone exchange."

I turned my desk telephone around to face Miss Bouvier and gave it a push in her direction. She picked up the handset and dialed a number. After a short time that wasn't long enough for more than two rings, she said, "Hello, Henry, this is Lillian. I need to speak with Madam."

I practiced balancing my dagger-shaped letter opener on the tip of my index finger while she waited for Henry, whoever he might be, to find Madam, whoever she might be. I almost had the balancing trick perfected when Miss Bouvier said, "Yes, ma'am. I am in Mister Spicer's office and he has informed me he will not work for an anonymous client."

Pause. "No, ma'am."

Pause. "Yes, ma'am."

Pause. "Yes, ma'am."

After the last "yes, ma'am," she handed me the telephone handset, saying, "My employer wishes to speak with you directly."

I took the handset and said, "Spicer here."

"Mister Spicer, I prefer not to say my name over this telephone connection, but perhaps I can give you a hint that will reveal my identity."

By that time I didn't need any hints. Even a non-movie fan like me could easily recognize the familiar voice coming over the telephone line. Still I thought it might be amusing to play her game, so I said, "Okay, give me the hint."

"Mister Spicer, you and I have met. The location of our meeting was the Warner Brothers commissary and you were in the company of an actor named Humphrey Bogart. As I understood the story, you had just saved Mister Bogart from an early demise by pushing him from under a falling soundstage spotlight. Does that ring any bells?"

I couldn't help grinning as I said, "Yes, it does."

"Good. Not long ago your employer at that time told me that, should I ever need the services of a discreet private investigator, you were the person to call. He seems to think very highly of you, Mister Spicer."

"The feeling is mutual. I think very highly of the checks he signs."

That got a small chuckle out her, after which she said, "Then may I assume I can count on your help in this matter?"

"Well, that depends to a great extent on the nature of the matter in which you need help."

"Very well. I will hang up the telephone now so Lillian can give you the details. Goodbye, Mister Spicer."

"Goodbye."

I replaced the telephone handset in its cradle and turned to my office guest. "All right, Miss Bouvier, what. has been stolen from Miss Bette Davis that she wants me to recover?"

Lillian Bouvier cringed slightly at hearing her employer's name spoken out loud in such unholy surroundings, and then said, "The item taken is a priceless African object of art."

Leaning back in my desk chair, I said, "You know, Miss Bouvier, there is no such thing as a priceless object. Anything can be had if the person who wants it makes a high enough bid."

"All right, Mister Spicer, I stand corrected. I will rephrase. The object taken is an extremely valuable African statuette. Is that better?"

"It's more accurate. What does this statuette look like?"

Fishing around in the large black handbag that still hung over her shoulder as if she was afraid to set it down for fear of it being stolen in such a disreputable milieu, Miss Bouvier said, "It is called the Ivonya-Ngia Elephant. The name refers to Kenyan mythology regarding the origin of elephants. I have some photographs here taken when Miss Davis acquired the statuette about a year ago. Of course, she promptly had it appraised and these photographs were made by the appraiser."

I was handed a half dozen five-by-seven color photos of a black and gray elephant sculpture. Judging by the scale ruler included in some of the pictures the thing was between seven and eight inches in length and about six inches in height. "So what value did the appraiser put on this curiosity?"

That got Miss Frump all haughty again. "I would hardly describe a two-hundred-year-old piece of art worth more than a hundred thousand dollars a curiosity!"

"All right, we'll upgrade it to a knickknack. Where and when was it when last seen?"

Glaring at me to make clear her continuing disapproval of my flippant attitude, she said, "It was on display in Miss Davis's home last Friday evening while she was entertaining a few close friends. It was a member of Madam's domestic staff who noticed the display case was broken and the Ivonya-Ngia Elephant was missing. That was around eleven or maybe a little before."

"And being a law abiding taxpayer you immediately called the Los Angeles Police Department, right?"

With a guilty expression that put me in mind of a kid caught with her hand in the cookie jar, she said, "Well, no . . . not exactly. You see . . ."

"Of course you didn't call the police, Miss Bouvier. Your employer wouldn't allow it, which means Miss Davis acquired the knickknack by questionable means. That's the only reason she would spend a lot of money to have me locate her purloined pachyderm instead of letting the cops find it for free."

Of course Miss Frump had an answer for everything including that accusation. "Mister Spicer, Miss Davis is an upstanding member of the community. I assure you she has done nothing illegal. It is just that she is quite well known and prefers to keep her personal business out of the newspapers."

I nodded my best all-knowing nod and said, "I don't doubt that for a minute. Tell me, is Miss Davis still living in Beverly Hills, or has she moved again?"

That struck a chord and I suspected Miss Lillian Bouvier was beginning to wonder if I didn't know more about her employer than she did. That's no mystery, though. All she had to do was read the Hollywood Reporter, which always reported the movements of notables like Miss Davis, who have a penchant for changing homes almost as often as I changed shirts.

In a considerably less snooty tone, Miss Bouvier said, "Actually, she and Mister Nelson have moved twice since Beverly Hills. The Ivonya-Ngia Elephant was stolen from their current home just a few blocks from here at 5346 Franklin Avenue."

Sensing there might be an actual human being under all that snoot, I said, "Tell me, Miss Bouvier, when was the last time anyone called you Lilly?"

I said it just to see her reaction and she didn't disappoint me. Lillian Bouvier turned red as a beet and stammered, "Nobody . . . I mean I have never been called . . ."

I let her off the hook. With my friendliest smile, I said, "Well, Lilly, it's about time somebody did."

She quickly returned to Snootville, saying, "Let us just keep this on a business level with Miss and Mister, Mister Spicer."

Grinning now, I said, "I'll do my best, but I make no guarantees. Now tell me who else has keys to the house besides Miss Davis, Mister Nelson and you?"

Lillian thought for a moment, and then said, "Miss Davis's butler, Henry Gough; her maid, Doris Alpert; and Joyce . . . ah . . . Pimm, I think, Miss Davis's cook. But all those people were carefully scrutinized before we hired them, mostly by me. I am certain none of them have anything to do with this."

"Probably not, but investigations like this are often a process of elimination, so let's start out by eliminating all of the fine upstanding citizens employed by Miss Davis. Will they all be at the house around five this afternoon?"

"Yes, I see no reason why they would not be, but if you wish to come to the house, I should clear it with . . ."

"Just tell Bette I wouldn't take no for an answer. Now, let's get the discussion of my fee out of the way. In cases like this I receive seventy-five dollars per day plus actual expenses. We start out with a hundred dollar retainer. Is that Jake with you?"

Apparently Bette had told her cost was of no concern, because she immediately removed a checkbook from her bag and wrote my retainer check. As Lillian Bouvier left my office I smiled and said, "Take care, Lilly. See you at five."

She blushed again and crossed my outer office as if she couldn't wait to get out the door. Despite my first impressions of Miss Bouvier, I'd come around to thinking she was okay, a little pompous and naïve, but okay.

Two

4:45 P.M. – Monday – August 5, 1940

Bette Davis Residence – 5346 Franklin Avenue, Hollywood

It was still Monday and it was still too damned hot and muggy. In fact, the only positive things that had happened in my world during the past four hours were a pretty darned good pastrami and Swiss on pumpernickel for lunch and learning how to tell an African elephant from an Asian or Indian elephant.

The first of those two occurrences happened when I walked into Eli's Deli a few doors north of my office on Highland and Eli's kid, Danny, told me they'd just gotten some choice premium pastrami in. I remembered Danny from the days when he used to ride his bicycle to the Hebrew bakery on Hollywood Boulevard to get fresh pumpernickel whenever they ran low at the deli. Danny and I were old chums.

The pastrami and Swiss improved my disposition immeasurably and motivated me to walk ten blocks east on Hollywood Boulevard to Ivar, where I turned right and stepped into the new Hollywood Branch of the Los Angeles Public Library. There I acquired an extensive knowledge of African elephants.

I was only interested in African elephants because according to the appraisal photos, Miss Davis's elephant was of that persuasion. I knew that because the first thing I learned about elephants is that African elephants have much larger ears than the other varieties. Why, Jumbo, what big ears you have!

What I did not learn is anything of importance concerning elephant mythology. In her eagerness to be helpful, Miss Bouvier had let slip that the name of the statuette, Ivonya-Ngia, came from

Kenyan mythology about the origin of elephants. I found nary a mention of Ivonya-Ngia in any of the elephant tomes through which I slogged. I did, however, come to the conclusion that people who write about elephants must be the most boring folks on the entire planet. The elephants need to get themselves some new agents who are on the ball and in tune with the times.

Next stop, Miss Davis's digs at 5346 Franklin Avenue. Franklin is a major east-west thoroughfare that runs along the southern edge of the Hollywood hills, and as streets in Los Angeles go, there's nothing about Franklin that makes it particularly attractive as a street to live on. In fact, the way things have been going lately, it becomes less attractive on a daily basis. Heavy automobile traffic dodges around the Pacific Electric Red Line streetcars rattling back and forth under a jungle of utility wires so thick you can hardly see the sky. Add to that all the apartment complexes and commercial businesses springing up and Franklin's greatest benefit becomes providing a route to somewhere else. That made me wonder why Miss Bette Davis, who could live pretty much anywhere she wanted, moved there from swanky Beverly Hills.

I became even more curious about that when I got to 5346. What I found was a tropical jungle so thick the actual house wasn't even visible from the street. The buildings—it turned out there were two, a large home and a cottage—were set well back from the street at the end of a long driveway down the right edge of the property.

Since there were no signs telling me to go away, I drove into a primeval forest full of exotic trees and shrubs. The only flora I recognized were some Italian cypress and maybe a camphor tree or two. Otherwise I might just as well have been transported to deepest, darkest Africa or wherever such trees grow.

I pulled into a guest parking area in front of the larger building, a simple tan structure with dark brown trim and a raised front porch, and shut off the Chrysler's engine. As I sat there listening to the popping and creaking noises my engine made as it cooled, nothing in the virtually primordial scene around me moved. Nobody inside the house peeked out a window or opened the door to see who was invading their privacy.

I was within a hundred feet of a major Los Angeles thoroughfare, and yet I might just as well have been a million miles from civilization. The effect was so complete I actually felt a couple of hairs on the back of my neck standing up. Easy, Spicer. Big–time Hollywood gumshoes don't quake and quiver just because they can't hear any traffic going by.

On that note I stepped down from my car and walked to the house. I climbed the porch steps and gave the door a knock. Something that sounded like a dry twig snapped behind me and as I turned, the door opened and a small pointed object whistled past me about a foot in front of my nose. Even though I didn't get a good look at it as it went by, I knew it had a point because the thing embedded itself in the doorframe as I dove through the opening, knocking a balding, red-faced man flat on his caboose as I did so.

The red-faced man let out a yelp, more twig-snapping noises came from the yard, and I rolled over to kick the door shut as protection against . . . what? There was nobody out there, at least nobody I could see, and the twig-snapping sounds were growing more distant. That's when Lillian Bouvier decided to show up.

"Mister Spicer! What on earth . . ."

"Hello, Lilly. Lend me a hand helping this gentleman up, and then it might be a good idea if you introduced us."

After we got the fellow back on his feet and leaned against the foyer wall because he was looking none too stable, Lilly said, "Henry, this is Mister Johnny Spicer, a private detective Madam hired to look into the robbery. Mister Spicer, this is Henry Gough, Madam's butler."

Gough looked at me disapprovingly. "I must say, Mister Spicer, you do have a rather dramatic way of entering a home."

Lilly added, "Yes, Mister Spicer. What was that all about?"

Stepping out the still open front door, I pulled the little dart out of the doorframe and held it up. "It was all about this."

We all stared at the projectile for a moment before Lilly said, "What in heaven's name is it?"

The dart was about an inch-and-a-half long with tiny white feathers like an arrow might have at the back and a nasty looking needle at the other end. The needle had something orange on its tip, which of course had to be curare or some other exotic poison.

I said, "Unless I'm way off base, this is a blowgun dart. It was fired or blown or whatever one calls it at us from out there in the front yard somewhere. I heard the guy, but never saw him."

Frowning, Henry said, "A blowgun!? Who would shoot such a thing at us?"

"That's one of the things I intend to find out. Another would be why. Henry, would you please find a paper envelope for this ugly little dart so I can safely carry it to an expert on such things?"

Henry disappeared down a hallway and returned a moment later carrying a standard-sized business envelope. "Will this do, sir?"

As I dropped the dart into the envelope, Henry said, "I'm curious, sir. Where does one find an expert on blowguns? Surely they aren't listed in the telephone directory business section."

So as not to appear incompetent, I lied through my teeth. "Oh, I know a fellow here in town who is widely versed in primitive weapons. I'm sure he'll have some answers for us." Quickly changing the subject, I added, "Now, if you don't mind, let's get on with the business at hand. Can you show me the display case from which the elephant statuette was stolen?"

Lilly, who was looking dubious as she listened to our conversation said, "Certainly, Mister Spicer. It is back in the library, right where it was when the Ivonya-Ngia elephant was taken. Walk this way, please."

Watching Lilly as she marched off down the hall, the Nick Charles gag from one of the Thin Man movies popped into my mind—the one where he follows a butler using the butler's bowlegged walk after being told to "walk this way." Unfortunately, Lilly's walk left no room for gags. It and she were all business.

The library—rich folks always have libraries whether they can read or not—was a small room at the south end of the house in which one wall was covered with bookshelves. Miss Davis had eclectic tastes, including everything from Shakespeare to *A Detailed History of the California Missions* and a copy of Thornton Wilder's *Our Town* script. There were also some comfortable-looking chairs, a library table, and a swanky fireplace, which given our current weather, did not have a fire going in it.

Atop the table sat a wood framed display case measuring about fourteen inches in each direction. Four of its six sides were glass, the bottom and back panels being wood. The bottom panel was covered in padded white satin, carefully custom fitted with indentations for the statuette's four feet.

I concluded that the back panel was intended to be the accepted way in and out of the box because it was secured by a sturdy little brass lock, but whoever bagged the elephant used a speedier method. They simply smashed the glass top panel.

All that remained of the elephant display was a small brass plaque attached to the case's padded bottom panel and inscribed with these words:

IVONYA-NGIA ELEPHANT
Kenya, Africa
Circa 1700s

I didn't have my official detective magnifying glass with me, but I leaned close to the busted case and looked for clues anyway because that's what it says to do in mail order gumshoe lesson number two. Lesson number two seldom yields any results, but this time it did, even without my magnifying glass. There, snagged on the sharp point of a jagged shard of glass was a small fragment of cloth that appeared to be wool and dark blue in color. Chances are the thief used his elbow to break the glass and left a tiny piece of his suit behind.

Eureka! Now all I had to do was find out who wore a blue wool suit to Bette's event, which probably included every male there, and I had the culprit. Still, it was a clue worth noting, so I asked Henry for another envelope to hold the fragment of cloth.

Next I gave some thought to the idea the perpetrator might have left a fingerprint or two on the display case and decided looking for a print would be a waste of time. Someone, probably Henry, had polished the display case glass recently so it showed very few fingerprints, and those I could see were mostly smudges. Besides, if the thief was clever enough to break the glass and remove the statuette without attracting the attention of other party guests, it seemed likely he also knew how to avoid leaving fingerprints on the case.

When I figured I'd seen all the clues the display case had to offer, I suggested we sit down so I could ask my questions. Lilly had no problem with that idea, but Henry seemed uncomfortable sitting in Madam's fancy chairs in Madam's fancy library. Or he might have been feeling a little stiff and sore after landing on the tile floor of the foyer.

Pulling my notebook and a pencil from my inside jacket pocket, I said, "If one of you will please ask Miss Pimm and Miss Alpert to join us . . ."

Lilly interrupted, saying, "I'm afraid that is not possible. Miss Alpert, Madam's maid, has gone home for the day, and this is Miss Pimm's night off. That's one of the reasons Madam is not home tonight. She always dines out on Miss Pimm's night off."

I nodded and wondered why Lilly had forgotten to mention Miss Pimm's and Miss Alpert's schedules when she was in my office that morning. Looking at my notebook again, I asked, "Well, let's see what the three of us can come up with on our own. The statuette turned up missing the evening of August second, last Friday. Have I got that right?"

Henry nodded and Lilly said, "Yes, that is correct."

Next question: "And Miss Davis hosted a party of some sort here that night. Is that also correct?"

"Henry nodded again and Lilly said, "Yes, that is correct."

Seeking a more informative response, I asked, "All right, what was the nature of that party and who were the guests?"

I was looking directly at Henry when I asked the question, but all I got out of him was, "Something to do with a movie Madam is making I think."

Lilly offered a more complete response. "The guests were mostly people with whom she is working in her current film."

Nodding in appreciation for the wealth of information she'd given me, I said, "I see. Then the attendees were mostly Warner Brothers folks?"

She shook her head. "No, that is not correct. Madam is on loan to RKO Studios for this project, so most of the people here were from there."

"What's the production title of the film, and do you have a copy of the guest list?"

"The project is a motion picture version of Lillian Hellman's play, Little Foxes. And, yes, I have a copy of the guest list. I'll get it for you."

She walked across the library to a small desk in one corner and I watched Henry. He shifted in his chair a little, still looking uncomfortable.

When Lilly returned, she handed me a neatly hand-printed list of eight names, most of which I recognized. Madam was hanging out with a pretty classy crowd, at least they were considered classy among film people.

I asked Lilly if I could keep the guest list and she said, "Yes, you may. I have other copies for the files."

Wondering what sort of files Bette Davis kept on her party guests, I moved on to my next question. "What time did your guests begin arriving?"

This time Henry had something to contribute. "The first to arrive was Mister Roland Boland. He arrived about eight o'clock. I recall that distinctly because he mentioned he had to leave for another engagement in about two hours."

Lilly added, "Yes, that is correct. I remember him mentioning another engagement."

I asked, "And did he leave at ten?"

Looking thoughtful, Henry said, "Yes, sir, I believe he did. I did not note the exact time he left, but that seems about right."

"Did you notice if he was carrying a package or had something heavy in one of his pockets?"

"No, sir. I do not recall anything of that sort."

"I see. Now the big question, who the heck is Roland Boland? His is the only name on the list I don't recognize."

Lilly said, "Mister Boland is Madam's favorite cinematographer. He has been connected in some way with nearly every film Madam has made. He's more commonly known as Rolly."

I noted this fact in my notebook. "And when did the other guests leave?"

Lilly took this question, too. "When Madam learned the statuette was missing it upset her terribly. She made it quite clear the party was over at that point. That was between eleven and eleven-thirty. I think everyone was gone before midnight."

"And," I asked, "Who noticed the elephant was missing?"

Henry spoke up again. "I'm afraid I was the bearer of those sad tidings. Madam's parties have a tendency to spread out all over the house, so I check all the public rooms regularly to empty ashtrays and see if her guests need anything. I came in here around ten-thirty and noticed something sparkle on the carpet over there." He gestured toward the table on which the statuette had been displayed.

"I went over to see if one of the ladies had lost an earring or something and discovered it was a shard of glass. That made me wonder where a piece of glass could have come from, and that's when I noticed the display case was broken."

"What did you do then, notify Miss Davis of the theft?"

"No, sir. I told Miss Bouvier here and she informed Madam."

"All right, Henry. Do you happen to recall when you last saw the statuette?"

Putting on his thoughtful look again, Henry said, "Not with any certainty, sir. As I said, I move around the house quite a bit during one of Miss Davis's affairs and it's possible the statuette was missing on one of my previous visits to the library and I simply failed to notice it."

"You said some of Miss Davis's guests were in the library here, do you remember who they were?"

Henry was wearing out his thoughtful look. "It changed throughout the evening. The only guests I remember being in here for a period of time were Mister Wyler and Miss Wright."

I turned to Lilly. "What about you? Do you remember who was in the library before the knickknack disappeared?"

She frowned at my use of the term knickknack and said, "I was only in here once Friday night. That was about nine o'clock. Rolly

Boland cornered me and asked to see the elephant. Mister Boland fancies himself a ladies' man, so I don't know if he actually had any interest in the statuette or if that was just an excuse to get me alone for a few minutes."

Grinning, I said, "Now, why would he want to do that?"

Lilly's frown turned into a glare. "Mister Spicer, you may not be among them, but some men do find me somewhat attractive."

"I don't doubt that for a moment, Miss Bouvier. Now, I have one last question for the two of you. Did you happen to notice if any of the men at the party were wearing a blue wool suit?"

Henry looked like he was getting a kick out of the teasing I was giving Lilly. He also knew a little about blue wool suits. "Yes, sir. There were several blue wool suits here that night. It seems they are quite popular this season. I recall that Mister Goldwyn, Mister Westmore and Mister Wyler were all wearing dark blue wool suits."

I looked in Lilly's direction and she simply said, "So was Rolly Boland."

That made three-quarters of the males at the party suspects, although I couldn't convince myself that Sam Goldwyn, Perc Westmore and William Wyler were likely candidates to be elephant thieves. The jury, however, was still out on Mister Boland.

At that point I also ran out of questions, so closing my notebook, I said, "Thanks to both of you for your time and cooperation. Again, Henry, I apologize for the dramatic entrance I made earlier. It seemed like the right thing to do at the time."

"That's quite all right, sir. I understand that your actions were in my best interests."

Turning to Lilly, I said, "Would you please set a time tomorrow afternoon when I can come back and meet the other two staff members. It will also be helpful if Miss Davis is here. I need to ask her a few questions about how she obtained the knickknack. If I'm not in the office when you call, leave a message with my answering service. I check with them regularly."

Turning her glare back down to a frown, she said, "I'll certainly try, Mister Spicer, but I cannot make any promises about Madam being here."

"Tell Madam if she wants her fancy elephant back, she needs to answer my questions, otherwise we're wasting time and money."

On that note I left 5346 Franklin Avenue with a good deal less drama and a whole lot more caution than that with which I had arrived. Fortunately the Montero Apartments where I live a few blocks away on Yucca at Highland don't have enough foliage, exotic or otherwise, to conceal a small cat.

Three

8:00 A.M. – Tuesday – August 6, 1940

Montero Apartments – 6795 Yucca Street, Hollywood

Tuesday brought with it a break in the heat and humidity, which considerably improved my outlook and that of my fellow Angelinos. I felt ready to take on the world, or at least one ceramic elephant thief.

Over a couple of scrambled eggs and toast, I considered what I knew about Bette Davis's missing elephant to see if the picture was any clearer in the cold, hard light of day. It wasn't.

I needed to know a hell of a lot more about the situation than the skimpy notes jotted in my notebook so far. True, I was just getting started with my investigation, but I had the definite feeling Henry and especially Lillian Bouvier weren't being as forthcoming as they might be. If true, that could just be their loyalty to Miss Davis showing in a reluctance to talk about their famous employer.

Okay, I'd just find the damned elephant in spite of them . . . I hoped.

So I donned my favorite gray fedora at a rakish angle and slipped into my shoulder holster, adding my Smith & Wesson Police Special. I don't like carrying the darn thing, but it's a good precaution when people are shooting at you . . . even if they're only shooting darts.

Next I climbed into my car and turned left from Yucca onto Highland, following it south through downtown Hollywood about a mile-and-a-half to Santa Monica Boulevard. There I turned left again, and then right a few blocks later onto Cahuenga Boulevard where I pulled to the curb in front of the block-square Technicolor production and processing labs.

I walked into the three-story main structure just like I owned the place and headed toward the labyrinth of small labs at the back of the building. The fellow I'd come to see was Mike Winters. He was one of Technicolor's top technicians and he occasionally moonlighted as a forensic chemist when his employers weren't looking.

Mike is a tall, slender fellow with one of those swarthy complexions that make him look like he needs a shave, whether or not he really needs one. When I walked into his ten-by-ten laboratory space, he was busy pouring something brown and hot from a larger glass beaker into a smaller one. Mike looked up and said, "Hey, Johnny! Good to see you, pal. You're just in time for coffee."

We shook hands and I said, "Is that what you're concocting there?"

"Yup. I discovered a method they use over in France that involves something called a coffee press. It's a little complicated to explain, but I built my own version of a press and it makes the best coffee you ever tasted. Here, let me pour you a cup."

"No thanks, Mike. I'm already coffeed-out this morning."

Raising the beaker of coffee in a toast, he said, "Okay, it's your loss. Now, what can I do for you?"

I slid the envelope out of my pocket that contained the dart I'd removed from the frame around Bette Davis's front door and offered it to him. "Be careful, there's a very sharp blowgun dart in here."

"Blowgun dart? Where the hell did you come across a thing like that?"

"Someone just missed sticking it in me yesterday. I brought it to you because there's some sort of orange substance on the business end—probably curare or something equally deadly. I'd like you to find out anything you can about the dart and the poison. Something in there might give me a clue as to who blew it at me."

Turning the dart slowly in his fingers as he held it up to the light, Mike said, "I gather you have a good reason for not just taking this into the police crime lab?"

"Yeah, my client's privacy."

He looked at me over the dart. "Got a big one on the line, huh?"

Nodding, I said, "Yeah, you could say that. Can you do it?"

"Well, there isn't much of the stuff left on there, but I can give it a try. Say twenty bucks to cover my time and materials?"

Even though I suspected that Technicolor provided the materials and paid for his time, whether they knew it or not, Mike had me over a barrel. I said, "Okay, but only if you get results."

"I'll do my best, my friend. I should have something for you by this time tomorrow. That soon enough?"

I told Mike that would be fine and returned to my car parked out on Cahuenga. I drove south five or six blocks to Melrose, where I jogged east a block to get around the Wilshire Country Club, and then continued south on Rossmore Avenue through snooty Hancock Park and the Wilshire District.

When I got to Wilshire Boulevard, I jogged east another block and followed Crenshaw Boulevard three or so miles south through the apartment buildings and business of the Mid City District to Exposition Boulevard. There I turned east and completed the last leg of my journey to Exposition Park, where one finds the University of California, the Coliseum, and my destination, the Los Angeles Natural History Museum.

The entire trip had taken up about an hour of my morning. The experts tell us parkways and freeways are the answers to wasting time on the road due to traffic congestion and the state just opened the Arroyo Seco Parkway between downtown Los Angeles and Pasadena to prove that point. It is eight miles or so of divided, high-speed road with overpasses for all the streets it crosses and a speed limit of forty-five miles per hour. We'll see. Personally, I doubt that letting unskilled drivers travel at speeds like that in close proximity to one another will lead to anything but roadway carnage.

I was going to the Natural History Museum because I remember going there with my folks as a kid and seeing a really terrific elephant display. If it was still there, I hoped there was an expert to go along with it who could tell me something about elephant mythology. It might be a long shot, but I figured a Natural History Museum was as good a place to start as any.

At the top of fifteen wide concrete steps there was an elaborate entrance topped by three arches and a whole lot of gewgaws and other stuff that, as far as I could see, contributed nothing to the process of learning about natural history. Walking through the entrance, I found myself in a great chamber with marble walls and more echoes than the Swiss Alps. It was all I could do to refrain from yodeling.

There was a young woman at the information desk who was far more skilled at making popping sounds with her chewing gum than she was at providing information. Once we agreed that elephants were mammals and the person to see was probably the curator of mammalogy, however, things began to go more smoothly. Between gum pops she directed me to a Doctor Jessup, who is the museum's expert on African mammals.

I found Doctor Harvey Jessup, PhD in a small office on the museum's second floor. He was an average looking fellow of about forty with a graying beard and moustache. He was sitting in a gray metal frame chair behind a gray metal desk, both of which looked to be Navy surplus. A second gray metal frame chair sat opposite the desk and the office was neat as a pin.

Trying out a little explorer humor, I said, "Doctor Jessup, I presume?"

Standing, he replied, "You presume correctly, sir. And you are?"

Offering a handshake, I said, "My name is Spicer. I'm a private investigator in search of some elephant mythology."

"All right, have a seat. Asian or African?"

It took me a minute to realize he was asking me which kind of elephant I wanted to know about. I quickly said, "Oh, African."

He stroked his beard and looked contemplative for a moment before saying, "I'll do my best to help you, but I must admit that I am curious why a Los Angeles private detective is interested in African elephant mythology."

"It has to do with a case of theft I'm investigating. The object stolen was a supposedly priceless elephant statuette called . . ."

"Oh, yes, the famous Ivonya-Ngia Tembo."

Surprised, I asked, "You've heard that it's missing?"

"No, sir. I don't even know who owns it now. It's simply that the Ivonya-Ngia is one of the most famous objects in the world of elephant studies."

"A minute ago you called it the Ivonya-Ngia Tembo. Is that the technical name for it?"

"Not really. Tembo is the Swahili word for elephant, so it's often referred to in that manner.

"Do you happen to know the myth the statuette represents?"

"Certainly. Would you like to hear it?"

Removing my notebook and pencil, I said, "That's exactly what I'm here for."

Leaning back in his chair, Doctor Jessup said, "All right. It seems there was a shepherd back in the early times whose entire flock died due to a drought. Penniless and desperate, he went in search of a generous man in his region who was known for helping those in need.

"This man's name was Ivonya-Ngia, and when the shepherd found him, Ngia saw that he was worthy and ordered his men to give the shepherd a hundred sheep and a hundred cows, but the poor shepherd turned the gift down and instead asked for the secret of becoming rich.

"Ivonya-Ngia decided to grant the shepherd's wish and gave him a special bottle of ointment. He told the poor man to rub the lotion on the pointed canine teeth of his wife's upper jaw every day. Even though the shepherd couldn't see how this would make him rich he did as he was told, and before long his wife's canine teeth began to grow and became tusks, which the poor man cut off and sold when they had grown long. He repeated this process many times and eventually became as wealthy as Ivonya-Ngia himself.

"Now, what I just told you is more or less the Kenyan version of the story as told around Nairobi, which is where the Ivonya-Ngia elephant was supposedly found."

I finished writing the legend into my notebook and asked, "You said the statuette was found in Nairobi. Do you know anything else about its origin?"

"No, my interest is in the living, breathing sort of elephant. You'll need to see an expert in African art for information about the statuette itself. I've heard of a Kenyan fellow who has written a few books on the subject, but I'm afraid he's some distance away in Sacramento. I'll write his name and information down for you just in case you decide you want to look him up."

Jessup took one of his own business cards out of the desk drawer and on the back he wrote:

Joseph Kipchumba
724 Harbor Blvd.
West Sacramento, Calif.

Doctor Jessup handed me the card and I thanked him for his time and the information he provided. Then I returned to my car and thought about what to do next. It was a few minutes past eleven-thirty, so I decided to head back to Hollywood, check my messages, and stop by El Coyote for lunch. When in doubt, eat.

My route back from Exposition Park took me north on Figueroa, west on Washington Boulevard, and north again on La Brea to First, where I pulled to the curb and walked across the street to the El Coyote Mexican Café.

El Coyote is unique in Hollywood because it is one of the few good restaurants celebrities have found, but tourists haven't.

Personally, I go there because the food is good, and I can honestly say I've have never been pestered for an autograph while eating there.

It's a small place with an exterior mish-mash of columns and arches. The mish-mash continues on the inside with a long narrow dining room full of booths and a ceiling draped with those colored light bulbs they put on Christmas trees. Well, like I said, I go there because the food is good.

After being seated in the only empty booth left in the room, I ordered cheese enchiladas with rice and beans and a bottle of Dos Equis. Then, while my lunch was being prepared, I made use of the public telephone mounted in a narrow hallway that leads to El Coyote's back door.

Rosie, of Rosie's Professional Telephone Exchange Service, answered promptly, and gave me the two messages that had been left so far today. The first she read had just come in and it was from a Miss Lillian Bouvier who wanted to inform me that she had made a thirty-minute appointment for me to speak with her employer at four o'clock this afternoon. She added, "Please be prompt."

My second message came in earlier this morning and was from a Miss Susan Jackson who requested that I call her back. It was nothing urgent and she didn't leave her number because, as she explained to Rosie, I already had it.

Susan Jackson was, of course, Nurse Susan in Santa Barbara with whom I'd been spending so much delightful time lately. And, yes, I had her number.

My lunch and I arrived at the table simultaneously and it was delicious. I'm not a big fan of beer, but a Mexican beer with a Mexican meal can't be beat. Thus refortified, I paid my bill and headed for my car.

When I got outside, though, I noticed a piece of paper under my windshield wiper blade. Since I was parked perfectly legally, I wondered what horrible traffic crime LAPD's finest thought I had committed. It turned out not to be a ticket, though, but the silliest ransom note I have ever seen. In roughly formed capital letters it said:

DETECTIVE

IF YOU EVER WANT TO SEE THE ELEPHANT AGAIN PUT ONE-HUNDRED-THOUSAND-DOLLARS IN SMALL BILLS INTO A PAPER SACK AND WAIT FOR INSTRUCTIONS OTHERWISE ELEPHANT GOES TO HIGHEST BIDDER

I almost laughed out loud. First of all, ransom notes go to the person whose property you've taken. Sending one to somebody investigating the crime is just begging him to find you. Second, if you can get more from a higher bidder, why settle for a hundred thousand? And third, think about one-hundred-thousand-dollars in small bills for a minute.

If it was in twenties, for example, you would have fifty bundles of bills, each about three-quarters of an inch thick. That adds up to a stack more than three feet high—a hell of a lot more than you could jam into a paper grocery bag.

Now, could I be so lucky as to have the dummy who left the ransom note on my car still hanging around? He could be watching to make sure I got the note, in which case, he might appreciate a reply. Ripping a page from my notebook, I wrote:

Listen, Stupid,
I don't have time to fool with amateurs. Return the elephant by five this afternoon and all will be forgiven. Otherwise, you're looking at about 20 years of hard labor.

I placed my cleverly worded reply under the wiper blade and walked back into the restaurant, stopping near one of the front windows so I could see if the culprit took my bait. I had to wait a while, but after about ten minutes, curiosity got the better of him and I watched a black DeSoto two-door sedan pull up and double park next to my car.

While he slid over to open the passenger side door, I charged out of the restaurant and started across La Brea. Of course, I couldn't see much of him because his car was between us, but I had the impression of a fellow with a medium to small build.

He got out the passenger side door of his DeSoto and was retrieving my note when something made him look my way. The guy saw me and dove back into his car. I hollered, "Freeze, police," but he was already behind the steering wheel and shifting into first gear.

At that point I got a look at him through the driver-side window, but there wasn't much to see. He was wearing a fedora low over his forehead and dark glasses. Two seconds later he was around the corner and heading south on First Street.

I was prepared for that and had my car keys in my hand. The Chrysler started on the first try and I followed the DeSoto as it roared down First. He was going all out, but I could still see him two blocks ahead.

Now things would either get very easy or very tricky. If he didn't know First dead-ends at the Wilshire Country Club in seven or eight blocks, I had a good chance of trapping the guy. If he did know the layout, he'd have to make a turn off of First, and if I didn't have him in sight when he turned I could very easily lose him in the surrounding residential area.

First Street has only one stop sign between La Brea and the country club. It's at Highland, and he blew right through it. I was planning to do the same, when a Coca-Cola delivery truck heading north on Highland entered the intersection just ahead of me. I slammed on the brakes and managed to get the Chrysler stopped in time, but there wasn't more than an inch or two to spare between my front bumper and the truck. I didn't want to think about the sticky mess we would have had if my brakes weren't pretty darn good.

Of course, the truck driver stopped when he heard all my tire screeching. He looked down at me shaking his head and his fist, and then leisurely continued on his way. When the street ahead was finally clear, the DeSoto was nowhere to be seen.

I looked left and right at each intersection hoping to catch a glimpse of the car without any success, so I made a U-turn and headed back to Highland, where I turned right. By two o'clock I'd parked in the First National Bank Building's parking lot and was on the way up to my office on the second floor. I was also feeling pretty silly for letting our amateur elephant thief outsmart me.

Four

2:00 P.M. – Tuesday – August 6, 1940

Spicer Investigations – 1st National Bank Building, Hollywood

Feeling the need to hear a friendly voice, I placed a long distance call to Nurse Susan in Santa Barbara. She had the eleven p.m. to seven a.m. shift all this month, so at the risk of waking her, I called Susan's home number. Susan picked up on the second ring.

"Hi, Angel. Hope I didn't wake you up."

"Hi, Johnny! Oh no, you didn't wake me. I usually go to bed around three when I have the early morning shift."

"Good."

"It would have been okay if you had awakened me, though. After all, you are returning my call to you."

"I am indeed. Is everything okay up there in the land of millionaires?"

"Everything's swell, Johnny. I just called to let you know I have next Saturday and Sunday off. I was scheduled to work, but one of the other nurses really wanted a weekend off at the end of the month, so we traded shifts."

Teasing Susan was one of my favorite pastimes and that was okay because she could dish it right back to me and then some. I said, "How interesting. And you thought it was worth the price of a long distance telephone call for me to know this?"

"Well . . . actually, yes. I'm trying to get an out of town weekend date with this handsome Hollywood detective I know, and if I'm successful, I might ask you to stop by and feed Mister Whiskers. You and he get along so well, I know it would be a treat for both of you."

Mister Whiskers is an orange and white tabby Susan adopted, or vice versa. Whiskers and I tolerate each other for her sake.

"Gee, Angel, that would be terrific and I'd love to do it for you, but I've got a date with this classy nurse from Santa Barbara this weekend. Maybe another time."

Susan giggled. "How come, no matter how clever I think I am, you always one-up me?"

"Probably because I'm a natural smart aleck. Hey, I know just the place for us to go."

"You do?"

"Yeah, there's this fancy hotel that just opened on the waterfront in Santa Monica. Everybody who's been there seems to think it's really the place to stay on the coast."

"Nifty! What's it called?"

"They named themselves after James Hilton's earthly paradise, Shangri-La."

"Oh my, how exotic!"

"Well, I don't know how exotic the joint is, but from the outside it looks very modern and swanky."

"That would be really great, Johnny, but I hate to see you spending so much money on fancy hotels. We could just as easily stay at an auto court or even at your place."

"Angel, as long as I've got it, I plan to spend it. I set some aside for the future and I landed a new case yesterday that's paying top dollar, so we . . . so I can afford it. Do you want to come down on Friday?"

"Yes. I get off at seven in the morning and I was thinking of taking the train down after work. There's a Coaster that leaves here at nine-thirty and gets into Los Angeles at noon. Would that be okay?"

"Sounds fine to me. I'll go by Union Station and get you a will-call ticket for a deluxe parlor car seat. Then you can just . . ."

"Johnny! Didn't we just agree you shouldn't be spending so much money? I can buy my own train ticket."

"Maybe you agreed to that, but I didn't. Just pick up the ticket and have a fun trip. I'll see you around noon Friday."

"I just don't know what I'm going to do about you. You're way too generous."

"Just say goodbye, Angel. I gotta get back to work."

Our conversation over, I pulled the ransom note out of my jacket pocket and laid it flat on the desk. Then I took my magnifying glass out of the drawer and examined the slip of paper in minute detail. Problem was, there wasn't much detail to examine.

The note measured about eight inches in width by six inches in height and had been cut hastily from a larger sheet of paper because no two sides were precisely parallel. I suspected the note was printed first, and then cut out. The lack of a watermark and a rather course surface texture indicated the paper was an inferior quality of stationary, like the kind you find in hotels.

The text was printed using a pencil with wide, soft lead that smeared easily. The fact that the message was printed in all capital letters with no punctuation marks might be an indication that the author of the note knew block style capital letters are the hardest kind for a handwriting expert to match. The letters were formed crudely enough to have been printed by a right-handed person using his left hand, although that seemed like an unnecessary precaution.

Next I thought about what the content of the message told me about its author. For one thing, the guy knew I was a detective, although he could have guessed I was a police detective rather than the private kind. The guy was close enough to the case to know the missing knick-knack was an elephant statue. Given the curtain of secrecy Miss Davis and Lilly were using to keep the case out of the press that might be significant.

I also thought it interesting that the elephant-napper was asking for a hundred thousand. It was the same value Lilly claimed for the thing. That might mean nothing, however, if a hundred grand is the standard asking price for antique African elephant statuettes.

The bit about the small bills threw the whole thing into a cocked hat though. It told me the ransom note wasn't what it appeared to be. Only an idiot would ask for that many small bills in a paper sack that couldn't possibly hold them all, and whoever took the Ivonya-Ngia was no idiot.

So, if the message wasn't intended to be a real ransom note, why was it written and why was it given to me? The most logical answer to those questions would be that the message was supposed to scare me off the case, just like the blow gun dart was intended to do. Okay, who knows I'm on the case? The answer to that one pointed directly to an inside job.

To advance that theory a little further, I decided to put the message away in my office safe and not mention it to anyone at Miss Davis's home during my visit in an hour or so. If the elephant was an inside job, my not mentioning a ransom demand that was delivered to me personally could make someone very nervous.

I turned off of Franklin and down Betty Davis's primeval drive at precisely ten minutes before four. Lilly's instructions said to be prompt and that I was. It took a while for someone to answer my knock, and when Henry finally opened the door, he did so cautiously. Considering what happened the last time I was there, I didn't blame him.

"Good afternoon, Mister Spicer. Miss Bouvier is waiting for you in the library."

When we walked into the room, there were three people already there, but none of them was Miss Davis. Either she was planning a grand entrance or promptness was strictly a one way deal with her.

Lilly stood and said, "Good afternoon, Mister Spicer."

"Hiya, Lilly. How are you today?"

"Quite well, thank you, Mister Spicer." She emphasized the "mister" to let me know she still didn't like me calling her Lilly, especially in front of the hired help. Continuing, Lilly said, "I would like to introduce the two members of Madam's domestic staff you have not yet met, Miss Alpert and Missus Pimm."

I recalled Lilly telling me that Joyce Pimm was Bette Davis's cook. She was an older, heavy set woman who more than anything else resembled someone's kindly grandmother. Doris Alpert, the maid, was quite a bit younger, I guessed in her mid-twenties. She was trim with a flattering figure, but her face was rather plain, a minor fault she attempted to overcome with too much makeup. Back on the positive side, Doris had a ready smile and a cheerful personality.

"Good afternoon, ladies. I appreciate your taking time to talk with me." Then turning to Lilly, I said, "I was under the impression my appointment this afternoon was to include Miss Davis."

Looking just a little sheepish, Lilly said, "Well, yes it was. Unfortunately, she was detained at the studio. Madam telephoned and said she would be here by four-thirty."

I smiled a smile that meant I knew what she'd just told me was hogwash and turned to Doris Alpert. "Okay, Miss Alpert let's start with you."

She almost jumped to attention at the sound of her name. "All right, sir."

"My questions concern last Friday, the night the elephant statuette was stolen. Were you here that evening?"

"Oh my, yes. My first job at Madam's affairs is to see to the guests' coats and hats and such. I put them in the front bedroom as people arrive and return them when people leave."

"So you spent some of the evening in the front bedroom. Did you happen to go into the library that night?"

"No, sir. At least I don't recall going in there. When I'm done putting the coats and hats away, I see to the restrooms, making sure they are always clean and tidy. I also help Henry pass out the little sandwiches and what not when he needs me to."

My questions seemed to be making Miss Alpert a little nervous, so I tried to put her more at ease. "Very good, Doris. I only have a few more questions for you. When you were giving people their coats and hats at the end of the party, did you happen to notice if any of the men who were wearing blue wool suits had a tear in one elbow of their sleeves?"

After a moment's thought, Doris shook her head with conviction. "No, sir, I did not."

"Or did you notice anyone acting peculiar?"

Again she gave my question some thought. "I guess that would depend on what you mean by peculiar. Movie people are a little peculiar to begin with, and when they get a few drinks . . ."

Lilly interrupted her. "Stick to the facts, Doris."

Doris Alpert looked at Lilly with what was either an expression of surprise or one of anger, I wasn't sure which. Doris then turned to me again and answered my question. "No, sir, I did not."

I sighed and nodded. "All right, Doris, that's all the questions I have. You did a fine job. Thank you for your cooperation."

Doris gave me a pleasant smile and Lilly said, "Okay, Doris, you may return to your duties."

I thought about telling Miss Bouvier I would appreciate it if she would butt out. Often the best information you get from an interview shows up in impromptu comments people make when they wander from the subject, but taking a verbal poke at Lilly would antagonize her even more. There was nothing to be gained in doing that, so I turned to the cook. "Missus Pimm, were you here working last Friday night as well?"

"Yes, sir, I was."

"Did you happen to go into the library during the evening?"

"No, sir, I did not."

I could tell this interview was going nowhere fast. "So you spent the entire evening in the kitchen?"

"Yes, sir, I did until it was time to clean up. We all lend a hand when a party is over. It makes things go a little faster."

"And I don't suppose you saw any of the guests behaving peculiarly?"

"No, sir, I did not."

"Okay, Missus Pimm. Thank you for your cooperation."

Lilly dismissed the cook and I glanced at my watch. It was four-forty-five. "I thought you said Miss Davis would be here by four-thirty."

A familiar voice from the doorway said, "And so I was, Mister Spicer. However, I did not want to interrupt your interrogations, so I waited until you were through. That seemed the courteous thing to do."

I watched a look of relief spread over Lilly's face. She said, "Good afternoon, Madam. Unless you need me to remain here, I will return to my duties."

"You are dismissed, Miss Bouvier. Mister Spicer, it is good to see you again, but I would rather the circumstances were different. So have a seat and let us get your questions answered and you can get back to finding my elephant."

Still standing and in a very businesslike tone I said, "All right, Miss Davis, how long have you owned the Ivonya-Ngia statuette?"

Without hesitation she said, "I acquired it about two months ago . . . in mid-June."

"And from whom did you acquire it?"

"I'm afraid I cannot answer that question, Mister Spicer."

Lowering my notebook, I said, "Miss Davis, if you want your elephant back, you've got to give me the information I need to find it."

Miss Davis smiled at me with an expression she might use with a small child and carefully explained, "Mister Spicer you were not listening to me. I said 'I cannot answer your question, not 'I will not answer it.' The transaction was a very secretive business and I never actually met or learned the name of the seller."

"Really? How did you know you weren't being swindled or sold a fake?"

"The sale was handled through an intermediary; someone I trust. He arranged for an appraisal by some expert or other, and when the authenticity was certain, we finalized the purchase."

"And who was this intermediary?"

"A cinematographer friend I have known for some time."

Nodding, I decided to do a little name dropping and see what it got me. "That would, of course, be Rolly Boland."

If Bette Davis was surprised that I knew the name of her cinematographer friend, she concealed it well. I made a note never to play poker with this woman. She smiled pleasantly and said, "Yes, that would be Rolly."

Playing a hunch, I asked, "How were you contacted about purchasing the Ivonya-Ngia? I mean how did you even know it was for sale, let alone how to go about purchasing it?"

Still smiling, she said, "Rolly's hobby is collecting primitive art, and he heard through some grapevine or other that a rare piece of African tribal art might be available, and knowing that I also have an appreciation for unusual art, he passed the information on to me. He gave me the impression he would like to acquire the figurine for himself, but that it would be more expensive than he could afford. I asked him to find out more about it and he did."

"I see. Who did the appraisal?"

That question got a small reaction as if she wasn't expecting it. She looked down at the carpet for a moment before saying, "I do not recall his name. He was some distance away, though—San Francisco or maybe Sacramento. I remember Rolly making a couple of trips up that way to get the appraisal done. Rolly felt strongly about using this fellow because he has written books on the subject of African art and is quite knowledgeable."

I figured the "expert" appraiser was quite likely the fellow in Sacramento Doctor Jessup told me about, Joseph Kipchumba. That he had done the appraisal raised my interest level in him several notches.

Sensing I was running out of time with Miss Davis, I quickly asked another question to keep things moving. "Miss Davis, where do you keep the statuette when it's not on display in your home?"

"I keep it in a safe deposit box at the First National Bank. I have several boxes there containing small objects d' art."

"And who has access to those boxes besides yourself?"

"Only Lillian Bouvier and my sister, Bobby. Bobby is on the signature list in case I'm incapacitated."

Then the timer went off. "Mister Spicer, I must run along for another appointment. If you have more questions for me you can arrange another meeting with Miss Bouvier."

Standing, she offered me her hand, which I shook gently as I said, "Of course, Miss Davis. I think we covered all the important subjects today, so I'll try not to bother you further."

"No bother, Mister Spicer. Just please hurry and find my elephant."

Leaving Bette Davis's primeval forest, I turned right on Franklin, and headed east toward Vermont Avenue, where I turned right and drove south through Rampart Village to Wilshire Boulevard. The traffic was surprisingly light for the late afternoon hour, so I was able to do some thinking as I drove.

My tactic of not mentioning the fake ransom note had accomplished nothing. Doris Alpert seemed nervous at times during our conversation, but that could have simply been a case of nerves brought on by my interrogation. So much for that clever plan.

Next I tried to advance my inside job theory by picturing each of the principals in the case in a black fedora and dark glasses like the person who'd left the fake ransom note on my car was wearing. It certainly hadn't been Henry who left the note, nor could it have been Missus Pimm. That left Lilly, Miss Alpert and Bette Davis herself. I had to admit it could have been any of them.

The problem with any of the women as suspects was that it shot holes in my thought that the ransom note had been a spur of the moment thing, and few women of my acquaintance drive around with male disguises handy in their cars. There was, however, also Rolly Boland whom I had not met yet. I decided to correct that tomorrow.

At Wilshire Boulevard I turned left and continued southeast to Hill Street, which I took northeast up to Alameda Street and the new Los Angeles Union Station. The truth was that I could have purchased Susan's ticket at a couple of closer places downtown, but I always get a little thrill out of going to this monument to modern rail transportation.

When it opened about a year ago to replace the old Southern Pacific and Santa Fe depots, I read it was designed by the same architects who designed our monolithic City Hall, and the terminal was described in the papers as a combination of Dutch Colonial Revival, Mission Revival, and Streamline Moderne architectural styles. Okay, if that's what they want to call it, fine by me. I just call it an impressive, clean design that puts me in the mood to get on a train.

Inside, the place is huge with vaulted ceilings and what look like wooden beams, but I'm told are actually steel beams. The passenger waiting areas and the ticket counters are well lit by huge windows on both long walls during the day and, at night, by decorative chandeliers hung from the ceiling on chains. Either way, it's an impressive sight and an excellent place to begin an adventure by train.

Across a Spanish style courtyard garden from the terminal is an honest to goodness Harvey House restaurant. I've eaten in a lot of Harvey Houses in my time, and I was tempted to add this one to the list before the night was over.

Five

9:00 A.M. – Wednesday – August 7, 1940

Technicolor Labs – 1015 Cahuenga Boulevard, Hollywood

I found Mike Winters in his laboratory performing some sort of elaborate procedure with his coffee press. "Hi, Mike, still working on the perfect cup of Joe?"

"Hi, Johnny. You can't improve on perfection and every cup I brew is perfect. Say, I've got the analysis of the poison on that blowgun dart for you. Want to see what I found?"

"Yes, indeed."

Mike took the dart out of its envelope and held it up for dramatic effect. I noticed he'd stuck a rubber test tube stopper on the point to prevent any accidental deaths. He then unfolded a piece of paper from the envelope and said, "Your poison is organic and consists of Citrus sinensis, husk of Citrus x Meyeri, H2o, and disaccharide."

"Wow! I recognize the H2O part, but what about the rest of it? Is that a deadly combination?"

He grinned at me. "Absolutely, if your prey is a slice of toast."

"What?"

"Yes, my friend, your deadly poison is orange marmalade, plain and simple. It's made up of oranges, grated lemon zest, water, and sugar, and that's it."

Flabbergasted, I said, "You're kidding! The deadly African poison on the tip of this dart is nothing more than a breakfast preserve?"

"Yup, and what's more, you aren't even on the right continent. Blowguns and poison-tipped darts are used by South American natives, not African natives." Then he held his hand out and said, "I believe the agreed upon price for my analysis was twenty bucks."

I pulled a twenty out of my wallet and slapped it into his outstretched hand. "Marmalade to you, too, pal."

Mike's grin got even bigger. "Thank you, Johnny. It's been a pleasure doing business with you. Sure you won't have a cup of coffee before you go? It would be very tasty with some toast and marmalade."

I left Mike in his cubicle laughing his fool head off and returned to my car. I took the dart out of its envelope again and looked at it. The case of the missing elephant had just taken another weird turn. Now I had a phony poison dart to go with the phony ransom note. Well, at least there was some consolation in knowing whoever blew the dart at Henry and me wasn't trying to kill us. He was just inviting us to breakfast.

On my way back to the office, it occurred to me that having somebody not trying to kill you is infinitely better than having someone who is trying to kill you. That made me wonder if I've been taking this case entirely too seriously while everyone else is playing games. Oh, well, as long as Bette Davis was willing to pay my daily rate and expenses, I'd go along with the gag until her checks start bouncing.

I slid behind my desk and dialed Bette Davis's home number. After the second ring, Henry said, "Miss Davis's residence. Please state your business."

"Hi, Henry. This is Johnny Spicer. I need to speak with Miss Bouvier for a moment if she's available."

"Yes, sir. One moment please."

A minute or so later a click came down the line Lilly said, "Hello, Mister Spicer. How can I help you?"

I was listening for the second click that meant Henry had hung up the extension he used to answer my call. It never came. Interesting.

"Hello, Lilly. I called to ask how I can get in touch with Rolly Boland."

Several seconds of silence followed my request. Finally, she said, "Am I to assume you wish to interview him?"

"Yes, you may assume that."

More silence. "Would you like me to make an appointment with him for you?"

"If you don't mind, I'd rather do that myself. How do I reach him?"

With a good deal of resignation in her tone, she said, "Very well, Mister Spicer. Rolly lives at the El Royale apartments at 450 Rossmore Avenue, apartment number 802. His telephone number is Hollywood-one-one-three-one."

I wrote the information in my notebook and said, "Thank you kindly, Miss Bouvier."

"You're quite welcome, Mister Spicer."

She hung up, but I stayed on the line a few seconds, and sure enough, I heard the second click that meant Henry had listened to the entire conversation. I wondered if Lilly was aware Henry was in the habit of listening in to her telephone calls.

Fortunately, who was listening in on whose telephone calls was not my problem. Rolly Boland, however, was my problem and something about his address bothered me. I dragged my well-worn copy of the Thomas Brothers Los Angeles County map book out of the drawer and looked for Rossmore Avenue.

When I found 450 Rossmore, I immediately knew why Boland's address triggered an alarm bell in my head. He lives just on the other side of the Wilshire Country Club and only about a mile from where I had lunch and encountered the phony thief with the phony ransom note.

I had assumed the culprit must have followed me from my office this morning, but when I thought about it, that didn't make much sense because he could have simply left the note on my windshield while I was at Technicolor Labs. Now there was another possibility. If this guy knew what I looked like, he might have spotted me while I was having lunch practically in his backyard. He might have even been in the restaurant. It still seemed like a long shot, but it would explain a couple of things. I made a mental note to take a look around the El Royale for a black DeSoto.

Picking up the telephone receiver again, I dialed Hollywood-one-one-three-one and heard the annoying repetitious buzz that says the line I'm calling is in use. I tapped my fingers on the desk for about fifteen seconds and tried again. Still busy.

I gave it a little more time and tried again. This time I got a ring and an answer. Besides a silly nickname, Roland Boland had a deep, resonant voice and a hint of an English accent that might or might not be authentic.

"Mister Boland, My name is Spicer. I'm a private investigator looking into the recent theft of a piece of African art for its owner. She said you were helpful in the acquisition of the object and could provide me with a few details she doesn't know. Would you be willing to meet me for that purpose?"

"Certainly, Mister Spicer. I would be happy to help, however I would feel a great deal more comfortable if we had a member of the owner's staff—say, Miss Bouvier—here during the interview. As I'm sure you know, the owner is quite particular about her privacy."

Well, now I knew why his phone had been busy when I tried it right after talking to Lilly. That girl doesn't miss a trick. I said, "That's fine with me. Can we meet this afternoon?"

"Yes, as it happens I plan to be home today, so talk with Miss Bouvier and pick a time that's convenient for both of you. Whatever you decide will be satisfactory for me."

"Thank you, Mister Boland. I look forward to meeting you this afternoon."

As I sat at my desk thinking about it, I decided I was getting a little tired of having my investigation manipulated by Miss Frump. On the other hand, if I used my noggin and got a jump or two ahead of her, her manipulation might be turned into an advantage. One step in accomplishing that was for me to be a little less predictable. So instead of calling her to set up our appointment with Boland, I donned my fedora and headed out for lunch. Hopefully, Miss Bouvier and Mister Boland were sitting around waiting for me to call her and set up our appointment. Letting them wait a while might make them a little nervous. People who think they're smarter than the rest of us tend to get upset when things don't go exactly as they planned.

It occurred to me that I hadn't been to the Pig N' Whistle—or as we locals call it, the Pig—in a while. Since the Pig is only about a block and a half east of my office on Hollywood Boulevard, I left the car in its parking stall and hoofed it. Marco, the Pig's maître d', welcomed me by name and told me it had been too long since I was there last. I agreed with him because it's always a good idea to agree with Marco, and he seated me at a small table near the side door that leads out into the Egyptian Theater's forecourt next door.

Without the need of consulting a menu, I ordered one of my favorites, the Assorted Cold Plate, consisting of baked ham, Swiss and American cheeses, potato salad, coleslaw, and tomatoes. It gives me several flavors to enjoy and seems like a big lunch, when it's actually not a whole lot of food.

In a town where million dollar deals can't be signed without martinis on the table, Pig N' Whistle is something of an oddity because the bar running down the west side of the dining room is a soda fountain. You can't order a Snow White, but you can get yourself a Shirley Temple or a hot fudge sundae. What always surprises me are the people you see at the Pig's soda fountain.

Spencer Tracy is a frequent patron of the Pig's ice cream parlor and I've seen Clark Gable there on at least two occasions.

After lunch I sauntered back to my office, caught up on my mail, and finally turned to the telephone a little after one. This time Lilly answered my call herself, sounding a little breathless as she said, "Hello?"

"Hi there, Lilly. Have you been exercising or something? You sound a little out of breath."

There was a pause while she took a deep breath. "No, I was just at the other end of the house and Henry is off doing errands, so I had to run to answer the telephone."

"Maybe you should get a couple more extensions. They are certainly a convenience in many ways."

After another pause, Lilly said, "How can I help you, Mister Spicer?"

"Well, Lilly, a surprising thing has happened. I spoke with Rolly Boland about an interview and guess what?"

I gave her a couple of seconds to ponder my question before saying, "He would be happy to meet with me this afternoon as long as you are present. Isn't that a coincidence?"

She tried to sound puzzled, but not very convincingly. "Coincidence? What do you mean?"

"Never mind . . . just a little detective humor. Would you be available to meet me at Mister Boland's apartment about two-thirty?"

"Ah . . . that's . . . I don't know if . . . yes, I can meet you there."

"Wonderful, Miss Bouvier. Shall we meet in the lobby? That way you can show me the way to Rolly's apartment. You have been there before, I presume?"

"Oh, yes. I mean with Madam, of course. The lobby will be fine at two-thirty."

"Grand. See you then."

I set the handset in its cradle, smiled to myself, and donned my fedora. Ten minutes later I was eastbound on Hollywood Boulevard heading for the Wilshire district. The El Royale apartment building was a gray and white, nine-floor monstrosity designed in what I believe is called the rococo style, which seems to require that design figures—spirals, diamonds and such be stuck any place there's room for them. The management gets an A in landscaping, though. Little hedges, lawns and other shrubbery were all manicured within an inch of their lives.

Unfortunately, the management also provided an undercover parking garage on the first floor on the south end of the building.

That was unfortunate because it meant if Rolly Boland owned a black DeSoto, it would probably be in the parking garage, thus making it more difficult for me to get a look at it.

Parking at the yellow loading zone directly in front of the El Royale was not allowed, but I found a parking spot down the block where the neighbors were less particular about who parked in front of their residences. Cutting across the El Royale's grounds, I walked to the garage entrance and stared into the gloom. Noticing there were no "keep out" signs, I walked in a ways and looked around.

If the black DeSoto had teeth, it could have bit me. The darn thing was parked in the first slot north of the entrance facing the front of the building. It was locked, but I made a note of its license number—the black on yellow digits were 3Y5460. I walked around the car looking for distinguishing features and found nothing unique. It was simply a black two-door DeSoto Custom.

I couldn't say for sure it was the same DeSoto I chased this morning, but finding a look-alike in the parking garage of a principal in the case was a hell of a coincidence. Now I needed to find out if it belonged to Roland Boland. If so, that would pretty much cinch the deal.

Leaving the garage, I walked around to the El Royale's main entrance and waited for two guys in moving company overalls to make it out the door with the large divan they were carrying. Then I walked in for a look at how the other half lived.

Inside, the lobby was also loaded with more rococo designs, plus black and white ceramic tiles on the floor, an arched carved ceiling overhead, and moldings in places I've never seen molding before. There was also a concierge and a grand piano in the lobby. No, I don't know if the concierge plays the piano.

I'd made a point of getting there before Lilly so I could snoop around a little and if the opportunity presented itself, to ask questions. The concierge welcomed me the minute I set foot in the door and asked if he could be of help.

I said, "No, thanks. A friend and I are meeting here in the lobby to visit a mutual friend who lives in the building."

"Very good, sir. May I ask who you will be visiting?"

"Sure. Rolly Boland in apartment 802."

"Yes, that would be Mister Boland's apartment. I believe he is in this afternoon. I'll announce you as soon as your other friend arrives. Is he expecting you?"

"Yes, and I'm pretty sure he's here. He said he would be and I think I saw his car as I walked by your parking area. The black DeSoto?"

The telephone on the reception counter rang at that moment, so he answered my question with a nod and picked up the receiver. While he talked I wandered around the lobby taking in what is passing for luxury in the year of our Lord, one-thousand-nine-hundred-and-forty.

At about two-twenty-five a woman walked into the lobby and it took a second look for me to recognize Lillian Bouvier. She had traded her Miss Frump facade in for a considerably more glamorous look that included a touch of makeup and a nicely tailored and belted gray jacket over a skirt that ended about an inch below her knees. She was also wearing silk stockings, practical but stylish heels, and a hat with feathers in it.

If I still had any doubts about what sort of relationship Rolly and Lilly had going on, the concierge eliminated it, greeting Lilly by name and sending us off to the elevator for our trip to the eighth floor. On the way I said, "That's kind of a new look for you, isn't it?"

In a haughty tone of voice intended to tell me her look was none of my business, she said, "You don't wear the same shirt every day do you?"

I told her she had a point there, the elevator door opened, and she stepped in. Lilly told the young man operating the elevator that our destination was the eighth floor, and he was so busy looking at her, he almost closed the door in my face.

Apartment 802 was at the front of the building overlooking Rossmore Avenue. Lilly knocked on the door and I saw it move slightly as if it were ajar. Lilly noticed it, too. She didn't say anything, but looked at the door with a strange expression.

After waiting most of a minute and having no response to our knock, Lilly knocked again, a little harder. This time her knock was of sufficient force to push the door in a couple of inches.

Lilly looked at the door again and said, "That's strange. Rolly is obsessive about locking his door, whether he's home or not."

While she was saying that, I was getting a whiff of the air being pushed out into the hall by a ventilation fan in the apartment. People's homes have unique smells. They might smell like a pet, last night's fish, or the garlic in tonight's spaghetti sauce. There's one odor, though, that once you've smelled it, you hope to hell you never smell it again, and if you do, it turns your stomach.

That was the odor coming from Rolly Boland's apartment—a sickly metallic smell that tells you somebody in there has lost a lot of blood, more than enough to make them dead. I guessed Lilly hadn't smelled it yet, and I'm sure she wouldn't have known what it was if she had.

As I reached out to close the door in the hope of keeping her from going inside, she pushed past me. I said, "Lilly, you don't want to go in . . ."

I'm sure everyone from the concierge on up heard her scream. After the scream came some hysterical sounding sobs and the sound of someone falling to the floor. I rushed in and found Lilly just inside the door. Twenty feet away a man who I guessed must have been Rolly Boland in better times lay in a large pool of dark red blood on the hardwood floor of his living room.

Knowing from the amount of blood he'd lost that Rolly had to be long dead, I checked Boland's neck for a pulse anyhow. I found no pulse, so I pulled back his blood-soaked smoking jacket to see what had killed him.

Two small holes in the right side of his shirt told the tale. The bullets had not damaged his heart to the point where it couldn't continue pumping, so it did until there was little or nothing left to pump. The cops call it "bleeding out." I couldn't say whether or not he was conscious and aware of what was happening to him all that time, but I hoped not.

From behind me I heard Lilly stirring. She said, "Rolly . . . Rolly?"

Helping her up from the floor, I said, "I'm sorry, Lillian, but Rolly's dead. Let's get you out in the hall for some fresh air."

"No," she said weakly, "Rolly . . ."

Outside in the hall a few people who had heard Lilly scream were trying to get a peek through the doorway. I picked an older woman who looked like she had some sense and said, "I've got to call the police. Would you please take her somewhere quiet until the authorities get here?"

"Certainly, young man. To a fellow who was standing close by she said, "Edward, get hold of her other arm and help me get her to our apartment."

To the other three or four people who'd gathered outside Rolly Boland's door, I said, "Okay, folks, go back to your apartments. There's nothing more to see."

That wasn't quite true. Actually there was a lot to see in Rolly's apartment . . . if you didn't mind waking up to nightmares for the next month.

Six

2:45 P.M. – Wednesday – August 7, 1940

El Royale Apartments – Wilshire District, Los Angeles

After calling the Seventh Precinct to report Rolly Boland's murder, I used the time I had before the cops arrived to take a quick look through Rolly's desk in the library. Yes, even apartments have libraries these days; at least the luxury variety does.

I found nothing of particular interest except a tin box containing what looked like about two thousand in hundreds. It was in the bottom drawer of the desk, and I left the box right where it was after making sure I hadn't left any fingerprints on it.

Figuring it was about time for the police to show up, I went out into the hall and waited. The first cop out of the elevator was a patrol officer. He was followed by a big guy in a suit who figured to be a homicide detective. His jacket and slacks looked like he'd slept in them and his cigar only had about two inches to go. He held up a badge and said around the cigar stub, "Sergeant Salvino, Homicide."

I held up my P. I. Photostat in my right hand and said, "Spicer, private cop." At the same time I held the left side of my jacket open so my shoulder holster could be clearly seen.

Salvino promptly removed my Smith and Wesson from its holster and took my license for a closer look, saying, "I'll hold onto your piece for the time being because this piece of paper don't carry no weight with me. You know anyone in the Department who'll vouch for you?"

"Yeah, call Detective Lieutenant Winfield at the Sixth."

The detective flipped my Photostat to the patrol officer with him and said, "You heard the man. Go downstairs and make the call. See if Winfield knows this guy."

As the patrol officer turned toward the elevator I said, "Hey, if Winfield's not there, ask for C. K. Mackie. He and I have worked together a few times, too."

Salvino said, "Yeah, Murphy, I like that idea even better. Talk to C. K. He won't pull any punches."

I was instructed to sit in a chair down the hallway and wait while Salvino took a look in apartment 802. I hoped he hadn't just finished lunch.

Just as he came out several more cops arrived. One of them was carrying a large format press camera and the others had equipment cases and such that told me the crime lab guys had arrived. Looking just a little green around the gills, Salvino directed the lab people into 802 and put an officer on the door with instructions to keep everyone out until the lab guys were done.

The El Royale's elevator operator was earning his pay this afternoon. Patrol officer Murphy stepped out the next time the elevator arrived. He headed directly for Salvino and so did I. As I approached, Murphy was saying, ". . . Winfield says this guy is a straight-shooter, but he likes to be a cowboy sometimes."

The term "cowboy" is cop slang for a loner who goes in for grandstand plays. I wouldn't call that a fair assessment, but nobody was asking me.

Salvino said, "So did you talk to C. K.?"

"Yeah, for just a minute. He was on his on his way out. Mackie said Spicer's top drawer in his book." Then Murphy looked at me and grinned. "He told me to tell you to get your tail back up to the Sixth and stop botherin' us hard workin' cops down here in the Seventh."

The sergeant sighed as if it was painful for him to accept that a private cop might actually be on the level. Then he handed me my Smith and Wesson and Photostat, saying, "Well, I can see how you might con Winfield, but not Mackie, so I guess you're okay. But just so ya know, we play by the rulebook down here. That means no cowboy tricks."

"Got it, Sergeant."

"Okay, then. Tell me what the hell you were doin' here when you found the body."

"I'm working on a case involving a piece of African art that was stolen Friday night."

Salvino raised his thick, bushy eyebrows. "And you were likin' the guy in there, Boland, for the heist?"

"No, at least not yet. He was instrumental in helping my client purchase the art so I was coming over to get some of the background about the piece that was stolen. It's a ceramic elephant statuette about so by about so."

I held out my hands to indicate the size of the Ivonya-Ngia Tembo and the sergeant said, "And this thing is valuable?"

"If the estimates I've been given are accurate, its worth about a hundred Gs."

Salvino whistled. "Yeah, I'd call that valuable. Just who is this client of yours? And don't give me any guff about client privilege 'cuz that only applies to lawyers, not gumshoes."

I looked around to see if there were any ears pointed out way. There didn't appear to be, so I said, "I know you're under no obligation to keep this confidential, but I would appreciate whatever you can do along those lines. My client is really touchy about publicity."

"I'll try, but no promises."

"My client is the actress, Bette Davis."

"Talk about high jingo! How the heck did you ever get hooked up with her?"

High jingo is another phrase in the cop slang book referring to a case that has to be handled cautiously because it involves well known people, usually actors or politicians. Now I was having some fun with the sergeant. "Jack Warner recommended me to her because he's happy with the work I've done for him."

Salvino's eyebrows went up another notch. "You mean Jack Warner as in Warner Brothers?"

"Yeah, I guess he was pleased I saved Humphrey Bogart from being crushed by an overhead spotlight on one of Jack's sound stages."

The sergeant's eyebrows were now up about as high as they could get and still be on his face. "Geez, Spicer, talk about bein' connected! You're in with the studio big boys, the guys up at the Sixth think you're the second coming, and the biggest actors in town are standing in line waiting to hire you. You must be one clever P. I."

I grinned at Salvino. "Or a damned lucky one."

Shaking his head, Salvino got on with his questioning. "Okay, so what time did you get here?"

"I met Miss Bouvier, my client's personal secretary, in the lobby a few minutes before two-thirty. We came straight up here, so we knocked on the door no later than two-forty."

"Whoa. You mean there was someone with you when you came up here? Where is this dame now?"

"Yeah, I kinda forgot about her with all the excitement here. Her name is Lillian Bouvier, that's B-O-U-V-I-E-R, and I can't prove it yet, but I suspect she and Boland were involved romantically. Either way, she took his death pretty hard, so I asked the elderly couple who live in 803 over there to take her into their apartment where she could calm down a little. That's where she is now so far as I know."

Salvino was busy making notes. Sometimes I think if there's ever a shortage of notebooks and pencils the crime solving business would come to a complete halt. Exaggerating the French pronunciation of Lilly's name, he said, "And this Boo-vee-ay dame let you into his apartment?"

"In a manner of speaking. We knocked on the door and noticed it was ajar. When she saw that, she said something must be wrong because Boland was obsessive about locking his door because of all the bits and pieces of art he's collected."

The sergeant nodded and said, "And she barged right in and got a hell of a surprise, right?"

"Yup, then she passed out cold about two steps inside the door. I followed her in and took a look at Boland. He had no pulse that I could find and given the location of his wounds, I'm guessing he bled to death right there on the floor."

"And you didn't touch him or move him, right?"

"I looked for a pulse in his neck and lifted his jacket lapel up a little for a better look at his wounds. Then Miss Bouvier started coming round, so I got her out of there and called you fellows. The only places you'll find my prints are around the telephone on the desk in the library and on the inside of the front doorknob."

"You said Boland has a lot of expensive artwork in his apartment. Is that his business?"

"No, Sergeant, he was a cinematographer. Miss Davis likes his work, so he had a job every time she made a film. Needless to say, he got paid top dollar when he was working."

"No doubt about that if he could afford to live in a joint like this. What do you suppose the rent is on a swanky joint like this?"

"I'd guess it goes for at least four times the average Hollywood apartment, which would make the monthly rent somewhere around eight-hundred to a thousand bucks."

Salvino shook his head in amazement and closed his notebook. "All right, Spicer. I'm clearing you on this one, but if you come across anything that ties this shooting to your missing elephant caper, I expect to be the first one after you to know about it. In return I'll try to keep the lid on your client's identity. Fair enough?"

I offered my hand and we shook. "Fair enough, Sergeant Salvino. "And if you need to reach me, here's my business card. I have an answering service and I check in with them regularly, so if I'm not there, leave a message."

He accepted my card, saying, "Okay, Spicer. Got it."

"You gonna talk to Miss Bouvier now?"

Salvino sighed like there were about a thousand things he'd rather do. "Yeah, if she's through passin' out and bein' hysterical."

"Mind if I tag along while you talk with her. A friendly face might put her more at ease."

"Sure, Spicer. I'll take any help I can get. I hate talkin' to weepy dames."

That's when the coroner's medical examiner came out of 802. Salvino asked, "What's the word, doc?"

"The cause of death was exsanguination—he bled to death from two bullet wounds that hit a vital artery or two around his heart. I'm going to put the time of death tentatively between one-forty-five and two. It's always a little tricky placing a time of death for exsanguination cases, but he was certainly dead before two o'clock. My guess is he was probably shot earlier, say one-thirty or so."

The sergeant was writing in his notebook again. "Thanks, doc."

"You're welcome, Nick. I'll have a full report for you tomorrow morning. We bagged up the contents of the victim's pockets and turned the stuff over to Murphy so you can look it over before the lab gets it. Just be careful how you handle it. Okay if my boys take the body now?"

"Sure."

Five minutes later the El Royale's elevator door closed behind Rolly Boland for the final time and I followed Sergeant Salvino over to apartment 803, where we fetched Lillian. It seemed I was right about her appreciating a friendly face, even if it was only mine. She held onto my arm to steady herself as we walked across the hall to 802.

When we got to the door she stopped. I said, "It's all right, Lilly. Rolly has been taken downtown."

She nodded and followed Salvino into the apartment's foyer. From there we went down a hall to the library, carefully avoiding the sticky puddle of coagulating blood in the living room.

I sat Lilly in a comfortable chair and stood back to let Sergeant Salvino do his job. I imagine he's good at his job, too, but today his heart just wasn't in it. He covered Lilly's basic information, although she was reluctant to give up her employer's name.

Salvino let that question go. Really there was no need to press her on the subject because he already knew the answer.

Finally, he said, "Okay, Miss Bouvier, that's all the questions I have for now. Here's my business card. I would appreciate you letting me know if you need to leave town during the next couple of weeks. Now, can you get home all right, or would you like one of my officers to take you?"

Lilly shook her head. "No, thank you, Mister Salvino. I live close by. I think I can drive there without difficulty."

Salvino had a few more details to wrap up, so he stayed in the apartment with some of his crew and I walked Lilly down to her car. When we got to a maroon and wood-paneled Buick station wagon that no doubt belonged to Miss Davis, Lilly said, "Thank you for handling things in there. I would not have known the first thing to do."

"You're welcome, Lilly. I'm sorry you had to see what you saw. I'm sure it was quite a shock."

"Yes it was, but you handled it all as if it were something you did every day. How is it that things like that don't upset you?"

"Oh, they upset me all right. Something like that would upset anyone. I've just learned how to set the emotions aside long enough to do what needs to be done. I still have to deal with them sooner or later, though."

As she slid behind the steering wheel, Lilly got an odd look on her face. "Mister Spicer, I don't think I care much for your line of work."

I was going to say there were times I didn't much care for it either, but that wasn't the sort of comment that inspires confidence in clients. I just gave Lilly a wave and watched her drive off past the ritzy apartments and elegant homes where the rich folks live. Funny thing about rich folks, though, they bleed just like the rest of us.

On the way back to my office, I thought about how Boland's death effected my case. Whether or not it had anything directly to do with the missing statuette, Boland's demise meant one source of information was no longer available to me. Since I had damned few sources to begin with, Boland's death increased the value of whatever the African art expert in Sacramento might be able to tell me.

Back at my desk I checked messages—there were none—and found the business card Doctor Jessup at the Natural History Museum gave me. Then I got the operator on the line and placed a long distance call to Joseph Kipchumba.

The woman who answered Mister Kipchumba's telephone spoke very proper English with just the hint of an accent I didn't recognize. "Yes, Mister Spicer, how is it that we may assist you?"

"I'd like to interview Mister Kipchumba regarding a particular piece of African art."

"And, Mister Spicer, what would your interest be in this particular piece of African art?"

I already decided there was no purpose in lying about why I wanted information on the Ivonya-Ngia Tembo. It figured that the African art community was probably small and close knit, so it was possible the word was already out about the theft.

I said, "I'm a private investigator looking into the theft of this particular piece of art and Mister Kipchumba was recommended to me by Doctor Jessup at the Los Angeles Museum of Natural History as being someone who would be knowledgeable about its history and value."

"I see. And when would you be available to come in for this interview?"

"I was hoping to conduct the interview via the telephone. Would that be possible?"

Her reply was emphatic. "No, Mister Spicer, it would not. Mister Kipchumba would not discuss a subject so sensitive over the telephone."

"All right, I can appreciate that. Would he be available next week, say on Tuesday?"

"No, Mister Spicer, Mister Kipchumba only has time available for such an interview on Saturday. He has no other openings on his calendar."

I knew damned well this gal was giving me the runaround. I couldn't imagine why, but it made me all the more determined to beat her at her own game. "Very well, what time will Mister Kipchumba be available on Saturday and at what address should I meet him?"

She gave me the same address Jessup had given me—724 Harbor Boulevard, West Sacramento. I was instructed to be there promptly at 10 a.m. Given her mania about promptness, I thought she must be related to Lillian Bouvier.

Now all I had to do was convince Susan that a weekend trip to the state's capital would be much more fun than lounging around in a classy new hotel overlooking at the beach in Santa Monica. Having been to Sacramento a few times, I knew that was going to be a challenge. There is absolutely nothing fun about Sacramento.

Seven

8:00 A.M. – Thursday – August 8, 1940

Spicer Investigations – 1st National Bank Building, Hollywood

There comes a time in every case when you have to try and make sense out of what you've got and decide whether or not you're on the right track, or even any track at all. I had the definite feeling the choo-choo had jumped its track and I was going nowhere.

Pulling a fresh sheet of paper from my desk drawer, I made a list of the facts I had to work with so far:

1) A valuable piece of African art was stolen Friday night from the home of Bette Davis.

2) The missing art is an eight inch ceramic statuette known as the Ivonya-Ngia Tembo

3) The statuette was taken from a display case in the library during a small party.

4) The glass display case was broken to remove the statuette.

5) A piece of dark blue wool was found snagged on the broken glass.

6) Of the six men at the party Friday night four were wearing dark blue wool suits.

7) Someone blew a marmalade-tipped blowgun dart at Henry and me on Monday.

8) Someone driving a black DeSoto left what seems like a phony ransom note on my car Tuesday.

9) Rolly Boland drove a black DeSoto, lived near where the ransom note was delivered, and wore a blue wool suit to the party.

10) Rolly Boland was shot dead in his apartment a few hours ago.

Those were the facts of the case—ten pieces of a much larger puzzle. If I could fit some of the pieces I had together, they might point me toward new pieces I didn't have. The difficulty was that some of the pieces appeared to be completely unrelated. For example, it's a hell of a step from a marmalade-tipped blowgun dart to a bloody corpse in the living room of a swanky apartment.

Okay, instead of looking for similarities, try looking for differences. Going down that path, I might conclude I was dealing with two separate individuals—one that has no qualms about killing in cold blood, and another that was trying to scare me off without actually hurting anyone. Or I could be dealing with one individual who just upped the ante in a big way. I liked the first conclusion better.

All right, how do those conclusions get my investigation on track? According to the law, you need evidence providing conclusive answers to three questions in order to convict a culprit. Those questions are:

1) Did the suspect have the means to commit the crime?
2) Did the suspect have a motive for committing the crime?
3) Did the suspect have the opportunity to commit the crime?

That stuff is all fine and good for the lawyers, but what I had were too many people who had the means and opportunity, plus a hundred Gs makes a hell of a motive in just about anybody's book. So to narrow the field I need more information, which brings me right back to fitting puzzle pieces together so they will lead me to more puzzle pieces.

Okay, let's try this: If I had the statuette sitting on my desk right now, how would I turn it into a hundred thousand dollars? If I came up with the answer to that question I'd have a better idea where I ought to be looking for the damned elephant. The only person I knew of who might shed some light on how to fence a hot elephant was Mister Kipchumba up in Sacramento with whom I already had an appointment day after tomorrow. It always amazes me how much can be accomplished by sitting down and thinking things through. Hogwash.

It was time to get off this train of thought and get on one that would take me to the capital of our fair state. Sacramento is about four hundred miles to the north, so how do I get there as efficiently as possible? Driving would take about eleven hours without stops. The Coast Daylight train made the trip to San Francisco in around nine and a half hours, but that left you in San Francisco, a hundred miles west of Sacramento.

The remaining mode of transportation is the airplane, and I'd seen advertisements for an outfit calling itself Central Valley Air Lines that makes regularly scheduled trips up the San Joaquin and Sacramento valleys from Glendale. Flying certainly had to take less than ten hours, but was the cost prohibitive? I knew only one way to find out.

I got CVAL's Los Angeles ticket agency's number from an information operator and gave 'em a call. After a couple of rings, a woman with a smile in her voice said, "Central Valley Air Lines, we take you where you really want to go."

For the next five minutes or so I asked questions and she answered them. The fastest flight from Glendale to Sacramento took four hours because it included stops in Bakersfield and Fresno. The one-way fare was twenty-three dollars. According to her passenger manifests, there were seats available on tomorrow's two o'clock flight to Sacramento, and also on a three o'clock return flight Saturday.

Ninety-two bucks for a pair of roundtrip tickets didn't seem too steep, plus the two o'clock flight north would fit with Susan's noon arrival in L.A. on the Coaster and getting back here Saturday evening would still allow us some beach time on Sunday before I took her home.

I booked two roundtrip tickets. Now came the hard part. Telling Susan our plans had undergone a small change. Actually, they'd undergone a rather large change.

A helpful AT&T operator connected me to Santa Barbara about ninety miles up the coast. Susan answered promptly and I said, "Hiya, Angel."

"Hi, Johnny! This is a surprise. I didn't expect to talk to you until tomorrow. Is everything okay?"

"Everything is fine, except we have to make a bit of a change in our plans for the weekend."

"Uh, oh. Do you have to work?"

"I have to interview a fellow up in Sacramento, so how do you feel about flying up there with me?"

A little trepidation crept into her tone of voice. "Flying? You mean like in an airplane?"

"Yeah. Being an angel you could just fly up there on your own, but I'm not equipped with wings."

With a smile I could hear, but not see, she added, "Or a halo. Maybe it would be okay. Tell me how we do this."

"Well, it starts off just as we already planned with you coming down here on the Coaster. I'll meet you at Union Station and we'll drive up to Grand Central Air Terminal in Glendale, where we catch a two o'clock flight to Sacramento. Then we fly back after my interview on Saturday and get some beach time in before I take you home on Sunday. Does that sound okay?"

A few moments of silence came down the line before Susan said, "Ah . . . I guess so . . . I . . . Johnny, I've never gone anywhere in an airplane before. Aren't they kind of dangerous?"

"Not really. We're flying on an established airline with experienced pilots in a well-maintained airplane. Besides, I wouldn't suggest this if I thought it put you in any danger."

After a few more moments of silence, Susan said, "Okay, Johnny, but only if you promise to hold my hand if I get scared."

"I bet you'll be too busy looking out the window to be scared, but I will happily provide all the handholding services you require."

Susan laughed, but I heard some apprehension in her voice. "I sort of thought I might be able to count on you for that. What's it like in Sacramento? Do I need to dress differently or anything?"

"It's usually warmer in Sacramento than what you're used to on the coast, so you won't need a heavy jacket. Just pack light, and we can leave a jacket or anything else you won't need up there in the car so you'll have it when we get back here."

"Okay. Then I guess I'll see you tomorrow around noon at Union Station."

"No guessin' about it. I'll be there. Oh, and if you only take an overnight bag and don't check it, you can go straight through the terminal building. I'll be parked out in front waiting for you. That will save us some time in case the Coaster is late."

"All right, Johnny. Thank you for including me in the weekend. Lord only knows how much extra it's costing you to bring me along."

"We're gonna have an adventure. It'll be fun!"

On that cheery note we said goodbye and I called a downtown travel agent I've used before to make the rest of the reservations we needed. They included a rental car to be picked up at Sacramento Municipal Airport, rooms for Friday night at a hotel in West Sacramento called The El Rancho, and a Saturday night reservation at the Shangri-La Hotel in Santa Monica.

My next telephone call was to the Seventh Precinct. When I got Salvino on the line I said, "Hello, Sergeant. Johnny Spicer here."

"What have you got for me Spicer?"

"Just the news that I'm flying up to Sacramento this weekend to talk with a fellow who should be able to tell me how to fence a hot elephant. I'm hoping that will give me more to work with."

In a tone of voice dripping with sarcasm, Salvino said, "Wonderful. Have a swell trip."

"I'll do that. In the meantime, has your coroner come up with anything new?"

"Naw, everything was just about how he figured it at the scene. He did recover the slugs from the body, though. They're thirty-eights, but that don't mean much. These days everybody and their grandma has a thirty-eight revolver."

"Sergeant, do you still have a man on the door of Boland's apartment?"

"Yeah, the crime lab people will be in and out of there all day. Why?"

"I'd like to go back to the El Royale and take a look in Boland's closet."

Salvino let some silence come down the line before he said, "What aren't you telling me, Spicer?"

"Probably nothing. I just want see if he had a dark blue wool suit with a small piece of material missing from one sleeve."

"Why?"

"Because the guy who stole the elephant knickknack left a little piece of his clothing behind, probably from around the elbow of his jacket. If Boland's dark blue wool suit has a tear it would tie him to the theft in an entirely different way."

"How do you know he even owns a blue wool suit?"

"He was seen wearing one last Friday night."

More silence came down the line. Finally, Salvino said, "Okay, Spicer. Meet me outside the apartment in twenty. And don't keep me waitin'."

I stepped out of the El Royale's elevator on the eighth floor at ten-twenty. Salvino got there about five minutes later.

"Hi, Sergeant."

Salvino growled something that sounded like "Hello, Spicer" as he walked over to the patrol officer standing guard outside apartment 802. The officer opened the door and the sergeant walked in without a word. I followed him and headed straight for the master bedroom and its huge walk-in closet.

Sergeant Salvino strolled along behind me and watched as I looked for dark blue wool among the suits hanging in one area of the closet. There were lots of suits there, but no blue wool. That might mean he noticed the tear and tossed the suit into a trashcan somewhere, or he took it somewhere to have the sleeve repaired, or the suit was at the cleaners. I expressed those thoughts to Salvino who grumbled something about a waste of time and walked out of the bedroom.

Following on his heels, I noticed a laundry ticket in amongst some business cards and receipts on top of a chest of drawers near the door. Under the circumstances I did what any competent private eye would do. I palmed the laundry ticket and dropped it into my jacket pocket.

As we left the apartment, I noticed a ring of keys in a decorative ashtray on a small table near the door. I stopped, held up the keys, and asked Salvino for one more favor. "Sergeant, would you mind if we went out through the garage on the first floor and took a look in Boland's automobile?"

Salvino gave me a go-to-hell look. "Spicer . . . oh, hell. Bring 'em along, but you'll have to bring the keys back up here and put 'em where you found 'em when we're done."

"Will do."

In the garage I went straight to the black DeSoto two-door sedan and unlocked the passenger-side door. That's when I finally had a little luck. I saw a piece of paper sticking out of the crack between the front seat cushions. It was the page torn from my notebook on which I'd written my smart aleck reply to the phony ransom note.

I said, "Bingo!"

That got Salvino's attention. "Whatcha got, Spicer?"

"I've got proof positive that Boland was involved in the elephant heist."

"Yeah?"

"Yeah. Tuesday I had lunch at the Coyote Café and while I was there someone left a ransom note for the elephant statuette on my windshield. It was the silliest ransom note you've ever seen—I still have it in my office.

"Anyway, I tore a page out of my notebook and left this smart aleck reply where the ransom note had been and went back into the restaurant in the hope whoever left the ransom note was watching and would take the bait to see what I'd left. He did and I tried to stop him from leaving, but he had a head start. He was also wearing dark glasses and a hat low on his forehead, so I couldn't really see what he looked like."

Salvino read the note and smiled. "You got a real way with words, Spicer. A note like this might just tick the guy off and you'd lose the elephant gizmo for good."

Shaking my head I said, "No. I knew the ransom note was a phony from the beginning, so ticking the guy off wasn't a concern."

"What makes you think it's a phony?"

I went through the litany of points that convinced me the ransom was a phony and Salvino said, "Yeah, good points. You say you've still got the original note Boland left?"

"Yup. It's in my office safe. I kept it because it's proof that the ransom scheme is just a gag to cover up something else that's going on, although I have no idea what that might be."

"Okay, hang onto it for me, will ya? I still don't know if your elephant thing-a-ma-jig has anything to do with why Boland was killed, but it's looking more likely."

"Will do, Sergeant. And as long as we're here, let's check the backseat and trunk. I'd hate to think we walked away and left the damned statuette behind."

My luck had run out on this gambit. There was nothing in the trunk but a flat spare tire and the jack. The backseat held a neatly folded car robe. That was it.

Salvino pulled the keys out of the trunk lock and said, "I just thought of something I need to talk to the guy on the apartment door about. I'll take these back up. And stay in touch, will ya? Let me know what you find out in Sacramento."

"Will do, Sergeant."

According to the address on the laundry ticket I stole from Boland's bedroom, the Lee Dry Cleaning Service was located on the same side of La Brea Avenue a block north of the El Coyote Cafe. Hell, Boland might have been dropping his suit off at the cleaners when he spotted me going into lunch.

Lee's cleaners was one of half a dozen small businesses located in a two story building. I pulled to the curb and walked into the shop where I was greeted in broken English by an elderly Chinese woman.

I smiled and handed her Boland's ticket. She looked at it, smiled a mostly toothless smile at me, and disappeared into a forest of clothes racks. A moment later she returned and I knew my luck was working again. Most of the suit was hidden by a brown paper wrapper, but the part I could see was definitely dark blue and wool.

The Chinese woman pulled the wrapping back and showed me the right sleeve. Of course, it had a small tear in it near the elbow. She said, "You rip here. You bring back, we fix like new."

Apparently Rolly Boland didn't know he'd torn his sleeve on the display case. If he had known, he would have had the jacket repaired while it was in for cleaning. My luck was holding.

After I promised to bring the suit back for repairs, she collected the fifty cent cleaning charge, and I walked back out to my car with the evidence that essentially proved Rolly Boland had broken the elephant's display case. Okay, Spicer, you've got the goods on a dead guy, what now?

My first inclination was to stash the suit in my office somewhere, but I chucked that idea and decided to do something the easy way for a change. I made a U-turn on La Brea and headed for the Seventh Precinct. Sure, Salvino was gonna yell at me for taking the cleaning ticket, but overall we were ahead of the game because we now knew something about Boland that tied him to my case and might be helpful to Salvino, too.

When the patrol officer manning the front counter returned with Sergeant Salvino in tow, I laid the suit out on the counter and said, "I thought you might want to see this."

Salvino leaned over and examined the tear in the sleeve. I said, "The matching piece from the elephant display case is in my office safe."

"Good. Bring it in with the fake ransom note and we'll put all the pieces together in an evidence box."

With that, Salvino turned and started back to his office. I said, "You're welcome, Sergeant."

Salvino turned around and turned on his glare. "Don't get smart with me, Spicer. You're lucky I'm not arresting you for tampering with evidence in a police investigation. The only reason I'm not is you passed the test."

Puzzled, I asked, "What test?"

"When I took the keys back to Boland's apartment after we looked in his car, I checked the dresser in his bedroom to see if the laundry ticket was still there. It wasn't and you were the only one who could have taken it, so I've been waiting to see what you'd do with it. You did the right thing, so you passed my little test, but the next time you pull a stunt like that, I'm runnin' you in, period. Got that, Spicer?"

"Very clever, Sergeant. If you applied as much cleverness to catching bad guys, the Seventh's crime rate would drop by about fifty percent."

With his glare turned up to full power, Salvino said, "You're pushin' it, Spicer. Get the hell out of here before you make me do something you'll regret."

I got the hell out of there feeling rather silly about the whole situation. I'd been feeling that way a lot lately and it wasn't doing my self-esteem much good, but how the hell was I supposed to know Salvino set a trap for me with a damned laundry ticket?

It was almost one by the time I got back to the office, so I stopped in at Eli's Deli. Danny was behind the counter, so I asked, "Hey kid, what's the blue plate special today?"

"Corned beef and cabbage. I had some and it was pretty good."

"All right, I'll have the corned beef and cabbage."

As usual Danny's recommendation was a good one. After eating every morsel on the plate, I headed for my office, and by one-forty-five I was in my desk chair and contemplating what I needed to do next. I looked at the stack of mail—mostly bills—in my in basket and decided I'd better deal with them next. But first, I thought it might be a good idea to see if Rosie had any important messages for me.

The only message in my slot was from a Mister Henry Gough. I didn't recognize the name right away until Rosie read me the call back number. It was Bette Davis's number and Henry Gough was Henry the butler.

Henry answered my call and I said, "Hello, Henry. You wanted me to call you?"

"Yes, sir. I have a dilemma and I'm not sure what I ought to do about it."

Something about the tone of his voice told me Henry was more than a little concerned about whatever dilemma he was facing. I said, "I'll help if I can. What's your dilemma?"

Using language he figured was safe for a telephone conversation, Henry said, "A member of Madam's staff is missing. We haven't heard a word from her since this morning."

Eight

2:00 P.M. – Thursday – August 8, 1940

Bette Davis Residence – 5346 Franklin Avenue, Hollywood

As I drove up Highland to Franklin, I cursed Ivonya-Ngia and all his relatives. Every time I thought I was making progress with this case something came along to kick the slats out from under me. Now I not only had a dead suspect, but another principal in the case was supposedly missing.

So it was that my mood was none to cheerful when Henry opened the door. We went into the library and I got out my notebook and pencil.

"Okay, Henry, tell me what's going."

"Well, sir, Miss Bouvier seemed quite upset when she came in yesterday afternoon."

"What time was that?"

"It was around three o'clock, perhaps a little later."

"And did she tell you why she was upset?"

"Yes, sir. Miss Bouvier said Mister Boland had been murdered. She said something about him being shot in his apartment."

"All right, Henry. What happened next?"

"She said she wasn't feeling well and went home."

"That all sounds understandable. Why do you think she's missing?"

"Miss Bouvier called this morning to say she would be in late because she had some errands to run for Madam. That was the last time we heard anything from her, and when I asked Madam if she knew what errands Miss Bouvier might have been doing for her, Madam said she had no idea what errands those could be."

"So the last time you heard from her was this morning. What time was that?"

"It was perhaps fifteen or twenty minutes before eight."

"All right, Henry. I'll look into it. Where does Lilly live."

I was looking in my notebook, prepared to write down an address, but when Henry didn't respond, I looked up at him."

With a somewhat sheepish expression on his face, Henry said, "I'm sorry, sir. I am reluctant to give out such private information."

That was the last straw! "Damn it, Henry, if you want me to find Lilly you have to tell me where to start looking. I'm about two seconds away from telling you, Madam, and everyone else connected with this fiasco to go take a hike. So either give me her address . . ."

Making another surprise entrance, Bette Davis's voice came from the hall door. "Lillian rents a small cottage on Van Ness, number 1835, and I would consider it a personal favor if you would check on her for us, Mister Spicer. Henry has been over there twice today and Lillian wasn't there either time."

As I wrote the address in my notebook, I said, "Very well, Miss Davis. I'll see what I can find out. I have to tell you, though, I'm going to Sacramento tomorrow for an interview concerning the statuette. Saturday is the only day the fellow will see me, so all I have is this afternoon and evening to look for Miss Bouvier. I may not be able to accomplish much in that time."

"I understand. Please do what you can."

"I don't suppose anyone has a key to Miss Bouvier's apartment."

Miss Davis saved the day again. "I do, Mister Spicer. It happens I own the property. She rents it from me." She held up a key with a small cardboard tag tied to it. "This will open the front door."

Eighteen-thirty-five Van Ness Avenue was about half a mile from Bette Davis's digs. It turned out to be a symmetrical little bungalow with a front door perfectly centered between two windows. The peak of the shingled roof ran from left to right and, for reasons unfathomable to me, the builder had stuck something like a dormer window in the middle of the roof section facing the street. Aside from having a roof dormer window on a single story building, the cottage fit Miss Frump to a T. Maybe the odd roof protrusion represented an odd facet of Lilly Bouvier's personality.

I climbed three steps to a small uncovered porch and announced my arrival just in case Lillian had returned since the last time anyone checked. I pressed a small white button set in the right side of the doorframe and chimes sounded somewhere inside the house. I had a sudden case of déjà vu when I recognized what the chimes were playing. It was a phrase from Handel's *Messiah*, although most people simply know the tune as the Big Ben Chime. I could even tell you what four notes are needed to play it, but not because I'm a music expert. The intelligence work I'd done in England required that I know such things because the four quarter chimes that played the tune before the big bell rang the hour were occasionally used as part of a code sequence.

When nobody answered the door, I used the key. It opened the front door without difficulty and I walked into Lilly's domain. The living room was severely Spartan and orderly to a fault. It was furnished with an armchair and a couch, both upholstered in a decidedly neutral tweedy tan material. There was also a coffee table in front of the couch and a magazine stand next to the armchair. The magazines in the stand were recent copies of *Life*, *Saturday Evening Post*, and surprisingly, *Popular Science*. Miss Bouvier, it would seem, has eclectic tastes in reading material.

The only decorations in the room were two inexpensive art deco design prints on two of the walls and a small, delicately shaped ceramic bud vase in a sea green color on the mantel above the fireplace in the wall to the left of the front door. The bud vase had a homemade look about it, so I walked over for a closer look. The sculptor had signed and dated her work on the bottom: Lilly B./'26.

The kitchen was next. Its walls were painted a pale yellow to match the ceramic tiles on the counter top and a pattern in the linoleum on the floor. The cabinets were painted white to match the Kelvinator refrigerator and a four-burner Wedgewood gas stove.

I've found you can learn a lot about people by snooping in their refrigerators, so I snooped. Lilly Bouvier's fridge was mostly stocked with fresh vegetables—carrots, tomatoes, celery, and the like. The cold box also held half a quart of milk, a jar of Del Monte dill pickles, an egg carton with five eggs left, and a few condiments. It was enough to make a meat and potatoes guy like me cry.

The cabinet nearest the refrigerator held canned goods, like peas, corn, lima beans, peaches, and pears. One shelf was loaded down with Campbell's soups, including tomato, vegetable, and green pea. Up another shelf was a box of Sunshine Krispy Crackers, a package of Kellogg's Rice Krispies, and a can of Hills Brothers coffee.

I noticed the edge of a pale yellow box showing on the top shelf. I reached up and brought down a one pound Whitman's candy box. Inside there remained three chocolates in their little brown paper cups. I suspected they'd been put out of sight to make the candy last as long as possible. Apparently Miss Frump had at least one vice, but she was careful to keep it under control.

The upper cabinet on the other side of the sink held precisely four dinner plates, four salad plates, four soup bowls, four cups with saucers, and four nested serving bowls in primary colors. The drawer below it contained Lilly's flatware in a nifty divided organizer with spaces for forks, knives, and spoons. She'd chosen the kind of flatware with the colorful plastic handles, so the drawer was a cheery rainbow of orange, green, blue, and yellow handles. It seemed a shame that the most colorful spot in the house was inside a kitchen drawer.

Other cabinets and drawers held pots and pans, cooking implements, and the staples that came in larger packages, like flour, sugar and rice. The last items of interest in the kitchen were a small kitchen table and two chairs with chrome frames and yellow cushions. The table top was yellow and white Formica.

The table was of interest to me because of what was on it. Besides a bowl with two oranges and a lemon, there were the telephone and a three-by-five notepad. I held the notepad up so the light from the kitchen window reflected from the surface of the paper and found what I hoped to find. The last note written on the pad left indentations in the next page—the one I was looking at. By using my pencil to apply a light shading to the surface of the paper, I highlighted the indentations so I could read most of what had been on the previous page.

What I had when I was done were two lines of letters and numbers. The first line was "98 8A-545P." The other line was "MU7747." The second line could very easily be a telephone number, but the first line meant nothing to me except the letters A and P might be part of a time reference.

Okay, so dial the one that looks like a telephone number and see who says hello. I dialed and waited while the number rang and rang. Either nobody was home or . . .

"Good afternoon. Southern Pacific Railroad ticketing. How may I help you?"

I apologized for dialing a wrong number and replaced the handset in its cradle. Now the first line of printing made sense. Ninety-eight was the train number of the northbound Coast Daylight. Eight o'clock this morning is when it left Los Angeles and five-forty-five P.M. is when it pulls into San Francisco, and since Lilly—assuming she wrote the note—included the San Francisco arrival time, it was a good bet she planned to stay on until the end of the line.

All right, Spicer, so far so good. Now see if you can find more evidence around here to support your theory that Lillian Bouvier was at that moment on her way to San Francisco. The most likely places to find that sort of evidence were the bathroom and the bedroom.

In the bathroom I found a toothbrush holder, but no toothbrush or toothpaste. Since Lilly didn't wear a whole lot of makeup, I couldn't say what, if anything, was missing from the sparse collection of items in the cabinet behind the bathroom mirror. Okay how about the bedroom?

Two clothes hangers on the bed were out of character with Lilly's neatness obsession and could be an indication she packed in a hurry, not taking time to put the hangers back on the closet pole. Of course, I didn't know Lilly's wardrobe well enough to guess what clothes might be missing, but I noticed a set of matched luggage on the right side of the closet floor. There were a large suitcase, a medium-sized one, and a space where a small overnight bag might have been stored.

It was possible that I was trying too hard to make the evidence fit my theory, but it certainly looked as if Miss Lillian Bouvier was nearly four hundred miles north of where I was and, unless I was way off base, on her way to see a man about an elephant in West Sacramento.

I drove back to Bette Davis's house where Henry met me at the door and ushered me into the library where Miss Davis was seated at the desk, apparently waiting to hear my report. She said, "Thank you for reporting back so quickly, Mister Spicer. I hope you have some good news for us. Henry, you may remain to hear what Mister Spicer has to tell us."

I settled into an armchair. "I guess the good news is that I don't have any particularly bad news to tell you. Beyond that, it is my best guess that Miss Bouvier is about four hundred miles north of us on her way to San Francisco. That's the most likely conclusion I could draw from the evidence I found in her home."

That wasn't quite the conclusion I'd come to, but it was close enough. I didn't mention West Sacramento and stuck with what the evidence I'd found supported.

Miss Davis appeared mildly surprised at hearing that news. Of course she's also an excellent actress so one never knows which emotions are real. "San Francisco? Good heavens, why on earth would she go there?"

Henry, on the other hand, wasn't an actor and the news I had just delivered definitely worried him. Looking in his direction I asked, "So neither of you has any idea why Miss Bouvier might be going to San Francisco?"

The butler shook his head vehemently and Miss Davis said, "I haven't the foggiest notion why she would do such a thing."

Standing, I said, "Well, she apparently went voluntarily, so nobody kidnapped her or anything along those lines, and since Lillian is an adult and free to do whatever she wishes, I think we've done all we can do for now. Hopefully she will have an explanation for you when she returns.

"In the meantime, I need to prepare for my trip tomorrow. If you should hear from her tonight, please let me know. Goodnight, Miss Davis."

Henry saw me to the door and I had the impression he was on the verge of telling me something. When he didn't, I turned and looked him in the eye. "Henry, I'm pretty sure you either know what's going on around here or have a pretty good idea. If that's the case, you'd be wise to tell me what you know. This case is no longer just a theft. The cops are looking for a murderer. They aren't going to take kindly to anyone withholding information that would have helped them find the killer."

There was sweat on his forehead. "I swear I don't know anything about Mister Boland's death. Honestly, I don't."

I gave him a look that said, "I know you're lying," and put my hat on. He was still watching from the doorway when I pulled out of the jungle and headed for Highland Avenue and my apartment on Yucca.

After climbing the stairs to Montero Apartments' number 213, I locked the door behind me and poured a stiff shot of Vat 69 Scotch in a nifty double glass I swiped from Musso and Frank a while back. Then I lit a Lucky Strike—I like to enjoy my vices two at a time—and tossed the match into a gold and black Cinegrill ashtray that needed cleaning. Either that or I had to go across the street to the Roosevelt Hotel and steal another one.

Then I leaned back in a kitchen chair and gave some thought to Lilly Bouvier. She was a nut, no question about that, but a smart nut. I just couldn't see her swiping Bette Davis's elephant. I could see Rolly Boland talking her into some crazy scheme or other, but that would still have to be something legal.

So how does it all fit together? With a little more of the kind of luck I had today, I might just have an answer to that question by Saturday night. If not—if Joseph Kipchumba didn't come up with a lead I could follow, I'd be at a dead end. That's a phrase I've never liked.

I swallowed the last of my Scotch and stubbed out my cigarette. I took another look at the Cinegrill ashtray and decided to remodel my kitchen décor by swiping a new ashtray from Musso and Frank while I put away one of their steaks.

Nine

12:00 P.M. – Friday – August 9, 1940

Union Station – 800 N. Alameda Street, Los Angeles

I pulled into the tree-lined circular drive and parked smack dab in front of the Union Terminal entrance at noon. I wasn't there more than a few minutes when passengers from the Southern Pacific Coaster began pouring out through the station's large entrance doors.

When I saw Susan come through those doors, I got out of the car and met her. We shared a quick hug and a kiss before I stowed her overnight bag next to mine in the trunk and we were off to Glendale.

She was sitting in the center of the seat, right next to me and it felt good to have her there. I said, "How was your train ride, Angel?"

"It was great. Those parlor car seats are really slick. You can swivel them toward the windows and lean back for a great view of the scenery going by. I could see great views of the ocean and the beach and all the little towns along the way. Thank you for getting me a seat in that car."

"You're welcome. I thought you might enjoy some deluxe treatment."

"Oh, I did, but the seat I have right now is even better." She leaned over for a kiss, and then said. I hope you didn't have to wait too long at the depot."

"I didn't wait at all. I pulled into the parking lot a couple of minutes before noon, and before I got out of the car, you were coming out of the terminal."

I turned north onto San Fernando Road and we were rolling along next to a bone dry concrete channel about a hundred feet wide. Susan noticed it. "Johnny, what's that canal or whatever it is over there?"

"That, my dear, is the infamous Los Angeles River. The entire river bed was paved during the last couple of years to help control flooding."

"But there's no water in it!"

"That's the way it is most of the year, except during the winter. Then it fills right up to the banks and becomes a real raging torrent all the way to where the water runs into the ocean near Long Beach."

"To Long Beach? That's a pretty long way isn't it?"

"Yeah, the river starts out northwest of here around Canoga Park—you'll see where it turns south in a minute—and ends up in the ocean at the port of Long Beach. The way the river winds around, I'd guess it's close to fifty miles long."

"Wow! And it's all paved over like this?"

"Yes, all but a couple of small sections."

I stopped for a red light at Broadway and Susan's curiosity came up with another question. "What town is this?"

"This is Glendale. In another minute or two we'll jog over to a street called Air Way and we'll be at Grand Central Air Terminal. The official Los Angeles municipal airport is Mines Field over to the west near Inglewood, but Grand Central is a lot more convenient for people in Hollywood, Burbank, and Pasadena."

A moment later we were parked in one of the spaces provided just north of the circular drive in front of the airport. I opened the trunk and asked, "Is there anything you want to leave here instead of carrying the extra weight to Sacramento and back?"

Susan's attention was riveted to the terminal and a Trans World Airlines DC3 taxiing out to the runway. Then I remembered her trepidation about flying and wondered if keeping her mind off of what was ahead had anything to do with her sudden interest in the Los Angeles River. After all, the L.A. River isn't all that fascinating.

I took Susan by the arms and turned her to face me. "Hey, Angel, relax. We're going to be perfectly safe and we're gonna have fun. There's nothing to worry about."

She leaned forward into my arms. "I'm sorry, Johnny. I'll be okay. Promise."

I gave her an encouraging hug. "You've got nothing to apologize for. Most people are a little nervous on their first flight. Now, is there anything in your bag that you want to leave here?"

"Yes, there's a pale blue cotton jacket and a light green cardigan sweater in the bag that could stay here."

Inside, the Spanish and Deco terminal building was busy, but not crowded. The wall opposite the entrance was taken up with airline ticket counters—TWA, American and United were there, plus some lesser known airlines, including Central Valley Air Lines.

The first thing I did after giving the woman behind the counter my name and reservation information was to present my state private investigator's Photostat and open my jacket far enough for her to see my shoulder holster. She looked closely at my Photostat, and then returned it to me, saying only, "Thank you, Mister Spicer."

Next she sold us our tickets and assigned our seats from a printed seating chart. Their DC-3s were laid out with a single row of seats down the right side of the aisle and a standard double row on the other side, which is far less claustrophobic than the two and two arrangement with a narrow central aisle some airlines use to cram more passengers into the planes.

We were given the two seats in the last row closest to the boarding hatch. In a "Three" the ride tends to be a little rougher in the rearmost seats. On the plus side, the rear seats are closest to the restroom and the boarding hatch, which Susan might count as advantages.

Next the agent checked our bags, carefully weighing them and writing the weights down on a form. Finally, she stapled our baggage claim checks to our tickets and informed us our flight would be boarding on the ramp outside in about thirty minutes.

I escorted Susan to a small coffee shop on the terminal's second floor. It offered a nice view of the aircraft parking ramp and the runways. I ordered two cups of Java, and after the waitress left them on our table, Susan leaned across and whispered, "Johnny, do they have restrooms on these airplanes?"

With a grin I couldn't resist, I said, "They sure do, Angel. You can drink your coffee."

Blushing slightly, she said, "Well, I didn't know."

Eventually the public address system told us Central Valley Air Lines flight number 107 to Bakersfield, Fresno and Sacramento was ready for boarding through terminal gate two. When we got to gate two, we found our friendly ticket agent there to verify our tickets and tell us to follow the white line on the pavement to our airplane.

Susan already had a firm grip on my hand by the time we got to the silver CVAL DC-3. The boarding hatch was toward the rear of the ship on the left side and folded down when it was open to provide a set of stairs for passengers to use when boarding or deplaning.

At the top of the stairs we were greeted by a woman in a spiffy blue and white stewardess uniform who looked at our tickets and directed us to our seats. I urged Susan into the window seat, figuring she would enjoy seeing the landmarks we passed on the ground. Then, while a dozen or so more passengers filed aboard, I showed Susan how to fasten her seatbelt, turn on the reading light, and adjust the overhead ventilation outlet.

Once all of the passengers were aboard, our stewardess, who according to her name badge was Eileen, closed the hatch and walked to the front of the cabin. There she explained most of the things I had just shown Susan. Finally, as the pilot fired up the port and then the starboard engines, she walked the length of the cabin to make sure everyone was strapped in and ready to fly.

When she got to us, Eileen apparently sensed Susan's nervousness. She stopped and, as if making conversation, said, "We're in for a great flight today. My favorite captain is in the cockpit. He's the best!"

Next she returned to the front of the cabin and strapped into her jump seat. By that time we had taxied to the takeoff position at the south end of the runway. The pilot ran up the engines and Susan tried to break every bone in my right hand. That girl has a strong grip!

Then the brakes were off and we were rolling down the runway. I leaned toward Susan so she could hear me better over the engines and said, "See if you can feel when the tires leave the runway."

Her eyes were closed and I'm not sure she was breathing, but she nodded. A few seconds later the ship's nose came up and in a barely audible voice, Susan said, "Now?"

I said, "Great, Angel! You got it right on the money! Now take a look out the window. We're flying right over Highway 99. Go ahead, take a look."

Still holding on to my hand, she leaned a little toward the window risked a look down. I wasn't sure how she was going to react to the view below us, but getting her to look out the window was the right thing to do. After a couple of moments, she pointed west and said, "Then that one must be Highway 101, right?"

I felt her grip on my hand relax a little as I said, "Right as rain! And those mountains up ahead on the right are part of the Los Angeles National Forest."

Susan's grip on my hand tightened again. "It doesn't look like we're high enough to go over those mountains."

"We don't have to go over them. We fly through the Tejon Pass where the Ridge Route goes."

At that point our stewardess stood and asked for our attention. "Ladies and gentleman, Central Valley Air Lines would like to treat you to an in-flight snack." She raised her right hand in which she held a small bag of Planter's Peanuts and a bottle of Coca-Cola. In just a few minutes I'll be coming by with peanuts, soft drinks, orange juice, and coffee." The stewardess then raised her left hand and held up what I knew from previous experience was a tiny box containing two Chiclets. "If any of you are having difficulty clearing your ears from the altitude, we also have chewing gum that will help relieve the pressure."

I noticed Susan looking across the cabin to get a peek out the other side of the plane. I asked, "Whatcha looking for, Angel?"

"Home. I think I see the highway that goes through Santa Paula, so the town on the coast beyond it must be Ventura. Santa Barbara should be the next big city up the coast."

"It should be if it isn't too hazy to see it."

As I expected, the farther we traveled over the mountains, the bumpier it got. Susan was noticing it, too. She asked, "It's getting kind of bumpy, isn't it?"

As her hand tightened around mine, I said, "Yes, but try not to let it worry you. That's normal over the mountains because of the vertical wind currents. The biggest danger is spilling your coffee if you aren't prepared for the bumps. We're nearly to the pass though, so in a few minutes we'll be flying into the valley and beginning our descent for landing at Bakersfield."

Susan wasn't entirely sure about the bumps, but she seemed to relax a little. I had to give her credit for having faith in what I told her. The next big change in scenery came at about ten minutes before three. Suddenly the mountains were behind us and the pilot lowered the ship's nose for a very long straight-in approach to Meadows Field in Bakersfield.

I said, "There's the valley. We should have smooth sailing from here on."

"Oh, my! Everything is so flat. What valley is it?"

A little surprised that she didn't know that answer to that one already, I said, "In general terms it's known as the central valley, but on the map it's actually considered two valleys. Everything south of Stockton is known as the San Joaquin Valley and everything north of there is the Sacramento Valley. There is no real physical boundary between them. They're named for the watersheds that carry water down from the Sierra Nevada Mountains out there to our right. The primary drainage occurs through two rivers, the Sacramento River and the San Joaquin River. They come together beyond Stockton and form what's usually called the Delta."

Our landing at Bakersfield was smooth as silk and I asked Susan, "Well, what do you think Angel? Do you want to get out and hitchhike the rest of the way or is flying a little less scary now?"

"I'm still getting used to it, but it isn't nearly as frightening as I expected, thanks to you. You put me at ease." With a little smile, she added, "I'll even give you your hand back if you want."

I smiled back and gave her a wink. "Naw, I think you'd better keep it a while longer, just to be on the safe side."

Susan leaned over and gave me a kiss on the cheek just as our stewardess arrived to open the boarding hatch. She, too, gave Susan a smile and a wink. Susan grinned and winked right back.

We weren't on the ground in Bakersfield for more than fifteen minutes—just long enough for two passengers to deplane and a new one to come aboard. Then the hatch was closed, the pilot taxied out to the runway and we were back in the air.

I said, "I'm afraid the valley isn't very interesting to look at. It's mostly just farms and rural communities named for local pioneers like Visalia, Tulare and Hanford. Do you mind if I ask you for your opinion about an aspect of the case I'm working?"

Asking Susan for help with case always seemed to please her. She smiled. "Of course I don't mind. How can I help?"

After giving her the basic details about the missing Elephant without revealing the client's name, I went into greater detail regarding Lillian Bouvier. I told Susan about her behavior, mannerisms and about what I'd found during my search of her home. Then I asked, "What would you think makes a person like that tick the way they do?"

She tilted her head as though in thought for a few moments, and then said, "I'm not a psychiatrist, Johnny, so I'm not really qualified to give that sort of opinion, but as a female, my sense of the situation as you described it is that your young woman didn't get enough love and recognition as a child, so she ended up with a low opinion of herself. It may also be that she feels alone in the world, and with no one around to share her problems, she may have created a set of strict rules to maintain control of her life.

"Remember, I'm just guessing at these things based on what little information I have to go on. If I'm right about her childhood, though, no child deserves that sort of upbringing. You see the damage it can do. Mostly, I feel sorry for her. Does that help?"

"Yes. Thanks. I was thinking along the same lines, but it's nice to have a more qualified opinion."

About that time we landed in Fresno. Again our time on the ground was no more than fifteen minutes. As we took off on the last leg of the journey, I looked at Susan and sensed something was bothering her.

I said, "Hey, Angel. You're looking a little glum. What's on your mind?"

With trepidation showing on her face, Susan came right out with what she was thinking. "I was just wondering about the woman you were asking me about and hoping your interest in her is professional."

I smiled. "Now who's being insecure?"

"I don't mean to pry . . ."

"Sure you do and I'll put your mind at ease. My interest in Miss Bouvier is purely professional. She's part of a case that's got me stymied and if I don't make some sense out of it soon, I'm gonna get sacked."

That earned me another kiss on the cheek. Then Susan said, "You'll figure it out. I noticed you didn't mention who your client was, though. I take it that part is super-secret."

"Sort of. It's what the cops call a 'high jingo' case—one involving a celebrity or public official that requires special handling so the department doesn't end up with egg all over its face."

"And you're afraid of ending up with egg on your face? Somehow I don't believe that. You're more the sort who says 'damn the torpedoes, full speed ahead.'"

"Oh, I can be tactful if the situation requires it."

"Okay, Mister Hollywood Private Detective, if you say so."

"I say so."

The sun was getting low on the western horizon by the time I felt the pilot reduce engine power and begin his descent into Sacramento. Eileen stood up and reminded everyone to fasten their seatbelts, and then walked through the cabin to be sure everything was in order for landing.

When she got to us, Eileen looked at Susan and said, "Would I be right if I guessed this might be your first airplane flight?"

Susan nodded. "Yes. Did it show that much?"

The stewardess smiled warmly, "Oh, heavens! You should have seen me on my first flight, and look at me now."

Susan grinned. "I can see how you could get addicted to flying."

"You can, and to commemorate your first of what I hope are many enjoyable flights, here are your own Central Valley Air Lines Junior Pilot Wings. Wear them with pride!"

Eileen handed Susan a small silver replica of a commercial pilot's wings. They were emblazoned with the CVAL emblem and the words "Junior Pilot."

Susan said, "I will. I'll pin them on right now!"

She did pin them on and she definitely wore them with pride for the rest of the day. I couldn't help feeling a little proud of Susan, too.

Ten

6:00 P.M. – Friday – August 9, 1940

Sutterville Aerodrome – 6151 Freeport Boulevard, Sacramento

We stepped down out of the DC3 and into an oven turned up to "broil." It was a little after six o'clock and Sacramento's temperature still felt well above the ninety degree mark. Fortunately the small terminal building's lobby had refrigerated air. That made waiting for our bags a lot more pleasant, although we still had to go back outside into the oven to claim them.

Sacramento's municipal airport was called Sutterville Aerodrome, and it had two unpaved runways, although there was a sign in the terminal announcing plans to pave the runways and add a third one within a year. Paving would be a welcome change, because the current runways were hard to distinguish from dusty cow pastures.

Judging by the ticket counters in the terminal, two airlines besides CVAL would be using the new runways—Pacific Airlines and United Airlines. You would think that the capital city of a wealthy state like California would have a modern, well-equipped airport, but you'd be wrong.

The airport was located six or seven miles south of the downtown area, and our destination, West Sacramento, was another mile or so beyond that. From past visits to this Godforsaken place, I knew public transportation in outlying areas was scarce, which is why I reserved a rental car.

We found the Hertz Car Rental Company operating out of a small kiosk near the street entrance to the terminal. It took us longer to find the Hertz clerk, who was hiding out in a small room off the terminal lobby. Then it took another fifteen minutes to complete the paperwork before I was handed the key to a black Cadillac four-passenger coupe.

As we walked toward the parking lot in search of the Caddy, Susan said, "They had Chevrolets, you know. You didn't have to rent the most expensive car they have."

"Actually, I did. Think about it this way: First, the client pays my expenses, so the cost of the rental car doesn't come out of my pocket. Second, I have learned to rent cars with enough power to get away from trouble if necessary and strong enough to survive if it doesn't. Third, driving an expensive car seems to make people I encounter more respectful and cooperative."

"Oh."

"Angel, I wish you'd stop worrying every time I spend a dime."

Susan put on an expression that was somewhere between apologetic and pouty. "I'm sorry, Johnny. It's just that my folks drummed it into my head that I should save every nickel I could for a rainy day."

We came to the Cadillac—a Model 62 four-passenger coupe— and as I unlocked the trunk and put our bags in, I said, "And your folks were right—to a point. There's nothing wrong with spending a buck or two on fun and relaxation if it helps keep your mind alert and your body fit for the job you do. It's sort of a motivational treat."

As I opened the passenger door for her, Susan took my arm. "Johnny, I guess the truth goes a little deeper. Sometimes I'm afraid you don't save for the future because you figure you aren't going to live that long. I want you to be around for a long, long time."

"Angel, when we get back to L.A., I'm going to show you my savings passbook. That should convince you that I plan to be around for a long, long time. Okay?"

She gave me a hug. "Okay, I'll take your word for it."

Inside, the Cadillac was about as plush and stylish as you expect a Caddy to be. The seats were covered with a comfortable leather in a light brown color. The dashboard was a similar color with a pushbutton radio at the top of chrome waterfall that concealed the radio's speaker. The instruments were in the usual place on the left side in front of the driver while a clock and the glove compartment filled up the space on the passenger side of the dash.

The shift lever for the three-speed, all-synchromesh transmission was mounted on the steering column within easy reach, and the steering wheel was mounted at a comfortable angle and distance from the seat for long distance driving. The big 135 horsepower V8 started on the first try, and made a healthy rumble that clearly said, "Let's go!" We went.

Sacramento Municipal Airport is on a street called Freeport Boulevard, a major north-south artery. I turned north and followed it for three or four miles until we came to a major east-west street named Broadway. There I turned left and drove a few more miles until we got to Front Street, which runs along the riverfront in the older part of town. Here the streets could use the same treatment they planned to give the airport runways. Part of the street was actually still paved in cobblestones, for crying out loud.

To our left was a wide expanse of water and Susan asked, "Is that the Sacramento River, Johnny?"

"Yeah, that's the mighty muddy Sacramento. The American River flows into it up here a ways, but we're going to turn left and go over that bridge up ahead to cross the river before we get there. That will take us into West Sacramento."

"That's a funny looking bridge. I don't think I've ever seen one like that before."

"It's called a vertical lift bridge. The part of the bridge between the towers goes up and down to let large ships go through."

"Large ships? Why would large ships come here?"

"Well, until a few years ago they used to run passenger riverboats up and down the river. Long before that freighters brought mining supplies up the river from San Francisco and unloaded them on the docks here.

"Building the city right next to the river was convenient, but not too bright because every spring the snow up in the mountains melts and the river floods down here. The city fathers' brilliant solution to that problem was raising the whole damned town one story, so the first floors became basements and entrances had to be put in on the second floors. These people were not the sharpest saws in the tool box."

With a note of surprise in her voice, Susan said, "How on earth do you know all this stuff? Every time I ask a question you not only know the answer, you know all kinds of other stuff about it, too."

"I suppose you'd have to blame that on curiosity. Like when I go to the library to research something for a case, I always get sidetracked by other subjects I encounter along the way."

The sound of our tires changed as they rolled over the metal plates forming the bridge roadway, and then we were in West Sacramento. I said, "The hotel we're looking for should be coming up on the left soon. It's called the Hotel El Rancho. I don't know anything about the place except that my travel agent said it was the closest decent hotel to where I need to be tomorrow."

"There it is! Up there where that neon windmill is."

"Good eye, Angel. Let's see how big the cockroaches are in this joint."

Because it was situated out in the middle of a lot of nothing and could spread out, the Hotel El Rancho was built in the western motel style with single story wings containing guest rooms around a central building that housed the hotel lobby, restaurant, and lounge. A large swimming pool and cabana-style patio were adjacent to the central building.

While Susan wandered through the gift shop off the lobby, I filled out a registration card for each of the two rooms I'd reserved. We were given rooms eight and nine which were close to the central building and overlooked the swimming pool.

Along with our room keys, the clerk also handed me a brochure. "This pamphlet will tell you about some of the hotel's amenities. Be sure to enjoy a western-style dinner in the Round Up Room. Our steaks are world famous!"

We parked in front of our rooms and Susan, still proudly wearing her Junior Pilot wings on her blouse, led the way to our rooms. She unlocked both doors so I could put our overnight bags in the correct places. Then she left my room only to come trotting back a minute later to open my side of the connecting doors between the two rooms.

"There," she said, "That's better."

Grinning, I said, "Immeasurably." Then my stomach growled and I looked at my watch. It was already seven-fifteen. "Are you getting hungry, Angel?"

"I'm starving." Susan had picked up the amenities brochure the desk clerk gave me and was looking through it. "Since I'm no longer worrying about every dime you spend, I think you should take me to the Round Up Room and get me one of these world famous steaks, a big one."

"Okay, you've got it. Let's go."

The Hotel El Rancho's Round Up Room was a large dining room with a fake beamed ceiling, wooden tables with colorful table cloths, and western décor on the walls. Even the plates had western scenes on them. It all made me want to holler "Yee-Ha" and swing a lasso over my head, but I restrained myself so as to not embarrass Susan.

Our waitress arrived dressed in a cowgirl costume, complete with ten gallon hat. A name badge in the shape of a steer informed us she was Beth. The menu, also looking very western, listed every way of preparing every cut of beef known to man. Susan actually did pick out a steak and I ordered a slice of rock salt rubbed prime rib. A huge prime rib roast was delivered to our table in a charcoal broiler on wheels and my portion—enough to feed at least three—was sliced off by a tall fellow in a white chef's outfit. I would have attracted less attention by hollering "Yee-Ha" and swinging the lasso.

The food, however, was delicious. The Hotel El Rancho could claim "world famous" steaks without argument from me. Susan wisely saved a little room for dessert and was rewarded with a slice of terrific strawberry pie topped with whipped cream. I'm not a big fan of sweets, but the taste she gave me of her pie almost made me wish I'd saved room for a slice, too.

We took a walk around the grounds after dinner to work off some of the overindulgence we just consumed. The temperature had dropped down into the low seventies, which made for a pleasant summer evening. We also had a bright half-moon to light the way, although the Hotel El Rancho's grounds were plenty well lit to begin with.

On our way back to our rooms, we stopped at a driveway to let a car go by. I couldn't see the driver clearly, but something about the silhouette of the woman behind the steering wheel struck me as familiar. I was just opening my mouth to mention it when three gunshots popped in quick succession, followed a few seconds later by the crashing and grinding of sheet metal.

I pulled Susan back behind a large bush and we ducked as I drew my Smith and Wesson in order to return fire at the bad guys, only there were no bad guys in sight to shoot at. As I peeked around the bush, I could see the car—a white or light gray Chevrolet sedan—that passed us. It was crashed into at least two parked cars, but the shooting was over and a few people were coming out of their rooms and looking into the crashed Chevy.

"Susan, I've got a bad feeling about that car and its driver. Do you feel up to going over there and telling those people you're a nurse, and then checking on the driver's condition?"

"Sure. I was about to do that anyway. Aren't you coming with me?"

"No. I'm going back to our room and take off this shoulder holster before the cops get here. I know we didn't do anything wrong, but it usually takes all night to convince a bunch of hardheaded local cops that a private investigator is innocent of anything. It has something to do with their breeding I think."

"All right. I'll see what I can do. Anything else?"

"Yes, when you come back to our rooms, give me as good a description of the driver as you can. Here's your room key."

"Okay, on my way."

I watched her trot across the driveway and smiled. For a gal who was afraid to get on an airplane, Susan showed a lot of gumption when the chips were down. As she approached the small crowd gathering around the wrecked car, I headed to our rooms. At the same time I heard a siren begin to wail not too far away.

In room nine, I removed my jacket, took off my shoulder holster, and stowed it in my overnight bag. After putting my jacket back on, I walked to the window and pondered the meaning of what I thought I'd just seen. If my hunch was right, the Ivonya-Ngia Tembo had just claimed its second victim, and an unlikely one at that. If this kept up I wasn't going to have anybody left to investigate.

An ambulance, followed closely by two sheriff's cruisers with "Yolo County" painted on their doors, pulled into the parking lot. Then Susan walked past my window and I heard her opening the outside door to room number eight. A few seconds later she popped through the connecting door between our rooms and said, "Well, the good news is I'm fairly sure she's going to live. The bad news is her face is badly cut up from the crash. A good surgeon might be able to repair the damage, but her face will be a mess for a while."

"Besides that, what does she look like?"

"She's a slim woman in her mid-twenties, no makeup, and dark hair pulled up into a bun. Did I just meet your Miss Bouvier?"

I nodded glumly. "Yes, I'm pretty sure you did, but how did you figure that out?"

Susan held up some folded papers. "That's the name on these forms. They were on the ground just outside the driver's door of her car. I think they're rental papers from that Hertz Company, except they came from San Francisco."

I noticed smeared blood on the papers as I looked through them. "Good work, Angel. I knew she took this morning's Coast Daylight up to Oakland and I figured this was her destination, but I was wondering how she planned to get here from there."

Then Susan surprised me by assuming an angry posture with her fists on her hips, and saying, "You know, Mister Hollywood Detective, you've got a lot of nerve putting my life at risk without any warning."

Nodding again, I said, "I honestly didn't think there was any real risk. Obviously I was wrong."

"Well, you must have thought there was some danger or you wouldn't have been wearing that gun all day. And by the way, if you don't want a girl to know you're carrying that thing, don't hug her!"

"I wore the pistol because that's safer than putting it in a suitcase that's going to be out of my sight for several hours. That's the only reason I had it on. The truth is I underestimated the situation. I'm sorry to have put you in harm's way."

Susan smiled. "You know you're kinda cute when you make apologies." Then going back to a serious expression, she said, "Johnny, I understand there's sometimes danger associated with what you do. Remember how we met? Somebody had just blown a great big hole in your head for heaven's sake.

"The thing is I have complete faith in your ability to keep me safe. If I didn't, I wouldn't be anywhere near you. I'm just asking you to let me know what we're getting into before the shooting starts. Okay?"

"Okay, Angel. I promise."

She put her arms around my neck and whispered, "Now quit fooling around and take me to bed."

I did as the lady asked.

Eleven

7:00 A.M. – Saturday – August 10, 1940

Hotel El Rancho – 1075 West Capitol Avenue, West Sacramento

Susan and I were both awake by six. She because we'd loused up her sleeping schedule and I because I had a lot of questions that needed answers. So at seven we were back at the Round Up Room for coffee and breakfast.

She wanted French toast with maple syrup and I ordered my usual breakfast, scrambled eggs with some ham and/or cheese stirred in. Susan asked me to pass the cream to doctor her coffee and when she had to ask a second time, she said, "Hey, Mister Hollywood Detective, what are you thinking so hard about?"

"What happened last night and how it effects our plans for today."

Susan grinned a mischievous grin. "Are you talking about what happened before we went to bed or after?"

"Before, smarty."

She put on her pouty face and said, "Oh."

"I'm sorry I'm distracted, Angel, but in about three hours I'm supposed to meet with the people who may have killed one person involved in this case and just tried to kill a second. I'm supposed to go to their shop here in West Sacramento, but I'm not sure that's such a good idea."

Susan nodded enthusiastically. "Now you're showing some sense. I'm certainly no expert on these things, but letting those people get you alone doesn't seem like it will promote the long life we were talking about yesterday." After a short pause, she added,

"Besides, I'd have to find someone else to hold my hand on the airplane trip home."

I made a face at her and said, "I'm sure you'd find no shortage of volunteers."

"I was just kidding!"

"I know. I'm trying to work out an idea that might be more productive and a whole safer than keeping that appointment. Do you think you could find out where the ambulance took Lilly last night?"

"I imagine so. The desk clerk would probably know which hospital she would have been taken to."

"That's assuming there's more than one hospital in this cow town. If we do find her, do you think she would be in any condition to travel this morning?"

"Well," she said thoughtfully, "Unless there was something I didn't spot last night, most of her injuries are to her face where her head hit the dashboard or steering wheel or who knows what else. It's possible she also has a concussion and got a broken rib or two in the deal. If the concussion is minor, though, the other injuries just need time to heal before anything can be done about the scars on her face. So, if they got all her lacerations and abrasions dressed and taped up, I guess she could travel if there was a good reason."

"Would being in another hospital—say one closer to home—be considered a good reason?"

Susan grinned. "I get it. You want to kidnap Miss Bouvier and hide her somewhere, but what purpose does that serve besides getting her closer to home?"

"It will make her a whole lot safer. If I've got this thing figured out right, Miss Bouvier knows where some bodies are buried and whoever shot at her last night was trying to make sure she never got to tell anyone what she knows."

Susan nodded thoughtfully. "Didn't you tell me this is a . . . what did you call it? High jingo case?"

"Yes, very much so."

"Is there money available to pay medical bills?"

"I'm pretty sure there is, but we can find out. What are you thinking?"

"That she'd be much better off at the Casa Sobre El Mar."

"Your clinic in Santa Barbara? That's not a bad idea. You think you could get her in?"

"If there's money to pay for her care, I can get her in. They rarely handle charity cases." Grinning, she added, "You were an exception."

"And damned lucky for you I was or you'd be missing out on all this fun and excitement. Okay, let's take things one step at a time. First, please talk to the desk clerk and find out where the ambulance took her. Also, if you can, find out if she was a registered guest here and what room she was in."

"All right, but if you add one more piece of information to that list, you'll have to put me on the payroll."

Putting a few dollars in the plastic tray for our breakfasts and a tip, I said, "Fair enough."

While Susan went into the hotel lobby, I went to our rooms and loaded our bags into the Cadillac. On my way by, I noticed that the previous night's crash scene had been cleaned up pretty well, leaving only some oil stains and skid marks on the pavement to show anything unusual had happened.

By the time I drove around to the front entrance, Susan was out front waiting for me. She jumped in and said, "Miss Bouvier was most likely taken to a place called Sutter Hospital. It's less than five miles from here and I have instructions for getting there."

"Good work, Angel! Let's go pay Lilly a visit."

Shaking her head in mock exasperation, Susan said, "You have to do something about this obsession you have about women in hospitals. First, go back across that bridge we crossed last night."

Turning right out of the Hotel El Rancho onto Capital Avenue, I said, "Not all women in hospitals, just the kind that look like angels. Did the desk clerk say if she was a registered guest?"

"He said she had just registered. He doesn't think she'd even gotten to her room yet."

"That means the police have whatever was in her car. Hopefully they won't recognize anything that's evidence as evidence, like a ceramic elephant statuette. Ya done good, Angel."

"Thanks, but are you sure this is the best way to handle the situation, assuming we can even pull it off?"

"I have no intention of marching into Leo's den until I've seen the size of his teeth, but not keeping my appointment with Kipchumba eliminates what might be an important source of information. That leaves Lilly as my only lead. If I'm wrong and she doesn't know anything about the damned elephant, or if she knows something and just refuses to tell me, I'm out of business."

As we started over the bridge in the eastbound direction, Susan said, "Well, you get paid for looking, not necessarily finding, right?"

"I suppose you could say that, but it's not about getting paid. It's about doing my job well, which means finding out who the bad guy is and, in this instance, recovering the stolen property. I've had a couple of successes lately and my reputation is riding high right now. I'd like to keep it that way."

Susan said, "I guess that makes sense. Oh, the desk clerk said Seventh Street would be a good place to cut over to L. That's the next left turn."

After turning east on L Street, we followed it all the way from Seventh to Twenty-Ninth, where we found the remains of the fort John Sutter built just before the California gold rush. It was in worse shape than his aerodrome. We also found an impressive multi-floor building designed in a Spanish motif. The sign out front read, "Sutter General Hospital."

As I pulled to the curb in front of the place, I asked, "You have any idea how we go about finding out what room she's in, or even if she's here for sure?"

"That's easy, I'll tell them the truth. Well, part of the truth. You just do your best to look like a policeman of some sort. Okay?"

"I'm not exactly sure how you think a policeman should look, but I'll do my best."

"And how do you plan to move her to the new place? By airplane?"

"No, the connections to Santa Barbara would take us almost as long to get there as driving and would be harder on someone who isn't feeling well. We'll do it by automobile, and then I can return the Cadillac at Glendale and pick up my car."

"All right. When do you want to this?"

I glanced at my wristwatch. "It's about quarter to nine. Can we have her out of here by ten?"

"That's pushing it. Remember, Johnny, there are a lot of 'ifs' involved in pulling this off, and I won't do anything that will harm the patient, but I'll do my best and we'll see what happens."

Susan went straight to the reception desk in the hospital lobby and showed the woman behind the desk a card of some kind. "Hello. I'm Nurse Susan Jackson. I rendered first aid to a women out in West Sacramento last night before the ambulance arrived. I believe she was brought here, so I thought I would stop by and see how she's doing this morning."

"Certainly, Miss Jackson. I believe you are referring to a Miss Bouvier. She came into Emergency last night around ten o'clock. She was brought in following an automobile accident at the Hotel El Rancho that involved some shooting."

"That's her."

"Okay, but we have a very strict policy about giving out patient information to anyone but immediate family. I can give her room number to you, of course, but I shouldn't . . ."

The receptionist was looking at me and Susan said, "Oh, this is detective Spicer. He's assigned to the case and came along to make sure all the necessary security precautions were being taken."

On cue, I held up my Special Los Angeles County Sheriff's Deputy shield. It was legit, but on my home turf, it only identified me as a qualified volunteer deputy with little to no authority unless temporarily deputized for a special assignment. Here I hoped nobody would know the difference.

The woman behind the counter nodded and told us that Miss Bouvier was in room 211 on the second floor. We thanked her and climbed the stairway at the back of the lobby. Room 211 was a two-person room, but only one bed was occupied. Most of Lillian's face was covered with tape and gauze, but enough was showing for me to recognize her.

I walked to the side of her bed and said, "Hello, Lilly, do you know who I am?"

In a tone that told me I wasn't at the top of the list of people she wanted to see at that moment, she said, "Yes, Mister Spicer, I know who you are."

"Good. This is Susan Jackson. She's a nurse from Santa Barbara."

Lilly turned her head a little so she could see Susan more clearly and said, "Hello, Miss Jackson. You were at the hotel last night."

"Yes, Mister Spicer and I came up here on business and stayed at the El Rancho last night. We saw the . . . we saw what happened to you. I came over to check on you and give first aid if there was anything I could do before the ambulance got there. Do you mind if I look at your chart here?"

Susan lifted a clipboard from a hook at the foot end of the bed and Lilly said, "No, go right ahead. Maybe you can tell me what my ailments are. Nobody else has so far."

Smiling, Susan said, "Well, the worst of it seems to be multiple lacerations on your face, two broken ribs on your left side, and a minor concussion. Those are things that will heal in time, although you may choose to have some of the scars repaired with surgery, depending on how things look when everything is healed."

Lilly said, "Despite all that, I guess I was fortunate last night. Somebody was shooting a gun out there. I thought they were shooting at me. I was sure of it."

I said, "So am I. That's one of the reasons we're here. I think you'd be a lot safer in another hospital closer to home. In fact Susan thinks we can get you into the private clinic in Santa Barbara where she works. What do you think?"

"That sounds wonderful, but I doubt if I can afford . . ."

Susan said, "Johnny and I will make some telephone calls and see what we can do about that part of it. You just sit tight for a few minutes."

Outside room 211, Susan said, "Okay, Johnny, are you ready to tell me where the money will come from?"

"My client. Miss Bouvier is her employee and they seem quite close. I think Lilly's employer will want to help."

Susan looked doubtful. "And just who is your client?"

"One Miss Bette Davis. Lilly is her private secretary."

Now looking surprised, Susan said, "You mean the actress Bette Davis?"

"Yup. I'm gonna call her and get her okay on the medical expenses. How much do you think we're talking about?"

Susan thought for a moment, and then said, "Of course I can't give you an exact amount, but with daily care for several weeks, doctor visits, specialists, procedures to insure proper healing without infection, and additional surgeries to eliminate some of the scaring, I'd estimate we are talking about at least five thousand dollars. You think she'll go for that?"

"Trust me, she'll go for it. She may want to talk with you, though, so stand by, okay?"

She nodded and I got the long distance operator to bill the call to my office number. Henry answered and I said, "Henry, I need to talk with Madam right now."

"Yes, sir. I'll get her on the line."

A few moments passed before I heard that familiar voice in my ear. "Hello, Mister Spicer. I hope you have good news for us. We could certainly use some."

"For the most part, yes. Your missing employee showed up last night. She checked into the same hotel at which I'm staying and someone shot at her in the hotel parking lot."

"Oh, my. Was she badly hurt?"

"Not too badly. All of her injuries are the kind that will heal with time. The main thing right now is to get her out of the hospital she's in and into a place where we know she'll be safe."

Sounding a little incredulous, Miss Davis asked, "She isn't safe in the hospital?"

"That wasn't a random shooting last night. Somebody was targeting her specifically and while this is a very nice hospital, their security is almost nonexistent. She would be a whole lot safer somewhere more private and farther away from here."

"Do you have such a place in mind?"

"In fact, I do. It's a private clinic and I can assure you from personal experience that the care is first rate."

I winked at Susan and Miss Davis said, "I'll bet it is also expensive. Am I right?"

"You are correct. The costs could go as high as five thousand or more depending on the amount of scar repair required. Her face was cut up badly in the automobile accident caused by the shooting. I have a nurse here who is familiar with the place I'm thinking of if you'd like to speak with her."

"No, Mister Spicer, that won't be necessary. Your recommendation is good enough for me. Five thousand is a lot of money, but Lil . . . but she is very precious to me. I will pay her medical bills regardless of the cost. How soon would you move her?"

"I was planning on doing it today if you approved of the idea. The longer she stays where whoever shot at her can find her, the greater the risk."

"Then by all means move her at once, and please let me know where she is when you get her moved. I want to see her as soon as possible."

"I can arrange for you to do that. The location is within driving distance for you. I don't want to be more specific on the telephone because I have reason to believe your phone is bugged."

"Bugged?"

"Yes, someone has tapped into your line and could be listening right now."

"Then how will I know where she is?"

"We'll play another little game like we did once before. How familiar are you with Junipero Serra?"

There was a pause before Miss Davis said simply, "I know who he was and what he did."

"Good. Unless you hear otherwise, please meet me at the only one of his places that was started on December Fourth. I'll be there at ten o'clock tomorrow morning. Okay?"

"I have it. Goodbye and thank you, Mister Spicer."

I hung the handset back on its cradle and said, "Pack her up, we're in business."

"All right. But first, I need to make sure we have room for Miss Bouvier. Will Bette Davis sign a financial responsibility form for her?"

"She said she would take financial responsibility for all of Lilly's medical expenses. I'm meeting her at Mission Santa Barbara tomorrow morning at ten to bring her over there. I'm sure she'll sign your forms then."

"So that's what all that Father Serra mumbo jumbo was about."

"Yeah. On my first visit to her house we were in the library and I noticed a book about California missions on the shelf. I figured that was as good a basis for a code as any, and I remembered the Santa Barbara Mission was founded on December Fourth because that was my mom's birthday and we went on a trip to the mission for her birthday one year. Of course, Serra founded the mission in Seventeen-something and mom came along quite a bit later."

Susan leaned over and planted a kiss on my cheek. "That," she said, "Is for being a nice guy with a great memory."

She made the call, a room was available at Casa Sobre El Mar, and Susan went to work on the paperwork involved in springing a patient from Mister Sutter's hospital. Fortunately she knew the lingo and all the shortcuts. Otherwise we'd still be there today.

While she dealt with the hospital, I got on the telephone again and cancelled our flight reservations and our room reservation at the Shangri-La. Lillian Bouvier owed me big time for that one. Next I called the Hertz auto rental at the Sutterville Aerodrome and told them I would like to return their fine Cadillac tomorrow at the airport in Glendale. I was told the car I had rented was a "premium" automobile and could not be returned anywhere but where I rented it. If I wanted to stop by and swap the Caddy for a non-premium car, however, I could return it anywhere for a small additional fee. I told them that sounded good and to please have a large four-door sedan ready for me to pick up in an hour or so.

Next I stuck my head in Lilly's room and asked if she had a suitcase and if she knew where it was. She explained that she had a small bag in her rental car, and after going through its contents, the police dropped the bag off at the hospital. I checked another item checked off my list.

Finally, as the hands of the big white clock near the nurse's station approached ten o'clock, I sat on a chair in the hall studying a California roadmap provided courtesy of Mister Hertz when I rented his car. I was figuring out which route to take and how long the drive to Santa Barbara would be. It made no difference how I figured it, the trip to Santa Barbara was about four-hundred miles, or at least an eight-hour drive if we could average fifty miles per hour including rest and food stops. The best route in terms of driving conditions was one that took us down U.S. Highway 99 until it intersected State Route 41. Forty-One would take us southwest to the town of Paso Robles on U.S. Highway 101. From there it was about three more hours down the coast to Santa Barbara.

I was just trying to refold the map when there was a commotion in Lilly's room. I stood and turned to see Lilly in one of the hospital's wheelchairs with one of Sutter's nurses pushing it and Susan tagging along with Lilly's overnight bag.

Susan said, "Johnny, if you'll bring the car around to the front entrance, we can be on our way."

I headed off down the stairs and looked at my watch. It was five minutes after ten. As the nurse helped Lilly from the wheelchair into the Caddy's passenger seat, I asked Susan, "Can she get around without that wheelchair?"

"Yes. Quite well. It's just the hospital's policy to escort departing patients from the grounds by wheelchair."

A few minutes later we were rolling south on Twenty-First Street toward the airport, where it took about fifteen minutes to swap our Cadillac coupe for a LaSalle sedan with wide back doors to make getting in and out easier for Lillian.

At twenty minutes past eight that night we parked in front of Casa Sobre El Mar and I was bushed. Susan, who'd gotten a little sleep during the drive took charge of the situation and got Lilly admitted. While she took care of those details, I called Bette Davis's number and told Henry I wanted to speak to "Madam."

"Hello, Mister Spicer. Have you arrived at your destination?"

"Yes, we just arrived. Everything is going according to plan and the patient is doing well."

"Very well. Then I will see you tomorrow at ten as arranged. Thank you again, Mister Spicer."

I told her she was welcome. Then Susan and I headed to her place where she put me up for the night. I was too tired to protest and take us to a hotel.

Twelve

8:30 P.M. – Sunday – August 11, 1940

Casa Sobre El Mar, Santa Barbara

The Casa Sobre El Mar is nestled in a pine grove on the coast at the southern end of Santa Barbara. The neighborhood was a mostly residential area known as Montecito—an area lousy with large expensive homes, but that would describe almost any part of the Santa Barbara. It's a year-round paradise for folks who can afford the best.

The same could be said for the clinic. You didn't check into the Casa Sobre El Mar unless you could afford the best, and you got the best in return. The clinic's overall appearance was rustic so it looked right at home among the pine trees. The inside matched the exterior with extensive paneling, beam ceilings, and colorful Catalina tiles here and there to give the place some color. The overall feeling was one of peace and serenity.

Casa Sobre El Mar means house on the sea and it lives up to its name with fabulous views of the Pacific Ocean. You even had the refreshing ozone smells like you get at the beach. My impression is that the clinic must also be a great place to work because the employees are cheerful and almost feel like family. The staff isn't large, but consists of the most skilled people in the medical field. Casa was prestigious and attracted the best.

Susan and I arrived just as Lilly was finishing her breakfast. I figured we had about an hour before I'd have to leave to meet Bette Davis at the mission and I wanted to make the best use of the time I could. With Susan observing, I began asking questions to see what I was up against.

"Lilly, are you comfortable here? Anything you need?"

She looked at me with suspicion showing in her eyes, which were about the only parts of her face I could see. Apparently Lilly figured if I was being nice, I must be up to something. "Yes, the room is very comfortable."

"Good. The other day when we were talking out in front of Rolly Boland's apartment, you said you didn't care much for my line of work. Do you recall that?"

Lilly started to nod, but it must have hurt because she stopped the nod and said, "Yes, Mister Spicer, I remember."

"Unfortunately, you didn't get to hear my response. I was going to say, 'There are times when I don't care much for it either.' This is one of those times."

Still looking suspicious, but also a little curious, she said, "Why?"

I glanced at Susan. She was looking at me the same way, as if she was trying to figure out where I was going with this approach. I said, "Yesterday I was forced to make a tough decision. I had an appointment to see the African art expert, Joseph Kipchumba, in West Sacramento. I am certain he was involved with Rolly Boland in the theft of the Ivonya-Ngia Tembo and my intention was to get tough with him and see if he'd spill the beans about Rolly's involvement in the theft and the whereabouts of the statuette.

"But I didn't keep that appointment because I decided it was more important to get you somewhere safer than that Sacramento hospital. In doing that I gave up the only solid lead I had to locating the statuette. That is unless you know something about the theft you haven't told me. My instincts tell me you do or you wouldn't have been in West Sacramento last night. Am I right?"

I could tell Susan didn't approve of me using guilt as a persuasive device, but time was short so I had to play what I thought was my strongest hand. Lilly stared at me for quite a while and I was thinking about what to do next when tears appeared in her eyes and she said, "Yes, Mister Spicer, you are right. I saw and heard some things that convinced me Rolly was involved in the theft."

"What things are those?"

"You have to understand how things were with Rolly. He was a very handsome man and he was interested in me . . . plain, boring me. Rolly swept me off my feet and we began seeing each other on an almost daily basis. Falling in love with him was foolish, but . . ."

"I can see how that might have happened. Rolly was a pretty charming fellow."

Lilly laughed sarcastically. "Charming does not begin to describe Rolly Boland. He had me thoroughly hooked until a couple of clues tipped me off that our situation was not exactly what I thought it was. For example, I spotted some things in Rolly's apartment that clearly were left by another woman—I don't smoke, but I found cigarette butts in the waste can with lipstick on them and there was a woman's hairbrush in the bathroom that was not mine—things like that.

"I knew Madam had a fling or two with him, but that was different. That was business. This was . . . well, just a tawdry affair."

I wasn't quite sure how she differentiated between a tawdry affair and any other kind of affair, but I didn't ask. Instead, I asked a question that was more to the point. "Do you know who the other woman is?"

"Yes, I found that out by accident. The other woman was Doris, Madam's maid. I overheard her say something to Joyce Pimm about a unique—she called it sexy—brass table lamp her boyfriend has in his apartment. She described it as a brass sculpture of a nude woman reclining between two colored glass globes. I happened to know that lamp quite well. It is on a nightstand in Rolly's bedroom, and I remembered he once told me the lamp was a one-of-a-kind casting worth several thousand dollars, so there is not likely to be another one in some other man's bedroom."

I said, "Well, those things may prove he was having multiple affairs, but what makes you think he had anything to do with the Ivonya-Ngia Tembo theft?"

"Several things. First, at one point Rolly asked me to help him with his business bookkeeping—write his checks to pay bills and such—because that is part of what I do for Madam. That meant I saw his telephone bill every month. There was a long distance number in West Sacramento he was calling at least once a week, sometimes more often. I asked him who it was to make sure the telephone charges were legitimate and he told me it was an expert in African tribal art and the calls were definitely business expenses.

"The thing about that was I had seen the same West Sacramento telephone number on Madam's telephone bill at least twice. Also, I knew from something I heard Madam say that an African fellow by the name of Kipchumba had something to do with her buying the Tembo statuette.

"Rolly being close to Kipchumba combined with the piece of blue wool from his suit—yes, I noticed the tear in his elbow when he left that night—you found on the display case glass made me think something very wrong was going on, and then Doris Alpert said something that clinched it. She was in a tiff over some duty she was asked to perform and said she would not need Madam's 'lousy' job much longer because she and her boyfriend would soon be coming into a large amount of money. That's when I realized that she and Rolly were in on it together. They had to be."

Looking back through the notes I'd taken, I said, "All right, that means we have at least three people involved in the theft: Rolly, Doris Alpert, Joseph Kipchumba, and possibly the woman who answers his telephone."

Lilly said, "There is no question about that woman being involved. She is Kipchumba's wife. I think Rolly said her name was Damaris, or something like that."

"Okay, that gave us four suspects in on the theft and four people who could have had the elephant or knew where it was. Rolly's murder reduces the number of suspects we can question to three. Since I suspect the Kipchumbas likely went underground when I didn't show up for our appointment, Doris is the next person to interview."

Lilly looked puzzled. "But I still do not understand why those people tried to kill me, or even how they knew I was coming up there to confront them."

I'd given that one a lot of thought on the drive to Santa Barbara yesterday, but the only explanation I came up with was pretty weak. "I don't think they did. I think what happened last night is a case of mistaken identity."

With a frown, Lilly asked, "Mistaken identity? Who in heaven's name did they think I was?"

"My money's on Doris."

Looking surprised now, Lilly said, "Why would they want to kill Doris? She is one of them!"

"So was Rolly. The Kipchumbas are tying up loose ends and cutting themselves a larger slice of the pie. If they have the statuette, and their behavior makes me think they do, they had no further use for Rolly and they have no more use for Doris."

Lilly was still confused. "But what made them think Doris was in Sacramento?"

"Henry might have inadvertently been responsible for that. I'm fairly certain somebody has installed a listening device on Miss Davis's telephone. Henry called Thursday afternoon to tell me you were missing, except he didn't use your name. He was trying to be careful what he said over the telephone, so he just said 'a member of Madam's staff is missing' and he referred to you as 'she.'"

Susan joined in, asking, "But how did they recognize Lilly as a member of Miss Davis's staff when she checked into the Hotel El Rancho?"

I shook my head. "This part of it is pretty vague, but they were probably keeping a close eye on Rolly when the theft was being planned. He would have told them he had recruited a female member of Miss Davis's staff to help plan the heist. He probably even hinted that he had an intimate relationship with the woman. The Kipchumbas wouldn't have known he was fooling around with two of Miss Davis's women employees, so if they saw Lilly with Rolly during that time, they would assume she was the girlfriend he told them about."

I noticed Lilly cringe a little when I said Rolly was fooling around with two of Miss Davis's women employees. Obviously she thought her relationship with Boland was above "fooling around" status. I liked Lilly, but she had a bad habit of making judgments in which she conveniently deceived herself.

"My guess is they staked out the Hotel El Rancho because it's the most likely place to stay for someone who was unfamiliar with the area and could afford the price. Then, when Lilly got there to check in, the Kipchumbas jumped the gun and shot at her thinking she was Doris."

Lilly said, "Well, I sure hope they have discovered their mistake!"

I shook my head. "We have no reason to think they have unless the real Doris showed up, and I don't think that's likely. If Doris figured out that, like Rolly, she's expendable, and if she has a lick of sense, she's headed for parts unknown as fast as she can get there."

Again looking as if she was on the verge of tears, Lilly said, "Then they still want to kill me."

"That's why we moved you away from Sacramento, Lilly. Nobody except the clinic staff knows you're here, not even Miss Davis."

That surprised Lilly. "Where does she think I am?"

"When I told her what happened to you in Sacramento, I also said we were taking you someplace safe. In fact, I need to go meet her nearby and show her where you are and how to get here. By the way, she's picking up the tab for your care at the clinic."

Another surprised look. "She is?"

"Yup. Your employer seems to think plain, boring you is worth quite a bit more than you do. Now, just one more question before I go to meet Miss Davis. A moment ago you said you were up in

Sacramento to 'confront' the Kipchumbas. With what did you plan to confront them?"

Suddenly Lilly went pale and got flustered. She stammered, "Just that . . . just that I . . . that Rolly had told me the whole story about stealing the elephant and I would take what I knew to the police if they didn't return the statuette."

That was a load of hogwash. There was no question in my mind that Lilly still wasn't telling me the whole story. What the hell could she have that she could use to confront the Kipchumbas and make them return the elephant? I had the feeling knowing the answer to that one could put me a whole lot closer to recovering the statuette.

At least it was a direction in which to go. At that point, though, I needed to go meet Miss Davis. I said, "All right, ladies, I'm off on my Mission mission. I'll be back soon."

Not being expert in architectural styles, I'll simply say Mission Santa Barbara was built in the California Mission style. I can say that with some certainty because it looks like every other California Mission I've ever seen—a big white building with a red tile roof, lots of arches, and a bell tower or two. The only notable difference was this one had a scummy pond out in front with a fountain that wasn't working.

I parked near the scummy pond and watched the parking lot. Miss Davis wasn't there yet and that was exactly how I wanted it. This way I could see if anyone appeared to be following her when she got there. If she had picked up a tail somewhere, the last thing I wanted to do is lead them straight to Lilly.

When Miss Davis arrived, she was alone in the same maroon, wood-trimmed Buick station wagon Lilly had driven the day I saw her at Rolly Boland's apartment. I waited several minutes and nobody appeared to be taking the slightest interest in her, so I drove over and parked next to the Buick.

She rolled the driver-side window down and said, "Good morning, Mister Spicer. I must say you are very good at giving clues."

"And you're very good at figuring them out." I handed her a simple street map I'd drawn and said, "Here's a map that shows how to get directly to the clinic where Lilly is from Highway 101, but you can follow me this morning. Just don't leave this map laying around where anyone else can see it. Okay?"

"Okay, Mister Spicer, I shall take utmost care in that regard. I take it you think Miss Bouvier is still in danger."

"She is if the wrong people figure out where she is. Also, you need to know that Rolly Boland stole your statuette. He was in cahoots with an African art expert up near Sacramento—a fellow called Joseph Kipchumba. Is that name familiar to you?"

I noticed Miss Davis responded to the part about Boland, but ignored my question about her knowing Kipchumba. "Rolly was a fine cinematographer, but otherwise he was worthless. Poor Lillian. She must have been devastated when she found out what an utter scoundrel he was. Okay, Mister Spicer, lead the way. I want to see Lillian."

It took about fifteen minutes to cover the five-and-a-half miles between the mission and Montecito, and when we got to the clinic, Susan was waiting for us in the lobby. I introduced her to Miss Davis and explained that Susan needed her signature on some financial forms and such.

Susan said, "I apologize for these forms, Miss Davis. Unfortunately my employers require things to be done by the book."

Miss Davis smiled at Susan. I think that might be the first time I saw Bette Davis smile, but I shouldn't have been surprised. Susan has that effect on people. Bette Davis said, "No reason to apologize, Miss Jackson. Remember, I work for a living too. I know how business is conducted."

Once the forms were signed and Susan was preparing to take Miss Davis back to Lilly's room, I said, "With your permission, Miss Davis, I . . ."

"For heaven's sake, Spicer, stop calling me 'Miss Davis.' It makes me feel like an old spinster lady. You call me Bette and I'll call you Spicer. Deal?"

I chuckled and said, "It's a deal, Bette. With your permission I'd like to stop by your place and have another talk with Henry. Okay with you?"

"Do whatever it takes, Spicer. I intend to stay over here in Santa Barbara a few days to spend time with Lillian. I'll be at the Hyatt Hotel on the beach. It's not far and I've lodged there before. Stay in touch."

"Will do. Susan, I need a word with you when you're done."

Susan nodded at me, smiled at Bette Davis, and said, "I'll be right back. This way, please, Miss Davis."

Susan returned five minutes later and when we stepped out on the clinic's broad wood-planked veranda, she said, "Call me Bette? Good grief! That Rolly character wasn't the only charmer around here."

"You aren't jealous are you?"

Susan shook her head. "Of her? That will never happen. You're too smart to fall for a woman like that."

"Thanks . . . I think. How are Bette and Lilly getting along back there?"

"Like long-lost cousins. They were both crying big tears of happiness when I left. You really did a very good thing by arranging for Miss Davis to take responsibility for Lilly. I know it means a lot to both of them. Heck, if you did that for me, I'd tell you to call me Bette, too."

Grinning and wiggling my eyebrows up and down ala Groucho Marx, I said, "Okay, Bette, but this could get confusing."

Susan gave me a playful shove. "Oh, you! I was being serious."

"I know you were, Angel. I was just having some fun with you, but now I need to get on my horse, or in this case, LaSalle, and head back to Glendale."

Looking a little sad, Susan said, "I understand. Boy, this weekend sure didn't turn out the way we expected, did it?"

"No, it sure didn't. I feel bad about that."

"Don't. There have been times when my work has gotten in the way of something we wanted to do, too. Besides, I got to help you in your work. It was fun."

"I'm glad to hear you say that. You were singing a different tune Friday night."

"And with good reason! When will I see you again, Johnny?"

"That's hard to say. It won't be long, but I have to find out what Doris Alpert is up to, assuming I can locate her. I'll stay in touch by phone in the meantime."

"Thanks, Johnny. Remember, I work early tomorrow morning. Take good care of my favorite Hollywood gumshoe."

"Only if you promise to take good care of my favorite angel."

I used up the next two hours and change driving the ninety-some miles between Santa Barbara and Glendale. After filling the gasoline tank as per the rental agreement, I turned the La Salle over to the Hertz folks at the Grand Central Air Terminal and got back behind the wheel of my Chrysler, pointing it at Franklin Avenue in Hollywood. It was time for a heart to heart chat with Doris Alpert.

Thirteen

1:00 P.M. – Sunday – August 11, 1940

Bette Davis Residence – 5346 Franklin Avenue, Hollywood

Bette Davis's primordial front yard no longer raised the hairs on the back of my neck, but I was still very curious about who blew that marmalade dart at Henry and me. It could have been a prank having nothing to do with the Ivonya-Ngia Tembo, but the case was already so goofy, I had no doubt about it being connected. I even had my own idea about who was responsible.

Stepping up on the porch, I rang the bell and Henry opened the door promptly. Good morning, Mister Spicer."

"Good morning, Henry. I spoke with Miss Davis about three hours ago and told her I would be stopping by to ask a few more questions. First, though, I have a piece of news for you."

"Would that news be about Miss Bouvier?"

I gestured for him to step on the porch. He did and closed the door behind us. I said, "Yes it would. You need to keep this under your hat for now, but I found Miss Bouvier a couple of nights ago. I'll let Miss Davis give you the details, but for the time being I can tell you she is well and safe."

"Oh, I'm so glad to hear that. Lillian is a lovely young woman. She deserves the best."

"Believe me, she's getting the best, but I came here to have a second talk with another staff member, Miss Alpert. I trust she's here today."

From Henry's expression I could tell I was putting my trust in the wrong place. He said, "No, sir, she is not. Miss Alpert is no longer in Madam's employ as of last Friday morning. I thought Madam might have told you."

"No, we didn't discuss Miss Alpert. You say she resigned last Friday?"

"Yes, sir. She came in a little late—after Madam left for the day—and told me she was resigning. Then she demanded the pay she had coming. After that she got back into her auto and drove away. That was about eight-fifteen."

"That's just swell. Do you know where she lives?"

"Yes, sir, and I have no qualms about giving you that information. Come inside and I will write it down."

I followed Henry into the library, and as he wrote on a piece of stationary, I noticed Miss Davis's book on the history of the California missions was in a different place on the shelf than when I first noticed it. I'd wondered if she knew which mission was founded on a December Fourth or if she had to look it up. Now I knew. Small victory.

When Henry finished writing, he handed me the page and I read what he'd written. Doris Alpert lived in apartment number 201 at 1857 Wilton Place. It was less than a mile away.

"Henry, do you recall what sort of car she was driving?"

"Yes, I do, sir. It was an older Hudson two-door coupe', dark blue in color. I also wrote down the license plate number. It was 4J3871. I will add that information to the note with her address, if you wish."

I said I wished he would and handed him the note. While he was writing, I asked, "I don't suppose you know what model year the Hudson was."

"No, sir, I do not. I am afraid I am not very expert at identifying automobiles."

"All right, do you happen to remember what color the license plate was?"

He thought for a moment, and then said, "Why, yes I do. The background was yellow and the numbers were black."

"You have an excellent memory, Henry. That color combination was only used recently during three years, 1934, 1936 and 1938, so assuming the Hudson was purchased in California, odds are it is the model for one of those years."

Henry beamed. "Thank you, sir, and might I add that is a very clever way of identifying the model year of an automobile."

"It isn't foolproof, but it gives us a little more to go on. Now, did Miss Alpert give you any hint as to where she was going?"

"No, sir. She said very little. Just what I told you."

"All right, Henry, I'm going to see if Miss Alpert is at home, although I'd bet money she's long gone. Thanks for your help."

"You are quite welcome, sir. I am delighted to be of service."

Eighteen-fifty-seven Wilton Place was barely half a mile from Bette Davis's home. It was also the strangest looking apartment building I've ever seen. The place was a tall, narrow brick block that was either five or six stories in height—I couldn't tell which because the window placement was odd. Apparently there was enclosed parking on the first floor or in the basement.

The front was decorated with a stucco façade in two shades of pink and a fire escape that zig-zagged down the top four floors. An American flag flew from an angled flag staff near the front door, which was dolled up with a couple of phony columns and topped with some other design doodads, including an oval window in a fancy decorative frame.

After sizing the place up and concluding it must have been designed by somebody's brother-in-law, my next step was figuring out how to get inside the monstrosity. I started by climbing the steps to the entrance. Of course there was no directory or intercom system, but such devices apparently weren't considered necessary. When I tried the door it swung open invitingly.

Inside I found a narrow stairway at the back of the first floor and climbed it to the second floor. The stairs were a steep climb, and by the time I arrived huffing and puffing on the second floor, I was very glad Doris Alpert didn't live on the top floor.

When nobody answered my knock on the door to apartment 201, I tried the knob. It turned, so I committed a felony by entering the apartment and taking a look around. I was grateful I didn't stumble on any dead bodies in the living room and hoped that was a sign that Doris Alpert had the good sense to get the hell out of town before she suffered the same fate as Rolly Boland.

The apartment was a smallish two bedroom crammed full of souvenirs from places she'd been—like a miniature covered wagon from Knott's Berry Farm down in Buena Park and a big pin-on ribbon that said, "*I went to the San Bernardino County Fair!*" I looked for a desk or some other piece of furniture that might be used for storing correspondence and other documents, but found nothing.

I did, however, find a clue that answered one question. It was a length of bamboo sticking up from behind a chair in what seemed to be her main bedroom. Examining the bamboo, I discovered it was a three-and-a-half foot long tube that was about an inch in diameter. There was a tiny woven wicker basket attached to the bamboo and it contained two small darts identical to the one somebody shot at Henry and me. It would seem Miss Alpert was that somebody or knew who was. I wondered if looking further would turn up a jar of orange marmalade.

Instead, I peeked into the closet and found several empty hangers on the pole, which I suspected might be there because the clothes that normally hung on them had been packed for a trip. A look around the bathroom revealed not so much as a lipstick. Miss Alpert wasn't the sort who would go traveling without her makeup.

My next stop was her telephone. It was in a hallway niche similar to the one in my apartment. Next to the telephone was a notepad, so I tried my shading with a pencil trick to see if there were any impressions in the top sheet. There weren't, so I was about to move on when I realized the notepad page I'd shaded wasn't the top sheet of the pad. The previous top page was still there, it had simply been folded over and didn't require pencil shading. Whatever clues it held were clearly visible, if not clearly understandable.

It appeared Miss Alpert was a doodler. The notepad page was covered with drawings. Some of the shapes she'd drawn were familiar, others were not. I looked at the scribbling and scratched my head for several seconds before I got it. Miss Alpert didn't know how to read and write! When she needed to remember something, she drew pictures to remind her of . . . of what? The symbols meant nothing to me. Maybe they would when I had more time to study them.

I pocketed the notepad and went back to the living room for one last look before getting the heck out of there. What I noticed this time that I'd missed when I came in was a snapshot in a small frame on a teetering end table. The photo was of two women who bore a strong resemblance to one another. One of them was Doris Alpert and the other looked enough like her to be her older sister. I slipped the photograph into my pocket with the notepad. I would return it to Miss Alpert when and if I ever saw her again.

Then I slipped out of the apartment and back down the stairs. Before leaving the building, however, I took a quick peek out into the basement garage. There were lots of spiders down there, but no dark blue 1934 Hudsons.

By two-fifteen I was back in my office picking up the mail from the outer office floor where it falls when the mailman drops it through the slot in the door. I tossed the bills into my inbox and the circulars into the trash.

Next I picked up my telephone and dialed the Seventh Precinct's number. When I got Salvino on the line I said, "Hiya Nick. I thought you'd want to know I was back in town."

"Hell, Spicer, I didn't even know you were gone."

"It's nice to be missed. You got anything new on the Roland Boland murder?"

"Nope. I been waitin' on you to solve it for us."

"Well, at the rate I'm going you won't have much longer to wait."

"Oh yeah? You got something going?"

"Yup. Actually, a couple of somethings. You remember Miss Bouvier?"

"Yeah. What about her?"

"She showed up in West Sacramento Friday night and someone used her for target practice when she checked into the Hotel El Rancho."

"No kiddin'? She hurt bad?"

"No. The shooter or shooters were lousy shots, so Miss Bouvier just got banged up some when her car crashed into some other cars in the hotel parking area. I thought you might want to get a hold of the West Sacramento cop shop and see if they recovered any of the slugs that were fired—I only heard three—to see if they match the ones the coroner found in Boland."

With enough sarcasm to bog down a Mack truck, Salvino said, "What a grand suggestion, Detective Spicer. We'll get right on that. So now are you figuring this Bouvier dame for being in on the heist?"

Ignoring the sarcasm, I said, "Nope. I got her to open up and tell me what she knows about the missing statuette, which is essentially who stole it. The culprits were Boland and another gal who worked for my client, one Doris Alpert. I think the shooting of Miss Bouvier was a case of mistaken identity. I'm betting the shooter thought she was Miss Alpert."

"So it was an inside job. I figured it had to be. You got an address for this Alpert dame?"

"It's 1857 Wilton Place in Hollywood, apartment 201, but it you're looking to talk to her, don't bother rushing over there."

"Hell! Did somebody shoot her already, too?"

"Nope, at least not that I know about. Apparently she had enough sense to figure out that what happened to Boland was also likely to happen to her."

"Well, good for Miss Alpert. This business of shooting at suspects and witnesses is bad form. Okay, so where is the Bouvier dame? I need to get the story from the horse's mouth so to speak."

I chuckled. "I don't think you'll get very far calling her a horse."

"Never mind the humor, Spicer. Just tell me where I can find her."

"You can't. At least not for a few days. I've stashed her in a safe place until I'm sure the heat's off."

"Spicer, in case you've forgotten, this is Detective Sergeant Salvino you're talkin' to. I'm one of the good guys. You know, on the side of the angels and all that. Now tell me where the hell you stashed this dame."

"In a few days, Sergeant. I'll be in touch."

I heard him scream "Spicer" just before I dropped the telephone handset into its cradle. True, hanging up on Salvino wouldn't earn me his undying love, but the last thing I needed was an entire police department full of crooked cops parading back and forth from the Casa Sobre El Mar. Was Salvino a crooked cop? I had seen no evidence that he was, but if he wasn't that would make a total of three cops I knew out of the entire department who weren't on the take from somebody.

Turning my thoughts to a more pleasant subject, I dialed O for operator and placed a long distance call to Susan's home. She answered promptly.

"Hello?"

"Hiya, Angel. How are things on the rich folks' side of the tracks?"

"Hi, Johnny. Everything is good here. I just left the clinic a little while ago to get some sleep before my shift. Miss Davis—Bette to you—was still having a quiet afternoon with Miss Bouvier."

"You aren't going to let me forget that, are you, Angel?"

Susan's laugh came over the line like bubbles in champagne. "Not if it gets your goat. It's too much fun making you suffer."

"And after I went out and drummed up some new business for your clinic. That's gratitude for you!"

"Hey, speaking of the clinic, I got some good news a little while ago. The General Manager of Casa Sobre El Mar called me in to tell me I'm getting a promotion."

"Say, that *IS* good news!"

"It really is! I'll be the Supervising Nurse with a substantial raise in pay and regular weekday hours—no more strange shifts or weekends unless there's a major emergency of some kind. Isn't that swell?"

"It couldn't be sweller. When does this happen?"

"They're looking for a replacement for me. As soon as they find one, we make the change."

Trying to sound dismayed, I said, "Oh, oh. This could take a while. As far as I'm concerned you're irreplaceable."

In a softer tone that sounded like love talking, Susan said, "Oh, what a nice thing to say. Thank you, Mister Hollywood Private Eye."

"Just a little praise where it's due. I'll let you get some rest now. I just wanted to let you know I'm back in the office. Also, we've got another suspect who seems to have disappeared. Miss Davis's maid, Doris Alpert, resigned last Friday morning and when I went by her apartment a little while ago, I saw indications that she'd packed up and left on a trip to somewhere."

"Okay, do you think she's been . . ."

"It's a possibility, but so far no more bodies have shown up. I'm hoping it stays that way."

Sounding relieved, Susan said, "I'm glad to hear that. When do you think you'll be coming up here?"

"Soon, but I need to see if I can get a lead on where Miss Alpert has disappeared to. If I'm not headed back there tomorrow, I'll at least give you a call."

"Thanks, Johnny."

"Sleep tight, Angel."

I considered taking my own advice and catching up on my sleep, but there was a piece of paper burning a hole in my pocket. I took Doris Alpert's notepad out of my jacket pocket and just stared at it for several minutes.

She had drawn six symbols in two rows—three in each row. That much I remembered from the quick look at the drawing I took in Doris Alpert's apartment. What I noticed this time that I hadn't seen when I first looked at the drawing were arrows—one between each pair of symbols and all of them pointing to the right. Then there were three more arrows, one under symbols four and five indicating a ninety-degree angle to the right, and one under symbol number six that just pointed right.

I thought the straight arrows between the symbols implied a sequence, which could mean the six symbols were instructions for doing something and each instruction had to be in sequence with the others. Okay, what kind of instructions would she be likely to noting during a telephone conversation? How about directions for going somewhere Doris had never been before?

Since she seemed to have taken a trip somewhere, that made some sense, so go with that assumption and see where it takes you.

Of the six symbols three stood out as obvious. The fourth symbol was a fierce looking cartoon bee, the fifth symbol was a fire hydrant, and the last symbol might have been a set of tally marks. Since all three of the last symbols had either right angle arrows or a straight arrow to the right, the symbols might be landmarks indicating places to turn.

Doris Alpert's cartoon map.

I could see using a fire hydrant as a landmark, but unless it was on a sign, I couldn't imagine what sort of bee might serve as a landmark. B Street? No, if Doris couldn't read or write, it wasn't likely she would use a symbol for the name of the street because a street sign with the name on it would mean nothing to her. I had no clue what to think about the tally mark looking things, except that there were eight of them.

Okay, figure out the other symbols. At first glance, the symbol in the upper left corner of the page looked like a pair of coil springs, but when I took a closer look I saw that each spring was actually four sixes strung together as if each was hanging from the one above it. If Doris could draw a six on her map, she would probably recognize one if she saw it on a street sign, so that made some sort of cockeyed sense.

The second symbol was the strangest of the bunch. It looked like three toothpicks with ovals drilled in their wide ends. What on earth would be the purpose of drilling holes in toothpicks?

The third symbol in the upper right of the page was two rows of lower case Ts. After looking at the layout of the Ts for a minute I realized what else they might be; rows of crosses in a cemetery. That made sense in my driving directions theory because a cemetery would make a large landmark that could be easy to spot.

All right, I had a bunch of sixes, toothpicks with holes in them, a cemetery, an angry bee, a fire hydrant, and some tally mark-looking things. Where were they telling me to go? It seemed like the first two symbols were the critical ones indicating in which town I should look for a cemetery, an angry bee, a fire hydrant, and a count of eight somethings. The problem was the critical first two symbols meant nothing to me at all.

Phooey on Doris Alpert and her stupid map. I didn't need a damned map to find Eli's deli and a sandwich to take home for dinner.

Fourteen

8:00 A.M. – Monday – August 12, 1940

Spicer Investigations – 1st National Bank Building, Hollywood

My Monday morning in the office routine had recently been expanded to include listening to Elmer Davis reporting the news on KNX, the Columbia Broadcasting System radio station in Los Angeles. My theory was that if I listened to all the bad things going on in the world, my problems looked pretty small by comparison.

For example, this particular morning Elmer was going on and on about how all those folks who were supposed to get the first social security checks next month were waiting on pins and needles to see whether or not Uncle Sam's checks would actually arrive in their mailboxes. I wished all those folks good . . . pins and needles!

Sometime when I see pieces of what seems like an unsolvable puzzle from a different angle and the solution is suddenly so obvious I can't understand why it took me so long to see it. The things in Doris Alpert's doodles I'd been calling toothpicks were needles! I grabbed the notepad and a Thomas Brothers map book from my desk drawer and poured another cup of Joe.

Needles is the name of a town on U.S. Route 66 along the California-Arizona border. That also explained the strings of sixes in Doris Alpert's wordless driving instructions. She was supposed to take Route 66 to Needles, where she was to keep going past a cemetery—the rows of crosses in the drawing. Then she was to turn right when she saw . . . what? An angry bee? Several angry bees? Okay, come back to that.

After turning right at the bee, she was supposed to turn right again when she passed a fire hydrant. Then came the eight tally marks. Eight what? Eight blocks? Eight miles? Eight maids a milking?

Okay, I didn't have the complete solution, but I had enough so that the meaning of the bee and tally marks might be more apparent when I got there. The question that still puzzled me most was what's in Needles that would cause her to drive across a large stretch of desert to get there? Could it be Doris Alpert just picked out a little berg in the boondocks where she thought Kipchumba wouldn't be likely to look for her? No, someone wanted her to go there because they'd given her instructions and she'd "written" them down. There had to be more to it.

One of the souvenirs in her collection was a ribbon pin from the San Bernardino County Fair. Needles was in San Bernardino County, so there was some history for her there, but what kind of history? Did she know somebody . . .

The picture of Doris and a woman I thought could be her sister might be the answer. Did Doris have a relative—a sister, maybe—living in Needles? Without her married name, assuming she was married, I had no way of knowing the answer to that one without driving to Needles and showing the picture around to see if someone recognized Doris or the other woman. Okay, how far is it to Needles?

According to my Thomas Brothers Southern California Guide, the distance between Hollywood and Needles is a little more than 260 miles, which translates into about a six-hour drive across a lot of nothing. Was it worth the time to go there? Did I have a choice?

By nine o'clock I'd packed an overnight bag, strapped on my shoulder holster, and topped off the tank in my Chrysler. Route 66 begins—or ends depending on which way you're going—in Santa Monica and follows Santa Monica Boulevard through Hollywood, where I picked it up. After that it runs north to Foothill Boulevard and turns east again.

In San Berdoo the route jogs north for the Cajon Pass route to the town of Daggett. From there the highway runs east over South Pass to Needles and on across the Colorado River into Arizona.

The farther away from Los Angeles I got the lighter the traffic became until, a little past Pasadena, I was out in the wide open spaces. Looking around, I got an idea of what a hell of a lot of people saw heading in the opposite direction since 1926 when the highway was completed. They came to California, especially during the drought and dust storms of the 1930s, in search of a new start. A writer named Steinbeck wrote about some of them. A few of those folks found what they were looking for, but a lot more traded their automobile license plates for a meal at Barney's Beanery and settled for jobs that were a lot less than what they'd been given to expect.

As a result of all that coming and going, Route 66 became known as "America's Main Street," or the "Mother Road." No matter what you call it, Route 66 winds from Chicago to Los Angeles, nearly two thousand miles all the way, but it does so by a strange, off-the-beaten-path southern route. That's what they get for putting a guy from Oklahoma in charge of planning a cross-country highway.

Around eleven-thirty I rolled into Barstow and made a "comfort" stop that included filling my tank at a Standard service station, and having some lunch at joint called the El Rancho Restaurant. It was not related to the Hotel El Rancho in West Sacramento. I could tell that because nobody was shooting at anybody in the parking lot.

It was about three o'clock when I finally hit the outskirts of Needles. I stayed on 66, which is called Broadway as it passes through Needles, and kept my eyes open for a cemetery. When I got to the south end of town without seeing anything resembling a cemetery, I began to wonder if I was interpreting Doris Alpert's map correctly. Then I passed Cemetery Road and the Riverview Cemetery.

With my faith in Doris's instructions restored, I began looking for bees. I found them almost immediately. They were employees of the Mystic Maze Self-Serve Honey Company. While I didn't actually see any bees, I saw about a hundred of the white wooden boxes beekeepers use to house hives. The instructions seemed to be telling me I should take the next right turn, which turned out to be Victory Drive.

My next landmark was a fire hydrant. I found it on the left side of the road and the next right turn was Cherry Drive. I made the turn and looked for something to count with the tally marks. The most logical application for them was a count of the houses from where I'd turned onto Cherry Drive. Since there were only three houses on the left side of the street, I counted the houses on the right side.

The eighth house on Cherry had the number 1225 painted on its mailbox. The neighborhood in which I found myself wasn't ever going to be confused with Beverly Hills or Bel Air, but 1225 had one of the neatest yards on the street.

The house was white with a blue awning on the street side to serve as a sun shield. Like most of the houses in this part of the world, this one had an evaporative cooler—more commonly referred to as a swamp cooler—stuck on the side, and metal lawn furniture out on what actually looked enough like a lawn to be mowed. A large shade tree kept the right side of the house cool and two young trees had been planted to eventually perform the same job out front.

I saw no movement in or around the house, so I circled the block and parked a house or two away to see if anyone showed up. I hadn't been there more than ten minutes when I noticed I was being noticed. The residents of the house to the right of 1225 were peering out their front window and so were the folks across the street. I thought about knocking on their doors with the photograph of Doris and the other woman, but judging by the neighborhood, I got the idea that acting like a nosey detective knocking on doors might not be the best way to win friends and influence people. I decided to swing by again later and left.

I retraced my steps to Broadway and looked for a place to stop and decide my next move. For a street called Broadway, there was very little commercial activity going on. Mostly what I passed were vacant lots and empty spaces that seemed to be parking lots. Needles had enough parking spaces on its main drag to handle every car in Los Angeles.

Finally I spotted Uptown Liquors at the corner of Broadway and E Streets. Thinking an ice cold Coca-Cola might go well about then, I pulled into their large paved parking area and looked for the shadiest parking spot available when I spotted something I wasn't looking for. It was a dark blue 1934 Hudson coupe', and it was parked by itself along the E Street side of the parking area. I parked in the shade of the liquor store and walked over to the Hudson. The license number was 4J3871, the same number Henry had written down for Doris Alpert's plate.

As I peered in the driver's side window my hand brushed the door sheet metal and it was so hot it darn near raised a blister. The dark blue paint was sucking up heat like a sponge. I saw nothing of interest through the driver's side, so I walked around to the passenger side, and as I did, the screech of tires close by made me look up.

The car doing the screeching was a black four-door Ford sedan, and as it slewed into the parking lot from E Street, I saw gold county sheriff's stars on its white doors. That made sense. If the local deputy sheriff thought there was something fishy about the Hudson, he would tell the guys in the liquor store to call in if anybody showed a particular interest in the Hudson.

The Ford's tires skidded again as it pulled up next to Doris Alpert's car. I was walking around to greet the deputy when he jumped out of his with a chrome plated, pearl handled, long barrel Colt forty-five caliber revolver in his hand. He pointed it in my general direction and said, "All right, pal, lean on the hood and spread your legs."

For a Podunk county sheriff's deputy, he knew all the big city tricks. I said, "I'm a private cop from Los Angeles. This car figures in a case I'm . . ."

"A private cop ain't no kind of cop at all in these parts. Now hands on the hood and spread your legs nice and wide apart."

I said, "That damned hood is hot enough to raise blisters. How 'bout I just stand here and be docile?"

The deputy pointed his big forty-five right at my face. "Boy, if I gotta tell you again, I'll shoot your damned ear off."

Shooting suspects' ears off must be a local variation on big city police techniques I hadn't heard about. As gingerly as possible, I put my hands on the hood and leaned forward to spread my legs. Next he patted me down, taking my Smith and Wesson from its shoulder holster.

"Well, well. What do we have here? The big city detective's got himself a little toy gun."

"And I have a license to carry it concealed. My private investigator Photostat is in my badge case—inside coat pocket."

He grabbed my badge case and saw the Special Los Angeles County Sheriff's shield. It threw him for a minute, but not for long. He must have figured he was still on safe ground since I hadn't identified myself as an official law enforcement officer. He said, "How about that? I didn't know you could get fancy badges like this here in Cracker Jack boxes."

I said nothing and continued sizing the deputy up. His own badge was a star pinned on a filthy khaki uniform shirt which was partly tucked into blue denim work pants. On his head he wore a sweat-stained straw cowboy hat. Mostly, he just plain stunk.

"Okay, pal, stand up straight there and put your hands behind you."

I did as I was told and he snapped a pair of handcuffs on me. Of course he cinched them up a lot tighter than was necessary. Finally, he said, "Okay, now get your big city butt in the back of my cruiser. We're gonna take a little ride downtown."

I wondered where the hell he thought there was a "downtown" around here, but again I kept my yap shut. He grabbed my coat collar from behind and shoved me toward his Ford. Then he opened the back door on the driver's side and told me to get in and watch my head. That told me exactly what to expect.

As I bent over to get in, he shoved me hard into the door frame. The blow knocked my hat onto the seat and caught me just above my right ear. I saw stars for a moment or two while the deputy picked up my hat and pulled it down hard over the injury.

My head cleared fairly quickly, but I felt some dampness up there on my scalp. I didn't think bleeding was a good sign. By that time, though, we'd covered the block and a half to "downtown" and he pulled up next to a small storefront office. An official-looking sign painted in gold on the front window said "San Bernardino County Sheriff - Needles Substation."

He escorted me past an older man in civilian clothes and a pair of glasses sitting at the office's only desk and said, "This here big city private cop was tryin' to get into that Hudson over to the liquor store, but I got there first."

As the deputy shoved me into the station's single holding cell and slammed the door, the older man stood up and said, "Okay, Elmer, give me his paperwork and let's see who you caught here."

The deputy slammed the outer door to the one-cell cell block and I heard them having a lengthy conversation in the office, mostly the deputy was thinking up new lies to make himself sound like a hero. Then it was quiet for a while.

Finally, after what probably wasn't half-an-hour, but seemed much longer, the older man opened the outer door, and then unlocked the cell door. As it swung open on squeaky hinges he said, "Mister Spicer, if you'll kindly turn around, I'll remove those handcuffs."

Still keeping my mouth shut I did as he told me to do and he unlocked the cuffs. When they were off and I was rubbing my wrists trying to get the blood flowing to my fingers again, he offered his hand and said, "Mister Spicer, I'm Deputy Sheriff Bob Collins, and I'm afraid we owe you an apology. I did some checking by telephone and it seems you are very highly thought of in Los Angeles.

"So I hope you'll forgive my deputy Elmer. Sometimes he gets a little over zealous in his enforcement of the law. If he injured you, the sheriff's office will pay any medical expenses and Elmer will give you a ride back to your car."

In the office Sheriff Bob handed me my gun, badge case, and the other items Elmer had taken from me. Then Elmer came over and offered his hand. I didn't shake it.

Somewhat defensively he said, "Mister Spicer, I'm sorry I had to rough you up back there, but we never know how a suspect is gonna . . ."

The next sound that came out of Elmer's mouth was a loud "whoof" as my fist sank a good six inches into his beer belly. He slumped over, groaning, and although I hated to touch his filthy shirt, I grabbed his collar and held him bent over while I removed his fancy six gun from its holster.

I took a quick glance at Sheriff Bob. He was leaning on the edge of his desk with his arms folded watching the proceedings with what might have even been amusement. Since it didn't appear that he was going to intervene in his deputy's behalf, I jerked Elmer upright and stuck the barrel of his revolver right into his ear.

I said, "Okay, listen carefully now, Elmer Fudd. Even though your brain can't be much bigger than a pea, it's pretty unlikely I'll miss it at this range. So you'd be wise to do exactly what I tell you. Now, reach down, carefully remove your hide-away gun, and slide it under the desk there."

He quickly protested, "I ain't got no . . ."

"Sure you do, Elmer. Any deputy who carries a chromium plated forty-five is bound to have a hide-away gun. Now take it out of your boot and slide it under the desk like I told you."

Elmer looked up at his boss. "Sheriff, ain't you gonna . . ."

"Look here, Elmer, I'm running out of patience. You want me to shoot your ear off to prove I mean business? If I remember correctly, that's what you were going to do to me if I didn't burn the hell out of hands on the hood of that Hudson. What about it?"

Elmer carefully lifted a tiny twenty-two caliber pistol out of his right boot and slid it under the desk. It was also chrome plated. I said, "See, Elmer, you really can learn to follow instructions despite your tiny pea brain. Now walk into that cell and close the door."

By this time Elmer had run out of bravado and was being cooperative. He walked over to the cell, stepped in, looked at me with a lot of hatred, and pulled the door shut. With Elmer Fudd parked safely away, I handed his Colt to the Deputy Sheriff and said, "If you don't mind, Sheriff, I could use a lift back to the Uptown Liquor Store's parking lot."

"It would be my pleasure, Mister Spicer. My car is right out front."

As we got into his Mercury sedan, Sheriff Bob said, "That was quite a maneuver you pulled in there when you disarmed Elmer. You get a lot of practice slugging law enforcement officers where you come from?"

"No, Sheriff. In fact, I don't recall ever slugging a law enforcement officer before. On the other hand, Elmer Fudd there isn't much of a law enforcement officer."

Starting the Mercury's V8 and looking over his shoulder as if he expected the deserted street we were parked on to suddenly be crowded with traffic, Bob said, "True, but with budget cuts and all . . ."

His voice trailed off and as we pulled into the Uptown Liquors parking lot a moment later, I retrieved the snapshot of Doris Alpert and the woman I thought might be her sister from my coat pocket and held it up for the Sheriff to see. "By any chance do you know either of these women?"

He parked in the shade next to my Chrysler and looked closely at the photo. Handing it back to me he said, "That's an old picture, but I know both those women. I should know 'em. They grew up right here in Needles. The one on the left is Doris Alpert and the other one is her older sister Helen, but now it's Helen Valdez, not Alpert.

"She married a Mex named Miguel who ran a tamale stand during the summer when the tourists come through town. Helen convinced him they should open a real sit-down restaurant instead of just running the stand. They did and everything went fine for a few weeks until Miguel Valdez discovered running a restaurant was work. When that happened, he took all the money they had and went back to Mexico. Helen got herself a divorce but kept the name because it makes her Mexican restaurant sound more authentic or some such thing."

Nodding, I said, "Did you know that Hudson belongs to her sister Doris?"

Sheriff Bob shook his head. "We sent off a registration request to Sacramento when we figured the car was abandoned. That was last Friday evening and we haven't heard nothin' back yet. You sure it belongs to Doris?"

"I don't know if the car is actually registered in her name or not, but when she pulled up stakes and left Hollywood Friday, that's the car she was driving. A fellow where she works wrote down the license plate number because she's a suspect in a case of grand theft."

"Yeah? What did she steal?"

"A piece of African art. The case is being handled out of the Seventh Precinct in L.A. They can give you the details if you want them. Tell me, Sheriff Bob, have you searched that car, especially the trunk?"

"No. You think the missing art might be in it?"

"Probably not, but it might be good idea to see what *IS* in it."

"Okay, I've got a pry bar in my trunk. We ought to be able to pop the lock open with that."

"All right, Sheriff. Have at it."

He got the pry bar out of his trunk and I moved a respectful distance away. You might even say I moved a long respectful distance away.

Fifteen

5:00 P.M. – Monday – August 12, 1940

Uptown Liquors Parking Lot – Broadway & E Street, Needles

The Hudson's trunk lid was hinged at the bottom like a rumble seat. The latch was up at the top of the trunk lid and reaching it required leaning over the spare tire carrier. Sheriff Bob got the flat end of his pry bar under the trunk lid and put his back into it.

His first effort didn't yield more than some groans from the sheet metal. The next try got him a definite "clunk." Glancing over at me, Sheriff Bob reached up, grabbed the trunk handle and pulled. Then he puked his guts out.

Doris Alpert was last seen in Hollywood Friday morning, so she couldn't have been in the trunk of her Hudson longer than three days, but daytime temperatures consistently above a hundred degrees accelerated her decomposition, so what Sheriff Bob saw and smelled when the lid opened was a horribly grotesque decomposing body. I covered my nose and mouth with a handkerchief and took a close enough look at the stinking mess to be sure it was Doris Alpert. It was.

Then I walked over and helped Sheriff Bob up off his knees. "Sorry about that, Sheriff. I should have warned you, but I didn't really think we'd find her body in there." The last part was a lie.

The Sheriff shook his head. "How the hell can you look at something like that and keep your stomach from churning?"

I remembered Lilly Bouvier making a similar comment once. I said, "There's a lot about this job that isn't fun, Sheriff. I just wish your Deputy Elmer was here to see what real police work is like. Shall we call the county coroner?"

"Yes. Would you mind closing the trunk while I go over and make the call from the liquor store?"

"I'll take care of it, Sheriff."

He let out a gagging cough as he walked away and choked out a single word, "Thanks."

Using my handkerchief again, I took another look in the trunk. This time I was interested in what might be in there with Doris. What I got for my trouble was a big nothing. Her purse wasn't even there. The killers probably took that with them to look through when they weren't busy trying to dispose of a body. At this point it was going to take a coroner to figure out what killed her, but I'd bet money it was the same thirty-eight revolver that ended Rolly Boland's life.

To nobody, I said, "Well, Doris, now you and I have something in common with Lamont Cranston. We, too, know what evil lurks in the hearts of men." Then I slammed the trunk lid, put my handkerchief back in the breast pocket of my sport coat, and waited for Sheriff Bob to return.

When I saw him coming, he had a cardboard cup in each hand. He gave me one of the cups, saying, "Maybe a little coffee will make that awful smell go away."

"It will help, Sheriff, but nothing can completely eliminate it. That's something you'll remember as long as you live."

He nodded and glanced over at the Hudson. "The coroner will be here in about an hour. Things move a little slower out here than in the city."

"That's not a problem for Doris. She's not going anywhere, but if you don't mind another suggestion, you might want to send a deputy over to Helen Valdez's home to make sure everything is okay there. I don't think anyone is out to hurt her, but they might have searched her home."

"Good suggestion, Spicer. As soon as some help arrives from San Berdoo, I'll do that."

Writing Nick Salvino's name and telephone number on the back of my business card, I said, "This fellow Salvino is an LAPD Homicide Detective. He can fill you in on the case he's working and the one I'm working. It seems like they're all the same case, and now you've got a piece of it." With a grin, I added, "You can mention me if you want, but it might be easier to understand Salvino if you don't. For some reason he starts hollering incoherently whenever he hears my name."

We both got a chuckle out of that and I made a decision. Originally I'd planned to stay overnight in Needles and head back in the morning, but I changed my mind. I was tired, but not tired enough to make me spend another minute more in this miserable hell-hole than I absolutely had to.

I said, "Well, Sheriff, if you don't need me anymore, I'd like to head back to Los Angeles and get on with my work. On my way out of town I thought I might stop at Doris's sister's restaurant and give her the bad news. I'd also like to give her that picture of the two sisters. That all right with you?"

"Sure, Spicer. Just don't fall asleep on the road."

"I won't, Sheriff."

"Helen's joint is called La Cocina de Valdez and it's on the east side of Broadway just as you leave town toward L.A. on Route 66."

"Thanks. I'll tell her you'll be in touch."

As we walked across the lot to where my car was parked, Deputy Sheriff Bob said, "Listen, Spicer. I really am sorry about what happened with Elmer. He had no business treating you like that."

"Forget it, Sheriff. Maybe he'll think twice before he pulls something like that again."

Thinking that Elmer Fudd wasn't the kind who learns lessons from experience, I didn't really have any hope that he would change his ways. I gave Sheriff Bob a wave and pulled out onto Broadway heading northwest.

Helen Valdez's restaurant was small, but nicely decorated with a homey touch. Well, it was homey if you happened to be from a Mexican home. The food smelled wonderful and reminded me I had a long drive before arriving at the next outpost of civilization.

After ordering a couple of hamburgers and some wedge-shaped fried potatoes to go, I asked to see Helen. The waitress looked at me with a lot of curiosity. She was wondering what business a guy from out of town had with her boss, and since everybody in a little jerkwater berg like this knows everybody else, she knew I had to be from somewhere else. I sat at an empty table and waited for Helen Valdez.

I recognized her from the photo in my pocket. A little tentatively, Helen came up to my table and said, "I'm Helen. They said you wanted to talk to me?"

Standing, I said, "Yes, Helen. My name is Johnny Spicer, and I'm afraid I have some bad news for you. You should probably sit down."

She slid into the chair across the table from me and said, "It's my sister Doris, isn't it? She's dead, isn't she?"

"Yes, Helen, I'm afraid she is. The sheriff just found her a little while ago. He'll be getting in touch with you, but I knew Doris in Los Angeles and . . ."

Sounding a little hysterical, she interrupted me. "Somebody killed her, didn't they? She got in with the wrong people and it got her killed didn't it?"

"Helen, I don't know the details. I'm sure the sheriff will investigate her death and give you a complete report."

Helen nodded, but her expression told me she really didn't care to know the details. She knew more than she wanted to already. I changed the subject. "I stopped by Doris's apartment yesterday because I've been looking for her in connection with a robbery." I reached into my pocket handed her the photo of Helen and Doris and Doris's instructions on how to find Helen's home in Needles.

"While I was in her apartment, I took a couple of things to help figure out where she'd gone. I thought you might like them back. I've also written her Hollywood address down on the back of my business card. Her apartment wasn't locked, so you ought to locate the manager of the building and have someone lock up the apartment until you can get there. Also, feel free to call me if you need help with anything at that end."

My waitress chose that moment to bring my to-go order. She laid the check down next to the paper sack of food. Helen quickly picked it up and handed it back to the waitress, saying, "We don't charge our friends for a meal. Now, Mister Spicer, if you'll please excuse me. Thank you for coming. I know it wasn't easy."

After watching Helen hurry away toward the back of the restaurant, I left La Cocina de Valdez feeling like I'd just met one of the good ones. I hoped losing her sister wouldn't be a big setback in her life. Helen Valdez was the kind of person you wanted to see succeed.

My next stop was across Broadway at a Shell service station. There I filled up the Chrysler's tank again, bought an orange Nehi to go with my burgers, and made use of the restroom. It was six o'clock when I got back on Route 66 and headed for home.

Being a Monday night, there was practically no other traffic as I rolled along through the black endless desert, so I gave some thought to what I'd just accomplished. In exchange for eleven hours of driving I'd found another dead suspect in a heist case that was coming apart at the seams because the bad guys were quicker and smarter than me. I'd also been rousted by a hick sheriff's deputy and I'd ruined a very kind woman's day by bringing her rotten news.

August Twelfth would definitely not go into my diary as the best day I've ever had. It's a good thing I don't keep a diary.

It's one of those places about which people say, "If you blink, you'll miss it." The tiny community of Essex is about forty-five miles west of Needles and the whole town consists of a six-table café, a garage with a tow truck parked out front, a tiny market, a barn, and a few house trailers scattered along a two-block section of Route 66 at the exact center of nowhere. In fact, Essex is so small it makes Needles look like a major metropolis.

The only reason I mention Essex is that I had just passed through it when a pair of headlights appeared in my rearview mirror; and the only reason I mention the headlights is I'd only seen three or four cars since leaving Needles, and all the others had been going east. Also, this pair of headlights was closing the distance between us in a big hurry.

Suddenly another light—a red one—appeared between and a little above the headlights and the guy started flashing his high beams. By then he was on my rear bumper, and that's when he pressed the siren button. The situation was getting stickier by the minute. I'd already had one encounter with the San Bernardino Sheriff's Department. That had been in broad daylight and in the middle of town, and it wasn't a pleasant experience. Now it was dark and we were in the middle of nowhere. Not good; definitely not good.

I considered my options and decided that, if this was a legitimate stop, I was only making matters worse by not pulling over. That being the case, I took my foot off the gas and slowed down. At the same time, I pulled my Smith and Wesson out of its shoulder holster, just in case it wasn't a legitimate stop.

When I was going slow enough to pull off the road, I did so and stopped. The patrol car behind me did the same thing, leaving about ten feet between our two cars. At that distance I could make out the patrol car's grille. It was a Mercury, not a county squad car Ford. That made me feel a little better. Maybe Sheriff Bob had further business with me.

From my description of the surroundings, I probably don't need to mention there were no streetlights or any other kind of lights out there, so I couldn't see much of what was going on behind me until the driver got out and the reflection of his headlights bouncing off the back of my car flashed on something chrome. I took another look and recognized the shape of Elmer Fudd's straw cowboy hat. He stopped by my left rear fender, and through my open window I heard him say, "All right, Mister big city private cop, get yourself out of that automobile and keep your hands where I can see 'em."

I'd been sitting there with the car in gear, my left foot on the clutch, and my right foot on the brake. I slid my right foot over to the gas pedal and stomped down hard as I slipped the clutch. In the commotion that followed, I heard his big forty-five bark, but the slug didn't come anywhere near me because Deputy Elmer was getting a face full of the loose dirt and rocks being thrown up by my rear tires.

I expected him to fire again as I drove off, but a look in my mirror showed me the Mercury pulling onto the road after me. He wanted to play more high-speed fun and games, but this time when he began to close in on me, I put the gas pedal to the floorboard and let the big six cylinder engine in my Chrysler do what it did best.

The Mercury had a V8 engine under its hood, but I had the advantage of several more horsepower and at least two hundred pounds less sheet metal in my coupe than Deputy Elmer had in the sheriff's big four-door sedan. His advantage was that most V8 engines accelerate faster than straight six-cylinder engines. That meant he could get up to speed faster than I could, but once the speedometer needle got to the high end of the dial, I had him beat.

Slowly but surely, the distance between us began to grow. At one point I saw a muzzle flash on the driver-side of the Merc, but again his bullet missed its mark. Apparently Deputy Elmer had seen too many gangster movies or he would have known that in real life the odds of hitting anything by firing a weapon from one fast moving car at another are slim to none, especially when the driver is doing the shooting. Only a very lucky shot was going to hit me, and he was out of luck.

Then I realized his luck was about to improve when I felt the Chrysler begin to slow. We were starting uphill into the pass that would take us over the mountains to Barstow. The mountains meant curves and that would swing a lot of the advantage to his side of the ledger because we would have to slow for the curves and then accelerate while covering the short distance to the next curve. That's where his V8 engine gave him a big advantage. I still had one other advantage. My Chrysler was better sprung for taking curves at speed. I hoped it was enough.

Soon we were into the curves and I could see the distance between my car and his headlights begin to dwindle. After only a few curves, he had cut the distance between us in half. It was time to do something clever because letting him get to my rear bumper would be a fatal mistake.

As I went around a particularly tight bend to the right, however, I spotted a way out. I slammed on the brakes and pulled onto a wide section of shoulder on the inside of the curve. With the wheel cranked to the left, my rear tires slewed around to the right in the loose dirt and I ended up exactly where I wanted to be, perpendicular to and facing the road.

When the Merc came around the curve, Elmer saw me off the road to his right and stepped hard on his brake pedal. The big sedan skidded past me and its rear end spun 180 degrees counter-clockwise so he was facing the direction he'd come from. The big Mercury was still skidding toward the steep cliff beyond the left shoulder of the road. When he finally got the sedan stopped, its front tires were an inch from the edge and its front bumper was sticking precariously out over the embankment.

Coming that close to driving off a cliff was bound to shake anyone up, so I took advantage of his momentary confusion by accelerating across the road and stopping with my front bumper a few feet from his rear driver-side door. I jumped out and stuck my Smith and Wesson in his face through the Merc's driver-side window. "Why, if it isn't good old Deputy Elmer. I thought you'd learned your lesson the last time we met, but I guess that was taking too much for granted."

While keeping my thirty-eight in his face, I reached down and unlatched his door. Pulling it open, I said, "Get out with your hands raised."

He followed my directions slowly, looking for an opportunity to get out of the jam his overconfidence had gotten him into. I didn't give him any such opportunities.

When he was out of the car, I said, "Lean forward with your hands on the front fender there, and don't even think about trying anything cute because I'm just about sick and tired of fooling around with you."

Once he was where I wanted him, I carefully reached out to the black leather handcuff pouch on his pistol belt and unsnapped it. "Okay, right hand behind your back. I'm going to demonstrate how we big city cops deal with punk hicks from the sticks."

He did as he was told without comment and I snapped the cuff on his right wrist. "Very good, Elmer. Now your left hand." Again he did as he was told and I cuffed his left wrist.

Next I pushed the deputy's shoulders forward so he leaning over the driver-side front fender and I slipped the fancy chrome forty-five from his holster. Stepping around to where he could see me, I threw the revolver over the cliff.

Deputy Elmer let out a holler. "Hey, what the hell did you do that for? That was an expensive pistol!"

"It was? Gee, those things are a dime a dozen where I come from. All you have to do is find some dude ranch cowboy and take it away from him."

He glared at me just as he had done when I locked him in his own jail cell earlier. Elmer Fudd was a very good glarer.

Pushing him forward so he was leaning over the fender again, I pulled the hideaway gun from his right boot. It, too, went over the cliff and Deputy Elmer started to say something, but I interrupted him. "Shut up or the next thing to go over that cliff will be a pretty darn poor excuse for a San Berdoo County sheriff's deputy."

I was almost enjoying the situation, but I needed to hurry before any traffic happened along. I pointed to a large rock about ten feet away that was spotlighted by his headlights. "See that rock, pea-brain?"

"Yeah, I see it."

"Go sit on it and stay put."

Deputy Elmer walked slowly over to the rock and stopped, probably trying to figure out how to sit on the low rock with his hands cuffed behind his back. The technique he picked didn't work out and he ended up landing on the ground instead of the rock.

When I was sure he was staying put, I opened the driver door of the sheriff's cruiser and leaned in to do three things. First I removed his keys from the ignition, pleased to see that his handcuff key was on the same ring. Second and third, I pulled the shift lever into neutral and released the handbrake. Then I had to step back quickly because the sedan was nose down on an incline and immediately started to roll forward.

Elmer screamed, "What the hell are you doing? Are you nuts?"

Ignoring him, I watched the patrol car roll forward, hoping I hadn't overdone things. I hadn't. The Mercury did just what I thought it would do. The front wheels rolled off the embankment and the front end of the car dropped about a foot to the ground, sliding to a stop on its running boards and rear tires. With its front bumper, tires and engine hanging well out over the cliff, I would have been willing to bet that leaning on the front fender would probably finish the job, but I left things just as they were. It was time to get the hell out of there.

I pitched Elmer Fudd's key ring off the cliff and walked over where he was sitting on the ground. I removed his filthy straw cowboy hat and sailed it off the cliff for good measure. That was the most rewarding thing I did all night.

The rest of the trip home was a lot less exciting. After making a quick rest stop in Barstow, I pushed the speed limit a little the rest of the way and rolled into Hollywood a few minutes after eleven-thirty, despite my encounter with Deputy Elmer.

The strange thing was, I wasn't tired anymore. I was bushed when I left Needles, but now I felt like I could easily do a couple more hours behind the wheel, so I did. At one-thirty I pulled into Casa Sobre El Mar's parking lot.

She was talking to another nurse in the lobby as I strolled in, and when Susan saw me, she said, "Johnny! What are you doing here at this hour?" Then she looked more closely and rushed over, "What happened to your head? Your hat's all bloody!"

I took my fedora off and looked at the hatband on the right side. Sure enough, it was soaked with blood. I said, "I believe a sheriff's deputy named Elmer Fudd happened to my head. You think it's serious?"

"Oh for heaven's sake. Sit down over here and let me look."

I sat and she examined my scalp. Finally she said, "Johnny, the way you operate, it's a good thing you've got a hard head. It's just a minor scalp laceration. I'll trim your hair there and we'll put a patch on the wound. While I'm doing that you can tell me who the heck Elmer Fudd is."

It took Susan just about as long to repair my head as it took me explain the Elmer Fudd was Bugs Bunny's nemesis in the Warner Bros. cartoons. It might have been more than she actually wanted to know about Mister Fudd. When Susan was done with the patch job on my head, she made the rounds of her patients to be sure everything was in order. After that, we sat and drank coffee in a room that said "Nurse's Lounge" on the door and I gave her a summary of my activities since visiting Doris Alpert's apartment up to and including my final encounter with Deputy Elmer. After hearing all that, Susan shivered a little and then laughed. "Did you really throw all the deputy's stuff off the cliff?"

"Yeah. I did it just like Mister Whiskers knocks stuff off the table just to watch it fall."

Still smiling, Susan said, "I just can't let you out of my sight for a minute without you getting into some kind of trouble."

Grinning at her, I said, "Sorry, Angel. That's just my nature. Now, I should get out of here before you get into trouble for associating with undesirable characters on the job."

"Where are you going to go? Do you want to sleep at my place?"

"How about I check into the Hyatt and you come over there when you get off?"

"Okay, but Bette Davis is still staying there. What'll we do if she sees us there?"

"Invite her to the lounge for a drink?"

Susan shook her head in exasperation. "I get off at seven and I need to stop by my place for a couple of things and to give Mister Whiskers his breakfast. So I should be there before eight."

"Okay, Angel. I'll call here and leave a message for you with our room number so you won't have to stop at the desk."

She grinned and said in a quiet voice, "All right, Johnny, but for Heaven's sake, don't tell them it's a room number."

Then she gave me a kiss on the cheek and I headed out into the night again. In Santa Barbara they have much more pleasant nights.

Sixteen

9:30 A.M. – Tuesday – August 13, 1940

Hyatt Hotel – 1111 Highway 101, Santa Barbara

The Santa Barbara Hyatt is directly across Highway 101 from the beach so you'd expect the view to be good. It is. In fact, if you happen to have a deluxe suite on the second floor, you can see most of the harbor all the way to the commercial fishing boats tied up at Stearns Wharf.

Since it happened that Susan and I were checked into a second floor deluxe suite, we were sitting at a table on the small balcony outside our room enjoying both the view and some pretty decent coffee provided by room service. I'd gotten a few hours' sleep before Susan showed up around nine, so with a brisk shower and coffee, I was ready to go. The question was, where was I going?

Susan, looking more angelic than ever with a lot of shapely leg showing below a pair of shorts and a white cotton shirt, summed the situation up precisely. "What are you going to do, Johnny? You don't have anyone left to question unless you can find that fellow in Sacramento."

"And I'm not holding my breath waiting for his telephone call. Bette might know something more than she's told me, but she's skittish on the subject. There's something fishy there, too, but so far I haven't figured out how to crack that nut."

Susan giggled. "Better not let your pal Bette hear you calling her a nut!"

"Ha, ha. Very funny. I should probably stop in and see Lilly and Bette before I go back to Hollywood and let them know that

Doris Alpert is no longer with us, but I don't want Bette to conclude from Doris's death that it's safe to move Lilly back to L.A. just yet."

I thought there was some trepidation in her voice when Susan asked, "So when are you going back?"

"To tell you the truth, I haven't thought beyond my next cup of coffee. I don't see any reason to hurry back at the moment. I need to tell Sergeant Salvino what happened in Needles, but I can do that long distance. If you can put up with having me around for a couple of days, I kind of like this place."

Susan put a gentle hand on my arm. "I can put up with you here, at my place, or anywhere else you want us to be."

"Okay, how about putting up with me down in the restaurant while we get some breakfast? That seems like a good place for us to be next."

"Sounds like a good plan. Give me a minute to change into a skirt."

"Phooey. If I'd known you were gonna change, I wouldn't have suggested going downstairs. What's wrong with your shorts?"

"Good heavens, Johnny, what sort of girl do you think I am? I can't be seen wearing these in a place like this!"

Apparently there was still a lot I needed to learn about women's fashion and what you can wear where. I just said, "Okay, okay, Angel. Don't get your halo in an uproar."

On our way down to the restaurant we actually did encounter Miss Davis. She smiled at me and said, "Good morning, Spicer." Then she turned to Susan and said, "Hello, Susan. You're certainly looking chipper this morning."

"Thank you, Bette. Are you on your way to the clinic?"

"Yes, but I have to stop at a drugstore to pick up a couple of things for Lillian. Is there one close by?"

"Yes there is, Bette. Just turn right out of the hotel onto 101 and follow it to where Route 101 turns right and becomes State Street. From there Beach Sundries and Drugs is on your right two blocks up at Mission Street."

"Thank you very much, Susan. See you at the clinic later."

I could've sworn I saw them exchange winks just before Bette gave me a smile and headed out to the Hyatt's parking lot. I said, "Okay, I see how it is. You gals are ganging up on me."

"Why, whatever do you mean, Johnny? I thought Bette was quite cordial to you."

Realizing I couldn't win, I set my mind on enjoying a breakfast of sausages rolled up in pancakes. The menu called the dish Pigs in a Blanket. Despite the name, it was tasty.

Back in our suite I carried the telephone out to the balcony—it was equipped with a long cord for just that purpose—and placed a long distance call to the Seventh Precinct. As far as I was concerned, Susan made better use of the time changing back into her shorts.

Salvino was his usual charming self. "Spicer, you're lucky I'm even talkin' to you after you hung up on me the other day. I shoulda sent somebody over to haul your butt in for a round of the third degree."

"Good morning to you, too, Sergeant Salvino."

"Don't get smart with me, Spicer. I can still send some boys over to roust you."

"That would be a waste of the taxpayers' money since I'm about a hundred miles from my office right now. Besides, I've already been rousted a couple of times this week—by Elmer Fudd no less."

"What the hell are you talkin' about? You been at the bottle already this morning?"

"Get out your notebook, Sergeant. I have information for you."

After a moment of silence, Salvino said, "Okay, Spicer, shoot."

"First, Lillian Bouvier is at a private hospital near Santa Barbara called Casa Sobre El Mar. The address is 1184 Channel Drive in Montecito. It's southeast of town and off the beaten path."

"Sounds like a Mexican tamale joint, for cryin' out loud."

"Nope. The tamale joint is in the second story I have for you."

Sounding exasperated, Salvino said, "Of course it is."

I explained the tie-in between Doris Alpert and Rolly Boland, and that Doris had disappeared Friday morning. I pointed out that by means of extremely clever detecting I'd found Miss Alpert, but I'd found her too late. I also told Salvino about Helen Valdez's restaurant and recommended their hamburgers. Finally, I related my experiences with Sheriff Bob and Deputy Elmer.

"Holy cow, Spicer! Don't you know law enforcement officers frown on being handcuffed and having their weapons thrown off a cliff, and that's to say nothing about what you did to a deputy sheriff's car."

"I'd never do that to a real law enforcement officer, but Deputy Elmer is about as much a law enforcement office as you are a brain surgeon."

"Okay, Spicer, but I wish you'd go a little easier on our witnesses and suspects. We're running out of them."

"So I noticed, Sergeant. Anyway, you should be hearing from Sheriff Bob sometime soon. I told him you were the guy with all the answers."

"Yeah, don't I wish. I guess I'm going to take me a trip up to Santa Barbara. You gonna be there long?"

"I'm not sure. If I pick up a lead that will help me track down Joseph Kipchumba I'll be out of here in a flash, but I don't expect him to call anytime soon. I'm at the Hyatt Hotel. It's on the beach."

"Of course it is. You and your expense account! You're livin' the life o' Riley while us servants of the people are doin' all the work for peanuts."

"Yeah, Sergeant, it's a downright shame. Call me when you get into town and I'll buy you lunch."

My next long distance call was to Rosie's Professional Telephone Exchange Service.

While I was waiting for Rosie to answer, Susan came out onto the balcony and leaned a warm hip against my shoulder. "You making any progress out here?"

"Not much. I . . . hang on a sec."

Into the telephone I said, "Hi, Rosie. Johnny Spicer here. Got anything for me?"

"Yes, Mister Spicer. You had two calls yesterday. One was from the Chrysler automobile dealership. They want you to come in and look at the new 1941 Chrysler."

"I'll have to pass on that one unless the new 1941 Chrysler comes in a bicycle model. What else?"

Carefully sounding out the name, she said, "A Missus Kip-chum-ba called early this morning. She didn't care to leave a message. Said she would call back."

If you'd asked me to list the ten people from whom I was least likely to get a telephone call, Damaris Kipchumba would have been number two on the list right after her husband. I said, "Rosie, when she calls back tell her you don't expect be back for several days and see if she'll leave a call back number."

"Okay, Mister Spicer. I'll tell her."

I dropped the receiver into its cradle, put an arm around the angel leaning her hip against my shoulder, and said, "Now ain't that somethin'?"

"Isn't what something?"

"Rosie had a telephone message for me from Damaris Kipchumba. She called the office this morning."

Susan slid into the other chair and said, "Yes, that is definitely something, all right. What do you suppose she's up to?"

"About the only thing I can think of is she wants me to wear a bull's eye on the back of my coat so I'll make a better target."

Susan gave a little involuntary shiver. "Do you really think they want to kill you?"

I shook my head. "I don't know what that would gain them unless they think I know something I don't know I know. Hopefully she'll leave a call back number so I can find out what's on their evil little minds."

Susan stood to go in, saying, "I think I need to get back to catching up on my sleep."

"A good plan, Angel. I'll join you if that's okay."

She kissed me on the cheek, and grinning, said, "I guess I could move over and make room. But no snoring."

Susan made better use of the actual sleeping time than I did. My brain kept asking questions like why the heck did Damaris Kipchumba call me? What were they up to? Finally, I gave up on sleep about one-thirty and took the telephone back out to our little balcony. After closing the door as quietly as I could, I made another call to Rosie.

"Yes, sir, Mister Spicer. Missus Kipchumba called again at twelve-fifteen. She still wouldn't leave a call back number, but she did leave a message. The message is kind of strange. She said to tell you if you want the elephant, you are to meet her tomorrow evening at six in front of the Point Fermin Lighthouse.'"

"And you told her I wouldn't be back for several days?"

"I did, sir."

"Okay, Rosie. Thanks. Anything else?"

"No, sir. No other messages."

I hung up the receiver and lit a Lucky Strike. Then I blew a smoke ring and thought about what a nervy broad Damaris Kipchumba is. After that, I stared out across Santa Barbara Bay and thought about what a lonely place Point Fermin would be after dark.

Point Fermin is a small point of land sticking out into the Pacific Ocean at the southernmost tip of San Pedro. If you don't know where San Pedro is, it's a small town on the coast just west of Los Angeles Harbor that serves as home to commercial fishermen and stevedores who depend on the docks for their living.

The lighthouse, according to Miss Gleason, my eighth grade teacher who took us on a field trip to Point Fermin, was built in the 1870s and was the first light on that particular section of the coast. Originally the light burned kerosene, but now it's electrified and maintained by the City of Los Angeles instead of the Federal Light Keeper Service.

I'd just lit my third Lucky when Susan came out yawning. She put her hands on my shoulders and said, "Couldn't sleep?"

"Yeah. I kept wondering if Kipchumba had called back. I hope I didn't wake you."

"Not really, darling. Did she?"

"Yes. She called about twelve-fifteen. I'm telling you, that woman has a hell of a lot of nerve. Rosie told her I wouldn't be back in town for several days and Missus Kipchumba told Rosie if I wanted the elephant, I have to meet her at the Point Fermin Lighthouse tomorrow at six p.m."

"Point Fermin? I think I've been there. It's near San Pedro, right?"

"That's the one."

Susan frowned. "From what I remember it was out on a bluff all by itself . . . kind of a desolate spot."

"Well, there used to be a residential area right next to it, but there was a landslide and the part of the bluff where the houses were collapsed. I haven't been out there in a while, but aside from weekend picnickers, Point Fermin is a pretty lonely place."

"Johnny, I've tried hard not to be a nuisance about the things you do as part of your job, but this time I'm really worried. Please tell me you aren't planning to go out there tomorrow night."

"I'm still deciding on the best thing to do, Angel, but don't worry, I'm not going to do anything stupid."

With an expression I read as sheepish, Susan said, "I'm sorry, Johnny. I have no right . . . "

Standing, I put my arms around her. "Yes, Angel, you do have the right. I gave it to you. It has taken me a long time to learn that I can't expect a woman to be part of my life and not worry about what I do for a living. I've decided I want you in my life and I'm looking at how I can do things with more caution so you'll have less to worry about."

Susan looked up at me with tears in her eyes, said, "Oh, Johnny," and rested her head on my chest.

"Hey, hey. How come the tears?"

She looked up again, wiped a tear from her cheek, and said, "Another thing you need to learn about women is sometimes we cry when we're happy, too, and you just made me very happy."

We hugged again and I muttered, "Women."

Susan sniffed and said, "Yeah, I know. You can't live with us and you can't live without us."

I started back into our suite, but Susan said, "I need to call the clinic. They were already talking about moving schedules around to accommodate training my replacement. I'd like to know what they came up with."

"Sure. Then we can figure out when I should talk with Bette and Lilly and we can have some dinner or lunch or whatever it is at this hour."

Leaving Susan to her telephone call, I walked in and got myself cleaned up. I was still shaving when she came in and said, "Well, I've got good news and more good news. Which would you like to hear first?"

Rinsing shaving soap from my razor, I said, "Ah . . . how 'bout the good news?"

"Good choice! The first good news is that I am officially on the payroll as Director of Nursing starting tomorrow. The other good news that I also officially start a five day vacation tomorrow."

"Oh, you do, do you? How did that piece of good fortune come about?"

Susan put on her sheepish expression again. "My asking for the time off probably had something to do with it." Then speaking rapidly as if she had to get it out quickly, she added, "But I haven't used any vacation time in . . ."

"Relax, Angel. You're gonna give yourself one of those coronary things. It's okay. If you want, you can even come with me when I go back to Hollywood in the morning. Would you like that?"

Almost jumping up and down like a high school girl who just got invited to the prom by the captain of the football team, she said, "Can I, Johnny? Really? You wouldn't mind?"

"No, I wouldn't mind. I can't promise as much excitement as we had on our last trip, but that might be okay, huh?"

Throwing her arms around me, she said, "Oh, thank you . . . thank you . . . thank you!"

"You don't need to thank me, Angel, but next time you should probably talk with me about it before you take time off expecting we can spend it together. There will be times when that won't work out too well. Okay?"

Her sheepish expression was getting a workout. "Okay. I'm sorry, Johnny. I . . . I'm just worried about you and somehow being with you makes me worry less."

I told her I understood and gave myself a pat on the back for doing the right thing. We finished getting ready and headed out, taking both of our cars so Susan could leave her snazzy Pontiac Cabriolet at her place. Plus, Mister Whiskers needed some fresh kibble and a litter box change. I sat at her kitchen table scratching Mister Whiskers behind the ears while Susan did the other stuff.

By five o'clock we were both famished, so we headed to a place called Joe's Café on State Street just northwest of Haley Street.

Susan warned me it was expensive, but that Joe's was one of the oldest restaurants in town with terrific steaks and seafood. She was right on both counts.

When I saw Joe's Café I knew their food had to be expensive just to pay for all the neon lighting out front. Inside, though, the place was loaded with Italian ambiance—wooden tables and booths with red and white checked table cloths—and the smells coming out of the kitchen alone were worth the price of admission. They even had wicker-covered Chianti bottles with candles sticking out of them on the tables. Mama Mia!

From our secluded booth near the back of the dining room we could hear classical opera music being played on a radio somewhere. It was a perfect setting for some pretty fair veal scaloppini, and, of course, spumoni ice cream for dessert.

An hour-and-a-half later we walked into Lilly's room at the clinic. Lilly was still taped up like a mummy, but her spirits were high. I suspect that was largely due to Bette's presence. No one she respected had ever taken an interest in her, and that seemed to be exactly what she needed.

We chatted for about thirty minutes and my subtle attempts to wheedle information only earned me one fact I hadn't known before. Lilly recalled Rolly talking about wanting some sort of automobile called an SS Saloon like Joseph Kipchumba owned. That meant nothing to her, but as a performance auto nut, I knew "SS Saloon" could only refer to one automobile, an English Jaguar sedan.

In exchange, I told them a heavily sanitized version of Doris Alpert's demise. Bette took the news in stride and without a lot of comment. Lilly didn't have much to say, either, but what I could see of her expression under the dressings was fear. It naturally scared her when evil people who were capable of killing in cold blood intruded into her quiet, boring world. There were times when I wished to hell I lived in a boring world where people didn't go around killing each other quite so much.

Seventeen

3:00 P.M. – Wednesday – August 14, 1940

Point Fermin Lighthouse – Gaffey Street, San Pedro

Susan and I got an early start Wednesday morning because we had a lot to do. Our first stop was her place, where she packed a few more outfits into her overnight case and arranged for a neighbor to see that Mister Whiskers received the attention he rightfully deserved.

Then we headed south on U.S. 101, arriving in Hollywood around eleven a.m. We picked up some lunch at Eli's and spent the next two hours at my place while I did a load of laundry and repacked my bag.

While we were waiting for the Montero Apartments' fancy new clothes dryers to spin the water out of my shirts, I told Susan my plan for dealing with the Kipchumbas. Whenever possible I'd rather be the hunter than the hunted, so my plan was to turn the tables on them by staking out the Point Fermin Light from a concealed position. If we were lucky enough to spot the Kipchumbas without them spotting us, we might be able to follow them to wherever they were holing up and get Sergeant Salvino and his posse to round 'em up and haul 'em off to the pokey.

Susan asked what I thought our chances of success were and I gave her a straight answer. The plan's strongest virtue was its simplicity, but I emphasized the need for a lot of good luck to make it work. I also pointed out that there were some risks involved in getting within spitting distance of the enemy. I followed that thought with a question.

"I don't suppose you could be persuaded to wait for me while I watch for the Kipchumbas out at the lighthouse?"

She frowned and said, "I will do whatever you think is best, but I hope you'll let me come with you."

"I kinda figured that, and it's probably easier to keep you safe if you're with me."

Our next stop was the A & P grocery at Fairfax and Sunset, where I gave Susan a shopping list to fill while I filled the Chrysler's gas tank at a Shell station a few blocks up Sunset. My grocery list included:

Apples (4)
Block of Cheddar cheese
Beef jerky
Saltine crackers
Soft drinks (6)
Hershey chocolate bars w/Almonds (6)

After looking at the list, Susan frowned and said, "What is all this junk for?"

"Angel, those are called 'provisions.' They're what we stash behind the front seat of the car to keep from starving when we can't run into a restaurant."

"Well, your 'provisions' aren't the healthiest choices you could make. You'd be better off with some carrots and . . ."

"Take your cute little nurse hat off and save the advice for people who don't have to spend hours sitting in their cars staring at nothing."

Susan rolled her eyes and headed into the market. I yelled after her, "And there better not be any danged carrots in that bag!"

She looked back and stuck her tongue out at me and I drove off to fill the gas tank. When I returned to pick her up about twenty minutes later, I made sure there were no danged carrots in the grocery bag. Susan did sneak a box of raisins in, though.

It was nearly three o'clock when we started the thirty-some mile trek to San Pedro by heading south out of Hollywood on Highland. I stayed on Highland until it crossed Olympic and merged with La Brea Avenue. Eventually we got onto Figueroa and followed it to the harbor, where we took Gaffey through San Pedro to Point Fermin.

The trip had taken about an hour, which meant we were two hours away from the scheduled meeting time. I figured that was just about right. The Kipchumbas were certain to get there at least an hour early to make sure I wasn't setting a trap for them, which is exactly what I was trying to do. The next step was to find an observation point from which we could watch for the Kipchumbas without them spotting us when they showed up. Gaffey Street is the main route to Point Fermin. There is a second more roundabout route that required going through the harbor area, but I put my money on Gaffey.

As you approach Point Fermin, the east side of Gaffey is residential with a grid of east-west and north-south streets. The west side of Gaffey is mostly undeveloped land.

The sunken city landslide site sits to the southeast of the Point Fermin light. I considered the sunken city as an observation point, but rejected it because the view it offered of the lighthouse and its surrounding was too limited.

Our best bet turned out to be an alley off of Shepard Street, which was the last east-west street that crossed Gaffey before the lighthouse. It offered a view of the block of Gaffey just north of the lighthouse and there were no houses next to the alley so we wouldn't be upsetting anyone by parking there for a while. The alley also had a low wall between us and Gaffey that would make our car less visible. I pulled in, checked the view, and shut off the engine.

Susan looked around. "I bet you could get a real bargain on some of this property."

"Probably, but don't stand in one place too long, you're liable to slide right into the drink."

"What a delightful prospect."

I took a folded piece of paper out of my jacket pocket and showed her an advertisement drawing I ripped out of a March, 1939 issue of *Autocar Magazine*. The picture was of a Jaguar Saloon SS. I held it up and said, "This is what we're looking for."

"Well, that shouldn't be too hard to spot. It looks really different from most cars. Is that the Saloon SS thing Lillian was talking about?"

"Yes. The name the Brits gave it is 'Jaguar SS Saloon. That's where they make them—Great Britain, specifically in Coventry."

"What makes it so special? I mean why would anyone go all the way to England to buy a car?"

"Good question. European sporting cars are built for the way people drive in Europe, which is quite different from the way we drive our cars. For one thing, gasoline is an expensive commodity in England, so British cars are designed to use fuel more efficiently than our cars while still performing, as they say, in a sprightly fashion.

"This Jaguar, for example has a four cylinder engine with a displacement of two-and-a-half liters, or about a hundred and fifty cubic inches. Most American performance cars are powered by six and eight cylinder engines that displace between two and three hundred cubic inches. The surprising thing is that the manufacturer of the Jaguar gets more than a hundred horsepower out of that small engine, which is about the same as many of the larger, less economical American engines.

"Another difference is American cars are built for a smooth comfortable ride, while European cars are built to be agile for driving on curving roads at high speeds. To achieve that agility and those high speeds, European sporting cars are usually lighter than American cars, which often means they're smaller and not as sturdy as their American counterparts."

Susan said, "So if you want comfort and own an oil well, you get an American car. If you want speed and agility, and you are handy with a wrench, you buy a European car. Is that right?"

I nodded. "Generally speaking, yes. Like with anything else, there are exceptions."

Susan's next question was more to the reason we were there. "So where should I be looking for this Jaguar?"

"It will most likely be going through that intersection ahead of us from right to left. We can take turns watching. I'll start while you get the hang of recognizing the traffic that goes by."

"You want anything from the kitchen in the backseat?"

"No, thanks, but I need something out of the trunk. I'll be right back."

I climbed down from the driver's seat and walked back to the trunk. What I was after was a pair of field glasses. What I got was the biggest damned diamondback rattlesnake I've ever seen.

It was his rattle that saved me. I heard it the second I started to lift the rear deck lid, which was hinged at the top. I let go of the handle just as the snake stuck his head out of the trunk. I was hoping the trunk lid would catch him part way out of the trunk, but he was quicker and ducked back into the trunk.

For a couple of seconds I couldn't believe I'd seen what I just saw, but my clear memory of two black, beady eyes, a flicking forked tongue, and dark brown diamond pattern convinced me he was no hallucination. The raucous rattling that was still going on helped.

I yelled, "Angel, get out of the car. Now!"

She slid out the driver's side door which I'd left open. "What's wrong, Johnny?"

"Close the door, then come over here and stand behind me. We picked up a hitchhiker somewhere along the way."

Puzzled, she asked, "A hitchhiker?"

"Yeah, the biggest rattler I've ever seen. He's in the trunk, but there is a hole at each end of the back interior panel he could fit through, and they would allow him into the passenger compartment. We're damned lucky something attracted him to the trunk, probably the heat from the exhaust that passes right under the trunk floor on either side of the gas tank."

Ever following the logical path, Susan said, "Well, we have to get him out of there. How will we do that?"

"I have an idea that might work, but I need a long, sturdy stick, like a boom handle."

We started looking at the piles of trash that had accumulated along the fence on the driver's side of the car. After a few minutes of searching, Susan said, "How about a broken hoe?"

She held up a hoe handle that was broken at the metal shank below the wood. It was the perfect tool for the job because the broken shank formed a hook for catching the trunk handle. I said, "Perfect. I'm going to try to trap the snake half in and half out of the trunk so we can kill it. What I'd like you to do is stand back and look under the car while I open the trunk. I don't know if there are any holes in the bottom of the trunk big enough for him to get through, but if you see anything moving under there holler loud!"

"Okay, Johnny. Do you know where the nearest hospital is?"

Grinning, I said, "I'm sure San Pedro has a medical facility, but I don't know if they treat snakes."

Susan shook her head in apparent exasperation. "Not for the snake, silly. For you, in case you get bit."

"Oh. Well, we'll look in a telephone book after we kill the snake. Okay, here we go."

When I'd dropped the trunk lid earlier it had latched, so the first thing I had to do was use the key to unlatch the lid without actually opening it far enough for the snake to get out. Gingerly, I slipped the key in the lock and slowly turned it while applying downward pressure on the lid so releasing the latch wouldn't make it pop up.

I felt the latch release and still pushing down on the deck lid, I slipped the shank of the broken hoe around the trunk handle and moved to the driver's side and toward the front of the car as far as the length of the hoe handle would allow.

It took quite a bit of muscle to lift the trunk lid at that odd angle but I managed to get it up about two feet and hold it there. The snake took his damned time about it, but eventually, he slowly slithered through the opening. I was figuring him for at least six feet, so when about two feet of snake was out of the trunk, I pulled the hoe handle to the side and let the lid slam down.

For a panicky moment I wasn't sure the trunk lid was heavy enough to hold him, but it seemed to. Susan said, Good work! You got him. How do we kill him?"

That was an excellent question and one for which I didn't yet have a specific answer. I walked around where I could see him better and watched him struggling against the weight of the lid. I couldn't swear to it, but it sure looked to me like there was more snake outside of the trunk than there was a few seconds before. Now his head was actually on the pavement behind the car and his rattles were going like crazy.

I thought about shooting him, but a gunshot would attract unwanted attention, so I went for Plan B. There were some large chunks of concrete near where Susan found the hoe handle. I quickly hefted a couple of them and took the largest one I could carry over to the car. The snake had wriggled another inch or two out of the trunk, so I figured I'd better get on with it. Standing as close to him as I dared, I lifted the concrete slab as high as I could and slammed it down on his head.

A second later the rattling stopped and the snake went limp. I picked up my hoe handle and gave the damned thing a couple of pokes. It didn't move, so I opened the trunk all the way. There seemed to be a hell of a lot of snake in there. Using my trusty hoe handle again, I dragged the rest of him out. All in all he was at least seven feet in length.

Still watching him warily, I leaned against the side of my car and sighed a big sigh of relief. Susan came over to give me a hug. She said, "Wow! He was a lot bigger than I thought."

"Me, too. I guess we ought to get that concrete slab out of the road and move him where he won't scare the pants off of anyone."

"Okay, what do you want me to do?"

"Get back in the car and start looking for that Jaguar. I'll take care of the snake."

After another hug and a quick kiss on the cheek, Susan trotted back to the driver-side door and I hefted my handy-dandy hoe handle again. Then, poking the shank end of it under the concrete slab I'd dropped on the snake's head, I lifted. The wooden part of the handle was doing a lot of bending and I was afraid it would snap under the weight, but it held and the concrete rolled over toward the edge of the pavement. Underneath, the snake was flatter than a pancake, which was just fine by me. After rolling the rock once more to get it out of the road, I used the shank of the hoe handle to hook the snake and drag him into the vacant lot on the east side of the alley. He was one heavy snake—at least ten pounds.

I'm not ashamed to admit the snake gave me a pretty good scare, so much so that when I walked back to the trunk, I had to stand there for a minute trying to remember why I'd opened the trunk in the first place. Then I fished the field glasses out cautiously, hoping to hell we only had only picked up one hitchhiker.

When I slid back onto the car seat, Susan said, "How do you suppose that awful thing got in here?"

Looking back over the seat, I grabbed an apple and said, "Well, the Hollywood hills are lousy with them—so many that the investors behind the Hollywoodland development had to bring in a herd of hogs to roust the snakes before the men could begin construction up there.

"I've heard there are still a lot of them up there, so one might have come down to see how the hunting was in the big city. The hard thing to understand is how he got into the car. There are no holes that I know of that are large enough for a guy that size to get into the car, so somebody must have picked a lock and dumped him in. Want an apple?"

Susan shook her head. "So you think somebody was trying to kill us by snake?"

"It just about has to be that way. If he'd gotten in on his own, he would have used the same route to get out when we started driving. He wouldn't have liked the vibration and noise, but he acted trapped, so he must have had some help getting in."

"And you're thinking it was the Kipchumbas who gave him the help?"

"As far as I know they are the only ones who might think they have a reason to kill me, although I still don't know what makes them think that."

Susan was frowning again. "When could they have put snake in there? Wouldn't you have seen it when you put our bags in the trunk at your apartment?"

"You'd think so, but if the snake was in passenger compartment and saw or heard the deck lid open, he could have been on his way back there to investigate while we were getting in up here."

"All I can say is you sure have some scary enemies. I never heard of anyone using a snake as a murder weapon."

"Oh, it's been done before. In fact I doubt if there is any way a human being could kill another human being that hasn't been tried. It's the nature of the beast."

Tilting her head, Susan asked, "Well, if the Kipchumba's put that snake in your car, will they still show up out here?"

"That's hard to say, but if I were them, I'd show up just to make sure the snake did his job."

I finished my apple and flipped the core out my window and over the top of the car into the vacant field where I'd left the snake. Since my eyelids were getting heavy and Susan had gotten pretty handy at spotting the cars passing on Gaffey with my field glasses, I said I thought I'd take a nap. I suggested she wake me about half an hour unless the Jaguar showed up before then.

Then I took off my hat to relieve the pressure on the head wound Susan had patched for me and leaned back in my seat. I was out like a light, but it seemed like I'd only been asleep a few minutes when she tapped me on the shoulder and said, "Johnny?"

"Yeah?"

"What should I do if I see the Jaguar?"

Thinking she was kidding, I gave her a smart aleck answer. "If you see the Jaguar, tap me on the shoulder and say, 'I saw the Jaguar.'"

A few seconds later as I was just drifting off again, I felt another tap on my shoulder. "Johnny?"

Sometimes Susan's sense of humor can be exasperating. I said, "Yes, Angel, what is it now?"

"I saw the Jaguar."

Eighteen

5:00 P.M. – Wednesday – August 14, 1940

Point Fermin Lighthouse – Gaffey Street, San Pedro

That woke me up fast. "Where? When?"

Smiling at my reaction, Susan said, "Less than a minute ago and right where you said they would be; going from right to left on the street up there. I saw them through the field glasses. There were two people in the car; a man and a woman. The woman seemed to be driving, but she was in the passenger seat."

Reaching down to start the engine, I said "That would be correct. The crazy Brits still don't know which side of the street they're supposed to drive on."

"I see. What do we do now?"

"We get ready to follow them when they go back the other way and hope to heck they don't leave by another route. If they do, we're out of luck."

Grinning again, Susan said, "I'll keep watching if you want to take another nap."

"Thanks, wise guy. Besides, if I'm right about how that snake got in here, they won't stick around long. In that case, they're just here to see if I showed up."

About fifteen minutes later, Susan put the field glasses to her eyes and said, "You called that one right. There they go back in the opposite direction."

Shifting the Chrysler into gear, I pulled out of the alley and sped up to the intersection at Gaffey Street. From there we could see the Jag about a block-and-a-half ahead of us. I turned right and cruised sedately ahead until we were a car length in back of the second car behind the Kipchumbas.

Susan asked a pertinent question. "Johnny, how do you know they can't see us back here?"

"Pay careful attention, Angel, and I'll give you a quick lesson in tailing."

Nodding enthusiastically, she said, "Okay. Should I take notes? Will there be a quiz afterwards?"

"Yes. If they don't see us and shoot us dead, you pass."

"I'd better take notes."

"The trick to tailing another vehicle is to fix the rear view of the target car in your mind so you always know where it is with a quick glance ahead. That allows you to spend more of your attention on blending in with the other traffic and planning your next move. Susan asked another very good question. "How far behind is too far or too close?"

"That depends on conditions like traffic, visibility and whether the road is straight or has a lot of curves. If traffic is light, for example, you want to allow more space—sometimes as much as a block—between your car and the target car because you will be easier to notice when there are fewer cars for camouflage. If traffic is heavy, you can stay closer—maybe with only one or two cars between you and the target car so you won't lose it so easily. Also, on a road with multiple lanes going in your direction, you want to stay in the same lane as the target car so you don't get stuck in the wrong lane where you can't follow the target car if it makes a sudden turn.

"Guys who are really good at this will actually pass the target car and then let it catch up and pass them. The idea is that a car in front of you can't be following you. Of course that won't work if the suspects you're following will recognize you or your car."

"Got it. What can I do to help right now?"

"First, I'm going to get as close to the Jag as I can so you can write down its license plate number. Then keep your eyes on them so I can concentrate on the traffic. So far they're being predictable. My guess is they'll stay on Gaffey all the way through San Pedro and beyond it until they come to a major north-south highway. You'll know we've left San Pedro when you see a bunch of oil tanks on the right side of the road."

Keeping her eyes glued to the Jag, Susan said, "You must have spent a lot of time around here to know so much about the area."

"Not really, Angel. I just try to keep my eyes open and observe. Observing is a detective's most important skill. See and remember."

A few minutes before six the oil storage tanks appeared on our right and we came to the intersection of Gaffey and Anaheim Street. It's also the point at which Gaffey becomes Vermont Street. On a hunch I moved over into the left lane, preparing to turn left on Anaheim. A moment later the Kipchumbas did the same thing."

After taking off at a forty-five-degree angle to the northeast, Anaheim became Western and we arrived at the intersection of Western and Pacific Coast Highway. Once again I played a hunch and prepared for a left turn, and once again the Jag completed the same maneuver and we both turned left on PCH. The traffic was getting heavy because it was the time of day when the oil field and harbor workers got off work, so I moved up to a position three cars behind the Kipchumbas.

Susan was doing a little observing of her own and asked, "That's twice you anticipated a left turn before the Jaguar made any indication it was turning. How did you know where they were going to go?"

"I didn't really know, I just played the odds based on the route they seemed to be taking. My guess is they're headed north and the two left turns we made are on their most direct route through the mountains and into the San Fernando Valley or over to the coast."

We stayed on Pacific Coast Highway, which is also California Route One for a dozen or so miles, passing through the communities of Torrance and Redondo Beach. Then, as we entered Manhattan Beach, PCH turned inland and became Sepulveda Boulevard. A couple of miles later we passed Mines Field, Los Angeles's municipal airport.

I pointed the airport out to her and Susan said, "So there's this one and the one we left from in Glendale?"

"And one more in Burbank called Union Air Terminal. The towns of Burbank and Glendale are right next to each other, though, and there is no particular reason to have two major airports that close to each other. I'm guessing only one of them will survive. My money is on Grand Central Air Terminal in Glendale."

We continued on Sepulveda until we were almost to the point where the highway begins to climb over the Sepulveda Pass through the Santa Monica Mountains. There we left Sepulveda and headed more or less west on San Vicente Boulevard until turning right and winding around on Entrada Drive before it ended at Highway One and we were back northbound on Pacific Coast Highway just above Santa Monica. According to my odometer we had traveled a little over thirty miles since we began following the Kipchumbas on Gaffey in San Pedro. As we turned back onto PCH, the dashboard clock was showing ten minutes to seven and the sun was about to disappear below the western horizon.

Susan was having difficulty figuring out our route. "Wait a minute. We're back on Pacific Coast Highway and Highway One. Have we just been going around in circles for the past hour?"

"Nope, we're about thirty miles north of where we started out in San Pedro."

"Then how come they didn't just drive up Pacific Coast Highway instead of zigzagging around on all those other streets?"

"Because, despite its name, PCH doesn't always follow the coast. There are several places where the coast road stops and the restarts a few miles further on because of some obstacle or other. The route we took is actually quite a bit faster than staying on PCH."

"And you call the British crazy for not know which side of the street to drive on. I'd say that when it comes to driving, they don't have a monopoly on crazy."

"You'll get no argument from me on that score."

For a moment the three or four car lengths between us and the Jaguar were clear and I said, "Here's another Dick Tracy Crime Stoppers Tip. Earlier we were talking about how to keep the target car in sight by being aware of how it looks from the rear. Well, you might not think so, but sometimes that's easier to do in the dark."

That one puzzled Susan. "Why is that?"

"Take a look at the Jaguar's tail lights. They're dimmer than most of the American cars around it, and the right tail light is flickering on and off, probably due to a shorted circuit somewhere in the electrical system. Noticing those features make it a lot easier for us to keep the Jag in sight because after dark all they see in their mirrors are headlights, but from our position we have a pair of unique tail lights to follow."

"I see what you mean. I take it electrical stuff isn't the British car maker's strongest suit."

"No truer words were ever spoken."

"So do you know where this little parade of ours is going to end up yet?"

"Well, I've been giving that some thought and quite frankly, I haven't got a clue. At first I figured we were heading north to go back to West Sacramento, but that idea got thrown into a cocked hat when they headed over toward the coast rather than continuing north to the Ridge Route where Highway 99 goes over the pass into the San Joaquin Valley.

"The route they're taking is north, all right, but its north up the coast which is the long way to Sacramento, but the shortest route to San Francisco."

Surprised, Susan asked, "We're going to San Francisco!?"

"It's impossible to say at this point. There are a lot of destinations between here and San Francisco and even more beyond it. All we can do is stay back here and keep tagging along. However, if the Kipchumbas stay overnight somewhere, it might be Santa Barbara. We could stop by and say hello to Mister Whiskers."

"Oh, brother," she kidded. "The day you go out of your way to cater to a cat will be cold day in hell."

"Don't be so sure, Angel. Mister Whiskers and I are getting along better these days. I think he's taking a shine to me."

"Or maybe he's just figured out I'm not the only one who knows how to work the can opener."

"From his point of view that's a pretty sensible reason for being friendly to a human. And by the way, welcome to Malibu, the seaside home of the rich and famous who don't quite qualify for Santa Barbara—actors and show business folks."

"Rich people live in these little cracker box houses with no front yards?"

"True, they don't have much room for front yards, but you ought to see the beach they have in their backyards."

We'd been back on Pacific Coast Highway for about fifteen minutes and we were coming to the small commercial district that serves Malibu when I saw the Jag pull over to the right. "Oh, oh. They're up to something. Keep a sharp eye out."

Susan stored the field glasses in the glove compartment when the sun went down because they're not very useful after dark. Now she was relying on her eyesight, which was pretty darn good. "They're pulling into a parking lot . . . I can't make out the business yet."

"Okay, I'm moving into the left lane so we can find a place to wait them out on the opposite side of the road."

Susan said, "They pulled into a place called the Malibu Inn. It looks like a hotel and restaurant."

"All right. Now all we need to know is . . ."

"They parked in front of the restaurant. That could mean they're just stopping for something to eat."

Susan was getting better at this every minute. "Very good, Angel. I see a drive-in sandwich joint up ahead. I'll pull in there."

She continued watching them as we went by to be sure they stayed put. They did and I pulled around to the far side of a joint on the beach side of PCH called Johnny's Seaside Drive-In. A large sedan parked to my left helped hide us from the highway.

Susan kept her eyes on the Jaguar while I told the carhop we would have a clubhouse sandwich and a ham and Swiss on whole wheat, plus a side order of French fried potatoes. I also asked her to bag our order to go. The last thing I needed was to sit around waiting on her to pick up our money and take the car tray away while the Kipchumbas roared away from us on the highway.

"How are we doin' over there, Angel?"

"No change so far. I don't think the Malibu Inn is the sort of place where you order a club sandwich to go, so they should be there for a while."

When our dinner arrived, I paid the tab and pulled into a parking place near the highway, but behind a low fence. We still had a clear view of the road, but my Chrysler was almost invisible to people driving by.

I handed Susan her clubhouse sandwich and unwrapped my ham and Swiss. The ocean air was cooling down quickly, and Susan moved over to share some body heat. This was another of those times when the detecting business was getting in the way of things I'd rather be doing.

We'd been at Johnny's Seaside Drive-In for almost an hour when Susan said, "Johnny, they're coming out of the restaurant."

Starting the Chrysler's engine, I said, "Okay, which way are they going to go?"

"It looks like they're pulling out to go in the same direction we were going before . . . yes, they just turned right onto the highway."

Lots of light was spilling out of Johnny's parking lot onto the highway and that gave me my first look Joseph Kipchumba who was sitting in the Jag's passenger seat as they drove past us. He appeared to be a tall, thin fellow with dark skin and short cropped graying hair. Even at that distance he gave the impression of a man with determination.

Fifteen seconds later I pulled out onto Pacific Coast Highway behind the Jaguar, and we spent most of the next hour driving between the beach and moonlit breakers on our left and scrub-covered hills on our right. That's how long it took to get to the community of Oxnard. According to the Chrysler's odometer we had covered near eighty miles since leaving San Pedro.

I wasn't yet concerned about fuel, but it was a factor I would have to think about before too much longer. I knew the Jaguar had a more range than we did, so I was hoping the Kipchumba's bladders didn't match the range of their automobile.

Unfortunately, they did, and we were closing in on one-hundred-twenty miles from San Pedro when the Kipchumbas turned right onto State Street in Santa Barbara, and then turned right again into a Signal gasoline station in the block just past Gutierrez Street. I asked Susan if there was another gas station on State in the next couple of blocks.

"Yes. There's a Chevron station a block further up."

"Good. You keep an eye out for the Kipchumbas behind us and I'll get us to the Chevron and fill up our gasoline tank."

"All right, Johnny."

I made the best possible time through the traffic in the next block of State. Susan was right as usual. There was indeed a Chevron dealer at the southeast corner of State and Cota Streets and he was still open, although it looked as if the attendant was putting things away for the night. The Chrysler's dashboard clock said it was a minute or two before eleven p.m.

After I pulled up to the pump island farthest from the street, the attendant came over and said, "I'm sorry, fella, but I'm closin' up for the night."

I flashed my Photostat and badge at him, saying, "Police business. I'd really appreciate it if you could help me out this one time."

Looking startled at the sight of my badge, he said, "Why sure, officer. I'm happy to help the police. You guys are first rate in my book."

"Thanks. Don't worry about the oil or tires. Just pump it as full as you can get it."

"Yes, sir."

Susan was turned on the seat watching for the Jaguar out of the Chrysler's rear window. I was tapping my fingers on the steering wheel and watching the numbers go around on the pump. Then, just as the numbers were approaching the gallons I expected the Chrysler to take, the attendant came around to my window and said, "Excuse me, officer, but you ought to know you've picked up a nail in your right rear tire and it's causing a slow leak. Another ten miles and you'll be riding on the rim. I could patch it for you real quick."

I smacked my palm into the steering wheel. "Damn it! That's just what we needed."

Optimistically, Susan said, "They haven't gone by yet. Maybe they've got a problem, too."

"That would be too much to hope for." I turned to the attendant and said, "Thanks for spotting the nail, and yes, if you can patch it quick, I would appreciate it."

"Sure enough, officer. The gas pump just shut off, so you can pull it around and back right into the number one service bay there on the left."

I'd barely stopped when he chocked the front tires and I heard him roll his floor jack under the rear axle. No more than two minutes later he had the tire off and was removing the nail with a pair of pliers. Seeing how quickly the attendant was working made me almost optimistic, thinking he might actually get the tire fixed in time for us to continue after the Jaguar when it went by. That's when Susan came over and linked her arm with mine. "They just went by, Johnny."

Nineteen

11:30 P.M. – Wednesday – August 14, 1940

State Street Chevron Station, Santa Barbara

Sensing my frustration, Susan asked, "Is there any way we can tell where they went?"

I shook my head. "We know they headed north on Highway One and we could take off after them in the same direction, but if they stop or turn somewhere, we could end up in San Francisco without ever seeing hide nor hair of them.

"I think our best bet is to go back to the Signal station where they stopped and flash my badge to see if the Kipchumbas said anything about where they're headed or if they left any clues laying around. If we come up empty there, we might as well call it quits for the night. Talk about a wasted day! After twelve hours of driving up and down the coast we're right back where we started . . ."

Susan interrupted. "Don't be so hard on yourself, Darling. The flat tire wasn't your fault. You've done everything you could, but sometimes things just don't work out."

I was about to tell Pollyanna where to take her wisdom when the attendant came over and said, "Tire is back on. The gas was a buck-thirty-nine. How 'bout we call it two bucks even?"

After thanking the fellow for his diligence, we got in the car and backtracked a block on State Street to the Signal station. The lights were off and an older fellow was locking the office. When he came over to tell us the obvious—that the station was closed—I flashed my badge in his face.

"Yes, sir, officer. What can I do for you?"

Noting that the name embroidered on his overalls was Bud, I gave him a friendly smile and said, "We just need a little information, Bud. It won't take long. You just serviced a Jaguar sedan, right?"

"Yes, sir, I did."

"Did the folks in that car give you any idea where they were headed?"

"Well, no, sir; at least not directly. They were . . . ah . . . Negroes and they was talkin' some Jiggaboo language to each other. I didn't understand much of what they said. We don't get much business from Negroes here and that's okay by me."

I could sense Susan getting up a head of steam to blast the fellow, but I played along with his bigotry. I said, "Yeah, I know what you mean. They didn't say anything in English, huh?"

Bud pushed the brim of his Signal Gas cap up and scratched his forehead like that might help him remember something. Apparently it did. He said, "Well, the gal did. She was an uppity bi . . . person. You know, the kind that thinks just cuz they have some money they're just as good as white people."

Fearing that Susan was going to let the guy have it any second, I quickly said, "Yeah, what did the woman say?"

"She was all impatient about something. What she said was, 'How long will we have to wait at the light?' Well, sir, her husband, if that's what he was, just about clipped her one—I think for talkin' English in front of me. After that she kept her mouth shut."

"You're sure she said 'How long will we have to wait at the light'?"

"I'm pos'tive, officer. That's what she said."

"Okay, Bud. Thanks for talking to us. You've been very helpful."

"Glad I could help out, detective. You drive safe now, ya hear?"

I threw him a salute and said, "I sure enough hear you, Bud."

Then I pulled out of his Signal station and turned left. That took us back to Cabrillo Boulevard and the beach. I parked alongside a few other automobiles whose owners were either taking a stroll on the beach or petting in their backseats.

"Johnny, I don't know how you put up with people like that. I have no love for the Kipchumbas, but it has nothing to do with the color of their skin. I was about ready to get out and poke that mechanic in the nose!"

"I know, Angel. I could tell you were building up a head of steam. At that moment, though, getting information out of the man was more important than trying to change an ingrained attitude he's had all his life."

"Okay, what did we learn from that bigoted donkey?"

Chuckling at her fervor, I said, "We learned the Kipchumbas are headed for a place that has a light of some kind and they communicate with each other in a language other than English."

Leaning her head on my shoulder, Susan said, "The language part doesn't do us much good, but the part about waiting for the light might help if we knew . . ."

"Angel, according to Bud, she didn't say waiting FOR the light, she said waiting AT the light. There's a difference."

"Oh. Okay, what kinds of places have lights? Movie premieres? Grand openings? Streetlights? It could be almost anything."

An idea was fluttering around in my head and I was trying to get it to hold still long enough for me to grab it. A place with a light. That's what we were looking for and just a few hours ago we were at a place with a light—a huge light—the Point Fermin Lighthouse. The place with a light they were headed for now didn't figure to be the Point Fermin light because they were going in the wrong direction, but there were a lot of lighthouses up the California coast. Maybe they were going to one north of here.

"Angel, do you know anything about lighthouses?"

Shaking her head, she said, "No. Do you think that's the kind of light Missus Kipchumba was referring to?"

"It could be. Lighthouses are usually out somewhere all by themselves, and if the Kipchumbas are up to something illegal, an isolated place like that might be just what they need. I don't imagine there's anyplace open now where we could get a list of the nearest lighthouses to the north."

Susan sat up. "Now that I can help you with. Start the car."

"Where are we . . ."

"Just start the car, Darling. I'll show you the route. Go that way on Cabrillo."

I looked up and she was pointing west. I couldn't begin to imagine where she was taking us, but it didn't really matter much anymore, so I followed her instructions. After rounding a wooded point in the coastline about three miles later, we pulled into a driveway that was blocked with an official-looking white metal gate that said, "U.S. Government Property" on it.

Getting out of the car, she said, "Wait right here. Johnny. This will only take a second."

Then she closed the door and ran over to a protective metal box that contained a telephone. She picked up the receiver and dialed a short four digit number. A moment later she was having a conversation with someone. In the meantime I looked at our surroundings and realized we were at a Coast Guard facility. Half a block to the west beyond some eucalyptus trees I could see a narrow two story building with a light tower sticking up from its roof. Apparently Susan figured if you wanted to know about lighthouses, you went to one. Susan is never short on logic.

A moment later she walked over and stood next to the gate, giving me the universal thumb and forefinger gesture for "OK." A moment after that a tall, fit looking young man in a white Coast Guard officer's uniform came jogging up to the gate from inside the fence and removed a padlock. He and Susan hugged and he gave her a kiss. Then he waved me through the gate. After he locked the gate, the fellow signaled me to follow him and they walked off hand in hand toward a row of white buildings a hundred feet or so further up the road.

As I followed along, I told myself there was a perfectly good explanation for Susan's behavior with this guy and I was determined to find out what it was. Then I'd knock his block off.

He signaled me to pull up in front of the first of the white buildings. I did as instructed and stepped out of the car. Susan could tell from my expression that I wasn't happy about what I'd just seen. She came running over to me.

"Johnny, I want to you to meet my big brother, Jack."

That was a surprise. "Your brother? I didn't even know you had a brother."

Susan giggled. "And there are a few other things you don't know about me yet, like I'm a lousy cook, but all in good time."

Brother Jack offered me his hand and I shook it, saying, "Nice to meet you, Jack, but I have to tell you a minute ago I was ready to knock your block off."

Jack grinned Susan's mischievous grin and said, "I'm glad to hear that. I sure wouldn't want to think my sister was hanging around with a guy who wouldn't defend her honor." Then he sized me up, adding, "And ya know, I think you could do it, too. I'd rather we were friends."

"Me, too, Jack. Me, too."

Susan was hanging onto my arm. "Okay, now that we've got all the hoof stomping and antler rattling done, let's get down to business. You two can get acquainted some other time."

Jack nodded. "Sure, Sis. What is it you need to know about lighthouses at this hour of the night that couldn't wait 'til morning?"

Susan looked up at me and I said, "We need the locations of all the lighthouses north of here to, say, San Francisco."

He nodded again. "Well, as long as you aren't planning to blow them up, I can give you a list. With the likelihood of war in Europe growing stronger every day, the US armed forces are getting very protective of their facilities."

"So they are, but it seems to me they ought to be doing a whole lot more than putting up a few fences and getting Congress to vote on yet another selective service act, which I'm pretty sure is going to pass this time. Even with that, we're nowhere near a war footing."

Jack cocked his head to the side and said, "You sound like someone who might have some experience with the military."

"Yeah, I did a few years with the Army Intelligence Police."

"I kind of thought it might be something like that. You don't see many of those Longines European pilot watches a lot of our intelligence guys wear. What was your rank when you separated from the service?"

Jack was a sharp fellow. Few people would recognize my wristwatch as one of the unique Longines chronographs obtained from the Czech Air Force by the US intelligence services during the late 1920s and early 1930s. They were incredibly accurate, big enough to read at a glance in low light, and rugged enough to stand up to being used as brass knuckles if the need arose.

I said, "Oh, they got carried away and gave me a field promotion to major and it stuck."

He feigned worry. "Oh, oh. I'd better get another promotion before they call you back. It would be humiliating to have salute the guy who's dating my sister."

"Don't worry about that. They aren't going to want me back. They're still trying to straighten out the intelligence messes I created when they had me before. Anyway, to answer your first question, I've got nothing against lighthouses that would make me want blow one up."

"Then come on in and I'll make you a list."

The building we walked into was divided into apartments serving as base housing for bachelor officers. His apartment was near the front of the building and had what was probably a very nice daylight view of the lighthouse and the ocean beyond it.

Jack sat down at a small kitchenette table and began a list on a piece of binder paper. I used the time to take a look at the photos on his living room wall. They were all either of boats or men at sea. I gathered Jack was a photographer, and from the evidence in front of me, a pretty fair one at that.

Ten minutes later he handed me a list with about a dozen names on it. The first few were:

-- Piedras Blancas Light
-- Point San Luis Light
-- Point Arguello Light
-- Point Conception Light
-- Santa Barbara Light

Jack also handed me a tourist map showing the locations of all the lighthouses between San Diego and the Oregon border. He underlined the words "Santa Barbara Light" and said, "This is where you are right now. Everything above that line is north of here."

"Got it. How accessible are these lights? I mean could someone get to them in a regular sedan or something like that?"

He studied the map for a minute. "That's a good question. The next two north of here—Point Conception and Point Arguello—are a long way from the highway and the roads are rough. A good driver could probably make it to them, but it would take a lot of time, particularly at night, because you'd need to drive a dozen or more miles on rough dirt roads.

"The first one that's easy to reach is the next one on the list." He pointed to the words, "Point San Luis Light."

"The main highway goes pretty close to Avila Beach and the light is just the other side of the little village there. Getting to the light still requires driving on a narrow access road that was paved once, but hasn't been maintained. Still, if you're looking for the closest light that can be reached in an automobile, like Santa Barbara, San Luis would be my choice."

I nodded. "Makes sense to me. How far to Avila Beach?"

"It's at least a hundred miles, so two to two-and-a-half hours."

"Then that's our next stop. Thanks, Jack. I really appreciate this."

"I know you do. Susan wouldn't have asked for the help if she didn't know you really needed it." He paused for a minute, and then turned to Susan. "Are you going with Johnny tonight?"

"Yes I am, Jack, and that's my idea, not his. Johnny suggested I might be better off waiting here in Santa Barbara for him, but I nixed that."

Jack looked at me and I shrugged, saying, "Don't worry Jack, we're just going to observe. I'll keep Angel safe."

He nodded. "I'm counting on that. Then someday when we can sit back and open a couple of bottles of beer I hope you can tell me what this is all about."

"Count on it. I'd do it right now, but we're a little short on time."

"Okay, follow me and I'll let you out. And, if you don't mind," he added with a wink, "I'll give my little sister a hug and a kiss before you leave, and you can repay me for the light list by bringing her over to see me more often. She's always off cavorting with some guy she calls her Hollywood Private Eye."

I said, "Count on that, too, Jack."

We backtracked to State Street and rejoined Highway One there. As we headed northwest through town, Susan said, "I'm sorry for playing that trick on you, Johnny. That was mean, but I knew what Jack would do when he opened the gate and I couldn't resist. I hope you aren't angry with me."

"No, Angel, I'm not angry with you. Besides, who you choose to kiss and hug is up to you."

I could hear the smile in her voice as she said, "Well, you could always change that, you know."

"I suppose I could try, but at the moment we have other fish to fry. Please keep an eye on the oncoming traffic to make sure we don't pass the Kipchumbas coming back from wherever they've been."

"Yes, sir, ya old grump."

"And please reach back into the fridge and grab me a stick of beef jerky."

"Okay, but I don't know how you can eat that stuff."

"It's great for times like this. All that chewing makes me forget I'm hungry."

Once we were out of town, I pushed a little harder on the gas pedal and about two-thirty I spotted the turnoff for Avila Beach. It was a two lane paved road to our left called Avila Beach Drive.

The town—if you could call it that—of Avila Beach is about three miles from the highway. According to Jack's map the route to the San Luis light involved making a right turn onto Diablo Canyon Road, which was just past a large beach west of town. Immediately after that we needed to make a left turn onto Lighthouse Road. Then, after what looked like a mile or more of road that did a lot of twisting and turning through some low hills, we would come to the Point San Luis Lighthouse.

I made the turn into Diablo Canyon and pulled onto the shoulder opposite Lighthouse Road. It was barely a single lane wide and though paved sometime in the dim past, it was now full of the kinds of ruts and chuckholes that smash oil pans and poke holes in gas tanks. That was all I could tell about the road because it was dark as pitch out there. The only other thing I could see was Susan's face in the low light from the instrument panel. She was giving me a questioning look.

"Angel, this is a lousy situation. With all the twists and turns in that road, we would be an easy target for anyone who saw us coming from the lighthouse. The only way to get to the lighthouse without anyone seeing us would be to negotiate the road with our headlights off, which is a good way to bottom out in a chuckhole and bust the oil pan. And the worst part about it all might be that we manage to make our way out there in the dark only to find out this wasn't the lighthouse the Kipchumbas were headed for, if they are actually headed for a lighthouse."

Susan nodded her understanding of the situation. "Then what do you want to do, Johnny?"

I turned my head and looked over my left shoulder in the direction of the light. I couldn't see the lighthouse from where we were, but with the heavy fog out to sea, I could see the beam of light reflected by water droplets in the air.

"I think the only thing we can safely do is watch the road out of here to see if they come by. If they do, we can consider ourselves extremely . . ."

"What is it, Johnny?"

Shifting the Chrysler into gear and pulling ahead on Diablo Canyon Road, I said, "Maybe the answer to a prayer. I just saw a pair of headlights moving out there on the lighthouse access road."

The next curve on Diablo Canyon was about an eighth of a mile up the road. Just short of it, I pulled a U-turn, shut off the headlights, and parked alongside the road to find out if the car coming from the lighthouse had an intermittent short in its right tail light wiring.

Twenty

2:45 A.M. – Wednesday – August 14, 1940

Diablo Canyon Road, Avila Beach

Waiting with our engine running and headlights off, I tracked the progress the car moving along Lighthouse Road by the intermittent appearances of its headlights through the trees and between the hills. My plan—or what was currently serving as a plan—was to give the Kipchumbas, if it really was them, just enough time to get back on Avila Beach Drive before I began following them again. I had no intention of losing them twice in one night. The only problem was, whoever was driving the car threw me a curveball when they got to Diablo Canyon Road and turned left instead of right toward town. They were coming right at us.

Still not knowing whether or not the car coming in our direction was the Jag, I did the only thing I could think of that might be enough of a surprise to keep the Kipchumbas from realizing it was us they were passing. I said, "Get down on the floorboard, Angel," shifted the Chrysler into gear, stomped on the gas pedal, and simultaneously pulled the headlight switch on.

We shot out into the road, our headlights aimed right into the windshield of what I only then identified as a Jaguar. I kept my foot on the gas and waited until the last minute to swerve away from what must have seemed to the Kipchumbas as a certain collision.

I had a sense of the Jaguar swerving onto the shoulder, but I was too busy trying to stay out of a culvert on the other side of the road to pay much attention to what they were doing. It wasn't until I made a wide left turn onto Avila Beach Drive and pulled to the right into a beach parking area that I could look back up Diablo Canyon Road.

There was just enough time to see two dim tail lights—the right one flickering—disappear around a bend in the road. That was no surprise. The Kipchumbas had been up to no good at the lighthouse and now someone—hopefully they didn't know who—had nearly run them off the road. It figured they'd want to get the hell out of there as fast as they could.

What I did find surprising, however, was Susan. She had ignored my warning to get down on the floorboards and was still sitting on the passenger side of the seat looking up Diablo Canyon.

Susan saw me looking at her and shaking my head. She said, "I know, we lost them again."

"That's not what's upsetting me."

Looking puzzled, she said, "What then?"

"Angel, in situations like this—should I ever be dumb enough to allow you into another one—if I tell you to get down on the floorboard or something like that, you damned well do it! You could have been killed if they'd been on to us and started shooting."

"But that didn't happen. They . . ."

"We got lucky. That's what happened. If we hadn't, I could just as easily be headed for Santa Barbara to tell Jack he doesn't have to worry about saluting his brother-in- . . . that I just got his sister killed. I don't ever want to do that. I won't . . . I will not . . ." I was so damned angry I literally ran out of words.

Susan put her hand on my arm. "I'm sorry, Johnny. You are absolutely right to be upset with me. I'll do exactly what you tell me to do next time. I promise."

Taking a deep breath, I sighed and said. "It's okay, Angel. I apologize for losing my temper. I don't know why, but the thought of anything happening to you just . . . I don't know. It just upsets me beyond reason."

I heard rather than saw Susan's smile in the darkness. "Now maybe you understand why I get upset when I think you're in danger. It's because we've done something stupid and fallen in love."

"Oh, now you're really getting off the beam. That's . . ."

"When you start talking about Jack being your brother-in-law, I'd say that qualifies as being pretty close to the beam."

"I never said . . . I . . ."

"Yes you did, not more than fifteen seconds ago. There's no question about that. Now, I know you were upset when you said it, so I won't bring the subject up again unless you do. I'll just forget it happened. Okay?"

"Yes. No, I mean no. Oh, hell. I don't know what I mean anymore."

Susan gave me a kiss square on the lips that got my attention and then some. After that she said, "Let's use this time to figure out what we should be doing now to catch up with the Kipchumbas. We can talk about that mushy stuff later. All right?"

Turning to look back up Diablo Canyon, I said, "All right. I wish I knew if they turned up the canyon because they knew we were there somehow, or if they intended to go that way all along.

"All I can tell from Jack's rough map is that Diablo Canyon Road does a lot of twisting and turning and may or may not end up in a berg called Los Osos. I can't imagine why they'd go that way— the highway would be much quicker—but regardless of the reason, we can't go after them for the same reasons I didn't want to go up the lighthouse road. It's a great place for a trap."

A point of light moving just off the beach below us caught my eye as Susan said, "I'm still wondering why they went to the lighthouse to begin with. If they met somebody there, where is that person now? The Kipchumbas are the only ones who've come out of the area."

Gesturing toward the point of light, which was now crossing the bay toward open water, I said, "They're not quite the only ones. If the map Jack gave us is anywhere near accurate, it looks like a person could get to the lighthouse from that beach down there by climbing the end of the breakwater where it runs into the cliff. The boat you see out there is just leaving the bay. It's a small commercial fishing boat and it's too big to take right up to the beach, but I'll bet they have a skiff in tow for getting to and from the beach."

Susan leaned forward to look at the departing point of light. "Okay, so it is possible they met someone at the lighthouse who is now aboard that boat. What does that tell us?"

"Nothing. My original hope was that the Kipchumbas would lead us to wherever they're hiding so we could call Detective Sergeant Salvino and have his boys haul 'em off to the slammer on suspicion of murder and other assorted crimes. Instead we spent an entire night following them around and we haven't got one bit of information we didn't have before."

She held up my notebook and it took me a minute to remember I'd handed it to her in San Pedro about eight hours ago for some reason I couldn't remember at the moment. "Oh yes we do. We have the license number of their car. Could your cop pal track them down from that?"

"He probably couldn't track them down to a particular location, but he could put out a statewide all-points bulletin. Somebody might spot them somewhere. I don't have a lot of confidence in that happening, but it seems to be all we've got left at the moment. The only other thing we could do is an even longer shot."

Resting her head on my shoulder again, Susan said, "What's that, Darling?"

"We could take the highway up to this Los Osos place and see if they show up there. The problem with that is I don't know how many routes there are from Diablo Canyon to the highway. Those hills are probably loaded with little roads that end up at Highway 101. We could easily wait at the wrong one and never catch even a glimpse of them. I think the best plan is heading back to Santa Barbara where we can get some sleep and look at all this in the morning again."

Yawning, Susan snuggled closer and said, "I vote for that plan."

"Okay, the ayes, or yawns, have it. I'm just anxious to get back to civilization where the streets are paved, have names, and go in a straight line."

Susan mumbled something that sounded like, "City boy."

"And proud of it."

Santa Barbara was about a hundred miles back down Highway 101 and even without much traffic to speak of the trip took about two hours. We rolled into the Hyatt parking lot around five-thirty A.M., and by five-forty-five we were back in the same suite we'd occupied twenty-four hours earlier. A bed has never felt better.

10:30 A.M. – Thursday – August 15, 1940

Hyatt Hotel – 1111 Highway 101, Santa Barbara

It took nearly all the willpower I could muster to roll out of bed Thursday morning. Susan had already taken a shower and called room service for coffee. After a quick shower of my own and some fresh clothes, I joined her out on the balcony.

She poured a cup of coffee for me from the carafe room service brought up and I sat at the small table and stared out at the Pacific Ocean. Susan asked, "How'd you sleep, Darling?"

"Like a log. I don't think I moved for six hours."

With a grin she said, "I can vouch for that."

"Don't get smart with me, Angel. I've only had a sip or two of coffee, so I'm not responsible for my actions yet."

"I wouldn't think of getting smart with you, but speaking of smart, do you have any new thoughts on the Kipchumbas this morning?"

"If you mean do I have any thoughts about what I'd like to do to them, yes. If you're referring to thoughts about where they might be, no.

"I've been running around in circles on this case for ten days and I know who stole the elephant and I'm pretty sure who killed two others who were undoubtedly involved in the theft, but I don't have a speck of evidence to prove any of it. In fact, I don't even know where the suspects are. I'm seriously thinking it's about time to throw in the towel and tell Bette to put someone else to work on this mess."

Apparently that idea was disturbing to Susan. With a troubled look on her face, she said, "How about giving your cop buddy a little time to track them down? You said he might get lucky if someone saw the Jaguar."

I nodded. "Okay, I'll call him in a little while and compare notes to see what he's come up with in the past twenty-four hours. Then I'll make a decision. That okay?"

"Yes, that's fine, Johnny. I don't mean to tell you what to do. I just didn't think you were a quitter, that's all."

Glaring at her, I said, "There's a point in some cases where quitting is just plain good sense. These Africans have this scheme worked out so well that it's going to take catching them red-handed to put them away for their crimes. There are a lot more cops than there are Johnny Spicers, so let the cops do some of the work for a change."

Susan just nodded. I guess I was disappointing her, but you can't keep knocking on the same door and expect somebody different to open it.

Then she leaned over and took a close look at the patch on the side of my head. "How does your head feel?"

"Alright, except when I bump it, and I try not to do that very often."

With a grin that usually is a sign that some teasing is about to take place, she said, "Well, that's promising. You actually do show some common sense now and then. I think I'll put a new dressing on it."

She went in and returned with some gauze pads, a roll of adhesive tape, and a pair of those blunt-tipped medical scissors designed to cut tape without cutting the patient. While Susan was putting the new patch in place she said, "Hey, I just had a swell idea. Let's see if Jack is free to have dinner with us tonight. That would give the two of you a chance get acquainted."

With my mind mostly still on the Kipchumbas and what I might do to find them that I hadn't already tried, I said. "Sure. Maybe we can find a place with good food and a good view."

"I think we're looking at the best view in town right now."

"All right, invite Jack to come over here and, if he doesn't mind, we'll order dinner from room service."

Susan gave that a moment's thought. "All right, this is a pretty classy place, he'd probably get a kick out of it. Just one thing, though."

"You're worried about what he'll think of the sleeping arrangements, right?"

"Well, Jack's no prude and I'm glad we finally got past having two rooms all the time, but I'd rather not be too obvious about it. Let's let him wonder, okay?"

"Sure. Just pack your bag and stash it in the back of the closet, but leave your purse in plain sight. If you don't have a lot of stuff laying around here, he'll figure you're staying at your place."

Susan leaned over and kissed me. "Thanks for understanding, Johnny."

"Sure. Now I think I've had enough coffee to face Salvino. I'll get the telephone."

She popped up like a Jack-in-the-box, saying, "Stay there, Darling. I'll get it for you."

"Thanks, Angel."

She came back with the telephone, set it on the table, and turned to leave. I stopped her saying, "You're welcome to stay and listen in if you want."

"I'd like to, but I don't want to . . ."

I grinned. "Poke your nose where it doesn't belong? It's a little late for that. Sit down and listen to your heart's content."

Susan stuck her tongue out at me and sat while I got the operator to place a person to person call to Sergeant Salvino at the Seventh.

"Yeah, this is Salvino."

"Hi, Nick. How's it going this morning?"

"Well, things weren't particularly great, but now that you're calling, I'm sure everything is going to be just hunky-dory. I hope to hell you've got something useful for me."

"That bad, huh?"

"Yeah, Spicer, that bad."

"I know I'm stating the obvious, but it's becoming increasingly apparent to me that we're up against a couple of smooth professionals with a slick racket and a sick sense of humor."

"Yeah, I got the same feeling, except what's with the sick sense of humor?"

I told Salvino about our close brush with the snake in San Pedro. I ended the story by saying, "I know death by poisonous bug or snake isn't unheard of, but it sure isn't something you see every day."

"Thank God for that! You sure that was the Kipchumbas' work?"

"Pretty sure. First, besides you, there isn't anyone else around who'd like to see me get snake-bit and second, they conveniently set things up so they could check on whether or not the snake did his job. Fortunately, I managed to convince them he did, or they just got tired of waiting for me at the meeting place they suggested for last night. Otherwise, I wouldn't have the license plate number of the car they're driving."

"Seriously? You're getting' pretty good at playin' policeman, Spicer. But what do you mean the meeting place they suggested for last night? You had a meeting set up with the Kipchumbas and you didn't bother to tell me?

"It was kind of a last minute deal. Missus Kipchumba called and told my answering service that if I wanted the elephant back I had to meet them at the Point Fermin lighthouse down in San Pedro."

"Well, in the spirit of cooperation with brother law enforcement officers, you might have mentioned that little detail."

"I never seriously figured they were actually going to meet me there. I was pretty sure they were up to something that required either getting me out of Hollywood or into San Pedro. The most obvious explanation was they were setting a trap for me. I figured I could handle that without your help, and without a bunch of cops stumbling over each other out there, it might be an opportunity to follow them for a change and find out where they're hiding out."

In a tone dripping with sarcasm, Salvino said, "Oh. Well, that's different. Never mind their license number, just give me the address they led you to."

I ignored his attempt at humor. "They are driving a recent model dark green Jaguar sedan, or what used to be called an SS Saloon before they added Jaguar to the name."

"That's a British car, right?"

"Yup, as British as you can get without a cup of tea in your hand. Right-hand drive and the works. The model year is probably 1939 because that's when the license plates were issued, but it doesn't matter because all of the Jag models between about 1937 and 1940 looked exactly the same."

"What's the plate number?"

"It's got blue San Francisco exposition plates and the digits are two – c as in Charlie – seven – eight – two – one."

He repeated the number back to me and I said, "That's it Detective Sergeant Salvino. Now tell me how quickly we can expect you to have the Kipchumbas in custody."

"You're a regular Charlie McCarthy ain't ya, Spicer?"

"I can always hope. When last seen, the Kipchumbas and their Jaguar were bouncing along a back country road called Diablo Canyon up the coast in San Luis Obispo County near Avila Beach. That was around two-thirty or three this morning."

"Oh? How would you happen to know that?"

"Because I saw them." I described the previous night's adventure after following the Kipchumbas up the coast from Point Fermin.

Salvino's sigh came through the usual long distance telephone static. "You don't know what I'd give to have the freedom you've got."

"And you don't know how much I envy you your resources. If we could combine our advantages, the crime rate would be cut in half overnight."

"Yeah, and if wishes were fishes, or however that goes. What's your next step?"

Susan had been paying close attention to my end of the conversation, so now was my opportunity to make a point with her. "Sergeant, I'm all out of steps. I was hoping you'd have an idea or two."

Salvino sighed again. "Tell you what, Spicer. I'll put out an all-points bulletin for that British car. Call me back first thing tomorrow morning and let's see what I can come up with. We could get lucky."

I winked at Susan again and said, "Thanks, Sergeant. I gotta prove to someone I'm not a quitter."

Salvino grunted and I hung up. I looked down at the telephone and hoped to hell he came up with something useful.

Twenty-One

6:00 P.M. – Thursday – August 15, 1940

Hyatt Hotel – 1111 Highway 101, Santa Barbara

Susan's brother knocked on the door to our suite promptly at six. Walking over to answer his knock I looked at Susan. She was sitting in an armchair looking like she was about to come down with a case of the giggles.

I opened the door and said, "Welcome, Jack. I'm glad you could make it."

He was dressed in his Coast Guard whites and looking very shipshape. "Thanks, Johnny. I'm glad I could come, although it's a little embarrassing for a sailor, especially a Coast Guard sailor, to admit he doesn't already have a dinner date on such short notice."

Shaking the hand he offered, I said, "Don't worry. I won't tell. I don't know about your sister over there, though. She's behaving a little nutty tonight."

Jack laughed. "How could you tell?"

"Good point. Here let me take your hat—or cover if you want to do it by the book."

As I set his officer's cap on a small table near the door, Jack gave Susan a hug and she bestowed a kiss on his cheek. Then Susan took over the hostess duties, saying, "We have Lowenbrau Pilsner cooling on ice. Is that okay with you gentlemen?"

Jack looked in my direction and raised his eyebrows. "Wow, I was expecting something more pedestrian, like Falstaff or Acme, but you're pouring the best—imported, even!"

You bet! What more could a guy ask for?"

Susan said, "Are you referring to a woman who knows how to properly serve beer or Lowenbrau Pilsner?"

"I was referring to you, Angel."

As Susan poured, Jack said, "I'm anxious to find out how things went last night, but first, I notice you often refer to Susan as 'Angel.' There has to be a story behind that somewhere, if it's not too personal."

I looked at Susan and she made a 'go ahead' gesture, so I said, "Well, that goes back to when we first met. I was at her clinic recovering from a bullet wound to the head, and when I first came out of the anesthetic after my surgery, Susan was sitting in a chair in front of the window reading a magazine and keeping an eye on me. Now you have to understand my vision was pretty foggy at that point and I was looking around trying to figure out if I was dead or alive.

"Then I spotted a beautiful woman—Susan—in her white uniform with the sun behind her creating a sort of aura and concluded I must be dead because she had to be an angel. Eventually the error of my logic was made clear to me, but she's been 'Angel' to me ever since."

Jack laughed. "What a terrific story! Imagine, my little sister mistaken for an angel!"

Susan had just set his beer down on the coffee table between us. "Keep it up big brother and you'll be wearing your Lowenbrau Pilsner instead of drinking it."

I said, "Maybe we ought to move on to our trip to Point San Luis light last night."

Jack looked up. "You ended up at Point San Luis?"

"Yes. As you suggested, we skipped the next two lights north of here and went directly to Avila Beach, but I'm getting ahead of the story. For this to make sense you have to know what and who we were looking for."

While I filled in some background about the Ivonya-Ngia Tembo and the Kipchumbas' scheme for reselling the antique statuette over and over again to unsuspecting buyers at a hundred grand a pop, Susan snuggled in next to me on the loveseat. I concluded the story with a slightly cleaned up version of our encounter with the Kipchumbas' on Diablo Canyon Road.

When I finished the tale, Jack said, "You were smart not to follow those folks into Diablo Canyon. If they're as dangerous as you think, they would have had their choice of hundreds of places to lay a trap for you. Also, catching them returning to the highway would have taken a lot of luck. There are several ways they could have done it, which is probably why they left via that route in the first place."

Susan said, "I'm curious. Johnny thinks some people in a boat we saw crossing the bay were coming from the lighthouse because it looked like they could climb up to the light by way of the breakwater."

Jack nodded, "Johnny was right about climbing up to the light by way of the breakwater. Somebody even dug out some steps to make the climb easier. As for somebody meeting your people up there, it would be a good place. There's a keeper on duty there, but he's an older fellow and I doubt if he would hear or see a car approaching at night if you were careful how you did it."

I said, "If the Coast Guard is concerned about the security of their facilities, that light would be a good place to start."

"I already made myself a mental note to point that out to the area commandant."

As our conversation wandered around from one subject to another I found myself enjoying Jack. He was smart, quick and had his sister's sense of humor. Even though I was getting hungry, I hated to interrupt the proceedings when Susan passed out copies of the room service menu, suggesting we ought to get our order in.

Since I'd peeked at the menu earlier, I had already made my dinner choices: Jumbo Shrimp Cocktail, Cobb-Style Garden Salad, Grilled Pork Chops Marinara, and Cherry Cobbler. The Chops Marinara were two pork chops and a pile of spaghetti smothered in a rich tomato sauce that had some zest to it.

Jack turned out to be a meat and potatoes guy, ordering Minestrone, a huge New York Steak that came with a baked potato almost as big as a football and drowned in sour cream and butter. He also added a side dish of cauliflower in a Cheddar cheese sauce. His chosen desert was apple pie. I took one look at all that food and figured the Coast Guard must run him ragged in order for him to keep his slim shape.

Susan also ordered a Cobb-Style Garden Salad as I had, but for her entrée, she picked fillet of Halibut with a brown rice and a vegetable medley. Vegetable medley I found out was what you got in a restaurant around Wednesday or Thursday when the chef throws all the leftover vegetables from the past week into the same pot.

So I called room service and placed our order around seven. Dinner arrived a few minutes before eight. Our room service guys quickly set a table just inside the balcony doors so we could enjoy the view. They even added a candle as a crowning touch. When they left, Susan walked around the room shutting off all the lamps but one so the lights wouldn't reflect in the glass doors and ruin the view.

Then Susan assigned our seats. Jack, because he was our guest of honor, sat in the chair facing out onto the balcony and the harbor beyond it. I was to sit at his left and she sat on his right. I let him do the honors of holding Susan's chair for her, after which I sat and he remained standing, holding his beer stein up in a toast. He said, "To my little sister, the angel, and my new friend Johnny; may we all . . ."

In the next four or five seconds, several things happened almost simultaneously. I heard a faint "pop" some distance away followed by a "tink" that sounded like somebody lightly tapping a spoon on a drinking glass. Then Jack staggered a step to his right with a surprised expression on his face and fell to the floor.

Susan looked from Jack to me and I pointed to the floor. This time she did as she was told. I drew my Smith and Wesson, stepped to one side of the door, and looked out into the night. A raspy exhaust caught my attention and I saw a Jaguar that closely resembled the Kipchumbas' scoot away from the curb in front of the hotel. The Jag heading west toward State Street and winking its faulty right rear tail light at me.

By that time Susan had Jack's uniform shirt open and was using one of the Hyatt's fine linen napkins as a compress, trying to stop what seemed like a lot of blood pouring out of his chest. She saw me putting my Smith and Wesson back in its holster and said, "Call an ambulance, Johnny. Tell 'em we've got a gunshot victim and to make it fast."

The Santa Barbara telephone operator I got knew exactly what to do and quickly had an ambulance rushing toward the Hyatt. No more than two minutes later I could hear wail of a siren heading our way.

Susan said, "Thanks, now I need your help here."

I knelt on the floor next to her and she put my hands on the bloody napkin. "Put constant pressure on that wound until I get back. I'm calling the emergency ward at Cottage Hospital so they can get set up for him.

While I did as she instructed Susan placed her telephone call. She immediately identified herself as a nurse and started spouting medical terminology that I hoped the people she was talking to understood better than I did. Apparently they did because she didn't have to repeat any of it and sounded as pleased as one could expect under the circumstances.

Then she was back on the floor beside me to take over the pressure applying duties. "It sounds like the ambulance just pulled up out in front. Get the door open for them, will you?"

Opening the suite door, I turned to Susan and said, "The police will be on their way, too, and they'll have lots of questions to be answered."

I had turned my back to the door while talking to a Susan so I didn't see the first man into the room ahead of the ambulance crew. I only heard a voice say, "You bet I've got questions."

Turning around I looked into a friendly face, that of Detective Lieutenant John Walsh from the Santa Barbara Police Department. I knew Walsh from when I'd been shot last November by a nutcase with a very large revolver. I said, "Well, if they're the right ones I've got answers for you."

He offered his hand to shake, but I held up both of mine which were covered with Jack's blood. "Well, if anybody had to get shot tonight, I'm relieved it isn't you. You've already had your turn as a shooting victim."

The ambulance attendants relieved Susan at Jack's side and I said to John, "I suppose you'd like to know what the hell happened here."

"Yeah. My supervisors don't like it when I turn in blank shooting investigation forms."

I said, "Okay, standby to copy." He got out his notebook and I spent the next twenty minutes telling him what he needed to know, including how to get in touch with Sergeant Salvino for more background on the suspects. I only stopped long enough to talk to Susan as she went out the door behind the ambulance attendants.

She said, "With the right care I think he'll pull through. I'm going with him to be sure he gets that care. At best he's going be out of commission for a while."

"Better out of commission than the alternative. I'll get over to the hospital as soon as I finish up here. Anything else I can do?"

Kissing me on the cheek, she said, "Just say a prayer and get there as soon as you can. I need to lean on you some, Johnny. This is all just now sinking in."

"I'll be there soon, Angel."

As I returned to where Walsh was standing next to the dinner table, he said, "Say, isn't she the nurse . . ."

I grinned. "Yeah, we kinda got to be friends. I'm damned glad she was here."

"Then maybe something good came out of all that after all."

"I don't know if Jack would agree with you. She's his sister."

"Oops."

I nodded and said, "Worse yet, there's no doubt in my mind that the bullet Jack caught was intended for me. I don't know how the Kipchumbas found us, but there was no mistaking that Jaguar sedan parked out front."

Walsh was over at the balcony doors looking at the bullet hole in the glass. He said, "Small caliber, but it must have been a rifle. Not many people can shoot a handgun with any accuracy at that range."

"Yeah, for a job like that a twenty-two caliber target rifle would be a good choice, except they were shooting through a piece of glass. The slug lost some of its velocity getting through that glass, which is likely to save Jack's life."

Looking a little embarrassed, he said, "Speaking of which, you're carrying, aren't you?"

I held my jacket open and said, "Help yourself, John, but I need it back before we leave here."

He slipped the Smith and Wesson out of my shoulder holster, broke it open, and sniffed it. Then he handed the revolver back to me, saying, "Nobody's been shot with that piece tonight."

"Not yet, but if I see the Kipchumbas, that could change. Look, John, I'd like to get over to the hospital. Do you need me here any longer?"

"No. I don't think we even need to bring in a forensic team unless he . . . unless things don't go well for him. I will need to get a witness statement from Susan, though. I may show up at the hospital later tonight to talk with her. Think that would be okay?"

"I think it would be okay. Susan is a strong woman. Now I'll wash my hands and get going."

I came back from the bathroom drying my hands with a towel. "Susan had them take Jack to a place called Cottage Hospital. How do I get there from here?"

"Cut over to State Street and take a left at West Pueblo Street. Cottage is four blocks down on your right, but turn right just beyond the hospital and then make another right on Junipero Street. That will get you to the emergency entrance around back.

"Thanks. I would appreciate it if you could lock up on your way out and I'll check in with you and Salvino in the morning. Okay?"

"You've got it. Good luck!"

Figuring I had John Walsh's blessing, I pushed the speed limit all the way to the hospital and made it in ten minutes. My watch said nine o'clock as I walked through the emergency entrance. I stopped at a reception counter and asked for Jack.

The receptionist, who according to her name tag was Mrs. Carney said, "Would you be Mister Spicer?"

"I am."

"Miss Jackson asked that I send you directly back to her. She's in the emergency ward surgical recovery area. Go through that door and turn right, then go through the door at the end of the hall. She'll be in the third cubicle on your left. Don't forget to put on a surgical mask before you go into the recovery area. The masks are right outside the door."

Susan was sitting in a chair next to an empty bed, but she jumped up when she saw me. We hugged and she held on to me for all she was worth, saying, "Oh, Johnny, I'm so glad you're here. Jack's still in surgery, but it shouldn't be much longer before we know . . . if everything will be okay."

"Okay. Are you all right?"

"Yes, just a little shaken. I was doing fine when there was something helpful I could do, but this sitting around while somebody else takes care of Jack is driving me nuts!" Then she took a deep breath and asked, "How about you? Are you all right?"

"I'm fine, Angel, except it bothers me that Jack took a bullet intended for me. Otherwise I'm okay."

"Intended for you?"

"Yes. The Kipchumbas' Jaguar was pulling away from the curb when I looked out. All they could see from there was a man's silhouette in the window. They figured it had to be me. Unfortunately, it was Jack."

"Oh, God!"

"Yeah, I don't think he'll be accepting anymore dinner invites from me very soon."

She pulled me close again. "Johnny, how are we going to get you somewhere safe where those awful people can't hurt you?"

"I prefer to face this particular problem head on instead of hiding from it. I . . ."

A noise in the hall outside the cubicle made us turn. It was two orderlies pushing a gurney-style bed with a nurse following along. Jack was in the bed.

I got out of the way and let the important people do their jobs. Then Susan talked to the nurse for several moments, after which the nurse left. She promised, however, to be right back.

Susan stepped over to Jack's bed and placed her hand on his forehead. He opened his eyes for a few seconds and said something that included the word "Sis." Then his eyes closed again.

When the nurse came back, Susan came over to me and said, "Janet will be staying here with Jack. Would you mind if we went outside for a few minutes? I need some fresh air."

When we stepped out into the cool night air, I looked around to make sure there weren't any Jaguars of the four-wheel variety hiding in the bushes. Then I lit a Lucky and asked, "Well, what's the verdict? Is Jack gonna be okay?"

She took my arm and looked up at me. "Yes, he'll be fine. The bullet missed hitting anything really important. The rest will heal."

"With all that blood I was afraid . . ."

"A couple of blood vessels were nicked and they would have been serious if we hadn't been able to use compression to slow the bleeding down. Thanks for helping with that."

"I'm glad there was something I could do."

"You were great, Johnny. Really you were."

"Before I forget, Detective Lieutenant Walsh asked if he could stop by the hospital later tonight to get a statement from you. I said I thought it would be okay, but if you don't want to talk to him . . ."

"No that's okay. It will give me something to do while Jack sleeps. Is there anything I shouldn't tell him?"

"I don't think so. I just told him the story and gave him straight answers to his questions."

"Okay."

"Will you be taking Jack to the clinic when he can travel?"

"No. I called his commandant to let him know what happened and he said when Jack could be moved the Coast Guard will transport him to the naval clinic at Port Hueneme down by Oxnard."

I nodded. "How soon do you think?"

Susan thought about that for a moment before saying, "It might be as soon as tomorrow, but more likely on Saturday." After a pause, Susan tightened her grip on my arm and said, "Johnny, I'm going to spend the next few days with Jack. I really feel that's where I need to be."

"I figured that. It is exactly where you need to be."

"Do you know where you'll be?"

"Not yet. That mostly depends on what Sergeant Salvino has learned, if anything, when I talk to him in the morning. Would you like me to take you back to the Hyatt so you can pick up Jack's car and your clothes?"

Still holding on tight, she said, "Yes, if you wouldn't mind, Johnny."

"I don't mind at all, Angel. In fact I'll probably check out of the Hyatt while we're there and drive back to L.A. tonight after we get everything taken care of for you."

There was a sad tone to Susan's voice. "Tonight?"

Nodding, I said, "You need to be here and I need to get my mind back on track and figure out how to take these Kipchumbas out of the game."

Burying her face in my chest, Susan said, "Please be careful, Johnny. Please. I need you. I really, really need you."

"I will, Angel. That's a promise."

Twenty-Two

8:00 A.M. – Friday – August 16, 1940

Spicer Investigations – 1ˢᵗ National Bank Building, Hollywood

Driving back from Santa Barbara Thursday night was the best thing in the world for me. The trip gave me time to think without distractions; something I found difficult to do with Susan sitting next to me. Don't read me wrong on that. Having Susan with me is a pure pleasure, but there are times when a guy needs to do some serious thinking.

During the drive I sized up the enemy and concentrated on how to take advantage of my strengths and the Kipchumbas' weaknesses. What were my strengths? At the top of the list was intelligence—not mine, but all the information I had gathered about them. I knew how they ran their racket, that they had no qualms about killing anybody who got in their way, and I knew some physical details, like their car license and so on.

Further down my list of strengths were Los Angeles and Santa Barbara homicide detectives and their resources. Beneath Sergeant Salvino's gruff exterior was a lot of street savvy, and while John Walsh in Santa Barbara was younger with less experience, he had a strong education in law enforcement or whatever the hell they called it nowadays.

Finally, near the bottom of my strengths list, were my own experience and skills. Realistically, I knew I had the smarts to outfox the Kipchumbas. I just had to figure out how to put my advantages to work.

Okay, what were the Kipchumbas' weaknesses? For one thing, they thought they were clever, a way of thinking that usually leads to overconfidence. For another they tended to go in for complicated methods, which generally have a higher failure rate than simple, straightforward approaches. The snake and the long range shot through a pane of glass with a small caliber rifle were two good examples.

A third weakness was the Kipchumbas' apparent need to kill me, which was a waste of their time and effort. While I had figured out how their racket worked, I had no evidence to prove what I knew, so why waste time trying to kill me at this late point in the game?

The Kipchumbas did have one strength I found a little disturbing though. They had an uncanny way of finding me when I was being pretty careful about not leaving an obvious trail. For example, how did they know I would be in that particular suite at the Santa Barbara Hyatt? They seemed to have some pretty good detective skills of their own, or maybe they were just good at seeing behavior patterns and drawing conclusions from them. If that was it, I needed to be a little less predictable.

The night before I'd told Susan I preferred to face this particular problem head on instead of hiding from it, so I also needed to be more visible. The more time I spent in public places with lots of people around, the fewer opportunities the Kipchumbas would have to shoot blow darts at me or dump rattlesnakes in my car.

I still didn't know if the blow gun was the Kipchumbas' idea or Rolly Boland's. I suspected the later, but its use with marmalade showed how the situation had escalated from a more or less harmless warning to more deadly means. Regardless of whose idea it was, the escalation told me I needed to be more observant and less distracted. So, my new plan called for me to be less predictable, more visible, less distracted, and more observant.

I began the new program by skipping my usual breakfast at home and walking four blocks east from my office on Hollywood Boulevard to the Armstrong and Carlton Restaurant for flannel cakes and sausages. It was an unusually nice day and I enjoyed both the walk and the flannel cakes, especially since nobody tried to kill me on the way.

Next I returned to my office, opened the safe, and removed the envelope containing a tiny scrap of dark blue wool from Bette Davis's Ivonya-Ngia Tembo display case and the ridiculous ransom note Rolly Boland left on my car. I slipped these pieces of evidence into my jacket pocket and pointed my Chrysler toward the Seventh Precinct station on Venice Boulevard.

Inside the station, Salvino spotted me and promptly ushered me back outside, where he said, "Spicer, what gives with you? Every day I've got police officers and deputy sheriffs from other jurisdictions calling me to say somebody else was bumped off and you told 'em to call me. You gettin' paid off by the morticians' union or somethin'?"

"I take it you heard from John Walsh up in Santa Barbara."

"I did, but you're slippin'. This time the poor shmuck who got shot survived."

I lit a Lucky Strike and leaned back against the brick wall of the station. "That's good for a couple of reasons, one being that the intended shmuck was me."

"Yeah, that's what Walsh said. I hope you're takin' steps to be as small a target as you can be."

Exhaling a plume of smoke, I said, "Actually, I'm doing everything I can to be a bigger target."

"That's nuts, Spicer. Just take your girlfriend and get out of town for a while. We'll track these people down and then you can come back."

"For one thing, my girlfriend has nothing to do with this."

"That's not the way I hear it. I hear the guy who got hit last night was her brother."

Salvino took a Camel out of his pack and went through the ritual of patting his pockets looking for a match before I flipped my Zippo and held it out for him.

"And for another thing, unless there's something you're not telling me, your all-points bulletin hasn't turned them up yet. If I make myself visible, the Kipchumbas are more likely to take another swing at me, only this time I'll be expecting it."

"Spicer, using yourself as bait is only gonna get you killed. Now, I wouldn't consider that any great loss, but there's probably somebody—like that little gal in Santa Barbara—who would be happier if you kept on breathing."

Feeling the need for a change of subject, I took the evidence envelopes from my jacket side pocket and handed them over to Salvino. "Here are the two pieces of evidence I promised you. The little piece of cloth in one of those envelopes is a perfect match for the suit I brought you from Rolly Boland's laundry, and the other envelope contains the ransom note he stuck under the windshield wiper of my car."

Next I removed a sheaf of three typewritten pages from my inside jacket pocket. They were stapled together and folded vertically. I handed them to Salvino, saying, "Here's everything I've got on the Kipchumbas. There's nothing in here you don't already know, but sometimes I find it handy to organize this kind of thing on paper so I can refer back to it more easily."

Salvino took the papers grudgingly and I knew he was thinking I'd brought him this stuff because I thought I might not be around to do it later. There might be a little something to that. Better safe than sorry.

"Spicer, I wasn't kidding. You keep poking a stick into the hornets' nest and sooner or later you're gonna get stung."

"Well, Sarge, if that happens maybe you'll stop getting telephone calls about all the havoc I leave in my wake." Tilting my hat a little to take the pressure off the patch Susan put on to keep anything important from leaking out of my head, I said, "See you around, Salvino," and walked to my car at the curb.

I looked back as I opened the door and Nick was still standing there. He gave me a small nod. I gave him a casual version of a military salute in return and pointed the Chrysler back to Hollywood.

Driving back up Highland, I thought about my next move. Where does one go in Hollywood if one wants to be seen by crazy killers from Kenya, or wherever the hell the Kipchumbas were from? The Zebra Room at the Town House?

I was smiling over that poor attempt at humor when it reminded me of another advantage I had over the Kipchumbas. Because of their skin color most restaurants, night clubs, and other establishments in town were closed to them. I could go anywhere and they could not. The same would apply to the hotel or apartment where they were staying in Los Angeles. I wasn't sure how to use that to my advantage yet, but it was something to keep in mind.

In keeping with my new policy of being more observant and less distracted, I was driving with one eye on the rearview mirror, and just after I crossed Wilshire the new policy paid off. I caught just a glimpse of a brightly lit and distinctive Jaguar headlight three cars behind me.

Now that I had the tiger—or Jaguar—by the tail; what do I do with him? According to my new plan, what I do is the unexpected. The next cross street was Sixth and I turned a quick right onto it, and then pulled a U-turn that left me half a block up Sixth facing back toward Highland.

Not more than a second after I pulled to the curb, the Jaguar sped around the corner just as I had done. Joseph was driving and, and, through the Jag's windshield, I saw his eyes go wide when he spotted me sitting there facing the opposite direction. I gave him a friendly wave as he went by. Since I'd made him anyway, the logical thing for Kipchumba to do at that point was to make a U-turn and pull to the curb a few cars behind me so he could continue following when I pulled out.

I watched him in the rearview, but he just kept going. Apparently I had flustered him. Good! Now he could find me all over again. As I pulled out and prepared to turn back onto Highland, something about the Jag's image in my mirror flashed in my mind. The tail lights were on. There wasn't anything unusual about that. When I was in the Army and stationed in Europe I noticed that folks over there often drove with their lights on during the day to make themselves more visible to other drivers.

No, what was unusual about the Jag in my mirror was that the right tail light was no longer flashing on and off and it seemed like both lights were brighter than they had been, even in the light of day.

Either the wiring problem had fixed itself, which with a British car wasn't likely, or somewhere along the line since last night the Kipchumbas had gotten the wiring fixed. I wondered where they might have gotten that done. Joseph didn't look to me like the type who was handy with a wrench and a screwdriver, and I doubted the average repair shop would touch the thing with a ten-foot pole. So where does one take one's exotic European sport sedan when it needs repair?

In this instance, one would take it to a place like Los Angeles British Autos, a dealership in Beverly Hills that sold and serviced Jaguars, Rolls Royces, and other British cars. Since I was pretty sure there were no other Jaguar dealerships between here and San Francisco, the odds were good Joseph had gone there this morning to get his tail light fixed.

The only reason I knew where L.A. British Autos was or even that it existed is that I occasionally go over there to look around their showroom until they throw me out for drooling on their cars. I pointed the Chrysler west toward Beverly Hills to see if they'd had the pleasure of meeting Mister Joseph Kipchumba this morning.

Then I had another brilliant thought. Why had the Kipchumbas suddenly found it urgent to have the repair made? They probably didn't even know the problem existed unless someone pointed it out to them. Also, an intermittent tail light seemed like something that could wait until more pressing matters were resolved . . . unless . . . unless one of L.A.'s finest had stopped them and issued an equipment citation. The last thing the Kipchumbas needed was anything that made them stand out more than they already did. Now there was an advantage I might be able to take advantage of.

I pulled into the Shell gasoline station at Wilshire and Doheny to use their public telephone. When I got Salvino on the line, I told him I had encountered Joseph Kipchumba and what I suspected about the Kipchumbas suddenly getting the tail light wiring fixed because a cop had stopped them.

The Sergeant said, "That could be, especially with a Negro driving an expensive automobile, but it seems unlikely because we have an all-points bulletin out for that car."

"It's still possible, though, especially if the cop who wrote the citation hadn't seen the APB yet. Those things take a little time to circulate."

"I suppose that's true, but it would take a lot of manpower to check all the citations written by the LAPD since last night. Tell you what, though, I'll see if I can get somebody here to start with our citation log and I'll ask the Sixth if they can spare someone to go through their citations."

"Thanks, Nick. If they got a ticket, we might get an address from the car's registration. Even the location where the citation was issued might tell us something we don't know."

"Yeah, but just remember what I told you earlier. I don't want to be filling out any forms about your untimely demise."

"I'll do my best to save you from having to do all that laborious paperwork, Nick."

Los Angeles British Autos occupied a two-story building on Santa Monica Boulevard in the heart of Beverly Hills. It was high-priced real estate for southern California, but the owners apparently figured being right in their customers' backyard was worth the price.

The building was brick and had large windows across the fronts of both floors. A swanky brass plaque near the entrance read:

LOS ANGELES BRITISH AUTOS
9873 S. Santa Monica Boulevard
Beverly Hills

I pulled to the curb in front of the place and walked in like I owned it. The first person I saw was a fellow I'd talked with so many times we were on a first name basis.

He said, "Hiya, Johnny! You finally decide to move up in the world and get yourself a Jaguar?"

"Sure, Allen. Wrap up a gold-plated one."

"Say, I'm glad you stopped in. I've got something really swell to show you. Come over here."

I followed him to a smaller showroom off to the right of the main room. There, a highly polished black roadster with paint that looked a foot deep reflected small overhead spotlights. Allen stood there letting me look for a moment before saying, "Well, what do you think?"

"I think it's beautiful, but the badge above the grille says Triumph. I thought they were out of business."

Allen smiled his salesman's smile. "They were *almost* out of business, but fate stepped in and saved the day. Take a good look, my friend. You are admiring a brand new Triumph Dolomite Roadster, and it is the only one in the United States!"

"Well, how about that. Why did they call it dolomite? I thought dolomite was a pile of rocks or something."

"Dolomite, my friend, is an exquisite and rare pink crystal. Since the new Triumph is also rare and exquisite, it seems like an excellent choice."

I gave him a skeptical look. "What's under the bonnet?"

"The Dolomites are available with one of two engines, a one-point-eight liter four cylinder and a larger, more powerful two liter six cylinder engine like this one has. Suspension, of course, is traditional Triumph and feels as if you're riding on rails."

"I'm not even gonna ask what you want for it?"

"Well, Johnny, to tell the truth . . ."

Grinning, I interrupted, "Yeah. Try that for a change."

He glowered at me and continued, "To tell the truth, I'm not sure this car isn't already sold. We've had some offers, and if the dealership decided to accept one . . . well, it's gone and we'll just have to wait for the next one."

"It is definitely a beauty. I'd love to do a few laps around a course in it."

Allen laughed. "They won't even let me do that!"

I almost said I wasn't surprised, but decided to get down to business. "Allen, actually I'm here on business today."

That threw him. "Oh? I thought you were a private detective. What business do you have that involves us?"

"I'm interested in knowing whether or not a fellow brought an SS Saloon in this morning for a tail light wiring repair."

Allen gave me a sour expression. "Yes, he did, and I suspected there was something fishy about him from the moment he came in."

Giving him an innocent look, I said, "Oh? Why was that?"

Lowering his voice, he said, "The man is a Negro. I don't think I need to tell you we get very few colored customers. Oh, he talked good, with very proper English and all, but I ask you, where the hell would a Negro get the kind of money it takes to buy an SS Saloon? I can't even afford one of those!"

I thought it must have been very humiliating for someone like Allen to be in the position of having to serve a Negro customer, but that was neither here nor there. I said, "Do you have a work order with his address on it? Or by chance did he pay by check?"

Allen thought the part about a Negro paying by check was funny. After laughing sarcastically to show me how funny he thought it was, Allen said, "The service department didn't make out a work order. In fact, the fellow wasn't even charged for the repair. It was only a loose ground wire and they had it fixed in just a few minutes. The boss thought it was better to get him out of here before a real customer came in and got the wrong idea."

I couldn't help wondering what he thought the wrong idea was, but I stuck to business. "Was there anything else about the man or the car that you particularly noticed?"

"Nothing that comes to mind." After a momentary pause, Allen said, "No, wait. There was one thing. I didn't see it, but one of the fellows in the shop said he found the original invoice for the car in the trunk and he was surprised to see that it was purchased at a dealership in London and shipped over here at the new owner's expense. Naturally, being a dealership, we don't see many cars like that."

I thanked Allen for his time and walked out, feeling a strong need to be anywhere but Beverly Hills. Then I spotted my old friend, Joseph Kipchumba, parked up the block. I thought about walking up there and knocking on his window to be sociable, but I wasn't feeling all that sociable, so I slid behind the wheel of my Chrysler, made a U-turn, and headed northeast on Santa Monica toward Hollywood.

Twenty-Three

12:00 P.M. – Friday – August 16, 1940

Northbound – South Santa Monica Boulevard, Beverly Hills

I made a point of glaring at Joseph Kipchumba as I drove past the Jaguar, but my glare was wasted. That's a shame because it was a great glare. My glare was wasted because Kipchumba wasn't there to see it. I presumed he ducked down in the seat so I couldn't see him. Oh well, it was his loss.

Continuing on Santa Monica Boulevard, I watched my rearview mirror expecting to see the Jaguar pull out and follow me. When it didn't by the time I reached the end of the block, I made another U-turn and drove back to Los Angeles British Autos.

Kipchumba wasn't playing the game right. I was the one who was supposed to do the unpredictable, not him. I parked in the same spot I'd used earlier and looked through the large glass windows on the first floor. Nothing was moving among the shiny sheet metal in the showroom.

I got out of the driver-side door and moved cautiously toward the showroom entrance, my Smith and Wesson firmly in my right hand. I pushed the door open, and just as I did, I heard another door slam somewhere at the back of the building. I moved in that direction, using some very expensive automobiles for cover. One slug from a large caliber pistol could do several hundred dollars' worth of damage in there without trying very hard.

From my previous visits to Los Angeles British Autos I knew there was a hallway at the rear of the showroom that led toward the stairs, restrooms, and storage rooms further back in the building. There was also a door at the end of the hall that exited out to the service alley behind the building. If that was the door I heard slam as I came in, someone had just left in a hurry.

I turned to head out front, figuring to see Kipchumba driving away in his Jag. Then I spun back, realizing I could be falling for one of the oldest tricks in the book. As I turned, Kipchumba stepped through a storeroom door and into the hallway. He was raising a long-barreled revolver in his right hand. I had a choice. I could either fire a round at him or dive for cover.

Since getting shot myself while trying to shoot him didn't seem like very efficient detective work, I dove behind the hood of a two-tone blue Bentley as Kipchumba pulled the trigger. After the shot I heard a loud metallic "clink" followed by the door slam sound again. Deciding I wouldn't look very bright if I fell for the same trick twice, I worked my way to the Bentley's front bumper and took a look down the hall. Nothing moved in that direction for at least thirty seconds, so I turned and ran across the showroom toward the entrance. I was almost there when Kipchumba drove by. He gave me the same wave I'd given him earlier.

Seeing no reason to go speeding off trying to catch him, I holstered my revolver and walked back into the showroom to find Allen and see why Kipchumba came in. When I got to the small showroom housing the Triumph Dolomite Roadster I saw what I was afraid I would find. Allen Tremain was sitting on the floor leaning against the Triumph's large right front wheel with his legs straight out in front of him. His face was smeared with blood and I couldn't tell from there if he was breathing or not.

Expecting the worst, I leaned down and checked for a pulse. Kipchumba must have been feeling generous or I interrupted him before he was done because Allen had a good strong heartbeat.

I was just wondering where I might find a first-aid kit with some smelling salts, when Allen groaned. I said, "Just sit still for another minute or two and get your wits about you. Is there anyone else in the building?"

In a raspy, halting voice that matched his bloody appearance, he said, "No. It's . . . it's lunch time. Everybody's . . . out."

"Okay, you just stay put for a minute and I'll call the police."

Despite my sound medical advice about staying put, Allen was trying to get to his feet. "No! For heaven's sake don't . . . don't call the cops. If our customers read . . . read in the newspaper that we're having trouble with Negroes, they won't set foot in here. Just help me up."

I helped him to his feet and asked, "How do you feel? Any broken bones or other major injuries?"

"I don't think so. He was mostly hitting me in the face with his fists."

We took a slow walk over to a chair in the corner of the small showroom and Allen sat. I asked, "What the hell did he want?"

Allen blinked a couple of times as if trying to clear his vision. "Well, I was in here making sure the drip trays were properly in place under the Triumph when he came in. I didn't hear him until he grabbed me by the shoulder and spun me around. Then he hit me in the face and demanded to know what I told you about him."

That was the answer I expected. "I assume you told him what he wanted to know."

His head jerked up. "Hell, no! I'm not kowtowing to any damned Nigger!"

"Looks like he got pretty insistent."

Allen nodded. "Yeah. You got here just in time. He saw you coming back through the front windows and hit me on the back of my neck—like some kind of Jiu-Jitsu. I don't remember anything clearly after that until you woke me up."

"All right, Allen. If you won't let me call the police and you're physically okay, I'll get back to finding Mister Kipchumba and bringing him to justice."

"If you don't mind telling me, what's that guy wanted for?"

"Grand theft and at least two counts of murder."

"Oh, swell! I wish to hell I'd known that this morning when he brought his car in!" He paused for a moment, and then added, "That reminds me, I thought I heard something like a gunshot after you got here. Is everything all right in the main showroom?"

I shook my head. "I didn't stop to look, but Kipchumba took a shot at me and hit that blue Bentley instead. I think the bullet hit the left side of the bonnet. And while we're on the subject, your Dolomite Roadster over there has some pretty deep scratches and dents on the driver-side front fender."

Allen groaned. "Oh, no. Mister Canella will fire me for sure!"

"If he does, you send him to see me. I'll set him straight in a hurry. There was nothing you could have done to prevent what happened."

Allen nodded, but he didn't look convinced.

Outside on the street, I took a good look around and didn't see any sign of Kipchumba. I even checked my Chrysler before I got in, looking under the hood for a booby trap and checking behind the seat and in the trunk for any new hitchhikers. It was important to my survival that I keep in mind all the parts of my new policy for dealing with the Kipchumbas, especially the "more observant" part.

Next I lit a Lucky and thought about what had just happened. I had the distinct feeling Kipchumba wasn't really looking for information when he beat Allen up. He knew damned well why I showed up at the dealership. I wondered if, instead, he was giving me a warning. Maybe he was saying, "Don't get cute with us or more people will die. I also wondered why he didn't try to press home his advantage when he had me pinned down behind the Bentley in the showroom.

That could be explained by the Smith and Wesson I had in my hand at the time. Maybe Mister Kipchumba doesn't have much appetite for shooting at targets that shoot back. And, if he was giving me a warning it didn't have me shaking in my Florsheims. The situation did, however, warrant a couple of telephone calls.

With that and lunch on my mind I followed Santa Monica Boulevard—Route 66—into West Hollywood and parked out of sight from the road in the parking lot behind Barney's Beanery. Barney's isn't much more than a shack of a joint that has been here selling Barney Anthony's famous chili and French onion soup since 1920, six years before Route 66 was established as a federal highway. That's just what I needed right now, a homey place with some heritage and stability.

Inside Barney's I sat at my favorite table near a front window and when Lauren, my favorite waitress, brought a menu over, I told her that, as much as I enjoy reading the humorous descriptions of the four or five kinds of chili Barney serves, I already knew what I wanted. I asked her to bring me a cup of Texas-style chili and a tuna salad melt with iced tea to wash it all down. Then, while she took my order to the kitchen, I went to the public telephone near the back of Barney's small dining room and dialed the Seventh Precinct.

It was a few minutes before one o'clock and I hoped Salvino was back from lunch. He was and I told him I had another body to report. I noted, however, that the Kipchumbas were apparently slipping because, like the last one, this body was still breathing.

After I gave Nick the particulars, he said, "So in other words, I should expect a call from the Beverly Hills cops this time."

"No telephone calls this time. The salesman wouldn't let me call the cops. He was afraid of what their customers would think if the newspaper reported they were having racial troubles."

Salvino said, "Yeah, that figures. All those people see are the color of the man's skin." He paused, and then said, "Sounds like the Kipchumbas are still dogging your tail. Ya gotta wonder how he found you between here and Beverly Hills."

"I'm not sure he did. He could have been following me all the way from my office, although I've keeping a close eye on my mirrors when I'm driving and didn't see him until I got to Highland and Wilshire this morning. Right now, though, he's giving me a break. I haven't seen him since he left British Autos, so I'm hiding out at Barney's for some chili and a tuna salad melt."

"Any idea what you're gonna do next?"

"I'm going to check my service for telephone messages, and then I'm gonna eat my chili. To hell with Kipchumba until after that."

"Okay. Enjoy the chili, but keep your eyes open for trouble. These people are behaving like lunatics. We have no idea what kind of crazy thing they're going to come up with next."

I promised I would keep my eyes open and broke the connection. My second call was to Rosie's Professional Telephone Exchange Service, where Rosie had only one message for me. Susan had called about an hour earlier to say they had transferred Jack to the Navy hospital at Port Hueneme this morning and that she would be staying at a place called the Navy Lodge just inside the main gate at the base. Rosie recited the hotel's address and telephone number twice to be sure I got it. Then she said something that was a little out of character for her.

"Mister Spicer, I certainly don't mean to interfere in your business, but Miss Jackson sure sounded like she wanted to hear from you."

"Thanks, Rosie. I'll call her very soon."

While I was following Salvino's sage advice by enjoying my chili and sandwich, I gave some thought to how my new approach to Kipchumba had changed the situation, if it had actually changed anything at all. At first it seemed like my behavior confused him, but he caught on quickly. Now he might be upping the ante by threatening to hurt people I knew. At least that's one way I could interpret what happened at British Autos. Also, we had now met face to face for the first time, and I couldn't help wondering if our confrontation at the dealership was accidental. Salvino was right, Kipchumba's behavior was getting nuttier every time I encountered him.

I paid my bill and, as I walked out to Barney's parking lot, I heard a siren approaching from the direction of Hollywood. It was a common sound of my town—a sound that might mean the difference between life and death to someone, but not much to anyone else. Thinking I was in the "anyone else" category, I was opening the driver door of my Chrysler when the siren and the LAPD prowl car attached to it swung into Barney's parking lot and skidded to a stop alongside my car.

The patrol officer jumped out of his black and white Ford and jogged around to where I was standing. I recognized him as Murphy, one of the patrol officers Salvino had with him at Rolly Boland's apartment. In fact, he was the officer that Nick sent downstairs to call the Sixth and check up on me. Since he hadn't drawn his revolver, I wasn't too worried, but you never know.

"Detective Spicer, Sergeant Salvino at the Seventh sent me with an urgent message."

Noting the formal way in which he addressed me, I gathered my status at the Seventh had risen somewhat. "Yeah? What's up?"

"He would like you to meet him at 1183 Kingsley Drive in Hollywood. You know where that is, sir?"

"I've seen the street name, but I'm not sure where. Maybe over toward Los Feliz and Western?"

Nodding, Murphy said, "You're in the right area, but it's a maze of residential streets over there. Just follow me, sir."

I nodded and climbed into my car. We pulled out of Barney's parking lot onto Santa Monica Boulevard in the eastbound direction, and then Officer Murphy put his foot down and, with his siren wailing again, we tore along the boulevard like gang busters. I'll admit that running red lights and moving over to the wrong side of the road to pass vehicles that didn't yield fast enough was a kick, but knowing Los Angeles drivers as I do, it seemed like taking a few minutes longer would have improved our chances of getting there alive and in one piece.

Santa Monica Boulevard intersected Kingsley half a dozen blocks east of Western. We made the turn and Murphy killed his siren for the final two blocks to our destination. Eleven-eighty-three was a small, two-bedroom Spanish Mission style bungalow with the required red tile roof, stucco finish, and arches. If I'd had to guess, I would have put the age of the place at about twenty years. It was well maintained, but the yard was mostly gravel with a couple of spindly bushes for landscaping. In other words, it had the earmarks of a rental—in this neighborhood, an inexpensive rental. It might have even been the sort of place that would rent to a Negro.

As I got out of my car, Salvino appeared in the front door to the bungalow. "What do we have here, Nick?"

He lit a match and set fire to the remaining four inches of his cigar and said, "What we have here, Spicer, is the result of diligent detective work. The Sixth had a man they could spare for a few hours, so they put him to work looking through the traffic citations issued during the first part of the morning. We got lucky and he found that a Jaguar sedan with the right license plate had been cited out on Santa Monica Boulevard at one o'clock this morning for a faulty tail light. The address on the driver's license was West Sacramento, but the auto reg address was right here." Salvino finished with a flourish of his arm indicating the house behind him.

"You're right, Nick. Whoever came up with the idea of checking the traffic citations for a Jaguar with a faulty tail light should get a medal. On the other hand, you had them when the officer stopped the Jag. He needs to catch up on his bulletin reading."

Salvino grumbled, "Yeah, yeah. Come on in here and see what you make of this."

The bungalow must have been rented furnished. It was equipped with a bare minimum of cheesy furniture that had seen the inside of a secondhand store at least once already. That was to be expected, what I didn't expect was all the trash on the living room and front bedroom floors.

The kitchen, bathroom and the back bedroom were clean and tidy, but the living room and the front bedroom were full of clutter. When I took a closer look at the nature of the clutter and where it was, I realized the cluttering was done intentionally.

Nick said, "They weren't big on housekeeping, were they? This place is a mess."

"Yeah, a very artistic mess."

He looked at me. "What do you mean by that?"

"Look at the pattern, Nick. All that clutter was put down at the same time by somebody walking through two of the rooms dropping crumpled newspaper pages as they went. I bet you'll find they all came from the same edition of the Times."

The sergeant looked puzzled. "Why would anyone do that?"

"I've come to the conclusion Joseph Kipchumba likes to play games. It makes him feel clever to do things in a roundabout way so we have to figure out the puzzles he's created to play his game. In this instance, I'm betting he created the mess to hide something that would be in plain sight if the floors weren't cluttered."

Kneeling near the door, I slowly studied the debris on the floor for whatever Kipchumba wanted us to find. It didn't take long. A bit of color caught my eye among the black and white newspaper pages under a chair. I picked it up and flattened it out. When I saw what I had in my hands, my blood ran cold.

Twenty-Four

2:00 P.M. – Friday – August 16, 1940

Kipchumba L.A. Residence – 1183 Kingsley Drive, Hollywood

What I had in my hands was a map of Ventura County. That in itself wasn't especially noteworthy. What made the map significant was the part that wasn't there. The lower right corner had been carefully torn off.

Salvino was looking over my shoulder. "You think that's the message Kipchumba wanted to us to find?"

"No doubt about it, Nick."

"What's with the torn off part? Is that part of the clue?"

"Yeah. The torn off section includes part of Oxnard, Port Hueneme, and the Navy base there."

"What's so important about those places?"

"You remember that 'little gal in Santa Barbara' you keep referring to; the one whose brother the Kipchumbas shot?"

Nick's expression told me he already had it figured out. "She's there?"

"Yeah. She's staying on the base while her brother is in the hospital there."

"Damn! This Kipchumba is a real jerk. I'll get in touch with the authorities in Ventura County, Oxnard, Port Hueneme, and at the Navy Base and alert them to the likelihood the Kipchumbas will show up there. What are your plans?"

"Wherever the Kipchumbas are, there go I, but this whole thing has gotten way out of hand, so now I shoot first and ask questions later."

"How can I get in touch with you if we turn something?"

"My answering service would be the best bet, or maybe at that Navy Lodge on the base. Susan is staying there and I'll either be with her or she will know where I am. She should be registered as Susan Jackson. Otherwise, I'll check in with you."

Salvino offered his hand, and as I shook it, he said, "Good luck, Johnny."

By a few minutes after three I had stopped at my apartment and packed my overnight bag, filled the Chrysler's gasoline tank, and was headed over the Cahuenga Pass into the San Fernando Valley on Highway 101. Hollywood and Port Hueneme are about sixty miles apart and the drive typically takes an hour and a half if the traffic is light. By four-fifteen I was driving past the main entrance gate to the Ventura County Navy Base on Ventura Road in Port Hueneme.

When I had driven a mile or so past the gate without seeing any sign of the Kipchumbas or their Jaguar, I made a U-turn and drove back. I turned into the base access road and the Shore Patrolman responsible for checking people onto and off of the base stepped out of his shack and held up a hand to indicate he wanted me to stop.

I stopped and as I rolled down my window he said, "May I see your identification please?"

When asked that question, I usually hand over my driver's license, but on this occasion and particularly because of the Smith and Wesson revolver in my shoulder holster, I handed him the leather case containing my P. I. Photostat and Special Los Angeles County Sheriff's Deputy shield.

The young man looked at the Photostat, returned it to me, snapped to attention, and saluted, saying, "Good afternoon, Major Spicer. Welcome to Ventura County Navy Base, Port Hueneme, sir."

I managed to return his salute, darn near dropping my badge case in the process. Even though it is common practice in the services to address former officers by the rank they held when they left or retired, it had been seven years since anyone had called me major or saluted me. With no practice, I'd gotten a little rusty. Besides, who the hell told them I once held the rank of major?

"Thank you. I take it you were advised that I was coming?"

"Yes, sir. We've been expecting you. Please pull up into that temporary parking area ahead. The Officer of the Day will be with you in just a moment."

We exchanged salutes again and I was still wondering how he knew I'd been a major. Then I remembered Susan's brother asking me about my Army rank, so the major business was probably his doing. I also wondered how come the OOD wanted to talk to me. I figured he probably wasn't going to shoot me, or if he did, he would at least salute me first.

For those who are not unfamiliar with the term, the "Officer of the Day" or OOD, is a job that rotates daily among all of a base's officers and is similar in duties to those of a provost marshal on high-security bases and overseas installations. In other words, the OOD oversees the base's security and law enforcement activities for the twenty-four hour period during which he serves as Officer of the Day.

I pulled into the parking spot the Shore Patrolman had indicated, and before I could turn off the engine, a spit and polish Lieutenant wearing a black OOD armband on his freshly pressed white summer uniform and carrying a clipboard came striding purposefully toward my car. We went through the saluting routine again and he said, "Good afternoon, Major Spicer. I'm Lieutenant O'Keefe. Admiral Willets, commandant, Navy Base Ventura County, Port Hueneme, sends his compliments and hopes he will have an opportunity to meet you while you're visiting us, sir."

"Thank you, Lieutenant. I'll look forward to meeting Admiral Willets."

We exchanged looks that said we both knew that was a bunch of hogwash and he said, "I'll let you be on your way in just a moment, sir, but first I have some paperwork here for you."

First he handed me what appeared to be a street map. "This is a visitor map of the base to help you get where you need to be. With the exception of a few "need to know" locations, you have the run of the entire base. The base driving regulations are on the reverse side of the map. If anyone challenges you while you are on the base, show them your identification and this. "

On the next sheet of paper he gave me was a neatly typed pass authorizing one Major Jonathon Spicer, United States Army, to go just about anywhere on Navy Base Ventura County, Port Hueneme I damn well pleased. It was signed by Admiral Henry Willits. I was grateful for all the cooperation, but it was also baffling me. I didn't recall Coast Guard Lieutenants having the kind of clout it took to get admirals to sign passes like the one I was now folding to tuck into my badge case.

Lieutenant O'Keefe continued, saying, "A room has been reserved for your use at the VOQ. Just give your name at the reception counter. You also have privileges at the O Club."

In military parlance, VOQ stands for Visiting Officer Quarters; a sort of hotel for officers who find themselves temporarily on a base other than where they are normally stationed. "O Club" is slang for

Officer's Club, usually a restaurant and lounge reserved for use by officers. I thanked him and he handed me yet another item—a bright orange four-inch-by-four-inch card with large black letters on it that spelled out VIP. Below the letters were the words "Visiting Officer." The initials VIP were a recently coined military acronym for Very Important Person.

O'Keefe said, "This is your vehicle ID card. Place it so it is visible through the windshield of your car. Also, for security reasons, we urge you to keep your vehicle locked while this card is in it."

As I tucked the orange card into the windshield's rubber molding, Lieutenant O'Keefe said in a quieter voice, "I was given to understand that you would be carrying a personal weapon, sir. Is that correct?"

Holding my jacket open so he could see my shoulder holster, I said, "Yes, it's a point-three-eight caliber Smith and Wesson revolver, Police Special model."

"Very good, sir. May I see it long enough to copy the pistol's serial number on a Personal Firearms form?"

I handed him the revolver and he copied the serial number from its location on the frame at the bottom of the grip. Once O'Keefe had it recorded on the form attached to his clipboard he returned the revolver.

Next, O'Keefe said, "I also understand we have instructions to be on the lookout for a two or three year old dark green Jaguar sedan with California license number two – c as in Charlie – seven – eight – two – one. What would you like done if we see this vehicle or the people driving it?"

"First, treat them as armed and dangerous. We know of at least four people they've shot in the last few days. Two of them are dead and one of them is recovering in your base hospital right now.

"Ideally, we'd like it if you tossed them into your brig until someone from the LAPD can get up here and haul them back. Whatever the situation, though, please let me know immediately if they are spotted. Lives could depend on it."

"Will do, Major Spicer. If you would like to make your first stop the base hospital, its right over there." He pointed to a brick building across from what I thought might be the base lodge where Susan was staying.

"Thanks, Lieutenant."

O'Keefe snapped to attention and saluted again. "Welcome aboard, sir. Enjoy your stay at Port Hueneme."

I returned his salute and drove the short distance to the base hospital. After locking the car with its visiting officer card in the windshield, I walked in the main entrance and asked a Chief Warrant Officer behind the reception desk for the location of a patient named Lieutenant Jack Jackson.

The man looked through a typewritten list attached to clipboard on the reception desk and said, "We have a Lieutenant Orville Jackson. Could that the man you're looking for?"

Hardly able to suppress a grin, I said, "Orville? I've always heard him referred to as Jack, but . . ."

The CWO interrupted me, asking, "Excuse me, sir, but would you be Major Spicer by any chance?"

"That's me."

"Then Orville is your boy. May I see some identification please, Major?"

My badge case was getting a workout today. I handed it to him and he looked at my Photostat, along with the base pass signed by Admiral Willets. He handed it back, saying, "Thank you, sir. I apologize for the delay, but we have special security procedures in place for Lieutenant Jackson."

"I understand, Chief."

"Thank you, sir. Lieutenant Jackson is on this floor in room 115. Take a right at the end of that hall and it will be the third room on your right."

"Thanks, Chief."

He gave me a snappy salute, which I returned in an equally snappy manner. Whether I wanted to or not, I was getting back in the swing of things.

I found room 115 right where the Chief said it would be and walked in just as Susan was pouring Jack a cup of orange juice from a small glass bottle. I said, "Hey, Orville, how's it going up there in the clouds?"

Jack said, "Hey, Johnny! Good to see you, pal. And, please, let's keep that 'Orville' business between us."

Susan ran into my arms with such enthusiasm she darned near knocked me over. I hugged her and she said, "Oh, Johnny. I'm so glad to see you! I hope it was okay to call this morning."

I gave her a kiss on the forehead and said, "You can call me anytime and anywhere, Angel."

With my arm around her waist I pulled Susan along with me to Jack's bedside and we shook hands. "Seriously, Jack, how are you feeling?"

"Better every day, Johnny, and before we go any further, I've got something to say to you. I've heard that the bullet they dug out of me was probably intended for you. If that's true, I have to say there aren't many folks I would rather take a bullet for." Then with a big grin he added, "Now, having said that, I'll also say I'm gonna punch you right in the nose when I get out of here."

I think Susan was actually shocked. "Jack! Don't talk like that!"

"It's okay, Angel. That's a punch I deserve and I'll stand there and take it like a man."

Jack frowned. "Oh hell, don't get all noble about it. That takes the fun out of punching you in the nose. Now I'll have to find some other way to get even."

"Seriously, Jack," I said, "I'm very sorry this happened. If I'd thought there was a chance of somebody shooting at me last night, I wouldn't have been anywhere near either of you. I'll find a way to make it up."

"Just catch the SO . . . ah . . . the bum who shot me."

"I'm working on it, Jack, along with half the cops in Los Angeles, Santa Barbara, and now Ventura County. These people are as slippery as a couple of eels. In fact, that's the reason I'm here. We have reason to believe they're targeting people I know in order to get another shot at me, so I'm here to make sure they don't mess with two of the most important people in my life."

Susan had her arm looped through mine and I felt her tighten her grip. Jack said, "Well, if you're including me in that group, I appreciate it, but I've got the whole dang navy looking out for me. I heard Admiral Halsey was going to anchor the battleship Arizona right outside the hospital here to make sure there was no funny business."

We all got a chuckle out of that. Then Jack said, "You know, Johnny, there is one favor you could do for me."

"Sure, Jack. Name it."

"Would you please get my ever loving sister out of here for a while? Every time a cute nurse shows up, Sis comes charging in like the cavalry and runs her off. How am I ever gonna make any time with that going on?"

"All right, Jack, I'll take this cute nurse off your hands so you can catch a cute nurse of your own, but I don't think she's going to let me keep her away long."

Susan said, "No, no, Johnny, that's all right. I'll just tell 'em to send the cutest nurse in the place in here with the biggest, dullest needle they've got. Then maybe he'll appreciate me."

Jack quickly said, "Come on, Sis, it's not that I don't appreciate you. I do. I just . . ."

"Too late, big brother. The damage is done. Come on, Johnny. Help me find a really dull needle about the size of a ten penny nail."

Susan and I walked outside and sat on a bench in a small grove of shade trees. She gave me a kiss and said, "I'm sure glad to see you. I know we were apart for less that twenty-four hours, but I guess I got used to having you around. I've really missed you."

Grinning, I said, "I'm glad to hear that. I missed you some, too."

She looked up at me with disappointment on her face. "Only some?"

"I had a few other things on my mind part of the time. Joseph Kipchumba and I had a confrontation, for one thing."

"Uh-oh."

I told her about my encounter with Kipchumba at L.A. British Autos, and ended my story by saying, "When I changed how I dealt with him, Kipchumba was confused for a short time, and then he upped the ante by threatening people I know."

"That's what you said in Jack's room. How do you know that?"

"Two things. First, Joseph's attack on the salesman at British Autos points toward that conclusion. He had no other reason for nearly beating the poor guy to death.

"The second point came after Sergeant Salvino discovered where the Kipchumbas have been staying in Los Angeles—probably the whole time they were arranging to steal the elephant. The way he found the place was an L.A. cop wrote them a ticket for that tail light problem on the Jaguar and he wrote their address from the car's registration on the citation. When that happened, the Kipchumbas knew they had to move, but they figured out how to turn the situation around to their advantage.

"When Sergeant Salvino went to the address, the Kipchumbas had left us a clue. I guess Joseph likes to play puzzle games. Anyway, we found a Ventura County roadmap in the place they'd been renting, and the lower right corner of the map had been carefully torn off—that's the part of the map that includes Oxnard and Port Hueneme."

I'd never heard Susan sound so furious. "Oh! I want to get my hands on those two!"

"We have a lot of people on our side who feel the same. Salvino's working the case from L.A., John Walsh has the Santa Barbara police learning what they can from that end, and Salvino has the county cops here and the Navy looking for them as well. It won't be long before the Kipchumbas get a little too cocky and make a mistake. We'll be there when they do."

She leaned her head against my shoulder and said, "I sure hope that's soon. This is nerve-wracking."

"I know, Angel, but I'll be here until then. That might make you feel a little better."

"It does, Johnny. It really does. Where are you going to stay? I bet I could smuggle you into the lodge if you'd like."

"That's what I was hoping you'd say, but . . ." I suddenly realized that was a very strange question for her to ask unless she wasn't aware that Jack had made arrangements for me at the VOQ.

Susan cocked her head to the side and asked, "What's the matter, Darling?"

"Well, I have a room reserved at the Visiting Officers Quarters, and I thought Jack had arranged it for me, but . . ."

Looking even more puzzled, Susan said, "Jack? Jack didn't arrange anything like that. I've been with him practically every minute and we didn't even know you were coming up here until you walked through the door."

"That's right. They've also been using my old military rank ever since I got on the base and he's the only one who knew I was a major. So if he didn't do it, then who did? The only other person it could have been is Salvino. He told me he was going to alert the navy to me being here and get them watching for the Kipchumbas, but how did he know about my military service? Listen, Angel, I need to call Salvino anyway. Let's hunt down a public telephone and we'll find out from the man himself."

Twenty-Five

4:30 P.M. – Friday – August 16, 1940

Navy Base Ventura County, Port Hueneme

There were several public telephone booths just outside the hospital entrance and I used one of them to place a long distance, person-to-person call to Detective Sergeant Salvino at the LAPD's Seventh Precinct headquarters. I must have caught him at a good time because he was almost civil.

"Well, what do you know, it's our wandering boy. You make it to Ox Snort or whatever they call that place up there?"

"I did, Sergeant, and at least for the moment everything is quiet and peaceful here. You have anything new at your end?"

"Nope. Our crime lab crew went over the house on Kingsley with a fine tooth comb and all they found were fingerprints, and since we already know who lived there, prints don't do squat to help us, although we did send them off to the FBI's National Bureau of Criminal Identification, but getting anything back from them could take weeks or even a month. When the Kipchumbas left, they did a damned good job of making sure there was nothing left except what they wanted us to find. You make contact with the navy boys there yet?"

"Yeah, I have, and they're treating me like royalty, which makes me wonder what the hell you told them about me. For example, did you tell them that way back in the dim past I had been a major in the Army?"

"Seems to me I might have mentioned somethin' like that to 'em."

196

"Then you must have done a background check on me because I'm sure I never said anything about that to you."

"Geez, Spicer, you think I'm some hick from the sticks? Of course I did a background check on you. I had 'em start that the day you showed up at that ritzy apartment place where Boland lived. I figured you and I were gonna be stuck with each other and this case for a while so I wanted to know who I was dealin' with."

"Trusting soul aren't you?"

"I don't trust nobody 'til I know 'em. What's the matter, you don't like bein' treated like royalty?"

"I'm not complaining, Nick. I'm just a little surprised you have that much clout with the navy."

"Well, Spicer, if you'd done your homework like I did, you wouldn't be surprised because you might have found out that I served in the Navy, so I know the ropes. You might have even found out that my no good brother-in-law's name is Willets. That name mean anything to you?"

"If the rank that goes in front of that name is Admiral, yeah, it means something to me."

"Good. I was startin' to think you ain't as smart as I thought you were. You need anything else from me this evening or can I go home and get some dinner?"

"Go put on the feedbag, Nick. I think we're okay here."

"Well, just in case, you got a pencil?"

"Sure, hang on a sec."

I fished the notebook and pencil out of my inside jacket pocket and handed them to Susan. "Okay, Nick, what do I need to write down?"

"Walnut-one-eight-seven-eight."

After I repeated the telephone number so Susan could write it in my notebook, Salvino said, "That's my home telephone number. Don't give it to anyone or I'll toss you in a cell down here and lose the key."

Chuckling, I said, "Always with the threats, Salvino. Didn't anyone ever tell you you'll get more flies with honey than vinegar?"

"Swell, Spicer, I'll remember that next time I want some flies to keep me company. Anything else?"

"Yeah, if you need me call that Navy Lodge I told you about, the place Susan is staying. Officially I'll be at the VOQ, but I can't very well keep Susan safe from clear across the base."

It was Nick's turn to laugh. "Sure, Spicer, I get the picture."

"Have a good dinner, Nick. Talk to you tomorrow."

Susan was grinning when she handed me my notebook. "So you plan to stay in my room at the lodge to keep me safe, do you?"

"I can always stay at the VOQ and let the Kipchumbas do their voodoo on you."

"Voodoo is a Haitian religion, not African, but I'll take you over the Kipchumbas any day."

"Don't worry, Angel, I'll sleep in the bathtub."

She gave me an especially sweet kiss and said, "Not if I have anything to say about it, Mister."

We decided for propriety's sake that even though I didn't plan to actually stay there, I should at least check into the VOQ, so I headed out to find it while Susan checked on Jack. We agreed to meet back in his room when I finished taking care of my business at the VOQ.

Once I'd checked in, I took a look at my VOQ room. It wasn't the Hyatt, but it was a clean, comfortable, and efficient space that even had a view of the port. There wasn't much to see out there, though, because the base's primary function is training Construction Battalion troops, or Seabees as they like to call themselves, and since the Seabees do most of their work on land, the Navy didn't need a large harbor facility to support the base.

If you're curious about why the navy has a bunch of guys running around on bulldozers and such, they actually serve an important purpose. When the navy parks one of their battleships next to some remote island where they want to build a base or an airfield, they turn the Seabees loose to construct whatever needs to be built. These guys can build an entire airfield, runways and all, practically overnight. You might think of them as earthmoving tooth fairies. Now, if you're curious about why the navy needs airfields, you'll have to take that up with the War Department.

Next I used a public telephone in front of the VOQ to check in with Rosie. She had no new messages for me. After assuring her that I was in contact with Miss Jackson and telling Rosie that I would be out of town for a while, I found my way back to the hospital. When I got there Susan was sitting in the chair next to Jack's bed reading a copy of *LIFE* magazine. It was almost an exact recreation of the first time I saw her in the Santa Barbara clinic. I'd still swear she's an angel.

Jack saw me come in and said, "The O Club and the VOQ, yet! Man, I don't know where your pull comes from, but you've definitely got the navy on your side."

I suspected Susan told him about the VOQ for propriety's sake. Smiling, I said, "All I can tell you is what the man told me, 'It helps if your brother-in-law's last name happens to be Willets with 'Admiral' in front of it.'"

He nodded in a way that told me he knew the score when it came to pulling strings in the military. "That would do the trick, all right."

"Only thing is, I've had to learn to salute all over again. These Navy guys go by the book and then some."

"That they do, Johnny. That they do. You two going to the O Club for dinner?"

I looked in Susan's direction as she put down the *LIFE* magazine. "That's up to Angel. It's either the O Club or some leftover beef jerky and moldy cheese behind the seat in my car if she prefers."

"Oh no you don't, Mister. Jack's been promising to take me to an officer's club for years, and now that we are actually near one, he comes up with some cockamamie excuse about being shot. I'm not letting you get out of it as easy."

Jack snickered. "Looks like if you know what's good for you, you'll take her to the O Club, Johnny."

As Susan came over and took my arm, I said, "So it would seem. What about you, Jack? Can we bring you anything special for dinner?"

"Thanks, but that would be an insult to the hospital chef! They serve great chow here and I don't want to mess that up." He picked up a sheet of mimeograph paper from the nightstand beside his bed and added, "Let's see, tonight we're having Navy bean soup, pappardelle pasta with asparagus and salmon in a light cream sauce, and for dessert, Jell-O rainbow cups with whipped cream. Let's see the O Club beat that menu!"

I couldn't help smiling at his enthusiasm. "I see your point, Jack. Angel, you go ahead on over to the O Club, I'm gonna stay here and have dinner with your brother."

Susan figured I was kidding, but she wasn't taking any chances. "The heck you are, Mister! And, Jack, you just keep your big, fat mouth shut."

Looking thoroughly chastised, Jack said, "Yes, ma'am. Don't worry, Johnny, I'll save you some of my dinner."

Navy Base Ventura County's Officers Club was in an older building that looked like every other building on the base—a big gray box with windows that were mostly covered with curtains. Inside, however, a lot of effort had been put into making the place welcoming and comfortable.

Dark wood paneling covered the walls of a good-sized lounge, and the walls were decorated with Seabee unit insignia and photographs of construction battalions at work. A Wurlitzer jukebox over in the corner was flashing a rainbow of multi-colored lights and spinning a record by that crooner with Tommy Dorsey's orchestra. They were doing *I'll Never Smile Again*, while a few officers who brought their wives or a date to the club made good use of a small dance floor in front of the jukebox. The long mahogany bar had a genuine brass foot rail and a guy behind it I suspected of being an off-duty chief petty officer mixing drinks. If I didn't know better, I'd have thought I was back home in one of Hollywood's swanky watering holes.

No cost had been spared on the dining room, either. It looked as if it might have originally been an assembly hall of some sort, but the large space had been divided up with tall partitions to give the seating areas a more intimate feeling. The partitions were decorated with subdued but rich-looking wallpaper designs and large pots sprouting birds of paradise and other exotic plants were placed strategically around the room. The tables were set with fine linen, real silver and flickering candles. Again, I could easily imagine myself being in one of Hollywood's finer restaurants.

A tuxedoed maître d' greeted us cordially and we were seated at a table in a particularly secluded area of the room. He left us two leather bound menus with gold embossed covers featuring US Navy official seals and the words "Navy Base Ventura County, Port Hueneme Officers Club."

Our waiter took drink orders, Cutty Sark over ice for me and a Zombie for Susan, and then recommended the cioppino, an Italian seafood stew. In the end, Susan opted for sautéed sand dabs and I chose veal scaloppini.

When our drinks arrived, Susan's Zombie was decorated with a wedge of pineapple, a cherry, and a colorful little beach umbrella. My Cutty was decorated with ice, the way a drink should be served. We raised our glasses in a toast to good times and I watched Susan take a sip of her rum cocktail.

She smiled and I said, "You know, Angel, that's a pretty powerful concoction for such a health conscious person."

"Oh, don't be a poop. I'm a nurse, not a Methodist minister. Besides I know you would never take advantage of the situation in the unlikely event that I should become a little tipsy."

I winked at her. "Don't bet on it, Angel."

Our dinners included everything from soup to nuts, including scoops of tasty spumoni ice cream, and while I'm certainly no gourmet, I'd say the meal was some of the best chow I'd ever had. During dinner we talked about subjects that really didn't matter in the overall scheme of things just to get our minds off of the Kipchumbas and the situation in which we found ourselves.

I could tell the conversation was helping Susan relax. She was smiling and a good deal of the tension I'd seen before was melting away, although I suspect the Zombie might have had a little something to do with that, too. In order to continue in the same direction, I suggested we go into the lounge for brandy and some music. Susan thought that was a fine idea, so I signed our dinner tab and we strolled back to the lounge.

Being a Friday evening, the lounge was doing a pretty fair business, but we were able to find a corner table near the parquet dance floor and far enough from the jukebox that we could carry on a conversation without yelling. The overall ambiance was friendly and relaxing, despite Glenn Miller's brassy *Tuxedo Junction* trying to shake to rafters loose. The navy was having a good time tonight.

At Susan's urging I ordered a couple of Cusenier Apricot Liqueurs, which was something like drinking apricot-flavored Karo syrup. That was one reason I was particularly happy when somebody put a nickel in the box to hear *When You Wish Upon A Star*. It was the *Pinocchio* movie version sung by Cliff Edwards, and it was a ballad you could dance to, thus saving me from more apricot liqueur.

It felt good to have Susan in my arms and I got the distinct feeling she enjoyed being there. I found myself thinking, "Heck, for this I would even drink apricot-flavored Karo syrup."

We returned to our table and when nobody ventured forth to put another nickel in the jukebox, I figure it was my turn. I walked over to see what I could find that would give me another excuse to dance with an angel. I found what I was looking for almost immediately. I put my nickel in and pushed A6 which happened to be Glenn Miller's *Moonlight Serenade*—angel music if there is was such a thing.

When Glenn and the boys finished that one up and we returned to our table, Susan said, "I could stay here all night, but I'd like to see Jack before he goes to sleep for the night and I'm feeling a little sleepy myself. Is that okay with you?"

"Sure, Angel. Whenever you're ready."

In the car, Susan looked back at the O Club entrance and sighed. "I don't know what's the matter with me, Johnny. I was having a wonderful time in there. It was the first really fun time we've shared in quite a while, and I make us leave to see if my stupid brother is okay. That's ridiculous."

"No, Angel, that's being responsible to the people you love—it's part of what makes you a great nurse."

"But, I love you, too! The other night I couldn't stop worrying after telling you I needed to be with Jack because I was afraid you'd take it the wrong way."

"I know you love me, Angel. I know you also love Jack, and I know I have to share you with him. Right now he needs you the most, so he's got top priority. On top of all that, Jack's a nice guy and he's in that hospital bed because of me."

Susan gave me a kiss, smiled, and said, "Well, once we get back to the Lodge, I'm all yours. No sharing then!"

"Okay, Angel. And we'll come back here again, maybe tomorrow night. Okay?"

"I hope you meant that, Mister, 'cuz I'm gonna hold you to it."

We parked in front of the base hospital and I asked Susan if she'd rather spend some alone time with Jack instead of having me tag along. She said she didn't mind my being there, but she wanted to get some frank answers out of Jack about how he was feeling, and she thought he might speak more openly if I wasn't there. I told her that was okay with me and walked around to open the car door for her.

Leaning against my Chrysler's fender I watched her disappear into the hospital with the distinct feeling that I had one hell of a woman on my hands there. Since I have been known to mess up relationships in the past, I was determined to handle this one right. Maybe Johnny the kid was finally growing up.

I lit a Lucky Strike and blew smoke at a moon that was trying to hide behind some passing clouds. Something was going on. I could feel it in the air. My sixth sense for trouble was ringing alarm bells like crazy, but the trouble with my sixth sense is that it only tells something's wrong, not what the problem is.

The part of the base around the hospital was deserted and quiet as a graveyard. The only sign of life was an occasional car passing two blocks away on Ventura Road. The peace and calm was adding to my sense that something was going on. It was like the proverbial calm before the storm.

I heard one of the hospital entrance doors make a small sound as it opened, and I quickly turned to look, my right hand reaching inside my jacket as I did so. It was the Chief Warrant Officer who was behind the reception desk when I arrived three hours ago.

He saluted and I returned the favor. Then he lit a cigarette and said, "Major, I hope you don't mind me saying so, but you've got reflexes like a cat. For a minute there I wasn't sure you weren't gonna draw on me."

Laughing his comment off, I said, "There's nothing to worry about on that score. I haven't shot a Chief in a least a couple of days."

He laughed, too, and offered his hand. "I'm sure glad to hear that. Tom Nugent, sir. I'm happy to make your acquaintance."

"The pleasure is mine, Tom. And I'm sorry if I startled you earlier. I'm just feeling a little uneasy tonight. It's probably nothing, but . . ."

When you are close to a very powerful detonation, you feel it as much as hear it. There's a percussive hammer blow that gets you right in the chest. I felt this one and then some!

Twenty-Six

7:45 P.M. – Friday – August 16, 1940

Navy Base Ventura County, Port Hueneme

Tom Nugent was on the ground in front of the hospital entrance exactly where I would have been if I wasn't leaning on the fender of my Chrysler when whatever blew up went boom. I helped him up onto a pair of shaky legs and he said, "Seems like your sense of uneasiness was right on the mark. What the hell was that?"

A second explosion of lesser magnitude made us both flinch and I said, "Whatever it was, I'll wager it wasn't a good thing. Tom, this may be a diversion to give them a clear shot at Jack Jackson or his sister. Get back to Jackson's room and make sure he and his sister are okay and that they stay that way. I'll find out what blew and get back here as quick as I can."

One thing I always appreciated about the military was that when you told someone to do something, they didn't stand around asking questions. Without another word we headed in opposite directions.

By then I could see the base streetlights illuminating the underside of a large, dark cloud over the Navy Lodge. The lodge was about the equivalent of a block away if you went cross country. Hearing what I presumed were the sirens of fire trucks and ambulances getting closer, I decided not to add to the traffic jam. I left the Chrysler right where it was and sprinted across a lawn and through some trees to the perimeter of the lodge.

At the center of a chaotic scene right out of Dante's Inferno I saw all that remained of a Ford DeLuxe Coupe. Of course it would have been hard to tell that the twisted, charred hunks of steel had been a Ford DeLuxe Coupe unless you happened to have seen it parked there earlier and knew the car belonged to Jack Jackson. Just as I got to where I could see the situation clearly, the Ford's rear tires, which for some inexplicable reason were still inflated, popped in unison and the wreckage dropped with an audible "crunch" onto what was once its rear bumper. It put me in mind of a dying animal's last gasp.

The Ford had been parked alongside a wing of the lodge and there was now nothing left of the rooms behind the car but a few smoldering interior walls. The damage wasn't confined to the car and the lodge, though. I could see men from the Shore Patrol and base fire department tending to the injured and to some who were beyond tending.

That was when a young Shore Patrolman approached me with his sidearm drawn, and in a slight tremor in his voice that made me think he didn't have much experience at this sort of thing, he said, "State your name and business here, sir."

"My name is Spicer and you'll find my identification and a base pass signed by Admiral Willets in my inside coat pocket."

Nervously, he said, "Take it out and hand it to me. Do it slowly. No funny business."

Giving him a nod, I did as he ordered. Suddenly the seaman's eyes bulged when he saw my shoulder holster. He quickly said, "Put your hands over your head."

I did and he carefully removed my Smith and Wesson from its shoulder holster. Then he backed up a few paces to study my ID and the pass. He'd been doing a pretty fair job up until he saw my revolver. Had I been a bad guy, however, he'd given me ample time and opportunity to take his regulation Colt Model 1911 pistol away from him and disappear into the night.

He handed my stuff back, holstered his sidearm, and said, "Okay, Major Spicer, everything seems to be in order. I'm sorry for bothering you, sir, but . . ."

I held my hand up to stop him. "You were just doing your job, son. Next time, though, take your prisoner somewhere where you have help watching him while you study his identification. And finding out if your prisoner is armed is the first priority. If he is, get the weapon before the ID. Got it?"

"Yes, sir. I'll remember that."

"Good. Now point me in the direction of whoever is running this show."

"That would be Lieutenant Commander Arnold, sir. That's him over there talking to the fire chief.

"Thanks, son. As you were."

The young man threw me a snappy salute, which I returned before hiking over to a short fellow with gray hair and an SP armband on his white uniform sleeve. He was just finishing his conversation with the fire chief and he turned in my direction to glower at whoever the hell was coming to bother him next.

I said, "Lieutenant Commander Arnold, I'm Major John Spicer and I think this," I gestured toward the still smoldering wreckage, "Is part of why I'm here. I just wanted to check in with you and ask if there's anything I can do to help."

He offered his hand in a friendly gesture that contradicted my first impression of him. "Hello, Spicer. I heard we had the Army aboard today. To answer your question, so far all I have is a statement from my guy in the guard shack at the gate. He reports seeing a smaller, low-slung dark colored sedan parked out on the other side of Ventura Road. It was pointed north and took off in a hurry just before all hell broke loose here. It might not be related, but he remembered it because not many people have reason to park out there."

"Would your guy know a British Jaguar if he saw one?"

Arnold chuckled. "Spicer, that boy grew up on a farm near Omaha. He wouldn't even have known a battleship if he saw one when he signed up."

"Got it. Okay, I'll get out of your hair here, but let's see if we can compare some notes tomorrow."

"Okay. How 'bout lunch at the O Club about eleven-forty-five? That be okay with you?"

Nodding, I said, "I'll be there with bells on."

Chuckling again, he asked, "The Army wears bells to lunch?"

Giving him a shocked expression, I said, "The Navy doesn't?"

I spent the next few minutes taking a closer look at the scene of the crime while trying to stay out of the way of people who were actually doing something useful. I'm certainly no expert on arson, but the way it looked to me, the initial explosion occurred under the Ford's hood. The fact that the charred, bulging sheet metal of the hood was on the ground about twenty feet away seemed to confirm that.

From there, the fire had probably followed the fuel line back to the gasoline tank. That would account for the secondary explosion. That the fuel tank explosion came right on the heels of the first detonation told me whoever rigged the explosives knew their business.

I guessed the initial explosion had blown out the exterior walls of the rooms near where Jack's Ford had been parked, and the secondary explosion had sprayed the interiors of those rooms with burning debris, effectively spreading the fire. So, it seemed safe to assume that, if the arsonist had a human target, it was more likely someone inside the lodge rather than someone inside the Ford.

Of course, I knew very well who the 'arsonist' was and who his target was. The 'smaller, low-slung sedan' description fit a Jaguar saloon to a T. I figured Kipchumba had seen Susan driving Jack's Ford somewhere along the line, maybe even when we were still in Santa Barbara, so he knew what to look for. It is also obvious from the torn map he left in the house they were using Kipchumba knew she was here, either in Oxnard or on the base. When he saw the car parked outside the lodge, which was clearly visible from Ventura Road, he put two and two together and knew where to look for his target.

From there it made sense that Susan would park her car—or more accurately, Jack's car—close to her room at the lodge, so if he blew up the car in such a way as to destroy the nearest rooms, he had a good chance of getting Susan or me or both of us. That he would also kill and injure several other people didn't seem to be a matter of concern. What I still didn't understand about all this is why the Kipchumbas were so all-fired bent on killing me and the people who were close to me. What did I know that made the Kipchumbas fear me so much?

Recalling the promise I'd made to Tom Nugent—that I would get back to the hospital as quickly as I could—and figuring I'd seen all there was to see at the lodge, I retraced my route through the trees and across the lawn and returned to the hospital. When I arrived at room 115, I found Chief Nugent standing right outside the door keeping his promise to make sure nothing happened to Susan or Jack.

Nugent said, "They're fine, sir. I pulled the drapes on the window and suggested they shouldn't stand in front of it in case someone outside could see their shadows."

Thinking that was something Jack already knew from personal experience, I said, "Thanks, Chief. I appreciate you being on top of things here. The explosion was over at the lodge. Lieutenant Jackson's car was blown up. It was parked near a wing of the lodge and the bomb took out a couple of rooms as well as the car. There were a few deaths and several other casualties."

"Understood, sir. What can I do to help?"

"I think the real target of the bombing was Miss Jackson. For that reason I'm going to take her out of here for a while. Jack is also a possible target, but less of one. Besides, he needs to be where he can get good medical care."

The chief nodded and said, "I get it, sir. I'll be here until my replacement arrives, and I'll make sure he's someone I know and trust."

"Thanks, Chief. I appreciate your diligence."

By this time Susan heard my voice and came out to find out why I hadn't come in yet. She held onto my hand and said, "Did you find out what that big explosion was?"

"I did, but let's go inside so Jack can hear what happened and I don't have to go through the story three times."

Susan, still holding onto my hand headed into Jack's room. I gave Tom a nod and followed along.

Jack, sitting up in bed, said, "Hi, Johnny. Are they still celebrating the Fourth of July out there?"

"I'm afraid that was a little more than a firecracker. Somebody blew up your Ford."

"What? Somebody blew up my beautiful new car?"

Susan said, "Not just somebody. It was those African nuts, wasn't it?"

"It looks like it, Angel. The front gate guard saw a car matching the description of their Jaguar parked across Ventura Road until just before the explosion. They may have even had a radio detonator and set the bomb off themselves."

I spent another few minutes describing what I'd seen at the lodge before Susan reached for her jacket. Jack said, "Where are you off to, Sis?"

"I've got to go help treat the casualties. I have triage training, so I can . . ."

I took Susan by the shoulders and turned her to face me. "Not this time, Angel. The navy has that under control. You and I need to go where you'll be safe tonight."

Jack agreed. "He's right, Sis. You can help out at the next disaster you come across. This time you need to get out of here. And don't worry about me. I'll be fine."

"Jack," I said, "I talked to the CWO who has been heading up the security detail protecting you here. He's taking all the steps necessary to insure that you'll be safe. I'll do the same for Susan."

Susan looked up at me. "Are you sure Jack will be okay. It was his car . . ."

"Yes it was his car, but the explosives were positioned to do the most harm to people inside the lodge rooms closest to the car. Either way, Jack's Ford would be destroyed, but they were aiming for people inside the lodge."

"Like we would have been if they had waited until a little later."

I don't think she even realized she just let the cat out of the bag about where I had planned to sleep tonight. If Jack caught her faux pas, it didn't send him into a fit of moral outrage.

She sighed. "Okay, I guess you guys are right. I'm ready to go when you are."

"That's the best choice, Angel. Jack, start thinking about what you'd like to get as a replacement for that Ford. We need to get you something with some class."

He laughed. "Hell, Johnny, I could barely afford that Ford!"

Susan gave her brother a kiss and I tossed him a wave, saying, "We'll see. Talk with you tomorrow."

As we drove past the wreckage, Susan took it all in. I heard her gasp in what I presumed to be shock a couple of times, and then she said, "Those Kipchumbas are animals! No. They're worse than animals. They're just plain evil! I counted at least three bodies laid out and covered on the pavement . . . Johnny, two of those could have been you and me if we had been in our room when that bomb went off."

I nodded solemnly. "Yes. That's why we're getting the heck out of here. I don't know if this was supposed to be another warning or if they actually thought we were in your room, but either way, they didn't seem to give a damn who or what got blown up. I'm guessing Joseph is responsible for planning these things, and if that's the case, the man is just plain crazy."

In what was a good example of closing the barn door after the horse was already headed for parts unknown, the Shore Patrolman at the gate stopped us and asked to see our identification papers before allowing us to leave. While the guard was looking at my ID and pass, I looked up and down Ventura Road. There were no Jaguars in sight.

Past the gate, I turned left off of the access road and we headed north on Ventura Road. As she often does, Susan asked a very pertinent question: "Where are we going, Johnny?"

Fortunately, I had an answer for her this time. "We're going to a lovely dream vacation spot called the Sunset Motor Court up here on Highway One. I've never stayed there, but I've driven by it a hundred times and it looks like an okay joint."

"You think we'll be safe there?"

"Unless the Kipchumbas happened to pick the same place to stay, in which case I'll call the Ventura County Sheriff and have him take 'em away. Either way we win."

Susan sniffed, and in a voice that wasn't more than an inch away from a sob, she said, "I wish I could be as optimistic about all of this as you are. I don't know how you do it."

I'm not sure I completely believed what I told her, but I hoped she did. "I do it by having faith in myself; just like you have faith in your ability to help those people who were injured at the lodge. What we've got here is a contest of wills, and my will is stronger than Joseph Kipchumba's."

The drive to the Sunset Motor Court was no more than four miles, but Friday night traffic was slow so it was almost ten o'clock when we pulled into the court's graveled parking area. The rooms were arranged in the typical U-shaped court layout with all of the units attached instead of being individual cottages. Each unit had its own garage and the office was in the first unit on our right.

As I pulled in to a parking space facing the office, my peripheral vision caught a flash of reflected light somewhere at the back of the U. I was turning in my seat to take another look when an electric starter whined for two or three seconds. I was almost certain what the next sound would be and I was right. It was the crisp rasp of a high-compression six-cylinder engine coming to life.

I was already backing up to block the Kipchumbas' path out of the auto court's parking lot as the Jag roared out of a garage at the back of the U, its rear tires spraying gravel as Joseph Kipchumba swerved around behind us and shot out of the lot. Without thinking, I jammed the Chrysler's transmission into first and pointed us toward the Sunset Motor Court's exit.

It flashed through my mind that I'd been joking when I told Susan we'd be safe at the Sunset Motor Court unless the Kipchumbas happened to pick the same place to stay. Apparently my sense of humor was smarter than me.

Kipchumba pulled a quick left turn onto Highway One and I was about to do the same when another car appeared going the opposite direction. I had to wait until it passed, then I put my foot down hard on the throttle pedal and the chase was on.

That was when I remembered Susan was in the car with me. Bracing herself against the car's motion with her right hand on the dashboard and her left on the seat between us, she said, "I guess this means you won't be calling the sheriff to come and take 'em away."

I immediately backed off the gas. "Oh, hell, Angel. I wasn't thinking. I shouldn't be doing this with you in the car. I'll take you back to the base, and then . . ."

"The hell you will! C'mon, Mister Hollywood Private Eye, step on it! Catch that Jaguar! I want to give Mister Kipchumba a good piece of my mind!"

Against my better judgement, I stepped on it.

Twenty-Seven

10:00 P.M. – Friday – August 16, 1940

Southbound – California Route One, Port Hueneme

Leaving Port Hueneme, California Route One is a two-lane thoroughfare heading southwest toward the coast through scattered residential areas. Beyond the housing tracts we encountered some of Ventura County's vast fields of agricultural endeavor. What the local farmers were growing in those fields, however, was a mystery to me because we were traveling at a high speed through near total darkness. In other words, there wasn't much time for sightseeing and no moonlight to see anything by if we had the time to look. Earlier in the evening there was a full moon playing tag with the clouds, but now a layer of thick overcast almost entirely concealed the moon.

At that moment I was concentrating on two jobs—keeping the Chrysler going as fast as conditions would allow it to go and making sure we didn't lose the Jaguar's tail lights, which I gleefully noted were again dim with the right one blinking merrily as a Christmas tree bulb. Los Angeles British Automobiles had charged Kipchumba exactly what their repair job was worth.

I had to admit, however, that the fault was not entirely with L.A. British Auto's service shop. Most British cars and many other European marques use electrical components made by a company called Lucas, and I had to smile as I recalled a phrase British auto sport enthusiasts frequently use in reference to Lucas's reliability, or its lack thereof: "Lucas, the Prince of Darkness."

With the speedometer needle nudging the 90 mark, we were gradually gaining on the Jaguar, but not quickly enough. As one might expect of a road named the Pacific Coast Highway, Route One was headed for the coast and when we got there in a few miles the road was sure to start twisting and turning. Since going around curves was the Jag's forte, I needed to make up as much time as I could on the straight sections where I had the slight edge on speed.

Without taking my eyes off the road, I checked to see how Susan was holding up. "Angel, if we survive this and you tell Jack I had you in the car during a high-speed chase, I'll never speak to you again."

There was some nervousness in Susan's voice when she spoke, but I could also hear determination and she still had her sense of humor. "Good! Now I have something I can hold over your head. Either we do things my way or I'll tell my big brother and he'll beat you up!"

I mumbled, "Oh swell," and continued squeezing every mile per hour I could get out of the Chrysler's hundred and two horsepower. I was also thinking about the tire we had patched in Santa Barbara two nights ago and hoping to hell the guy knew what he was doing.

It was about then that I noticed the Jaguar's tail lights were undulating up and down periodically and it took me a moment to realize why. The reason had to do with roadbeds constructed in sandy soil. If the silt, sand or what have you isn't sufficiently removed and/or compacted before the roadbed cut is filled and paved, the road will most likely sink in some spots, creating an undulating surface, which in this instance was almost the answer to a prayer.

A light and tightly sprung car like the Jaguar suffers the effects of an uneven road surface much more than a heavier, softer sprung car like my Chrysler. In other words, when the Jag's suspension rebounded from a dip, a lot of the car's weight came off the tires, reducing their grip on the road. If he continued at the speed he was traveling and met up with a curve and an undulation at the same place, he was going to find himself going sideways. That appeared to be exactly what happened a few seconds later. Kipchumba caught it in time to straighten the Jag out before he completely lost control, but the experience must have given him a scare, because he immediately slowed down a little.

The Chrysler on the other hand was oblivious to the uneven road surface and roaring along like it was on rails. Now we were gaining on him by leaps and bounds, but we were also darn near to the beach.

There were steep cliffs and mountains on our left and I could see our headlights illuminating breakers up ahead. Then Highway

One did a zigzag to the left and we were twisting and turning with the coastline. We both slowed to take the curves and the advantage I'd had with the uneven road surface disappeared. Kipchumba was pulling away from us again.

Susan said, "What's the matter, Johnny? Can't you catch up to him?"

"No, Angel. I'm pushing it as hard as I dare. We'll just have to keep him in sight until he does something stupid or some traffic slows him down."

"I guess we'll have to hope he does something stupid, because there sure isn't much traffic out here."

I made no reply because she was stating the obvious. We hadn't seen another car since we entered farming country outside of Oxnard. I did, however, see some lights up ahead so we weren't entirely out of civilization.

The lights turned out to be a couple of ancient streetlights at Point Mugu Beach on our right and a roadhouse perched at the base of the cliff on our left. A red wooden sign illuminated by a spotlight announced the roadhouse as Stew Mugu's Chowder House and Bar. Apparently Joseph Kipchumba wasn't in the mood for chowder because I caught a glimpse of his tail lights up the road before he went around a curve.

I was going as fast as I could without the Chrysler losing its grip on the road, and every time we came to a curve I had to brake hard, which cost us time and, worse, my frequent use of the brakes was heating them up. The hotter drum-style brakes got, the less effective they are and I could already feel the pedal getting spongy.

Around the next curve I watched the Jag's tail lights slow, pull to the left, and disappear. Kipchumba had turned and it looked like a straight shot between us and where he turned, so I pushed hard on the foot throttle again.

We came up on Deer Creek Road so quickly I almost missed it. In fact, if I hadn't seen the Jag's taillights out of my peripheral vision, I'd have gone right by the turnoff. Deer Creek road was narrow, poorly paved, and full of tight turns. The good news was that it ran uphill—a definite advantage for the greater torque of the Chrysler's engine. Now if the brakes would just hold out.

The first curve was a wide one to the left about an eighth of a mile from the highway. We took it easily. The next curve was roughly a mile from the highway and it was a complete one-hundred-eighty degree U-turn that required slowing down to a crawl.

Still climbing, we went around another slightly wider one-eighty, and came out on a short straightaway. We were gaining on the Jag again! I saw his taillights disappear around the next curve, which was no more than an eighth of a mile ahead of us.

I had the Chrysler at full throttle and the curve ahead looked like a wide sweeper to the right. I was pretty sure I could take it at a fast clip, so I kept my speed up, hoping to gain a little more ground before I had to slow for the turn. Then we nearly had the Jaguar in our laps.

Just past the curve, the Jag was sideways in the road with its rear bumper hanging over the steep embankment to our right. Suddenly I was busy trying to get the Chrysler whoa-ed down, and I didn't see what Susan saw.

I heard her gasp and shout, "Johnny, up ahead. Someone's coming the other way!"

Her warning probably saved our lives. The oncoming vehicle looked like a small flatbed farm truck and I was sure had both feet on the brake pedal, but he was still going far too fast to stop before he got to Kipchumba. When he moved over to our side of the road, I saw exactly what he intended to do. There was a small gap between the Jaguar's nose and the cliff face on our right and the truck driver was doing exactly what I would have done—he was heading for that gap.

The problem was we were sitting right in the middle of the same gap. I slammed the Chrysler's shifter into reverse, and backed up as fast as we could go. That quiet piece of Deer Creek Road was suddenly very noisy with the truck's tires screeching, our tires squealing, and the crashing sound of the truck's rusty front bumper smashing into the Jag's left front fender. The impact spun the light sedan around and shoved it nose first down the embankment.

By backing up when I did, I'd made just enough room for the truck to get through without hitting us, and he did. The driver avoided hitting us and kept right on going down the hill. I didn't notice that he hadn't stopped until a few moments later because I was too busy watching the Jag disappear over the shoulder of the road.

I pulled ahead past where the Jaguar had been sitting so someone coming up behind us would have time to avoid hitting us. Then I pulled in close to the cliff face, set the parking brake, and grabbed a three cell flashlight I keep handy in a bracket under the front seat.

"C'mon, Angel. Your special skills might save a life tonight after all."

Susan slid out of the car behind me and we looked down the embankment. The Jaguar had traveled about seventy feet down the embankment, and its flattened roof indicated that part of that trip had been made upside down. The driver's side door was ripped off its hinges and laying about twenty feet up the hill from the rest of the wreck. Kipchumba, or what was left of him, was face down on the ground about halfway between the decapitated door and the rest of the wreck.

Looking for a way to get down there, I noticed the embankment was shallower to our left and would make the climb down to the motionless Joseph Kipchumba a lot easier. I took Susan by the hand to head down the hill, but she resisted, making me think for a moment she wasn't particularly anxious to give Kipchumba first aid, assuming anything could be done for him.

I said, "C'mon, Angel. I know the guy gave us a lot of grief, but we need to do what we can for him."

Susan pulled her hand away and put it on my shoulder to steady herself while she took off her shoes. "You're damned right we do. I want to see that guy and his wife behind bars, but these shoes weren't exactly designed for mountain climbing."

With her shoes off, Susan led the way down the shallowest section of the slope and I kicked myself for thinking she would be unwilling to do what she could to save a human life. We slipped and slid down the embankment until we reached a point opposite where Kipchumba was. After that the hike across the slope was fairly easy.

Kneeling at Kipchumba's side, Susan hunted for a pulse in his neck while I held the flashlight. I could see no indication he was still alive, but then again, I'm no expert on such things. Finally Susan said, "I'm not finding a heartbeat. Help me roll him over."

It took some doing to roll Joseph Kipchumba onto his back. It seemed as if he was stuck on something, and when we eventually got him rolled over, the reason she hadn't been able to find a pulse became more apparent. Kipchumba had landed on the sharp stump of a small tree that had snapped off about a foot above the ground.

Susan said, "That stump impaled him right through the heart. He probably lived for a minute or so after landing on it, but then he was gone."

She stood up and I said, "I know this is going to sound strange, but do you think we could put him back on the stump the way we found him?"

Susan looked at me strangely for a moment, and then caught on. "You don't want anyone to know we were here?"

"I'd just as soon not spend the rest of the night answering questions. I'll call this in from that chowder house we passed, but I'll do it anonymously. I'll give Salvino the straight scoop when I talk to him later, but until then let's just be the little people who were never here."

"What about the truck driver? He saw us."

"True, but he is also guilty of hit-and-run driving and manslaughter at the very least. I don't think he's going to be very anxious to tell his story to the cops. Besides, I'm pretty sure he didn't get a good look at us because everything was happening pretty fast. I doubt if he could even describe our car."

Susan nodded and we bent to the grisly task of re-impaling Kipchumba on the little stump. When we were done, she started back toward the car, but I said, "Hold on for just a minute, Angel. I want to have a look in the Jaguar's trunk."

Recalling Kipchumba's snake, I'll admit to feeling some trepidation when I turned the handle of the boot. When it wouldn't budge, I walked around to the driver's side and pulled the key ring from the ignition switch. Having the key always makes opening a locked trunk much easier.

With the trunk, or as the British call it, the boot, open I shined the flashlight around and saw nothing, or almost nothing. The only things in the trunk besides a spare tire, a crank-type jack, and a large wrench for removing the wire wheel hubs were three identical cardboard boxes about nine-by-nine inches square and maybe six inches deep. The printing on the boxes was the same: "Murakami Imports. Made in Japan."

I picked the closest box up and shook it. It didn't rattle, so I used my penknife to slit the shipping tape securing the box lid. After removing some crumpled tissue paper padding, I was face-to-tusk with Bette Davis's Ivonya-Ngia Tembo statuette. Curious, I opened another of the cardboard boxes and, lo and behold, it contained another elephant statuette identical to the first one.

The tape on the third box was already cut and I was pretty sure I knew what I was going to find in it. I opened the lid, and sure enough, it was yet another elephant. I couldn't help laughing out loud.

Concerned because I seldom found anything funny enough to make me laugh hysterically, Susan rushed over. What's the matter, Johnny? Are you okay?

Still laughing, I managed to say, "What we have here, Angel, is Bette Davis's hundred-thousand-dollar ceramic elephant."

Not getting the joke, Susan said, "That's the priceless knickknack you've been looking for from one end of the state to the other?"

"Yup, in fact, what we have here are three of the priceless knickknacks I've been looking for, all purchased by the Kipchumbas at their neighborhood five and dime."

Incredulously, Susan said, "You mean the elephant statue thing is a fake?"

Still on the verge of tears from laughing so hard, I said, "It sure is. That was the Kipchumba's real scheme. Being African art experts, they sold the elephant to Miss Davis—and who knows how many other suckers—in an-under-the-table deal she'd be reluctant to talk about, and then they set up Rolly Boland and Doris Alpert to steal the damned thing so some other African art expert didn't come along and louse up a very profitable confidence game."

Now Susan had the giggles. "There's nothing funny about several people, including Jack, getting shot, but it's a hell of a joke on a bunch of snobbish art collectors. And I see we're back to 'Miss Davis.'"

"We will be when she gets my bill for finding her buck-fifty curio."

Still giggling, Susan said, "Well, congratulations on solving the mystery, Mister Clever Hollywood Detective. Now let's climb back up to the car and get out of here before someone comes along. Besides, these rocks are killing my feet."

I closed the trunk and started to put the Jaguar's key back in the ignition. Then I realized there were other keys on the ring. Remembering one Kipchumba was still on the loose, I removed the other keys from the ring and dropped them into my pocket before returning the Jag key to the ignition switch.

Back at the Chrysler, I turned the car around carefully so as to avoid ending up down the embankment with the late Mister Kipchumba, and as we drove down the hill at a leisurely pace I checked the odometer. Our high-speed chase had lasted a little more than twenty miles. The way the extra adrenalin in my system was giving me the shakes, it felt more like a hundred. I turned north on Pacific Coast Highway and a short distance later, I pulled into a parking spot in front of Stew Mugu's Chowder House and Bar.

There I used a public telephone to tell the operator a car had gone over the side about a mile-and-a-half from Highway One on Deer Creek Road and it looked like there was a fatality. She told me to hang on while she connected me to the Ventura County Sheriff's office. I told her I had a train to catch and hung up.

When I climbed back into the Chrysler, Susan slid over to the center of the seat so she could put her head on my shoulder. I asked, "Tired?"

With a yawn, she said, "Yes. Is it still Friday?"

I read my watch by the light reflected from the Stew Mugu sign. "In fact it is for another hour-and-a-half. The night is still young. We still have plenty of time to go bar hopping."

Susan yarned again and said, "Oh, goody. Let me know when the fun starts."

By the time I pulled out of the parking lot and got headed north again she was asleep. Laughing to myself, I quietly said, "So much for bar hopping."

Twenty-Eight

9:00 A.M. – Saturday – August 17, 1940

Navy Base Ventura County, Port Hueneme

I was so tired Friday night I almost made what could have been a fatal mistake. When we got back to Port Hueneme I was about to turn into the Sunset Motor Court when I remembered that was where we'd found Joseph Kipchumba earlier. If he was there, his wife, Damaris, was likely to be there, too.

Being too tired to look for another place to stay, I drove back to the base lodge and got Susan a room on the side of the lodge that hadn't been as badly damaged by the explosion and fire. There were still a lot of Shore Patrolmen and firemen milling around the place. It would be a while before things got back to normal at the Port Hueneme Navy Lodge; if they ever got back to normal.

Now, following a restless sleep during which Susan woke me twice in the middle of nightmares in which I was yelling at someone, and breakfast at a coffee shop near the base, we were on our way to look in on Jack. At the hospital I told Susan I was going to use one of the telephone booths outside to call Sergeant Salvino. She asked if I would rather she went inside and gave me some privacy. I told her she'd been part of this caper since the beginning, so she was damned well entitled to get in on the rest of it. She liked that idea and rewarded me with a kiss.

I placed a long distance call to the Seventh Precinct and immediately knew Salvino had already gotten the word on Joseph Kipchumba. "I hear somebody saved the taxpayers a little money last night. Given your record with suspects, I kinda thought you might have had something to do with it, but the Highway Patrol officer I talked to said, judging by the tire tracks, somebody in a truck ran Kipchumba off the road and over a cliff. Trucks just aren't your style. Or are they?"

"Nope, not guilty on that one. It was a farm truck coming down the hill in the opposite direction. Kipchumba pushed it a little too far and spun out just as the truck showed up. The truck had nowhere else to go. To make things even better, the driver of the truck just kept going. I don't think he'll be mentioning the incident to anyone."

"If that's your story, you stick to it."

"Actually it's the truth, Sergeant. We saw it happen and went down to render first aid, but Kipchumba was already dead. There was nothing we could do. Of course, that wasn't in the police report."

"I see. Did you happen to take a look through what was left of Kipchumba's car?"

"Well, officially I wasn't even there, but while I was not being there, I did take a look in the trunk."

"Find anything in there I should know about?"

"Only if you think you should know we were selling the Kipchumbas short. Their scheme was much slicker than we figured."

"Yeah? What the hell did you find in that trunk?"

"I found three, count 'em, three identical one-of-a-kind priceless African elephants that the Kipchumbas probably bought right off the knickknack shelf at their local Woolworth's store. Would that interest you?"

"Not particularly, Spicer. But bring your herd of elephants in until we're sure we don't need 'em for evidence. In case you haven't noticed, we still have one primary suspect you haven't managed to get killed yet."

"Honest, Nick, I didn't . . ."

"Relax, Spicer. I believe your story. It's just this case has been so fouled up since the beginning it's like a Jack Benny radio show."

"Even a comedy show has to be somewhat believable. Stuff like this just doesn't happen in real life."

"It sure as hell doesn't. What are you up to next?"

"I'm going to meet with the Lieutenant Commander who runs the Shore Patrol here at lunch time, even though we don't have much to talk about now."

"True, but he's got paperwork just like I do, so help him out as much as you can without letting him know you were there when Kipchumba got it. Okay?"

"Fair enough. After that I'm going to take Susan up to Santa Barbara to get her car. While I'm up there I'm going to see my client and square things with her."

"You gonna give up on the case with one of the suspects still on the loose?"

"I'm not giving up on the case, but the job my client hired me to do—finding her stupid elephant—is done, so I can't go on charging her to find Missus Kipchumba."

"So you're going to keep looking for the dame?"

"I've got a few ideas about how I might find her, so I think I'll sniff around a little. Besides, I need to keep Susan and her brother safe until we wrap things up once and for all."

"Okay. Keep me informed and come in to see me when you get back to town. And bring all those damned elephant thingamabobs with you."

I hung up and Susan and I stood there looking at each other for a moment. Suddenly we both had smiles on our faces and I had a nurse with her arms around my neck. We kissed and she said, "It's just like last night, Johnny. I don't know what's so funny, but I just feel very happy and I can't help smiling."

"Me, too, Angel. We have to remember, though, Missus Kipchumba is still out there somewhere, and I have no reason to think she's any less dangerous than her husband."

"I know, Johnny, but we're way ahead of where we were before aren't we?"

Yes, Angel, we are."

On the way to Jack's room we encountered Chief Nugent. He was also in exceptionally good spirits. "Good morning, Major Spicer. I'm happy to report all is quiet here."

Returning his crisp salute, I said, "Thank you, Tom. I appreciate your extra diligence last night."

"My pleasure, sir."

In room 115 Jack was reading the morning edition of the *Oxnard Press-Courier*, and when he looked up at us he had a strange expression on his face. Jack put the paper down to give his sister a hug.

Susan gave him a kiss on the cheek and asked him a bunch of questions about how he was feeling. When her interrogation ended, he looked at me and asked a strange question to go with the strange expression that had returned to his face. "Johnny what was the name of that African art dealer you were looking for?"

"Joseph Kipchumba. Why?"

Holding up the newspaper again, Jack said, "There is an article in this morning's paper about a fellow by that same name. Seems he was going a little too fast in his expensive British sedan and went off the road in the coastal hills just south of here. He was killed in the accident and the paper said the accident was reported by an anonymous caller."

I said, "Really? Isn't that something? I guess I don't need to look for him anymore."

Jack looked over at his sister, but before he could speak, she said, "Jack, you know I would never lie to you, so unless you really want to know the truth, don't ask."

He sat there for several moments looking back and forth between Susan and me. Then he mumbled, "Geez, remind me never to blow up your car!"

Susan said, "Speaking of which, Johnny is going to drive me home so I can get my car since yours is . . . out of service. Are there any errands I can do for you while we're up there?"

"No, Sis, unless you can smuggle me out of here."

Susan laughed. "You're talking to the last person who'd do that for you. You need to be here and . . ."

"I know, I know, but I can't ask Johnny because I can tell you've got him . . . ah . . . "

Susan said, "You just watch your language, Sailor!"

Figuring this was a good time to change the subject, I said, "Well, if you think of anything we can do for you while we're up there, we'll be here until after lunch. I've got a meeting at the O Club at a little before noon."

"Holy mackerel! Now you're having meetings at the O Club. Next thing you'll be sitting in Admiral Willets' desk chair!"

"I might. This Navy of yours could use some new ideas."

"Hey, I'm Coast Guard! We just use the Navy for incidentals, like doctors and the like."

Susan said she would rather stay with Jack during lunch, so I took off for the O Club and my meeting with Lieutenant Commander Arnold. After some small talk, we got down to business.

I asked, "Have you seen the Oxnard paper this morning?"

"I looked through it quickly. Why?"

"Do you recall an article about a car going over a cliff on Deer Creek Road?"

Arnold thought for a moment. "Yes, I did see something about that. Why?"

"Unless I'm way off the beam, the guy driving that car is the fellow who blew things up at the lodge last night."

223

"What makes you think so?"

I gave Arnold the short version of the missing African art I'd been looking for and how Kipchumba fit into it. I finished with, "If you'll give Detective Sergeant Salvino at LAPD's Seventh Precinct a call, he can fill in the holes for your reports and so on."

"Great! If you're right, this could save me a lot of work."

"I'm ninety-nine-point-nine percent positive, but there's one thing I haven't told you yet. Kipchumba was in this with his wife, a woman named Damaris Kipchumba, and my impression of her is that she is every bit as dangerous as her husband maybe more so, and she's still out there somewhere."

Arnold was making notes on a legal pad. "Any description?"

"I've only seen her once and that was just a quick glimpse through a car window. She is a Negro and wears her hair in a kind of natural style, like all fluffed up."

"Okay, I'll get that description out. With her hair like that, she should be easier to spot. Was the car her husband crashed in the Jaguar sedan you had us watching for?"

"Yup. You can cancel that bulletin now."

"What's your plan at this point?"

"I need to make a trip up to Santa Barbara and back this afternoon. Then I'd like to take advantage of your hospitality for another couple of days while I try to turn up something locally on this woman. Think that will be okay?"

He nodded. "I'll make sure it's okay, Major Spicer. I'll let 'em know at Admin so they'll keep your pass active, and I'd appreciate knowing anything useful you learn."

"Count on it."

Susan was waiting for me outside the main entrance to the hospital, and when she saw me pull up, she trotted down the stairs and climbed into the car. Settling in, she asked, "How was the O Club today?"

"It lacks quite a bit when you're not with me."

"Then we'd better plan another visit together like we talked about last night, that is, if you're going to be around."

"I told you I'm not going anywhere without you until this mess is cleared up and I meant it. So another visit to the club would be easy to arrange."

It was right around one-thirty when we pulled up in front Susan's apartment. She asked if it would be okay to run in and pack some fresh clothes since all she had with her went up in smoke at the lodge. I told her I was going up to her apartment with her just to see my pal, Mister Whiskers.

I opened her apartment door cautiously. My caution was unnecessary, though, and Mister Whiskers was indeed happy to see us. He even gave my ankle a rub in passing.

With a new bag packed, Susan said she needed to stop at a sundries store for some toiletry items. I suggested we do that on our way to the clinic. Next we headed down to the garage where her sea green Pontiac De Luxe Six Cabriolet was parked. I inspected the car carefully, including giving the wiring under the hood a careful inspection. I couldn't find anything amiss, so we started the engine, let it warm up, and I followed her to a nearby drug store.

It took Susan a while to gather up all the items she needed, so I just followed her around the store and got an education about the toiletries preferred by the modern woman. For my lady's teeth she chose Listerine mouthwash, Ipana tooth paste, and a Doctor West toothbrush. For just the right shade of lipstick—Holly Berry Red—Susan selected Max Factor. Then there was Dew Deodorant, Halo Shampoo, and a perfume called Emeraude Encores by Coty that looked like it might be worth its weight in gold.

On our way out, Susan said, "All right, now that you are privy to my beauty secrets, you must take a vow of silence. If you ever reveal what you saw here today, I'll stop using this stuff and you'll see what an ugly old witch I really am."

I slipped my arm around her waist, made a careful scan of the cars and people around us, and said, "My lips are sealed."

She looked up at me and said, "Boy, did you just miss a perfect opportunity to make points!"

"That's because you were fishing for a compliment. When I tell you you're beautiful, it comes from the heart, not because it's expected of me." After a few steps, I added, "By the way, you're beautiful."

Susan gave me a bump with her hip and said, "That's better."

Our next stop was Casa Sobre El Mar. Inside, she chatted with her fellow nurses for a few minutes, after which we walked to Lillian Bouvier's room. Bette was reading a magazine and Lilly appeared to be napping, but they both paid close attention when Susan and I walked in and I set the cardboard box I was carrying down on the table.

Bette's famous eyes studied if for several seconds, and then she looked at me with a question on her face. I said, "Yes, that's the Ivonya-Ngia Tembo Joseph Kipchumba arranged for you to buy."

She took a tentative step toward the table and I said, "That's the good news. Everything else about the statuette is bad news. For one thing, it's a fake. I found two more just like it in the trunk of his car.

The Kipchumbas bought them at a five and dime or an import store somewhere and gave the one you had a little patina of age. Then they got Doris Alpert and Rolly Boland to help them sell it to you for about a hundred-thousand times what they paid for it."

If that surprised her, she didn't show it. Instead, she asked, "What else do you have to tell me about the Ivonya-Ngia Tembo, Mister Spicer?"

Susan winked at me when she heard the "Mister Spicer" and I said, "There isn't much more to tell that you don't already know. They arranged to have Rolly swipe the statue before someone who knew African art tipped you off that it was a phony. Rolly and Doris were killed to keep them from ever telling anyone what they knew and to increase the Kipchumbas' share of the hundred grand they collected when they sold you the statuette.

"I can let you take a look at the statuette if you'd like, but I need to hand it over to the LAPD for a while to use as evidence if the case goes to trial. You can have it back . . ."

Bette Davis's eyes flashed. "Of course it will go to trial. I'm going to see that crook spend the rest of his life behind bars!"

"Well, I'm afraid that's not going to happen. Joseph Kipchumba died in an automobile accident last night. Susan and I saw it happen. She even tried to give Kipchumba first aid, but he was already dead."

"You're just full of happy news, aren't you, Mister Spicer?"

I unwrapped the statuette and held it up in its last layer of tissue paper as I said, "I think that's the end of the bad news. Kipchumba's wife is still on the loose, but the deal you and I had was to find the elephant. Whatever work I do to find Missus Kipchumba will be on me."

"I see. What do you estimate I owe you at this point?"

"Well, we've been at this for twelve days at seventy-five per day less a hundred dollar retainer comes to eight-hundred-dollars. Expenses will add another four hundred or so to that, so roughly one-thousand-two-hundred."

"That's a great deal of money for recovering a dime store knickknack."

"True, but it wasn't such a great deal of money when you thought this knickknack was worth a hundred grand. If you had bought the real thing, the recovery cost would be less than one-and-a-half percent."

Bette Davis nodded. "You make a good point, Mister Spicer. However, I wasn't trying to cut you out of anything I owe you. To the contrary, I want to continue paying you until you get that dreadful man's wife behind bars. Is that acceptable to you?"

I was repacking the elephant and I darn near dropped it. I said, "That's very generous of you, Miss Davis. I'll put whatever extra there is toward replacing an innocent man's car that was blown up because he was in the wrong place at the wrong time. The details will be in my final report."

She smiled and said, "Oh, I can't wait to read that report. Maybe we can make a screenplay out of it."

The hands of my Chrysler's dashboard clock were pointing at three-twenty-five when we pulled out of Santa Barbara and headed south on Highway One. Susan led our little parade, and I kept my eye on the rearview mirror for any car that appeared to be following us. Now that the distinctive Jaguar was scrap, watching for the remaining Kipchumba was more difficult because I didn't know what I was looking for. Still, I saw nothing suspicious in my mirror.

We drove back on the base at four-forty-five and Susan parked her car at the lodge, but not directly in front of her new room. Since nobody seemed to be paying the slightest attention to us, I carried both bags in and plunked them down on the bed.

Susan said, "If you don't mind, I'd like to freshen up a little before we go out again."

"Gonna apply some of your famous beauty secrets?"

She turned and with her hands on her hips she said, "Why? Do I need them?"

"Not so as I could see. That would be like gilding the lily."

Susan smiled. "Why, what a nice thing to say!"

"See? I'm trainable."

Twenty-Nine

5:45 P.M. – Saturday – August 17, 1940

Navy Base Ventura County, Port Hueneme

It was quarter to six when we drove over to the hospital so Susan could see how Jack was doing. Everything was quiet and appeared to be in order there except Jack. He was in a stew about his automobile insurance.

". . . and they told me my car wasn't covered because I was on a military base when it happened. I can tell you I'll be getting a new insurance company if and when I ever get another car to insure. Those blankety-blank . . ."

Susan said, "Jack, calm down. You're getting yourself all upset. That's not good for your blood pressure or anything else. Besides, I have a feeling everything will work out just fine."

He grumbled, "I don't see how. The only thing I can do is buy myself a twenty-dollar jalopy and hope it holds together so I'll have something to run around in."

Susan put a hand on his shoulder. "Just relax for now. You've got family and a pretty darn good friend on your side."

We needed to do something to cheer Jack up. He'd had more than his share of grief during the past few days, and I had an idea that might be just the ticket. Turning to Susan, I said, "Angel, would you mind stepping out in the hall with me for a second? We need to have a quick discussion."

I could tell from her expression she was wondering what I was up to now, but she said, "Okay. Jack, I'll be right back. I want to see that frown gone by then."

Jack mumbled something about Little Goody Two Shoes and I followed Susan out into the hall, giving Jack a conspiratorial wink as I left. Out in the hall, Susan said, "Darn it, Johnny we need to cheer him up somehow. I hate seeing down in the dumps like this."

"I might know a way of getting a smile back on his face. How soon will Jack be able to get out for an hour or two, like in a wheelchair?"

I could see the wheels turning as she figured out what I had in mind. "I don't see any reason why he couldn't do that right now. He has a couple of uniforms here, so if we take it slow, we could get him dressed for an outing. We can borrow a wheelchair from the hospital; they have several of them around."

"Good. Do you think he would enjoy going to O Club for dinner with us tonight?"

She grinned from ear to ear. "I bet he'd love it! Go ask him."

Back in Jack's room, I said, "Jack, the last time I invited you to dinner you got cheated out of a meal, but according to this nurse I know, there's no reason you couldn't slip into a uniform and ride over to the O Club in a wheelchair. So how 'bout it? Join us for dinner?"

My question had the desired effect of instantly putting a smile on his face. "Really? I would love to! Are you sure I won't be a fifth wheel?"

Susan laughed. "Of course you will, but this big lug insists on bringing you along. So if I get a sudden urge to kiss him, you just look the other way. Deal?"

"Deal!"

I was sent in search of a wheelchair and Susan went to work helping Jack into a uniform. An orderly helped me procure a wheelchair we could use and keep in Jack's room for future outings. The orderly also took care of signing Jack out to the O Club for two hours, explaining the best way to get there with the wheelchair was down a ramp at the hospital's rear entrance.

Back in room 115, Jack was fully dressed except for his tie and hat. Susan was fussing with the tie and getting nowhere. She said, "Here, Johnny, you tie this darn thing. Apparently big brother can't tie his own tie without looking in a mirror to see what he's doing."

I said, "Sure, but first let's move to the wheelchair. That'll make it easier."

Taking my arm, Jack carefully stood up and we walked slowly to the wheelchair I'd brought back. Then I stood behind Jack and put my arms around in front of his shoulders so it felt like I was tying my own tie.

I thought I did a pretty swell job, but of course Susan had to fuss with it, claiming it wasn't quite straight. A minute later he was ready for his cap. The uniform he'd chosen was the white summer version and I have to say he looked pretty spiffy in it.

I said, "Okay, Jack, we're off like a herd of turtles!"

"No, wait. I have to sign out first."

"All taken care of, Amigo. You're officially at the O Club for the next two hours."

With a big smile on his face, he said, "Then what are we waiting for?"

The staff at the O Club was very helpful, seating us at a table that would accommodate Jack's wheelchair and making sure we had everything we needed for a pleasant evening. Jack was clearly enjoying being out of the hospital for a couple of hours, and I couldn't blame him one bit.

In a teasing tone, he said, "I guess I should ask if we're celebrating anything special tonight."

Susan looked at me and said, "That's my brother for you—subtle as a ton of bricks."

"Geez, Sis. I was just askin'."

Chuckling, I said, "Don't worry, Jack. You'll be the first to know when it's time to celebrate."

"Good, and I notice you said 'when it's time to celebrate,' not 'if it's time to celebrate.' I'll take that as a positive sign."

Susan shook her head in exasperation. "Jack, you are hopeless."

By seven-thirty we'd finished dinner and despite having a good time, Jack was clearly getting tired, so I signed the mess check and we took him back to his room at the hospital. Susan got busy helping him out of his uniform.

When he was back in bed, Jack said, "I want you two to know how much I enjoyed tonight. It was a real treat to have a night on the town, so to speak."

Susan gave him a kiss on the cheek. "Johnny's the one you need to thank. It was his idea."

I quickly said, "No thanks are necessary. Having you join us was as much a pleasure for us as it was for you."

The Chrysler was still parked out in front of the hospital, right where I'd left it. After looking the car over carefully, I started the engine and we drove the short distance to the base lodge.

As we drove, Susan said, "Johnny, I apologize for Jack. He was trying to make a joke, but sometimes his sense of humor leaves something to be desired."

"I know, Angel. He embarrassed you, but from my perspective he was right on the beam."

Susan smiled. "He was?"

"Seems that way to me."

"Okay, as long as we're doing true confessions, I'll admit I was hoping he was. Still, we don't want to rush into anything we'll regret later. If or when I get married, it's going to be for keeps."

"That seems like the right way to go about it. How 'bout we just keep talking in that direction from time to time and see how we feel after more time together?"

Smiling a pleasant sort of smile, she said, "I was just going to suggest the same thing."

I pulled into the parking spot next to Susan's Pontiac and we kissed. Then Susan suggested we go in and get some rest. I told her I thought that was another excellent suggestion.

There are several ways to enter a room when you are concerned about who might be waiting for you inside. In this instance I was dealing with a possible ambush rather than a likely one, so I didn't feel drastic measures were necessary.

I simply unlocked Susan's room and opened the door just far enough to reach the light switch on the wall to my right. With the lights on, I took my time looking through the opening to see as much of the room as I could. Then I grabbed Susan around the waist and ran from the door, slamming it behind us as I went.

Our hasty departure was followed almost instantly by two muffled "pops" from inside the room and the appearance of two splintered holes in the wooden door. Pulling Susan with me, I ran as far as I thought I could go before the shooter got out of the room. The direction I'd turned leaving the room put us next to the narrow space between my Chrysler and Susan's Pontiac. I was already pulling her down to the ground between our cars when another gunshot popped and small chunks of plaster exploded from the wall behind us.

The sun had set about thirty minutes earlier, so the night sky still had a hint of natural light in it, but not enough to do the shooter much good. There were, however, several lights in the lodge parking lot and the base gate about a block away was also well lit.

I took a quick glace in the direction of the gate and saw the shore patrolman on duty looking back in our direction. He'd heard the shooting, but he couldn't see where it was coming from. I risked giving away our location by yelling in his direction. "Shore patrol! Send help to the lodge!"

He apparently didn't hear me because he was still looking to find the source of the shooting. Okay, if they can't hear you find another method of communication. After checking to make sure the shooter was still looking around to see where we'd gotten to, I fished my car keys out of my pocket and reached up to unlock the passenger-side door of my car. Opening it, I grabbed the flashlight from under the seat. Then I turned the light on and pointed it at the shore patrolman. The way his head turned, I knew he saw the light. Now we could communicate.

Using the small pushbutton incorporated into the off/on switch just as it was intended to be used, I sent the shore patrolman a message in Morse code. I used short flashes for dots and longer flashes for dashes to send: ... . --- --- - . .-. / .- - / .-.. --- -.. --. . .-.-.- / ... . .-. -.. / ....-.. --. / - --- / .--. .- .-. -.- .. -. --. / .-.. --- - / ..-. .-. --- - - / ... --- ..- - .... .-.-.- / .... .--. .. -.-. . .-. .-.-.-

Susan said, "What the heck are you . . . Oh! You're flashing Morse code at him! What are you saying?"

"Geez, if you'd been a Boy Scout you'd know what I'm saying."

"If I'd been a Boy Scout, we probably wouldn't be hiding behind cars in front of our hotel room."

As I finished my message, I said, "Good point. I sent 'shooter at lodge / send help to parking lot from south / spicer.'"

While the shore patrolman spoke animatedly into his telephone. I checked on the shooter and caught a brief glimpse of a reflection in the window of the room on our side of Susan's. The shooter had moved out into the driveway and was coming toward us behind the parked cars.

When the shore patrolman hung up his telephone, the interior light of the guard shack began flashing on and off: -- . ...- --. . / ..- -. -... . .-. ... - --- --- -.. .-.-.- / ....-.. .--. / -.-. --- -- .. -. --. .-.-.-

Knowing help was now on its way, I moved as fast as I could to the back of my car, and aiming carefully to avoid hitting the shooter, I ricocheted a slug off the pavement to the right of my target. The shooter stopped and ducked between the closest parked cars.

Speaking softly so the shooter couldn't hear her, Susan asked, "Did you get him?"

"Nope. First, it's a her, not a him, and second, I want her alive. That shot was just to let her know we're armed and dangerous too."

While I got down on my belly and looked under my car to find out if I could see the shooter's feet under the cars between us, Susan said with astonishment, "Her? You mean that's the Kipchumba woman shooting at us?"

Still flat on the ground looking under my car, I found I could make out the woman's feet in the shadowy area between two cars a ways down the row. I said, "Or her twin sister."

"Oh, for heaven's sake! Don't those people ever give up?"

"They must think persistence is a virtue."

"What I don't understand is how you saw her in our room. I was right behind you and I would have sworn there was no one in that room."

As I watched her feet from under the cars, Damaris Kipchumba moved back toward the sidewalk in front of the rooms. I did the same and positioned myself for a shot over the hood of my Chrysler if she showed herself on the sidewalk between the cars and the rooms.

"That's because there wasn't anyone in the bedroom. She was in the bathroom."

That surprised Susan even more than the identity of the shooter. "The bathroom?"

"Yup. The door between the bathroom and the bedroom was open and when I turned on the bedroom light, enough of it spilled into the bathroom that I could see a dim reflection of someone in the bathroom mirror. I couldn't have told you who it was at that point, but I could definitely see someone standing in there."

"That was very clever of you. So what very clever thing are we going to do now?"

"It looks like we're going to do our best to stay alive for another minute or two until the shore patrol comes to our rescue. After that it's pretty much up to Missus Kipchumba."

No more than a minute later a gray four-door Chevrolet sedan with big white stars on its front doors came squealing around the south end of the building and slowed almost to a stop. The shore patrol's problem was they were driving into the middle of a gunfight and they had no idea who or where the shooters were.

Crouching, I ran to the back of my car, held up my badge case, and pointed my flashlight at the shiny gold shield. In the illumination of the parking lot lights I saw the driver of the Chevrolet was Lieutenant Commander Arnold.

He waved back just before another movement off to the right caught my eye. Pushing Susan down, I quickly moved to the front of my car and took aim. Damaris Kipchumba was walking straight toward me with her revolver in both hands and raised to fire.

The woman had great reactions. The instant she saw me pop up, she fired. Fortunately, her aim wasn't as good as her reactions. The slug went high and wide to my left. One of the shore patrolmen yelled at her to stop and drop her weapon, but she just walked faster. In another few steps she would have us at point blank range.

She was giving me no choice. I aimed for her left hip, hoping to stop the woman without killing her, and began to squeeze the trigger, but before I got the shot off, three things happened almost simultaneously.

First, the louder, more percussive "bams" of two large caliber pistol rounds came from the parking lot area off to my left. At the same time Missus Kipchumba fired a round at us that ended up ricocheting off the hood of my Chrysler with a high-pitched whine. Then she took a staggering step forward and collapsed to the sidewalk.

Susan started to go to the woman on the ground, but I grabbed her and held her back. "Just a second, Angel. Let me get that pistol away from her so we don't have any more surprises."

She waited impatiently while I kicked Damaris Kipchumba's long-barreled thirty-eight several feet from her motionless body. I said, "Okay, Angel, she's all yours. See what you can do for her."

While Susan knelt next to the unconscious woman and began examining her, I held the flashlight where I thought it might help her, and Lieutenant Commander Arnold and his three Shore Patrolmen trotted up.

The patrolmen went over to cover the Kipchumba woman, although it seemed fairly evident to me that she didn't need much covering in her present condition. I turned to Arnold and said, "Thanks, George. You brought the cavalry to our rescue just in the nick of . . ."

Susan interrupted saying, "She's still alive. We might save her if we can get her to a doctor quickly enough."

I turned to Arnold and said, "There you go, George. You've got yourself a prisoner who was at least an accomplice in the bombing last night; that is if you get her to a medic fast enough."

Picking two of his men he said, "Put her in the back of our car and get her over to the hospital. Then stay with her. I'll send someone over to spell you in a while, but I don't want that woman disappearing on us."

Susan jumped up, saying, "I'm going with them. I want to see that she survives to spend a long time in jail."

With our party thus reduced to Lieutenant Commander Arnold, the other Shore Patrolman and me, we set about making and taking statements and collecting information that would appear in Arnold's reports.

When we were just about done, Arnold asked to see my revolver. I handed him my Smith and Wesson and he inspected it. Then he handed it back to me and to the shore patrolman who was taking notes, he said, "One round fired, as testified to by Major Spicer." To me he said, "That revolver doesn't get much use, does it? In fact, I think I saw dust in the barrel. In the Navy we frown on those who don't take proper care of their equipment."

Smiling, I said, "Why should I worry? I've got you guys with all your properly maintained equipment to take care the bad guys for me."

Arnold shook his head as if he couldn't believe what he'd just heard. "That sounds like the Army, all right." Then he added, "What I don't understand is why you didn't shoot when she left cover and was marching in your direction bold as you please."

"I was about to, but I was aiming to put a round into her that would stop her, but not kill her."

"That was pretty cool-headed thinking under fire. What the hell did you do in the Army?"

Grinning, I said, "Mostly, I kept my head down and let the Navy do the shooting. You guys had a bigger ammo budget than we did."

At the hospital Chief Warrant Officer Nugent greeted me and said I would find Miss Jackson in her brother's room. I went to see if he was right. He was.

Susan got up and held on tight for a moment, and then she gestured toward the door. Jack appeared to be sound asleep and she didn't want to wake him.

"It looks like Missus Kipchumba will pull through. Who do you think will happen to her when she's recovered?"

"That depends on who brings the most serious charges against her. I'm betting on the Navy because they've got at least three murder wraps they can pin on her. Federal cases almost always take priority over other jurisdictions. Once they're through with her, though, there are still the murders of Rolly Boland in Los Angeles and Doris Alpert in Needles, plus it's likely some other jurisdictions will get in on the act. By that time, though, Missus Kipchumba's future will be pretty well determined. The Navy thinks cold-blooded murder in the first degree is a hanging offence."

Susan nodded. "That's sort of what I figured out, too."

"More to the point, Angel, how are you doing?"

She thought about the question for a moment. "It's very strange. When it was all happening and that awful woman was shooting at us, I wasn't really scared. I mean my adrenalin was pumping and my heart was racing, but I somehow knew we were going to be okay. Now, after it's all over and we're perfectly safe, my knees are shaking so badly I can barely stand up."

"That's often the way it goes, Angel. I'm just glad you weren't hurt. This business of having you close at the wrong times is scaring the hell out of me. When we were chasing Joseph, I almost stopped a dozen times because I was afraid you were going to get hurt."

"I know, Johnny, but please don't push me away. Being with you and sharing the risks is a lot better than sitting somewhere waiting to know if you're all right."

I didn't know how to respond to that one, so I just kissed her and we drove back to the lodge.

Thirty

9:00 A.M. – Monday – August 19, 1940

Spicer Investigations – 1st National Bank Building, Hollywood

I was just about to head over to the Seventh Precinct to see Salvino when the little bell on my outer office hall door tinkled. I opened the inner door and there stood the man himself.

"Hello, Nick. What brings you to this neck of the woods? Or are you just out slummin'?"

Removing three inches of stogie from his mouth, he said, "I got tired of waiting for you to bring those damned elephants in, that's what."

"Hell, Nick, I only found them Friday and I was just getting ready to bring them to you. They're right there on the desk. The top one is the statuette the Kipchumbas sold to Miss Davis. The other two boxes were sealed when I found them. They each contain an exact duplicate of the statuette sold to Miss Davis, except they haven't been monkeyed with to look like antiques."

He walked over to my desk and picked up the top cardboard box in the stack. As he opened it, he said, "Any chance of fingerprints on this thing?"

"As long as you don't smudge 'em up. It was wrapped just the way you see it, and I've made sure nobody handled the statuette itself."

Holding the elephant in its wrapping paper, he looked it over. "So this is what got three people killed and a few more shot?"

"Actually, six people were killed if you count the three who died in the Navy Lodge explosion."

He turned the elephant so he was looking it in the eye and simply said, "Amazing."

"My sentiments exactly."

Rewrapping the statuette, Salvino said, "I hear you got in on some shooting Saturday night. Thanks for leaving a suspect alive this time so we have someone to prosecute."

"Don't thank me; thank Susan. Those shore patrol boys were aiming to kill, but Susan gave Missus Kipchumba first aid and got her to the hospital in time for the doctors to save her."

"Well, good for her! I'll have to take her out for dinner to say thanks."

"Good idea. Why I'll bet she's never even been to that hot dog joint you like over on La Brea."

Picking up the boxes containing the phony Ivonya-Ngia Tembo and its replicas from my desk, Salvino turned and walked toward the door. On the way he said, "Thanks for reminding me about that place. Think I'll get myself a dog or two so this trip shouldn't be a total loss."

To his back I said, "What a classy guy!"

With delivering the statue crossed off my list of things that needed doing, I went downstairs and ran a finger over the dent in the maroon paint caused by Damaris Kipchumba's stray round. Getting it fixed was the next item on my list of errands, and the place where that job was going to get done was the dealership the car came from, Greer-Robbins over on Western Avenue.

Greer-Robbins was located in a smallish, two-story brick building with a showroom up front and the repair shop down a driveway that ran along the left side of the building. The guy who ran the repair shop was a tall, slender fellow in coveralls named Ralph who genuinely looked like a mechanic.

He looked at the dent and said, "That there looks like somebody took a shot at you."

I smiled, "As much as it grieves me to admit it, Ralph, not everyone thinks I'm a really swell guy."

That seemed to confuse Ralph, so he didn't reply, but set about writing an estimate for the repair. He figured fifty dollars and he could have it ready the next day at five. I told him that sounded fine and asked about the chances of getting a loaner to drive until then. He called up front to the showroom and Glenn White, Greer-Robbins' General Manager showed up a few minutes later.

"Hi, Johnny. Ralph here says you need a loaner until tomorrow afternoon. That right?"

"I sure do, Glenn. You have something I can use?"

"Johnny, I've got something you're gonna love. Come out here."

I followed him out front to the curb where he stopped next to a sleek, pale blue coupe. "This is the 1941 Royal Coupe. How would you like to drive this around for a couple of days?"

"I suppose it would be all right."

"All right? Johnny, you're gonna come back wanting to swap that nineteen-thirty-eight model of yours for this beauty. I guarantee it!"

Being an honest sort of guy, I lied and told him I really couldn't afford a new car right now, but Glenn insisted I was going to fall in love with his nineteen-forty-one Royal. I was pretty sure I wasn't, but I hated to disillusion him.

My next stop was the See's Candy store in the one hundred block of Western, about two miles north of the dealership. There, I splurged three-fifty on a five pound box of the best assorted chocolates made—or at least that's what my chocolate-loving friends tell me. Chocolate doesn't go real well with Scotch, so I don't eat a lot of it.

Then I drove over to Van Ness Avenue and let myself in to Lilly Bouvier's cottage with the key Bette Davis had given me. In the kitchen I bagged up a few items from the refrigerator, like the milk, that were well past their prime. I also added the nearly empty one pound Whitman's chocolate box I'd found on the top shelf of a cabinet during my last visit.

After taking the garbage bag out to the trashcan, I placed the fresh five pound box of See's on the top shelf where the Whitman's had been. Lilly deserved a hell of a lot more for what she was going through, but the candy was all I could think of that she would accept from me. I hoped the surprise of finding her chocolate stash re-supplied would put a smile on her face.

9:00 A.M. – Tuesday – August 27, 1940

Bette Davis Residence – 5346 Franklin Avenue, Hollywood

Bette brought Lillian Bouvier back to Hollywood from Santa Barbara over the weekend. Then Bette called me and arranged for a Tuesday morning meeting to discuss my bill and other matters. I arrived promptly at the designated meeting time. I always endeavor to be prompt when matters of money are on the agenda.

We sat in her library for our chat. She started the conversation by asking after Susan.

I said, "Susan is doing well. If all goes according to plan, we'll move her brother back to Santa Barbara next weekend. In the meantime Susan is going up to the clinic for a few hours every day to start her new job. That makes for some long days, but Susan feels obligated, especially since her boss is being extremely understanding about the whole thing."

"Would her boss be Doctor Rothenberg?"

"That's him."

"He stopped by a few times to look in on Lillian while I was there. I'm quite fond of him."

"So am I. I was at his home last year when I was shot. That's how I ended up at Casa Sobre El Mar and how I met Susan."

Smiling what I thought looked like a knowing smile, Bette said, "So I understand. Listen, Johnny, I'm going to give you a piece of advice you haven't asked for, and if you're the man I think you are, I'm preaching to the choir, but you've got yourself one very fine woman there. On top of being pretty as a picture, she's smart as a whip with a great sense of humor. Don't let her get away!"

"Thank you, Bette. I will heed your advice."

With a chuckle, she said, "See that you do! Now, let's get down to business. I've read your report and gone over your bill, but I have some questions about your expenses."

"They're all pretty standard. I did my best to keep them to a minimum."

"That's the problem. You left items off that should be here. For example I don't see any of the nights you were at the Santa Barbara Hyatt on here."

"True, but the Hyatt is a little steep. I didn't feel right about billing you . . . "

Glowering, Bette interrupted. "The only time I get upset about expenses is when the hired help is staying at a place I can't afford for myself."

She shuffled the papers and looked at the total on the last page. "Look, you've got a total of one-thousand-six-hundred here. I think this is more like it."

She held out a check, but I couldn't see the amount until I walked over and accepted it. Then my jaw dropped. She'd written the check in the amount of three-thousand-six-hundred; two thousand more than the amount I'd billed her.

Before I could think of something to say, Bette said, "Now, about this fellow who was shot and had his car blown up, he is Susan's brother, is that correct?"

"Yes, but about this check . . ."

"Hush, Johnny. You may speak when it's your turn. You are to give Mister Jackson this letter." She held it up for me to take and smiled. "To save you the effort of steaming the envelope open—that is what you private eyes do, isn't it? Anyway, to save you going to all that bother, it is a letter introducing Mister Jackson to Mister Jeremy Coberly who is the owner of the Ford dealership on Eighth Street downtown. Upon presentation of this letter Mister Jackson may pick out any new Ford on the lot without cost. Does that seem fair?"

By that time I was astonished at Bette's generosity. "That is more than fair, Bette. In fact it seems to me you're being overly generous."

"Johnny, generosity has absolutely nothing to do with any of this. You put your life on the line to recover a fake piece of art. To me, that seems overly courageous, but it is what you do. Think of it that way . . . this is what I do."

For some reason that reminded me of a key in my jacket pocket I'd almost forgotten. I took the key to Lilly Bouvier's house out and handed it to Bette, saying, "I've been carrying this around so I'd remember to give it to you when we got together. It's the key to Lilly's cottage."

She accepted the key, saying, "Yes, I recognize it. And this key reminds me of something else I want to discuss with you."

"What's that?"

"When I took Lillian home, someone had carried her garbage out so it wouldn't smell up the house. Was that you?"

I was pretty sure I knew what was coming, but I was guilty, and saw no reason to lie about it. "Yes, I stopped by a week or so ago to make sure everything was okay and decided there were some things in the refrigerator that needed to be tossed out."

"That was nice of you, Johnny, but the box of chocolates was a true act of kindness. I was watching her when she noticed that her almost empty box had been replaced. She asked if I had done it, and when I said I had not, she sat at her kitchen table with the box and bawled like a baby."

"Damn, I was hoping it would make her happy."

"It did, Johnny, it did. I think she was crying because that might have been the first time anyone—a relative stranger—ever did her a thoughtful kindness. And you did it without any ulterior motives or expectations other than to do something nice for someone who needs to believe in herself again. In my book that makes you a real classy guy."

"So she knows I left the candy?"

"She put me on the spot. Lillian asked me who else had a key to the house, and you were the only one who did. When I told her that she got suspicious, I guess figuring you were trying to sleep with her or something else equally terrible. I told her you and Susan had a strong relationship and I couldn't imagine you being interested in any other woman.

"Then she started crying again. I expect she'll come around to say thanks one day, but if she doesn't, I wanted you to know you've done something special for a young woman who desperately needs special things to happen in her life."

11:45 A.M. – Monday – September 2, 1940

Susan Jackson Residence – 3412 State Street #4, Santa Barbara

I spent a good part of Labor Day weekend helping Susan move Jack back from Port Hueneme to Santa Barbara. He would be staying with her for a couple of weeks before returning to his base housing at the Coast Guard facility, thus allowing her to work full time in her new job at the clinic.

Now, with Mister Whiskers making sure every inch of my dark blue slacks was decorated with at least one cat hair, I sat at Susan's kitchen table chatting with Jack while Susan made tuna salad sandwiches for lunch. After she brought the plate of sandwiches and three bottles of Lowenbrau to the table, I raised my bottle and said, "To Jack, may his recovery continue to be swift."

We all drank to that and Susan said, "Ah . . . Johnny, don't you have something for Jack to help celebrate his homecoming?"

"As a matter of fact, I do." I removed Bette Davis's letter from an inside jacket pocket and handed it to him. "This is from my client in the elephant case. She felt badly that you were injured and your car was blown up while I was working on her case, so she wants you to have this."

Jack opened the envelope, read the letter, looked up at Susan and me, and read the letter again. Then in a tone edged with astonishment, he said, "Is this for real? I mean was your client the real Bette Davis and did she really do this for me?"

I said, "Yes, it's for real and yes my client was the 'real' Bette Davis and yes she really wants you to have a new car at her expense. It turns out she owns a percentage of the dealership. That's why she set it up this way."

Holding the letter up Jack said, "This is just . . . just incredible!"

Winking at me, Susan said, "Bette is an incredible woman. I hope you'll get to meet her one day. She's been very generous to all of us."

I was wondering in what way Bette had been generous to Susan when Jack said, "When can you take me down to L.A., Sis? I want to pick out my new car!"

Susan said, "Maybe next weekend if a certain Hollywood Private Eye invites me down to spend some time on the beach and if you're feeling up to making the drive home alone."

"Great!"

It was time for me to head back to Hollywood, but before I left a thought occurred to me. I said, "Jack, when you pick up your car, talk the guy into letting you keep your copy of that letter."

"Why, Johnny?"

"Because in twenty or thirty years that piece of paper might be worth enough to pay for a college education."

10:00 A.M. – Tuesday – September 3, 1940

Howard Automobile Company – 6660 Sunset Blvd., Los Angeles

After getting back from Santa Barbara Monday evening, I relaxed with the current issue of *Automobile Monthly* magazine and came across a road test article that fascinated me. The car tested was something called a Buick Century Sedanette.

Besides having the silliest name ever given to an automobile, the thing that fascinated me about the car was the author's speculation that the Sedanette was possibly the fastest production car made in the United States. That's saying quite a bit, but the coupe is powered by Buick's Fireball 248 cubic inch straight eight with twin carburetors that develops 125 horsepower. If it wasn't really the fastest U.S. production car, all of that horsepower in a light two-door coupe ought to make it a close second. This, I decided, was a car I needed to see . . . and drive.

So, after coffee and a look at the *Times*, I drove down Highland to Sunset and turned left. Hollywood's Buick dealership was the Howard Automobile Company at 6660 Sunset, across the boulevard from the new Crossroads of the World shopping bazaar. The dealership was on my right, but there were no parking spots on Sunset, so I turned right at the next intersection—Cherokee—and found an empty slot alongside Howard's lot.

I spotted a Sedanette on the lot almost immediately, but it was a Super, not a Century. According to the article I read, the Century was just a little longer than the Super and, more importantly, had the one-hundred-twenty-five horsepower engine instead of the hundred-and-seven horsepower version. Another way of spotting a Century was that it had five Cruis-a-line Vent-a-ports—or portholes as they're more commonly called—above the front fenders instead of four.

After looking around the lot, I came to the conclusion that all of the Sedanettes they had were Supers. As I was drawing that conclusion, a roly-poly salesman headed in my direction. Maybe he knew where they hid the Centuries, although he looked more like he'd know where the donuts were stashed.

Offering a chubby hand he said, "Howdy, neighbor! I'm Andy Pruett. Who might you be?"

I ignored the offered hand because it was bound to be damp with nervous sweat—he looked like that sort of fellow. "I might be a guy who wants to buy a Century Sedanette. You got any?"

I've found that when dealing with car salesmen it's always best to keep them off balance. It didn't take much to achieve that condition with Mister Pruett. "Well, ah, I understand we have more of them ordered, so, ah . . ."

"Andy, it seems as if you have a sufficient grasp of the English language to understand my question, so I would consider it most helpful if you answered it. Do you have any Century Sedanettes?"

"In a sense, yes, but . . ."

"You know, Andy, getting a straight answer out of you is like pulling teeth. Now, I'm going to try one more time. If you don't give me a direct answer to my question, I will drive over to Greer-Robbins and buy another Chrysler Royal coupe instead. Now, do you have a Century Sedanette for sale on the lot?"

Before he could get his mouth open, a voice from behind me said, "Yes, sir, we do have a Century Sedanette available for sale. Andy, a couple of customers just showed up to look at a Special station wagon. I would appreciate it if you would take care of them and I'll help this gentleman."

Jovial Andy gave the new arrival a look of the sort about which they say, "If looks could kill," and waddled off to sell a station wagon. Meantime, the new fellow introduced himself.

"My name is Dave Anderson. I'm the General Manager here at Howard, and I apologize for Andy's behavior."

"He certainly didn't seem anxious to sell a car."

Dave smiled. "The Century Sedanettes are a limited production model this year, so if a dealer is lucky enough to get one, that's all he'll get until the 1942 models arrive. We received one, but Andy wants to sell it to an actress he's fond of. She, on the other hand, can't make up her mind whether she wants it or not, so Andy has been trying to keep the Century Sedanette under wraps in the hope she'll still buy it."

"I see. Do customers with money in their pockets take priority over actresses who can't make up their minds?"

"They do with me! C'mon, let's go take a look at the Century Sedanette."

We went into the service department and stopped at a service bay that was apparently used for detailing new cars as they arrived at the dealership. At the moment it was occupied by a dark green Century Sedanette with chrome plating so shiny it was almost blinding and a polish job that looked three feet deep.

I damned near whistled at the beauty of the car, but curbed my enthusiasm to keep Dave wondering if I was interested. I said, "Last night I read a road test in *Automobile Monthly* that said this thing was the fastest production car made in the U. S. You agree with that?"

Dave was a good salesman. He didn't try to oversell the car. "Ya know, I read that article, too and wondered the same thing. It's definitely peppy; no question about that, but . . ." He paused for a moment while he opened the hood. "By the way, this hood opens from either side. That's kind of handy.

"Anyway, I wouldn't want to go on record as claiming this is the fastest production car, but it's one of them, that's for certain."

He looked through the driver's window and said, "Good, the key is in it. I'll fire it up."

The big straight eight fired on the second crank and Dave said, "I always like to crank the engine twice in a car that hasn't been run in a while—gets the oil distributed faster. Look at how smooth that engine runs. You could set a glass of water on top of the air cleaner and it would sit there without spilling a drop. Say, climb in here and let's take it for a drive. The battery probably could use a little charging anyway. Here, you drive and I'll open the roll-up door."

Half an hour later we'd worked out a reasonable trade-in price for my Chrysler and I'd written a check drawn on my account at the First National Bank for the balance owed on the Buick. I handed Dave the check and became the proud owner of a spanking new green 1941 Buick Century Sedanette. Driving out of the dealership I smiled at Andy Pruett. He didn't smile back.

Thirty-One

12:15 P.M. – Tuesday – September 3, 1940

Spicer Investigations – 1st National Bank Building, Hollywood

After driving my new Buick back from the dealership, I carefully parked in the First National Bank Building's lot and stood there admiring the Green Hornet for a few minutes before heading up to my office. Yeah, I gave it a name. So what's it to ya?

Walking down the hall, I noticed my outer office door was slightly ajar. It could have been left that way by the postman delivering a package, but I'd gotten into the habit of being extra cautious lately and it seemed like a good habit to keep.

Standing to the right of the door, I pulled my Smith and Wesson and gave the door a push with my left foot. The door swung open and as I peeked through the opening Nick Salvino said, "If you're gonna shoot me, at least buy me lunch first."

Slipping my revolver back in its holster, I gave a little sigh of relief and said, "Sure, Nick. How 'bout one of the best Reuben sandwiches you ever ate?"

Standing, he put his fedora on and said, "What are we waitin' for?"

I took him over to Eli's deli and getting there required walking right by the lot where I'd just parked my new acquisition. I stopped to show it off and after walking around the Buick a time or two, he said, "That's really somethin'. Save me some time by telling me which bank you robbed to pay for it so I can arrest you right now."

"No banks were robbed. My client was grateful for the return of her dime store elephant and she threw in a little bonus."

"That's just swell. We do all the work and you get a new car!"

"What are you complaining about? The city gives you a car and you don't have to pay the rent for your office. Hell, they probably even buy your bullets."

"Yeah, and I'm gonna use one of 'em on you if you don't hurry up and get me that sandwich. I'm starvin'."

I made an "after you" gesture, and as I fell into step behind him, I said, "Not so you'd notice from this angle."

Over our Reubens the sergeant told me the reason for his visit—aside from a free lunch, that is. He said, "I had a visit from the federal prosecutor who's handling the Navy's case against that Kipchumba gal."

"So Washington gets the first crack at her? That's kinda what I figured was gonna happen."

"Yeah, they've got witnesses that saw her and her husband in that fancy car outside the navy base, plus her fingerprints were all over that elephant statue, but the part you will be most interested in is this."

He removed a business-size envelope from his inside coat pocket and handed it to me. The envelope held a photographic copy of a snapshot taken in front of the El Royale apartment building. At the far right of the scene was a familiar Jaguar sedan with the license plate 2C7821. Between the garage entrance and the Jag was a woman walking toward the car. There was no mistaking Damaris Kipchumba and her wild hairdo. A date was printed on the back of the photo by the processing machine. It was 8-8-40.

I handed the photo back to Nick, saying, "That's all fine and good, but you've got no proof of when the photo was made except that it was taken sometime before the eighth of August."

With a triumphal smile on his face, Salvino said, "You're slippin', pal." Holding up the photo, he said, "Take another look."

The only other thing in the photo that could possibly have anything to do with when it was taken was the back half of a moving van with the letters O and N and below them the word "storage." Then I remembered waiting for two movers who were carrying a divan or something out the main entrance as I was going in. I smiled back at the sergeant. "You called Lyon Van and Storage and found out when they made a delivery or a pick up at the El Royale apartments."

"I sure did. And they not only pinned down the time they left, two P. M., one of the movers remembered the Kipchumbas' fancy car. Now how's that for good detective work?"

"Impressive, Nick. In fact, darn good work. Lillian Bouvier and I can both vouch for the fact that Boland was dead by two-forty-five, so we know who was most likely the last one to see him alive."

"Exactly, except for one little detail."

"What's that?"

"I would be surprised if Lillian Bouvier will testify to anything about this photo."

That threw me. "Why?"

"Because we think she took the picture in the first place. They found the copy of the photo from which this copy was made in Missus Kipchumba's luggage at the Sunset Motor Court in Oxnard and when they looked for prints, they found two sets, one belonging to the Kipchumba woman and the other to Miss Bouvier."

"All that means is that she handled the photo at some point."

"Except for another one of those little details. One of Miss Bouvier's prints was under Missus Kipchumba's, which means . . ."

"Yeah, I know. Lilly had to have handled the picture first, but what would she be doing with it?"

Salvino leaned back in his chair and lit a brand new cigar. I think it was the first fresh cigar I'd ever seen him light. He said, "I might have an answer to that question. My guess is that she got to Boland's apartment house early that day you were to meet her there and for some reason the Kipchumba dame being there meant something to her. Apparently she had her Kodak with her—a lot of people never go anywhere without their camera—and she took the picture.

"Later, when she found out Boland was dead, Miss Bouvier put two and two together and realized Missus Kipchumba must have murdered him. Since she had the proof, or what to her mind was proof, she took the film to an overnight film developing company, and then she took this picture up to Sacramento intending to use it as a lever to recover her employer's elephant knickknack, which she still thought was worth a hundred Gs."

"Did anyone ask Missus Kipchumba where she got the photograph?"

"Yeah, and all she would say about it is they found the picture in the mail drop at their office in West Sacramento, but I think the Kipchumbas saw Lillian Bouvier drop the picture in the slot and figured she was the girlfriend Boland recruited to help pull off the heist, which gave them two good reasons to want her dead.

"Then something tipped them off to the fact that Miss Bouvier wasn't Boland's girlfriend, but she was hooked up with you somehow and you were working for Miss Davis and, therefore, must have the photographic negative, so they forgot about Miss Bouvier and went after you. I'll admit there are some holes in that theory here and there, but I think it's right for the most part."

I nodded my understanding of the scenario he'd just outlined. "The Kipchumbas also went after Doris Alpert to cut her out of her share, but she had already blown town. I don't suppose we'll ever know for sure how they tracked her to Needles. So what do the Feds want to do with Miss Bouvier?"

"Absolutely nothing. They searched her place while she was still up at that swanky clinic in Santa Barbara hoping to find the negative to the photograph. The investigators thought if they could find it, they might be able to scare her into testifying about what she saw that day, but they didn't find it."

"I hope they didn't leave a mess for her to come home to."

"No, I was there and they did a very tidy job of it. Anyway, unless something new comes up, Miss Bouvier is out of this."

"When did they conduct their search?"

Salvino pulled out his notebook and scanned a few pages. "It was on the twenty-first of August. So that would be what? Almost two weeks ago? Why?"

While I was busy counting days in my head, I said, "I was just surprised that the federal investigators were that speedy, especially since Missus Kipchumba was still in the hospital. That was only three days after she was shot."

If my count was right, the feds had searched Lilly's place two days after I was there. That realization resulted in one of those moments when a bunch of the puzzle pieces rotate in the right directions and fall into position, allowing me to see a new part of the picture. I suddenly realized I'd done Lillian Bouvier a bigger favor than I thought by carrying out her garbage.

Salvino got a look on his face that told me he wasn't buying my reason for wanting to know when Lilly's place was searched. He said, "Spicer, if you and I are gonna get along, you gotta shoot straight with me. Now, sure as we're sittin' here, you just told me a great big fib."

"Gosh, Sergeant what makes you think that?"

"I can tell by the dumb expression on your mug. Most wouldn't notice it, but I can hardly wait to get into a poker game with you!"

I smiled. "Nick, if it was important, I'd tell you what I'm thinking, but it doesn't make a lick of difference, so I'm keepin' it to myself. That okay with you?"

He laughed. "That time you were tellin' the truth, so I'm gonna fold my hand, say thanks for lunch, and get back to work."

We both stood up and as we turned to leave, I noticed the photograph was still on the table. I slipped into my jacket pocket and gave Nick a "thank you" nod. He gave me a "you're welcome" nod in return.

2:30 P.M. – Monday – September 3, 1940

Lillian Bouvier's Residence – 1835 N. Van Ness Ave., Hollywood

I'd spent several minutes debating the pros and cons of going to see Lilly. The deciding factor was the answer to a question: What day do they pick up the garbage on Van Ness in Hollywood?

Being a firm believer that even in matters of garbage it isn't what you know that matters, but what you know how to find out, I placed a call to the city's department of public works. The garbage on Van Ness Avenue north of Santa Monica Boulevard is picked up on Tuesdays.

So the trash was hauled away the day before the federal investigators searched Lilly's place. Why that suddenly became important was that the garbage guys picked up the negative along with the other trash I'd carried out of her kitchen because Lilly hid it in what from her point of view was a safe place; under that sheet of heavy paper candy companies put in the bottoms of chocolate boxes.

So Bette's conclusion that Lilly was reduced to tears because I'd done her a kindness wasn't even close. Lilly was upset because the negative for her photo proving, at least to her, that Damaris Kipchumba killed Rolly was gone and she had no idea who had it. Did it just get hauled off to the L.A. dump? Someone—maybe the police—searched her home while she was in Santa Barbara. Did they have the negative? Or did I find it when I came over to carry out her trash?

If I found the negative, I would know Lilly lied about why she went to Sacramento and that she withheld information important to a police murder investigation. Under the circumstances, her crimes weren't all that serious, but what if I told Madam?

All Lilly had really done was use what she knew in an attempt to recover the Tembo statuette and save her employer a great deal of money, but her carefully planned scheme went terribly wrong. Now she might be convicted of a crime and sent to jail, or maybe worse to her mind, she might lose her position with Miss Davis.

Like I said, all that was small potatoes under the circumstances, but to an insecure and tightly strung woman like Lilly, not knowing where she stood had to be driving her crazy. So off I went on yet another mission of mercy.

Before the chimes stopped playing their catchy little melody from Handel's *Messiah*, the door opened a few inches and Lilly peeked out. When she saw it was me, her hand immediately went to her face. "Mister Spicer!"

"I'm sorry to show up unannounced, Lilly, but I was driving right by, and seeing your place, I wondered how you were doing. If this is a bad time, I can . . ."

I could see in her eyes that she was making a decision. It was probably quite a different decision than she would have made under different circumstances. Lilly said, "No, no, Mister Spicer, please come in."

Removing my hat I stepped into the house and said, "It's good to see you back home again."

"It's good to be here. There's a fresh pot of coffee on the stove. Would you care for a cup?"

"Yes, I would love a cup, thank you."

I followed her into the tidy little kitchen where she poured coffee into two white mugs with yellow daisies painted on them. Of course, they matched the kitchen color scheme.

She said, "I'm afraid I don't have any sugar or cream for the coffee. The Adohr Farms delivery isn't until tomorrow and I need to make a trip to the market, but I just . . ."

Smiling, I said, "Understood. I drink my coffee black anyway. How are you feeling otherwise?"

"Quite well, thank you. Miss Jackson and the people she works with did a wonderful job of making me comfortable and giving me medications to hurry the healing process. I will still have to have some surgery for the scars . . ."

Lilly's hand went up to her face again and I again said, "Understood." Then, taking a business card out of my pocket, I wrote a Santa Barbara telephone number on the back. "This is Susan's home number. She told me to give it to you in case you had any questions about how you're feeling or about your medications. She now works more of an eight-to-five schedule, so if you don't catch her at the clinic, you can reach her at home in the evening."

If Salvino had been in the room, his Spicer Fib Alarm would be going crazy, but I wanted to mention Susan to make Lilly feel more comfortable about me being there. Now I had to remember to tell Susan I'd done it.

"Oh, goodness. That's awfully nice of her. Please thank Miss Jackson for me."

I'd been wondering how she was going to broach the subject of the negative. She wasted no time in coming up with a very smooth conversational segue. As an apparent afterthought, she said, "And while we are on the subjects of nice things, thank you for the lovely box of See's chocolates. They're my very most favorite."

"You're very welcome, Lilly. I noticed the box you had up there was nearly empty, so I thought I would restock your supply."

Now we were down to what she really wanted to know. For a moment I was tempted to see how she went about finding out the rest, but it didn't seem right to keep her in suspense.

"Lilly, I threw the old box of chocolates and the other trash from the kitchen into the garbage on the nineteenth of August. That was a Monday. Your garbage was picked up the next day. The federal investigators searched your place the day after that."

"You knew?"

I pulled the photograph of Damaris Kipchumba in front of the El Royale out of my jacket pocket and tossed it onto the table, then I took a long shot to find out if what I'd figured was right. "If you're asking me if I knew you hid the negative for this photo under the paper in the bottom of the Whitman's candy box, the answer is no— at least not at the time I tossed the box out. I only found out you'd taken the photo and that the Feds were looking for the negative an hour ago."

"Oh, God. Did you tell them?"

"Did I tell them what?"

She gave me a puzzled look. "That I had the negative?"

"Ah, what negative is that?"

She was starting to get irked with me when she realized what I was up to. "The negative for that . . ." Then a look of relief crossed her features and she said, "You didn't tell them. Oh, thank you, Mister Spicer."

"Lilly, in the first place, the feds already knew about the picture. They found it in Damaris Kipchumba's luggage after she was shot by the navy shore patrol. Missus Kipchumba told the investigators how she got it and they searched your house to find the negative, which was at the city dump by that time.

"In the second place, an investigator deals in facts and I have no first-hand knowledge of there being anything in that candy box but a couple of stale pieces of chocolate. Okay?"

Lilly suddenly stood up and did the least likely thing I would have ever expected her to do. She came over to my side of the table and kissed me on the cheek, saying, "Thank you, Johnny. Thank you so much."

"You're welcome, Lilly. What you did with this photograph was dangerous and foolish, but you didn't do anything that serious where the cops are concerned. And you're already paying a high price for your foolishness. So I figure you're even on the day."

She nodded. "I was just trying to . . ."

"You were just trying to do my job. The difference is, I have people around me I can trust to help me. You had nobody. If I could offer you two pieces of advice they would be get some people you can trust into your life and don't go into the private investigator business."

Lilly laughed a real honest to goodness laugh and said, "Thank you for that advice. I believe I have already made a couple of friends I feel good about trusting. Do you mind being one of those friends, and do you think Susan would mind being the other?"

"I think that's an excellent start, especially Susan. You'll never find a better friend than Susan Jackson."

That brought a puzzled expression to Lilly's face, and she said, "That's strange?"

"What's strange?"

The puzzled expression changed to a smile and Lilly said, "She said exactly the same thing about you."

We had a laugh at that, and then I excused myself, saying I had to get back to the office. Pointing to the photo on the table, I said, "Would you like to keep that copy for any reason?"

Lilly shook her head. "No, thank you, Johnny. Please take it with you."

I got back to my office around three-thirty and spent some time tidying up the place. Mostly, though, I was killing time. I wanted to talk with Susan as soon as she got home. For some reason spending time with Lilly had made me miss Susan even more than usual.

At five-thirty I sat at my desk and dialed the long distance operator who connected me to Susan's number. I felt a little disappointment when Jack answered the phone. When she's home, Susan usually answers the phone.

"Hi, Jack. Johnny here. How are you doing?"

"Real well, Johnny, but if I hear one more soap opera on the radio, I swear I'll throw the damn set out the window!"

I laughed. "Are you trying to say Stella Dallas and Amanda of Honeymoon Hill aren't your cup of tea?"

"Amanda of Honeymoon Hill? Are you kidding me?"

"No, sir, I am not. I've seen it listed in the newspaper radio log. It's on NBC Blue at three-fifteen. I made a note of that so I wouldn't accidentally turn it on."

"Good thinking, but I suppose you'd rather talk to Susan of Santa Barbara Beach instead of me?"

"If she's home, yes I would."

"She's right here trying to yank the telephone out of my hand."

Bringing Susan up to date, I told her Salvino's news about Missus Kipchumba and Lilly's photograph. She said, "You know, now that we have the facts, that makes a lot of sense. I was having trouble figuring out why Lilly thought she could recover the elephant. Now I see how her mind was working."

Then I told her about the chocolates and my visit to see Lilly today. In a tone with a smile, she said, "Giving chocolates to another woman, huh? And See's no less! I can see I have to keep a closer eye on you, Mister."

"Then you better get your cute fanny down here 'cuz you can't see what I'm up to from Santa Barbara."

"Johnny! Such language! Would Friday be soon enough?"

"No, but if that's the best we can do, I'll take it. But rather than you driving Jack down to pick up his car, how 'bout if I come up and bring you guys down Friday after you get off work?"

"That would be swell if you don't mind doing all that driving."

"I don't mind at all. Besides, I've got a surprise to show you."

"Oh? What's the surprise?"

"If I tell you it won't be a surprise."

"Phooey! Do you have to be so darn logical all the time?"

By then Susan and I talked long enough to raise American Telephone and Telegraph's stock a few points, so we said goodbye and I headed home to fix some dinner. Talking to Susan always makes me hungry.

Thirty-Two

2:30 P.M. – Friday – September 6, 1940

Cahuenga Pass – Southbound Highway 101, Hollywood

Since Susan had put in a few extra hours during the week on some sort of special project, she felt okay about only putting in a half day on Friday. I got to her place around eleven-thirty so Jack and I could load up the car and be ready to leave town when Susan got home a little after noon.

Jack was getting around with the help of a cane that he carried more as a precaution than a necessity. Since he was getting around so well we sent him in to a sandwich shop a block away on State Street to pick up sandwiches for lunch on the road while Susan and I had a short conference about an idea she had. Before he got back we had connived what she thought was a way of making her idea work. I wasn't so sure.

After spending a few moments admiring the Green Hornet before we headed out, we were rolling over the Cahuenga Pass on our way into Hollywood by two-thirty. It was time to put Susan's plan into action.

I turned off of Cahuenga Boulevard onto Highland and headed south to Sunset. There I took a right and went east to the A & P market at Sunset and Fairfax. Susan went in with a grocery list that included mostly fresh produce plus a few canned items and a tin of Hills Brothers coffee. I told her it was okay to get carrots this time.

With step one completed, we drove back east on Sunset a couple of miles to Van Ness, where I turned left and continued up to Lilly Bouvier's cottage. Susan had already explained to Jack that she was helping one of her former patients by dropping by with some groceries so the woman didn't have to make a trip to the store. As I parked in front of Lilly's place, Susan said, "Jack, would you please come with me and carry one of the grocery bags? It will only take a minute."

I was watching his reaction in the rearview mirror and his expression had some suspicion in it. On the other hand, Jack is the sort of fellow who is always ready to lend a hand, so he didn't hesitate to say he'd be glad to help. Thus, with Jack carrying one of the three bags of groceries, Susan marched up to the front door and pushed the Big Ben chimes button.

In case you haven't tumbled to it yet, Susan's idea was to introduce Jack to Lilly and see if anything came of it. She had the idea they might be good for each other. Susan even mentioned Lilly to Jack in passing a few times, preparing him for her appearance and explaining that after a couple of relatively minor surgical procedures Lilly would be just as pretty as she was before the accident. As I said before, I had my doubts about Susan's matchmaking scheme.

Of course, I couldn't hear the conversation from where I was in the car, but my impression was that things went more less the same as they had on my visit earlier in the week. The door opened a crack, at first, then it opened all the way and Susan and Jack went in with their grocery sacks. Either Lilly was getting braver or Susan had greased the skids beforehand without telling me. That girl can be sneaky when she puts her mind to it.

They were inside Lilly's for about twenty minutes. When they came back to the car, Jack was smiling broadly—pun intended.

As Susan slid onto the passenger end of the front seat I asked, "How'd it go?"

She winked at me and said, "Ask Jack. He did all the talking."

From the backseat: "Aw, Sis, c'mon. She's a nice person and very easy to talk to. And we have a lot in common, like being shot at by the same bad guys."

Susan said, "Needless to say, it went well. Lilly kept insisting that she wanted to pay for the groceries and I kept telling her she'd have to take that up with you, since you bought them."

"That's fine. I intended them as a friendly gesture, so I wasn't expecting to be reimbursed."

From the backseat: "Ah, Johnny, how far is it to the Ford dealership? I want to get there before they close."

Before I could answer, Susan said, "Don't mind big brother back there. He's got a hot dinner date later. Lilly invited him back for her famous vegetable chowder, whatever that might be."

I couldn't help laughing. "Angel, your brother is one fast operator. He talks to her for twenty minutes and they're an item. And to answer your question, Jack, we're less than five miles from Coberly Ford. We'll be there in a few minutes."

From the backseat: "Well, step on it will you!?"

I stepped on it and we pulled up to the curb in front of 1400 West Eighth Street at three-forty-five. As Susan climbed down to let Jack out of the backseat, I said, "We'll wait here for a bit while you talk to them. Give us a wave when you've got things worked out."

Susan said, "And pick out something really snazzy, big brother."

I leaned back in the seat and lit a Lucky Strike. When I turned to see how Jack was coming, I saw him talking to a fellow in a suit I guessed was the General Manager. He must have asked to see Jack's identification because Jack pulled out his wallet and handed a card to the guy.

The GM then made a sweeping gesture that encompassed the cars on the lot and the showroom. Jack nodded, they shook hands, and the fellow in the suit headed into the showroom. I suspected he'd just told Jack to pick out a car while he started the paperwork.

Susan was also watching Jack. "What do you think he'll pick out?"

"You see that maroon convertible over there next to the service entrance?"

She looked where I was pointing and said, "Yes. You think that's the one he'll pick out?"

"I'd bet money on it, but first he's going to come back over here and ask me what I think of his choice."

"Oh, really? What suddenly makes you such an expert on my brother?"

I shook my head. "I'm not an expert on Jack, but I am fairly knowledgeable about cars and I gather that Jack is not. Getting this right is important to him, so he's going to ask my opinion."

No sooner had I said that than Jack turned and walked in our direction. Susan and I got out and met him on the sidewalk. Jack said, "Johnny, can I ask your opinion on something?"

"If you want to know which one I think you should get, I say get that gray four-door sedan over there."

Jack turned and looked where I pointed, and when he turned back there was definitely disappointment showing on his face. Susan, said, "Don't you listen to him, Jack. He's kidding you! Aren't you kidding him, Johnny?"

"Yeah, I'm sorry, but when I saw you looking at that maroon convertible, I could resist recommending the plainest car on the lot."

Jack turned to me and said, "You know, you've got a real mean streak in you. Now tell me what you really think."

"Let's go over and take a look."

Jack's choice was a new 1941 model and when I opened the hood I saw something I liked right away. The convertible was powered by one of Ford's upgraded ninety-five horsepower Mercury V8 engines. Walking around the car, I discovered the car was what Ford called a Super Deluxe model. That was the top model in Ford's line, and it came with all the newest gadgets and a plusher interior than the less expensive models. It also was equipped with a long list of optional accessories, including a radio, heater, fog lamps, grill guard, mirrors, hubcaps, trim rings, fender skirts, tools and jack. This one even had an official Ford spotlight installed next to the driver-side wind-wing window. What on earth anyone would do with a spotlight besides have fun at drive-in movies I had no idea.

Turning to Jack, I said, "Do you know what you're getting into by picking a convertible?"

Nodding, he said, "Yes, I think so."

"The main things are keep the car inside when you're not driving it, and treat those leather seats with saddle soap about once a month. Also, don't park it in the sun with the top down for long periods of time. Do those things and keep up the factory recommended maintenance on that engine, and the car will look good and drive well for a long time."

Still nodding, Jack said, "I think I can handle that all right."

"Then go in there and tell that guy you've picked out your car. We'll stick around a little longer to make sure the car is serviced and ready to go."

Grinning from ear-to-ear, he said, "Thanks, Johnny," and took off toward the showroom.

Susan had nearly the same grin on her face. "You just made him one happy guy. I guess we're a two convertible family now."

Several minutes later, Jack came out of the showroom with the guy in the suit and waved a set of car keys at us. His grin still went from ear-to-ear. Now Jack would be off for some vegetable chowder at Lilly's and we were free to enjoy the rest of the weekend.

From the dealership I made a U-turn and then a left turn onto Western. We headed south on Western to Venice Boulevard, where I turned right. Venice zig-zagged around for a couple of miles before turning southwest toward our ultimate destination.

Eventually Susan's curiosity got the better of her, and as we went through Culver City she asked, "Where are we going, Johnny?

All this twisting and turning has me so confused I don't even know what direction we're going."

"Well, if it's any help, we're heading southwest."

Without turning my head I knew she was giving me her exasperated look. She said, "No, darling, it isn't any help. For all I know we're going by way of East Anaheim."

"Now that couldn't be if we're going southwest. Maybe I should check my compass."

"Okay, Buster, fair warning. You're about to get bopped."

"Golly gee whiz! You wouldn't really bop me, would you?"

With that she hauled off and slugged me in the right shoulder. "The next one lands on your nose!"

"Okay, okay, I'll tell you. We're going where we started to go nearly six weeks ago, but got sidetracked."

"Oh! We're going to that swanky hotel in Santa Monica? What was the name of it? Shangri-La?"

"That's the place."

"Thank you, Johnny. I've really been looking forward to this. How much further is it?"

"Geez, you're as impatient as your brother. We're just coming up to the coast highway which we will take north for a couple of miles through Venice and Santa Monica to the hotel. Enjoy the view."

I turned right on Pacific Avenue which changed names a few times before running into Ocean Avenue in Santa Monica. The view out my side of the car was a sandy beach and lines of white-tipped breakers rolling in. The view out Susan's side of the car was mostly high class beach hotels.

Because we were just in time to catch the beginning of the going-home traffic it took nearly fifteen minutes to cover the last couple of miles, so it was quarter past five when a big white building that looked like the upper half of a steamship parked alongside the road appeared to our right. We had arrived at Shangri-La.

There was a valet parking sign around the corner on Arizona Avenue and I pulled up to the curb next to it. A young man in an electric blue vest ran over to the car from his stool and opened the door for Susan while I got out and walked around to the sidewalk.

Now, you might be wondering why I was willing to trust a brand new, high-performance automobile to a kid who parks cars for a living. I was wondering that, too, so I employed a little intimidation ruse Humphrey Bogart taught me.

The young man was filling out the claim ticket as I approached and said, "Okay, kid, take a good look at this car." He looked at the car and then at me again as if wondering what I was talking about. I continued, "Beautiful piece of machinery, ain't it? I just picked it up last week, so there ain't no scratches or dents in it. I want it to look just like this when we leave on Sunday, and you really want to care about what I want, capiche?"

Part of the intimidation was reaching into my left trouser pocket for tip money in such a way that my coat was brushed back on that side to reveal my shoulder holster as I said, "capiche?" When he saw my shoulder holster, the kid's eyes nearly bugged right out of his head.

He half-stammered, "Yes sir, I'll take real good care of it."

I handed him two dollar bills—about four times the going tip rate for a valet—and said, "You're a smart kid. I predict you're gonna go far in the car parking business. Luggage is in the trunk; two small suitcases."

"Yes, sir, I'll make sure they get up to your room."

During that exchange Susan had taken my arm and was standing next to me. I could sense she was close to ruining my act by bursting into laughter. As we walked through a classy chrome and glass entrance opened by an equally classy doorman in a blue uniform, I said in my best Bogie voice, "You're gonna have to work on keeping a straight face, Angel, or you'll queer my act."

That was all she could take. The doorman must have thought Susan was nuts when for no apparent reason she started giggling uncontrollably.

The lobby of the Shangri-La was the ultimate in streamlined Art Moderne. Everywhere we looked were geometric shapes—circles and triangles mostly—done in chrome, glass brick and various polished woods. At the center of it all was a half-round wooden registration desk where I was greeted like royalty.

The fact that I had reserved a three-room suite on the top floor might have had something to do with the royal greeting. The nightly rate on the suite was eighty bucks—about twice the going rate for the best quality resort hotels on the beach. However, for our eighty bucks per night, we got the round ocean-view penthouse suite.

Yes, I said round. Our suite was at the front corner of the hotel above the entrance. Since that corner of the building was round, rather than square, the outer walls of the suite were curved, and because the hotel is right above the ocean, those curved walls were mostly glass, except for a door that led out to a terrace from which the view was spectacular, including the entire coastline from Palos Verdes to the south all the way up to Malibu on the north side.

The furnishings in the room were all streamline Moderne and good quality, as were the outdoor furnishings on our terrace. Our suite also had a fireplace, an excellent Zenith radio that wasn't bolted down, and a well-stocked bar.

Susan went through our rooms like a kid exploring a whole new fantasy world while I tipped the bellboy. After pouring myself a Scotch from the bar, I went in search of Susan and found her in the master bedroom stretched out on the bed like she was in the lap of luxury. For that matter, I guess she was.

We sat out on the terrace for a while and watched a pretty decent sunset. The view wasn't as spectacular as it would have been if the sun was setting behind a fog bank, but the lack of fog would make the night view even more spectacular. You just can't lose with the Pacific Ocean at your doorstep.

A few minutes past six I asked Susan if she was getting hungry. She said, "I thought you were never going to ask. What do the rich folks do for food around this swanky joint?"

She was giving me a taste of my own medicine with an impersonation of Myrna Loy playing Missus Nick Charles. I said, "Why as I live breathe; that sounds like Nora Charles over there."

"That's right, and you get to be Asta."

"Arf."

"You gonna answer my question or do I have to bop you again?"

"I think we've had enough bopping for one day. The dining room at the Shangri-La is called, strangely enough, 'The Dining Room at the Shangri-La.'"

Susan laughed. "How imaginative!"

"But it leaves little room for ambiguity. I understand, however, that one must 'dress' to dine in 'The Dining Room'. Are you prepared for that eventuality this evening or do we need to postpone the hotel restaurant and venture out to a dress shop tomorrow?"

With her coy look aimed directly at me, she said, "Maybe both, but I'll see what I can come up with tonight so I don't embarrass you too much."

On that note, we set off to change for dinner, with Susan mysteriously disappearing into the second bedroom and me dragging my dark blue pinstripe out of the closet, where it was trying to lose some of the wrinkles it had acquired in my suitcase. It was the closest thing to formal wear I had, but the cuffs weren't frayed yet, so I figured it would be okay. I'd donned said suit, with a white shirt and a classy dark blue tie and was checking myself in the mirror to see if my tie was straight when Susan came in.

She said, "Is this outfit sufficiently swanky to save you from embarrassment when we go downstairs to dine with the swells?"

I turned around to take a look and saw an honest to God true vision of loveliness. Susan was dressed in a black cocktail dress that had just the right amount of wow to make me say, "Wow!"

She did a fashion model turn, showing me that the dress was a perfect fit all the way around with a hem that came to exactly the right spot just below her knees. Completing her turn, Susan said, "May I assume that 'wow' means you approve?"

"You may assume that, but a question occurs to me. If you didn't know where we were headed today, how did you know you'd need to pack a fancy getup like that?"

Susan came over and gave me a kiss on the cheek. "Johnny, did you really think I didn't know this is where we were going?"

"Well, you asked, and . . ."

"You know, for a clever Hollywood Private Eye, you can sure be gullible sometimes!"

I slipped her wrap over her shoulders and we took the elevator down to "The Dining Room." As we followed the maître d' to our table I don't think there were more than two men in the room who weren't watching Susan go by. The thing about it was you'd never know from her poise that she noticed the attention she was attracting. I was pretty sure she did, though, and I sure as hell did. It made me feel like the luckiest fellow in the place.

Once we were seated a sparkle caught my eye at her neck. I'd been so busy looking at the whole package, I hadn't noticed the diamond pendant on a gold chain she was wearing. I said, "Angel, if it's none of my business say so, but I don't think I've seen that diamond pendant before."

She gave me another one of her coy looks and said, "Would it make you jealous if I told you some rich guy gave it to me?"

"You know damned well it would."

"Good. The truth is, though, it was given to me by a rich woman."

I remembered her saying Bette Davis had been generous to all of us. "Bette?"

She nodded. "Bette said it was a gift she received several years ago and she wanted me to have it because I'd been so kind and helpful to Lilly. I tried to tell her I was just doing my job, but she insisted."

"With a rock that size, you ought to have it appraised."

Looking a little sheepish, she said, "I did. I wanted to have it insured, so I took it to a jeweler I know. He said it weighed about

262

1.08 carats and the stone alone is worth almost two hundred dollars. The mounting and the chain brought the total value you up to almost three hundred dollars."

"Wow. That's a pretty nice gift to give another woman for being nice to a friend."

Susan looked at me for a moment and I knew we were wondering the same thing. She said, "Don't worry, Mister, you've got nothing to worry about on that score."

After a very well prepared seafood dinner in "The Dining Room," we returned to our suite and Susan walked out onto our terrace while I tuned the radio to a music station that was playing Glenn Miller's *Moonlight Serenade.*

Then I followed her out to the terrace and we danced until the Miller recording ended and Artie Shaw's version of *Frenesi* began. Since it didn't really fit the mood for dancing, we stood at the terrace railing and enjoyed the view together.

Always curious, it wasn't long before Susan was asking questions. "Johnny, what's that pier over there? It looks kind of like Stearns Wharf at home."

"It's the same idea, but I'll bet Stearns Wharf didn't start out as part of a sewage disposal system."

"Oh, I gotta hear that story!"

"Well, don't quote me on the date, but just a few years after the turn of the century Santa Monica was having trouble getting rid of their treated sewage, so they built a pipe line out into the ocean and ran the pier out above it to make installing the sewer pipe easier."

Susan shook her head in amazement. "They did that with a swimming beach right next to it?"

"That's the way the story goes. Then, in the 1920s they turned their municipal wharf into an amusement pier like Pacific Ocean Park down by Venice. They built rides and ballrooms, restaurants, the works. There's even a fleet of gambling ships out there. You can see the lights straight over there."

As I pointed to the Rex, or whichever of the gambling ships it was. As I pointed, Susan stood on her tiptoes and we kissed. I think I was still pointing when we finished because I forgot to lower my arm.

"Johnny, do you remember the first time we kissed like that?"

"If I remember correctly it was on the beach behind the Santa Barbara Biltmore."

"You do remember!"

"Of course I do, Angel. I wouldn't forget a momentous occasion like that!"

"Okay, Mister Hollywood Private Eye, have our kisses changed since then or are they the same?"

"Now that's a strange question to ask."

Looking a little pouty, she said, "I was just curious if . . ."

"Come to think of it, they have changed. Each one feels better and means more than the last one."

She cocked her head and said, "What a nice thing to say. I think you might actually be in love with me."

I smiled back at her. "I think so, too."

THE END

Meet H. P. Oliver

H. P. Oliver began his career with a degree in journalism from San Jose State University and spent the next twenty-some years writing award-winning entertainment and educational media. Now he applies his creativity and imagination to writing historical mysteries.

About mystery writing, Oliver says, "To be truly engrossing, a mystery needs a little meat on its bones—something more than just figuring out who done the evil deed. Taking a story back in time or even basing it on actual historical events is a great way to endow a good yarn with even more color and depth. Historical periods and locations give the writer an opportunity to take most readers where they've never been before."

H. P. Oliver lives in northern California and spends much of his time working on projects throughout the western states. In addition to his love of history, Oliver's interests range from vintage film to restoring classic cars.

For information about H. P. Oliver's books, including synopses, previews, video trailers, and purchase links, visit his fan site at www.HPOliver.com, where you will also find illustrated history articles and other fascinating features. Plan to stay a while!

Books By H. P. Oliver

CLASSIC MYSTERIES IN HISTORY

THE TRUTH BE TOLD
(E-book)

AND THE ANGELS SING
(E-book)

SILENTS!
(E-book & Paper)

GOODNIGHT, SAN FRANCISCO
(E-book & Paper)

WINGING IT
(E-book & Paper)

JOHNNY SPICER CAPERS

JOHNNY SPICER: THE FIRST CAPERS
(E-book)

PACIFICA
(E-book & Paper)

REVOLVER
(E-book & Paper)

TEMBO
(E-book & Paper)

www.ingramcontent.com/pod-product-compliance
Lightning Source LLC
Chambersburg PA
CBHW070901180626
46817CB00003B/864